CHARLES DICKENS

COMPLETE
WORKS

CENTENNIAL EDITION

Charles Dickens

CHARLES DICKENS

THE LIFE AND ADVENTURES
OF
MARTIN CHUZZLEWIT

II

Illustrations by
Phiz

Distributed by
HERON BOOKS

Edito-Service S.A., Geneva, Publishers

13 002 22 R3

CONTENTS

CONTENTS

CHAPTER XXXII

CHAPTER XXXIII

CHAPTER XXXIV

CHAPTER XXXV

CHAPTER XXXVI

CHAPTER XXXVII

CHAPTER XXXVIII

CHAPTER XXXIX

CONTENTS

CHAPTER XL

CHAPTER XLI

CHAPTER XLII

CHAPTER XLIII

CHAPTER XLIV

CHAPTER XLV

CHAPTER XLVI

CHAPTER XLVII

CONTENTS

LIST OF ILLUSTRATIONS

CHAPTER XXVI

AN UNEXPECTED MEETING, AND A PROMISING PROSPECT

THE laws of sympathy between beards and birds, and the secret source of that attraction which frequently impels a shaver of the one to be a dealer in the other, are questions for the subtle reasoning of scientific bodies: not the less so, because their investigation would seem calculated to lead to no particular result. It is enough to know that the artist who had the honour of entertaining Mrs. Gamp as his first-floor lodger, united the two pursuits of barbering and bird-fancying; and that it was not an original idea of his, but one in which he had, dispersed about the bye-streets and suburbs of the town, a host of rivals.

The name of the householder was Paul Sweedlepipe. But he was commonly called Poll Sweedlepipe: and was not uncommonly believed to have been so christened, among his friends and neighbours.

With the exception of the staircase, and his lodger's private apartment, Poll Sweedlepipe's house was one great bird's nest. Game-cocks resided in the kitchen; pheasants wasted the brightness of their golden plumage on the garret;

1

bantams roosted in the cellar; owls had possession of the bed-room; and specimens of all the smaller fry of birds chirrupped and twittered in the shop. The staircase was sacred to rabbits. There in hutches of all shapes and kinds, made from old packing-cases, boxes, drawers, and tea-chests, they increased in a prodigious degree, and contributed their share towards that complicated whiff which, quite impartially, and without distinction of persons, saluted every nose that was put into Sweedlepipe's easy shaving-shop.

Many noses found their way there, for all that, especially on Sunday morning, before church-time. Even archbishops shave, or must be shaved, on a Sunday, and beards *will* grow after twelve o'clock on Saturday night, though it be upon the chins of base mechanics: who, not being able to engage their valets by the quarter, hire them by the job, and pay them —oh, the wickedness of copper coin!—in dirty pence. Poll Sweedlepipe, the sinner, shaved all comers at a penny each, and cut the hair of any customer for twopence; and being a lone unmarried man, and having some connection in the bird line, Poll got on tolerably well.

He was a little elderly man, with a clammy cold right hand, from which even rabbits and birds could not remove the smell of shaving-soap. Poll had something of the bird in his nature; not of the hawk or eagle, but of the sparrow, that builds in chimney-stacks and inclines to human company. He was not quarrelsome, though, like the sparrow; but peaceful, like the dove. In his walk he strutted; and, in this respect, he bore a faint resemblance to the pigeon, as well as in a certain prosiness of speech, which might, in its monotony, be likened to the cooing of that bird. He was very inquisitive; and when he stood at his shop-door in the evening-tide, watching the neighbours, with his head on one side, and his eye cocked knowingly, there was a dash of the raven in him. Yet there was no more wickedness in Poll than in a robin. Happily, too, when any of his ornithological properties were on the verge of going too far, they were quenched, dissolved, melted down, and neutralised in the barber; just as his bald head—otherwise, as the head of a shaved magpie—lost itself in a wig of curly black ringlets, parted on one side, and cut away almost to the crown, to indicate immense capacity of intellect.

Poll had a very small, shrill, treble voice, which might have led the wags of Kingsgate Street to insist the more upon his feminine designation. He had a tender heart, too; for, when he had a good commission to provide three or four score sparrows for a shooting-match, he would observe, in a compassionate tone, how singular it was that sparrows should have been made expressly for such purposes. The question, whether men were made to shoot them, never entered into Poll's philosophy.

Poll wore in his sporting character, a velveteen coat, a great deal of blue stocking, ankle boots, a neckerchief of some bright colour, and a very tall hat. Pursuing his more quiet occupation of barber, he generally subsided into an apron not over-clean, a flannel jacket, and corduroy knee-shorts. It was in this latter costume, but with his apron girded round his waist, as a token of his having shut up shop for the night, that he closed the door one evening, some weeks after the occurrences detailed in the last chapter, and stood upon the steps in Kingsgate Street, listening until the little cracked bell within should leave off ringing. For, until it did—this was Mr. Sweedlepipe's reflection—the place never seemed quiet enough to be left to itself.

"It's the greediest little bell to ring," said Poll, "that ever was. But it's quiet at last."

He rolled his apron up a little tighter as he said these words, and hastened down the street. Just as he was turning into Holborn, he ran against a young gentleman in a livery. This youth was bold, though small, and with several lively expressions of displeasure, turned upon him instantly.

"Now, Stoo-pid!" cried the young gentleman. "Can't you look where you're a going to—eh? Can't you mind where you're a coming to—eh? What do you think your eyes was made for—eh? Ah! Yes. Oh! Now then!"

The young gentleman pronounced the two last words in a very loud tone and with frightful emphasis, as though they contained within themselves the essence of the direst aggravation. But he had scarcely done so, when his anger yielded to surprise, and he cried, in a milder tone:

"What! Polly!"

"Why it ain't you, sure!" cried Poll. "It can't be you!"

"No. It ain't me," returned the youth. "It's my son, my oldest one. He's a credit to his father, ain't he, Polly?" With this delicate little piece of banter, he halted on the pavement, and went round and round in circles, for the better exhibition of his figure: rather to the inconvenience of the passengers generally, who were not in an equal state of spirits with himself.

"I wouldn't have believed it," said Poll. "What! You've left your old place, then? Have you?"

"Have I!" returned his young friend, who had by this time stuck his hands into the pockets of his white cord breeches, and was swaggering along at the barber's side. "D'ye know a pair of top-boots when you see 'em, Polly? Look here!"

"Beau-ti-ful!" cried Mr. Sweedlepipe.

"D'ye know a slap-up sort of button, when you see it?" said the youth. "Don't look at mine, if you ain't a judge, because these lions' heads was made for men of taste: not snobs."

"Beau-ti-ful!" cried the barber again. "A grass-green frock-coat, too, bound with gold! And a cockade in your hat!"

"*I* should hope so," replied the youth. "Blow the cockade, though; for, except that it don't turn round, it's like the wentilator that used to be in the kitchen winder at Todgers's. You ain't seen the old lady's name in the Gazette, have you?"

"No," returned the barber. "Is she a bankrupt?"

"If she ain't, she will be," retorted Bailey. "That bis'ness never can be carried on without *me*. Well! How are you?"

"Oh! I'm pretty well," said Poll. "Are you living at this end of the town, or were you coming to see me? Was that the bis'ness that brought you to Holborn?"

"I haven't got no bis'ness in Holborn," returned Bailey, with some displeasure. "All my bis'ness lays at the West-end. I've got the right sort of governor now. You can't see his face for his whiskers, and can't see his whiskers for the dye upon 'em. That's a gentleman, ain't it? You wouldn't like a ride in a cab, would you? Why, it wouldn't be safe to offer it. You'd faint away, only to see me a comin' at a mild trot round the corner."

To convey a slight idea of the effect of this approach, Mr. Bailey counterfeited in his own person the action of a high-trotting horse, and threw up his head so high, in backing against a pump, that he shook his hat off.

"Why, he's own uncle to Capricorn," said Bailey, "and brother to Cauliflower. He's been through the winders of two chaney shops since we've had him, and wos sold for killin' his missis. That's a horse, I hope?"

"Ah! you'll never want to buy any more red-polls, now," observed Poll, looking on his young friend with an air of melancholy. "You'll never want to buy any more red-polls now, to hang up over the sink, will you?"

"I should think not," replied Bailey. "Reether so. I wouldn't have nothin' to say to any bird below a Peacock; and *he'd* be wulgar. Well, how are you?"

"Oh! I'm pretty well," said Poll. He answered the question again because Mr. Bailey asked it again; Mr. Bailey asked it again, because—accompanied with a straddling action of the white cords, a bend of the knees, and a striking-forth of the top-boots—it was an easy, horse-fleshy, turfy sort of thing to do.

"Wot are you up to, old feller?" asked Mr. Bailey, with

5

the same graceful rakishness. He was quite the man-about-town of the conversation, while the easy-shaver was the child.

"Why, I am going to fetch my lodger home," said Paul.

"A woman!" cried Mr. Bailey, "for a twenty-pun' note!"

The little barber hastened to explain that she was neither a young woman, nor a handsome woman, but a nurse, who had been acting as a kind of house-keeper to a gentleman for some weeks past, and left her place that night, in consequence of being superseded by another and a more legitimate house-keeper: to wit, the gentleman's bride.

"He's newly-married, and he brings his young wife home to-night," said the barber. "So I'm going to fetch my lodger away—Mr. Chuzzlewit's, close behind the Post-office—and carry her box for her."

"Jonas Chuzzlewit's?" said Bailey.

"Ah!" returned Paul: "that's the name sure enough. Do you know him?"

"Oh, no!" cried Mr. Bailey; "not at all. And I don't know her! Not neither! Why, they first kept company through me, a'most."

"Ah?" said Paul.

"Ah!" said Mr. Bailey, with a wink; "and she ain't bad-looking, mind you. But her sister was the best. *She* was the merry one. I often used to have a bit of fun with her, in the hold times!"

Mr. Bailey spoke as if he already had a leg and three-quarters in the grave, and this had happened twenty or thirty years ago. Paul Sweedlepipe, the meek, was so perfectly confounded by his precocious self-possession, and his patronising manner, as well as by his boots, cockade, and livery, that a mist swam before his eyes, and he saw—not the Bailey of acknowledged juvenility, from Todgers's Commercial Boarding House, who had made his acquaintance within a twelvemonth, by purchasing, at sundry times, small birds at twopence each —but a highly-condensed embodiment of all the sporting grooms in London; an abstract of all the stable-knowledge

6

of the time; a something at a high-pressure that must have had existence many years, and was fraught with terrible experiences. And truly, though in the cloudy atmosphere of Todgers's, Mr. Bailey's genius had ever shone out brightly in this particular respect, it now eclipsed both time and space, cheated beholders of their senses, and worked on their belief in defiance of all natural laws. He walked along the tangible and real stones of Holborn Hill, an under-sized boy; and yet he winked the winks, and thought the thoughts, and did the deeds, and said the sayings of an ancient man. There was an old principle within him, and a young surface without. He became an inexplicable creature: a breeched and booted Sphinx. There was no course open to the barber but to go distracted himself, or to take Bailey for granted: and he wisely chose the latter.

Mr. Bailey was good enough to continue to bear him company, and to entertain him, as they went, with easy conversation on various sporting topics; especially on the comparative merits, as a general principle, of horses with white stockings, and horses without. In regard to the style of tail to be preferred, Mr. Bailey had opinions of his own, which he explained, but begged they might by no means influence his friend's, as here he knew he had the misfortune to differ from some excellent authorities. He treated Mr. Sweedlepipe to a dram, compounded agreeably to his own directions, which he informed him had been invented by a member of the Jockey Club; and, as they were by this time near the barber's destination, he observed that, as he had an hour to spare, and knew the parties, he would, if quite agreeable, be introduced to Mrs. Gamp.

Paul knocked at Jonas Chuzzlewit's: and, on the door being opened by that lady, made the two distinguished persons known to one another. It was a happy feature in Mrs. Gamp's twofold profession, that it gave her an interest in everything that was young as well as in everything that was old. She received Mr. Bailey with much kindness.

" It's very good, I'm sure, of you to come," she said to her landlord, " as well as bring so nice a friend. But I'm afraid that I must trouble you so far as to step in, for the young couple has not yet made appearance."

" They're late, ain't they ? " inquired her landlord, when she had conducted them down stairs into the kitchen.

" Well, sir, considerin' the Wings of Love, they are," said Mrs. Gamp.

Mr. Bailey inquired whether the Wings of Love had ever won a plate, or could be backed to do anything remarkable ; and being informed that it was not a horse, but merely a poetical or figurative expression, evinced considerable disgust. Mrs. Gamp was so very much astonished by his affable manners and great ease, that she was about to propound to her landlord in a whisper the staggering inquiry, whether he was a man or a boy, when Mr. Sweedlepipe, anticipating her design, made a timely diversion.

" He knows Mrs. Chuzzlewit," said Paul aloud.

" There's nothin' he don't know ; that's my opinion," observed Mrs. Gamp. " All the wickedness of the world is Print to him."

Mr. Bailey received this as a compliment, and said, adjusting his cravat, " reether so."

" As you knows Mrs. Chuzzlewit, you knows, p'raps, what her chris'n name is ? " Mrs. Gamp observed.

" Charity," said Bailey.

" That it ain't ! " cried Mrs. Gamp.

" Cherry, then," said Bailey. " Cherry's short for it. It's all the same."

" It don't begin with a C at all," retorted Mrs. Gamp, shaking her head. " It begins with a M."

" Whew ! " cried Mr. Bailey, slapping a little cloud of pipeclay out of his left leg, " then he's been and married the merry one ! "

As these words were mysterious, Mrs. Gamp called upon him to explain, which Mr. Bailey proceeded to do : that lady listening greedily to everything he said. He was yet in the fulness of his narrative when the sound of wheels, and a double knock at the street door, announced the arrival of the newly-married couple. Begging him to reserve what more he had to say, for her hearing on the way home, Mrs. Gamp took up the candle, and hurried away to receive and welcome the young mistress of the house.

"Wishing you appiness and joy with all my art," said Mrs. Gamp, dropping a curtsey as they entered the hall; "and you, too, sir. Your lady looks a little tired with the journey, Mr. Chuzzlewit, a pretty dear!"

"She has bothered enough about it," grumbled Mr. Jonas. "Now, show a light, will you?"

"This way, ma'am, if you please," said Mrs. Gamp, going up stairs before them. "Things has been made as comfortable as they could be; but there's many things you'll have to alter your own self when you gets time to look about you. Ah! sweet thing! But you don't," added Mrs. Gamp, internally, "you don't look much like a merry one, I must say!"

It was true: she did not. The death that had gone before the bridal seemed to have left its shade upon the house. The air was heavy and oppressive; the rooms were dark; a deep gloom filled up every chink and corner. Upon the hearthstone, like a creature of ill omen, sat the aged clerk, with his eyes fixed on some withered branches in the stove. He rose and looked at her.

"So there you are, Mr. Chuff," said Jonas carelessly, as he dusted his boots; "still in the land of the living, eh?"

"Still in the land of the living, sir," retorted Mrs. Gamp. "And Mr. Chuffey may thank you for it, as many and many a time I've told him."

Mr. Jonas was not in the best of humours, for he merely said, as he looked round, "We don't want you any more, you know, Mrs. Gamp."

"I'm a going immediate, sir," returned the nurse; "unless

there's nothink I can do for you, ma'am. Ain't there," said Mrs. Gamp, with a look of great sweetness, and rummaging all the time in her pocket; "ain't there nothink I can do for you, my little bird?"

"No," said Merry, almost crying. "You had better go away, please!"

With a leer of mingled sweetness and slyness; with one eye on the future, one on the bride, and an arch expression in her face, partly spiritual, partly spirituous, and wholly professional and peculiar to her art; Mrs. Gamp rummaged in her pocket again, and took from it a printed card, whereon was an inscription copied from her sign-board.

"Would you be so good, my darling dovey of a dear young married lady," Mrs. Gamp observed, in a low voice, "as put that somewheres where you can keep it in your mind? I'm well beknown to many ladies, and it's my card. Gamp is my name, and Gamp my nater. Livin' quite handy, I will make so bold as call in now and then, and make inquiry how your health and spirits is, my precious chick!"

And with innumerable leers, winks, coughs, nods, smiles, and curtseys, all leading to the establishment of a mysterious and confidential understanding between herself and the bride, Mrs. Gamp, invoking a blessing upon the house, leered, winked, coughed, nodded, smiled, and curtseyed herself out of the room.

"But I will say, and I would if I was led a Martha to the Stakes for it," Mrs. Gamp remarked below stairs, in a whisper, "that she don't look much like a merry one at this present moment of time."

"Ah! wait till you hear her laugh!" said Bailey.

"Hem!" cried Mrs. Gamp, in a kind of groan. "I will, child."

They said no more in the house, for Mrs. Gamp put on her bonnet, Mr. Sweedlepipe took up her box, and Mr. Bailey accompanied them towards Kingsgate Street; recounting to Mrs. Gamp as they went along, the origin and

10

Mrs. Gamp has her Eye on the Future

progress of his acquaintance with Mrs. Chuzzlewit and her sister. It was a pleasant instance of this youth's precocity, that he fancied Mrs. Gamp had conceived a tenderness for him, and was much tickled by her misplaced attachment.

As the door closed heavily behind them, Mrs. Jonas sat down in a chair, and felt a strange chill creep upon her, whilst she looked about the room. It was pretty much as she had known it, but appeared more dreary. She had thought to see it brightened to receive her.

"It ain't good enough for you, I suppose?" said Jonas, watching her looks.

"Why, it *is* dull," said Merry, trying to be more herself.

"It'll be duller before you're done with it," retorted Jonas, "if you give me any of your airs. You're a nice article, to turn sulky on first coming home! Ecod, you used to have life enough, when you could plague me with it. The gal's down stairs. Ring the bell for supper, while I take my boots off!"

She roused herself from looking after him as he left the room, to do what he had desired : when the old man Chuffey laid his hand softly on her arm.

"You are not married?" he said eagerly. "Not married?"

"Yes. A month ago. Good Heaven, what is the matter?"

He answered nothing was the matter; and turned from her. But in her fear and wonder, turning also, she saw him raise his trembling hands above his head, and heard him say :

"Oh! woe, woe, woe, upon this wicked house!"

It was her welcome,—Home.

CHAPTER XXVII

SHOWING THAT OLD FRIENDS MAY NOT ONLY APPEAR WITH NEW FACES, BUT IN FALSE COLOURS.   THAT PEOPLE ARE PRONE TO BITE ; AND THAT BITERS MAY SOMETIMES BE BITTEN

MR. BAILEY, Junior—for the sporting character, whilom of general utility at Todgers's, had now regularly set up in life under that name, without troubling himself to obtain from the legislature a direct licence in the form of a Private Bill, which of all kinds and classes of bills is without exception the most unreasonable in its charges—Mr. Bailey, Junior, just tall enough to be seen by an inquiring eye, gazing indolently at society from beneath the apron of his master's cab, drove slowly up and down Pall Mall about the hour of noon, in waiting for his " Governor." The horse of distinguished family, who had Capricorn for his nephew, and Cauliflower for his brother, showed himself worthy of his high relations by champing at the bit until his chest was white with foam, and rearing like a horse in heraldry; the plated harness and the patent leather glittered in the sun ; pedestrians admired ; Mr. Bailey was complacent, but unmoved. He seemed to say, " A barrow, good people, a mere barrow; nothing to what we could do, if we chose ! " and on he went, squaring his short green arms outside the apron, as if he were hooked on to it by his armpits.

Mr. Bailey had a great opinion of brother to Cauliflower, and estimated his powers highly.   But he never told him so.

On the contrary, it was his practice, in driving that animal, to assail him with disrespectful, if not injurious, expressions, as, "Ah! would you!" "Did you think it, then?" "Where are you going to now?" "No you won't, my lad!" and similar fragmentary remarks. These being usually accompanied by a jerk of the rein, or a crack of the whip, led to many trials of strength between them, and to many contentions for the upper hand, terminating, now and then, in china shops, and other unusual goals, as Mr. Bailey had already hinted to his friend Poll Sweedlepipe.

On the present occasion Mr. Bailey, being in spirits, was more than commonly hard upon his charge; in consequence of which that fiery animal confined himself almost entirely to his hind legs in displaying his paces, and constantly got himself into positions with reference to the cabriolet that very much amazed the passengers in the street. But Mr. Bailey, not at all disturbed, had still a shower of pleasantries to bestow on any one who crossed his path: as, calling to a full-grown coalheaver in a wagon, who for a moment blocked the way, "Now, young 'un, who trusted you with a cart?" inquiring of elderly ladies who wanted to cross, and ran back again, "Why they didn't go to the workhouse and get an order to be buried?" tempting boys, with friendly words, to get up behind, and immediately afterwards cutting them down; and the like flashes of a cheerful humour, which he would occasionally relieve by going round St. James's Square at a hand gallop, and coming slowly into Pall Mall by another entry, as if, in the interval, his pace had been a perfect crawl.

It was not until these amusements had been very often repeated, and the apple-stall at the corner had sustained so many miraculous escapes as to appear impregnable, that Mr. Bailey was summoned to the door of a certain house in Pall Mall, and turning short, obeyed the call and jumped out. It was not until he had held the bridle for some minutes longer—every jerk of Cauliflower's brother's head, and every

13

twitch of Cauliflower's brother's nostril, taking him off his legs in the meanwhile—that two persons entered the vehicle, one of whom took the reins and drove rapidly off. Nor was it until Mr. Bailey had run after it some hundreds of yards in vain, that he managed to lift his short leg into the iron step, and finally to get his boots upon the little footboard behind. Then, indeed, he became a sight to see: and—standing now on one foot and now upon the other, now trying to look round the cab on this side, now on that, and now endeavouring to peep over the top of it, as it went dashing in among the carts and coaches—was from head to heel Newmarket.

The appearance of Mr. Bailey's governor as he drove along, fully justified that enthusiastic youth's description of him to the wondering Poll. He had a world of jet-black shining hair upon his head, upon his cheeks, upon his chin, upon his upper lip. His clothes, symmetrically made, were of the newest fashion and the costliest kind. Flowers of gold and blue, and green and blushing red, were on his waistcoat; precious chains and jewels sparkled on his breast; his fingers, clogged with brilliant rings, were as unwieldy as summer flies but newly rescued from a honey-pot. The daylight mantled in his gleaming hat and boots as in a polished glass. And yet, though changed his name, and changed his outward surface, it was Tigg. Though turned and twisted upside down, and inside out, as great men have been sometimes known to be; though no longer Montague Tigg, but Tigg Montague; still it was Tigg; the same Satanic, gallant, military Tigg. The brass was burnished, lacquered, newly-stamped; yet it was the true Tigg metal notwithstanding.

Beside him sat a smiling gentleman, of less pretensions and of business looks, whom he addressed as David. Surely not the David of the—how shall it be phrased?—the triumvirate of golden balls? Not David, tapster at the Lombards' Arms? Yes. The very man.

"The secretary's salary, David," said Mr. Montague, "the office being now established, is eight hundred pounds per annum, with his house-rent, coals, and candles free. His five-and-twenty shares he holds, of course. Is that enough?"

David smiled and nodded, and coughed behind a little locked portfolio which he carried; with an air that proclaimed him to be the secretary in question.

"If that's enough," said Montague, "I will propose it at the Board to-day, in my capacity as chairman."

The secretary smiled again; laughed, indeed, this time; and said, rubbing his nose slily with one end of the portfolio:

"It was a capital thought, wasn't it?"

"What was a capital thought, David?" Mr. Montague inquired.

"The Anglo-Bengalee," tittered the secretary.

"The Anglo-Bengalee Disinterested Loan and Life Assurance Company is rather a capital concern, I hope, David," said Montague.

"Capital indeed!" cried the secretary, with another laugh —"in one sense."

"In the only important one," observed the chairman; "which is number one, David."

"What," asked the secretary, bursting into another laugh, "what will be the paid up capital, according to the next prospectus?"

"A figure of two, and as many oughts after it as the printer can get into the same line," replied his friend. "Ha, ha!"

At this they both laughed; the secretary so vehemently, that in kicking up his feet, he kicked the apron open, and nearly started Cauliflower's brother into an oyster-shop; not to mention Mr. Bailey's receiving such a sudden swing, that he held on for a moment, quite a young Fame, by one strap and no legs.

"What a chap you are!" exclaimed David admiringly, when this little alarm had subsided.

"Say, genius, David, genius."

"Well, upon my soul, you *are* a genius then," said David.

"I always knew you had the gift of the gab, of course; but I never believed you were half the man you are. How could I?"

"I rise with circumstances, David. That's a point of genius in itself," said Tigg. "If you were to lose a hundred pound wager to me at this minute, David, and were to pay it (which is most confoundedly improbable), I should rise, in a mental point of view, directly."

It is due to Mr. Tigg to say that he had really risen with his opportunities; peculating on a grander scale, he had become a grander man altogether.

"Ha, ha," cried the secretary, laying his hand, with growing familiarity, upon the chairman's arm. "When I look at you, and think of your property in Bengal being—ha, ha, ha!—"

The half-expressed idea seemed no less ludicrous to Mr. Tigg than to his friend, for he laughed, too, heartily.

"—Being," resumed David, "being amenable—your property in Bengal being amenable—to all claims upon the company; when I look at you and think of that, you might tickle me into fits by waving the feather of a pen at me. Upon my soul you might!"

"It's a devilish fine property," said Tigg Montague, "to be amenable to any claims. The preserve of tigers alone is worth a mint of money, David."

David could only reply in the intervals of his laughter, "Oh, what a chap you are!" and so continued to laugh, and hold his sides, and wipe his eyes, for some time, without offering any other observation.

"A capital idea?" said Tigg, returning after a time to his companion's first remark: "no doubt it was a capital idea. It was my idea."

"No, no. It was my idea," said David. "Hang it, let a man have some credit. Didn't I say to you that I'd saved a few pounds?—"

"You said! Didn't I say to you," interposed Tigg, "that *I* had come into a few pounds?"

"Certainly you did," returned David, warmly, "but that's not the idea. Who said, that if we put the money together we could furnish an office, and make a show?"

"And who said," retorted Mr. Tigg, "that, provided we did it on a sufficiently large scale, we could furnish an office and make a show, without any money at all? Be rational, and just, and calm, and tell me whose idea was that."

"Why there," David was obliged to confess, "you had the advantage of me, I admit. But I don't put myself on a level with you. I only want a little credit in the business."

"All the credit you deserve you have," said Tigg. "The plain work of the company, David—figures, books, circulars, advertisements, pen, ink and paper, sealing-wax and wafers—is admirably done by you. You are a first-rate groveller. I don't dispute it. But the ornamental department, David; the inventive and poetical department—"

"Is entirely yours," said his friend. "No question of it. But with such a swell turn-out as this, and all the handsome things you've got about you, and the life you lead, I mean to say it's a precious comfortable department too."

"Does it gain the purpose? Is it Anglo-Bengalee?" asked Tigg.

"Yes," said David.

"Could you undertake it yourself?" demanded Tigg.

"No," said David.

"Ha, ha!" laughed Tigg. "Then be contented with your station and your profits, David, my fine fellow, and bless the day that made us acquainted across the counter of our common uncle, for it was a golden day to you."

It will have been already gathered from the conversation of these worthies, that they were embarked in an enterprise of some magnitude, in which they addressed the public in general from the strong position of having everything to gain, and nothing at all to lose; and which, based upon this great principle, was thriving pretty comfortably.

The Anglo-Bengalee Disinterested Loan and Life Assurance

Company started into existence one morning, not an Infant Institution, but a Grown-up Company running alone at a great pace, and doing business right and left: with a " branch " in a first floor over a tailor's at the West-end of the town, and main offices in a new street in the City, comprising the upper part of a spacious house resplendent in stucco and plate-glass, with wire blinds in all the windows, and " Anglo-Bengalee " worked into the pattern of every one of them. On the door-post was painted again in large letters, " Offices of the Anglo-Bengalee Disinterested Loan and Life Assurance Company," and on the door was a large brass plate with the same inscription: always kept very bright, as courting inquiry; staring the City out of countenance after office hours on working days, and all day long on Sundays; and looking bolder than the Bank. Within, the offices were newly plastered, newly painted, newly papered, newly countered, newly floor-clothed, newly tabled, newly chaired, newly fitted-up in every way, with goods that were substantial and expensive, and designed (like the company) to last. Business! Look at the green ledgers with red backs, like strong cricket-balls beaten flat; the court-guides, directories, day-books, almanacks, letter-boxes, weighing-machines for letters, rows of fire-buckets for dashing out a conflagration in its first spark, and saving the immense wealth in notes and bonds belonging to the company; look at the iron safes, the clock, the office seal—in its capacious self, security for anything. Solidity! Look at the massive blocks of marble in the chimney-pieces, and the gorgeous parapet on the top of the house! Publicity! Why, Anglo-Bengalee Disinterested Loan and Life Assurance Company is painted on the very coal-scuttles. It is repeated at every turn until the eyes are dazzled with it, and the head is giddy. It is engraved upon the top of all the letter paper, and it makes a scroll-work round the seal, and it shines out of the porter's buttons, and it is repeated twenty times in every circular and public notice wherein one David Crimple, Esquire, Secretary and resident Director, takes the liberty of inviting your attention to the accompanying statement of the advantages offered by the Anglo-Bengalee Disinterested Loan and Life Assurance Company : and fully proves to you that any connection on your part with that establishment must result in a perpetual Christmas Box and constantly increasing Bonus to yourself, and that nobody can run any risk by the trans-action except the office, which, in its great liberality, is pretty sure to lose. And this, David Crimple, Esquire, submits to you (and the odds are heavy you believe him), is the best guarantee that can reasonably be suggested by the Board of Management for its permanence and stability.

This gentleman's name, by the way, had been originally Crimp ; but as the word was susceptible of an awkward construction and might be misrepresented, he had altered it to Crimple.

Lest with all these proofs and confirmations, any man should be suspicious of the Anglo-Bengalee Disinterested Loan and Life Assurance Company ; should doubt in tiger, cab, or person, Tigg Montague, Esquire, (of Pall Mall and Bengal), or any other name in the imaginative List of Directors ; there was a porter on the premises—a wonderful creature, in a vast red waistcoat and a short-tailed pepper-and-salt coat—who carried more conviction to the minds of sceptics than the whole establishment without him. No confidences existed between him and the Directorship ; nobody knew where he had served last ; no character or explanation had been given or required. No questions had been asked on either side. This mysterious being, relying solely on his figure, had applied for the situation, and had been instantly engaged on his own terms. They were high ; but he knew, doubtless, that no man could carry such an extent of waistcoat as himself, and felt the full value of his capacity to such an institution. When he sat upon a seat erected for him in a corner of the office, with his glazed hat hanging on a peg over his head, it was impossible to doubt the respectability of the concern. It went on doubling itself with every square-inch of his red waistcoat until, like the problem of the nails in the horse's shoes, the total became enormous. People had been known to apply to effect an insurance on their lives for a thousand pounds, and looking at him, to beg, before the form of proposal was filled up, that it might be made two. And yet he was not a giant. His coat was rather small than otherwise. The whole charm was in his waistcoat. Respectability, competence, property in Bengal or anywhere else, responsibility to any amount on the part of the company that employed him, were all expressed in that one garment.

Rival offices had endeavoured to lure him away; Lombard Street itself had beckoned to him; rich companies had whispered "Be a Beadle!" but he still continued faithful to the Anglo-Bengalee. Whether he was a deep rogue, or a stately simpleton, it was impossible to make out, but he appeared to believe in the Anglo-Bengalee. He was grave with imaginary cares of office; and having nothing whatever to do, and something less to take care of, would look as if the pressure of his numerous duties, and a sense of the treasure in the company's strong-room, made him a solemn and a thoughtful man.

As the cabriolet drove up to the door, this officer appeared bareheaded on the pavement, crying aloud "Room for the chairman, room for the chairman, if you please!" much to the admiration of the bystanders, who, it is needless to say, had their attention directed to the Anglo-Bengalee Company thenceforth, by that means. Mr. Tigg leaped gracefully out, followed by the Managing Director (who was by this time very distant and respectful), and ascended the stairs, still preceded by the porter: who cried as he went, "By your leave there! by your leave! The Chairman of the Board, Gentle—MEN!" In like manner, but in a still more stentorian voice, he ushered the chairman through the public office, where some humble clients were transacting business, into an awful chamber, labelled Board-room : the door of which sanctuary immediately closed, and screened the great capitalist from vulgar eyes.

The board-room had a Turkey carpet in it, a sideboard, a portrait of Tigg Montague, Esquire, as chairman ; a very imposing chair of office, garnished with an ivory hammer and a little hand-bell ; and a long-table, set out at intervals with sheets of blotting-paper, foolscap, clean pens, and ink-stands. The chairman having taken his seat with great solemnity, the secretary supported him on his right hand, and the porter stood bolt upright behind them, forming a warm background of waistcoat. This was the board ; everything else being a light-hearted little fiction.

"Bullamy !" said Mr. Tigg.

"Sir !" replied the Porter.

"Let the Medical Officer know, with my compliments, that I wish to see him."

Bullamy cleared his throat, and bustled out into the office, crying "The Chairman of the Board wishes to see the Medical Officer. By your leave there ! By your leave !" He soon returned with the gentleman in question ; and at both openings of the board-room door—at his coming in and at his going out—simple clients were seen to stretch their necks and stand upon their toes, thirsting to catch the slightest glimpse of that mysterious chamber.

"Jobling, my dear friend !" said Mr. Tigg, "how are you ? Bullamy, wait outside. Crimple, don't leave us. Jobling, my good fellow, I am glad to see you."

"And how are *you*, Mr. Montague, eh ?" said the Medical Officer, throwing himself luxuriously into an easy-chair (they were all easy-chairs in the board-room), and taking a handsome gold snuff-box from the pocket of his black satin waistcoat. "How are you ? A little worn with business, eh ? If so, rest. A little feverish from wine, humph ? If so, water. Nothing at all the matter, and quite comfortable ? Then take some lunch. A very wholesome thing at this time of day to strengthen the gastric juices with lunch, Mr. Montague."

The Medical Officer (he was the same medical officer who had followed poor old Anthony Chuzzlewit to the grave, and who had attended Mrs. Gamp's patient at the Bull) smiled in saying these words; and casually added, as he brushed some grains of snuff from his shirt-frill, " I always take it myself about this time of day, do you know ! "

"Bullamy ! " said the Chairman, ringing the little bell.

" Sir ! "

" Lunch."

"Not on my account, I hope?" said the doctor. " You are very good. Thank you. I'm quite ashamed. Ha, ha ! if I had been a sharp practitioner, Mr. Montague, I shouldn't have mentioned it without a fee; for you may depend upon it, my dear sir, that if you don't make a point of taking lunch, you'll very soon come under my hands. Allow me to illustrate this. In Mr. Crimple's leg— "

The resident Director gave an involuntary start, for the doctor, in the heat of his demonstration, caught it up and laid it across his own, as if he were going to take it off, then and there.

" In Mr. Crimple's leg, you'll observe," pursued the doctor, turning back his cuffs and spanning the limb with both hands, " where Mr. Crimple's knee fits into the socket, here, there is—that is to say, between the bone and the socket—a certain quantity of animal oil."

" What do you pick *my* leg out for?" said Mr. Crimple, looking with something of an anxious expression at his limb. "It's the same with other legs, ain't it?"

"Never you mind, my good sir," returned the doctor, shaking his head, " whether it is the same with other legs, or not the same."

" But I do mind," said David.

" I take a particular case, Mr. Montague," returned the doctor, " as illustrating my remark, you observe. In this portion of Mr. Crimple's leg, sir, there is a certain amount of animal oil. In every one of Mr. Crimple's joints, sir, there is more or less of the same deposit. Very good. If Mr. Crimple neglects his meals, or fails to take his proper quantity of rest, that oil wanes, and becomes exhausted. What is the consequence? Mr. Crimple's bones sink down into their sockets, sir, and Mr. Crimple becomes a weazen, puny, stunted, miserable man!"

The doctor let Mr. Crimple's leg fall suddenly, as if he were already in that agreeable condition: turned down his wristbands again, and looked triumphantly at the chairman.

"We know a few secrets of nature in our profession, sir," said the doctor. "Of course we do. We study for that; we pass the Hall and the College for that; and we take our station in society *by* that. It's extraordinary how little is known on these subjects generally. Where do you suppose, now:" the doctor closed one eye, as he leaned back smilingly in his chair, and formed a triangle with his hands, of which his two thumbs composed the base: "where do you suppose Mr. Crimple's stomach is?"

Mr. Crimple, more agitated than before, clapped his hand immediately below his waistcoat.

"Not at all," cried the doctor; "not at all. Quite a popular mistake! My good sir, you're altogether deceived."

"I feel it there, when it's out of order; that's all I know," said Crimple.

"You think you do," replied the doctor; "but science knows better. There was a patient of mine once:" touching one of the many mourning rings upon his fingers, and slightly bowing his head: "a gentleman who did me the honour to make a very handsome mention of me in his will—'in testimony,' as he was pleased to say, 'of the unremitting zeal, talent, and attention of my friend and medical attendant, John Jobling, Esquire, M.R.C.S.,'—who was so overcome by the idea of having all his life laboured under an erroneous view of the locality of this important organ, that when I assured him, on my professional reputation, he was mistaken, he burst into tears, put out his hand, and said, 'Jobling, God bless you!' Immediately afterwards he became speechless, and was ultimately buried at Brixton."

"By your leave there!" cried Bullamy, without. "By your leave! Refreshment for the Board-room!"

"Ha!" said the doctor, jocularly, as he rubbed his hands, and drew his chair nearer to the table. "The true Life Assurance, Mr. Montague. The best Policy in the world, my dear sir. We should be provident, and eat and drink whenever we can. Eh, Mr. Crimple?"

The resident Director acquiesced rather sulkily, as if the gratification of replenishing his stomach had been impaired by the unsettlement of his preconceived opinions in reference to its situation. But the appearance of the porter and under porter with a tray covered with a snow-white cloth, which, being thrown back, displayed a pair of cold roast fowls, flanked by some potted meats and a cool salad, quickly restored his good humour. It was enhanced still further by the arrival of a bottle of excellent madeira, and another of champagne; and he soon attacked the repast with an appetite scarcely inferior to that of the medical officer.

The lunch was handsomely served, with a profusion of rich glass, plate, and china; which seemed to denote that eating and drinking on a showy scale formed no unimportant item in the business of the Anglo-Bengalee Directorship. As it proceeded, the Medical Officer grew more and more joyous and red-faced, insomuch that every mouthful he ate, and every drop of wine he swallowed, seemed to impart new lustre to his eyes, and to light up new sparks in his nose and forehead.

In certain quarters of the City and its neighbourhood, Mr. Jobling was, as we have already seen in some measure, a very popular character. He had a portentously sagacious chin, and a pompous voice, with a rich huskiness in some of its tones that went directly to the heart, like a ray of light

The Board

shining through the ruddy medium of choice old burgundy. His neck-kerchief and shirt-frill were ever of the whitest, his clothes of the blackest and sleekest, his gold watch-chain of the heaviest, and his seals of the largest. His boots, which were always of the brightest, creaked as he walked. Perhaps he could shake his head, rub his hands, or warm himself before a fire, better than any man alive; and he had a peculiar way of smacking his lips and saying, "Ah!" at intervals while patients detailed their symptoms, which inspired great confidence. It seemed to express, "I know what you're going to say better than you do; but go on, go on." As he talked on all occasions whether he had anything to say or not, it was unanimously observed of him that he was "full of anecdote;" and his experience and profit from it were considered, for the same reason, to be something much too extensive for description. His female patients could never praise him too highly; and the coldest of his male admirers would always say this for him to their friends, "that whatever Jobling's professional skill might be (and it could not be denied that he had a very high reputation), he was one of the most comfortable fellows you ever saw in your life!"

Jobling was for many reasons, and not last in the list because his connection lay principally among tradesmen and their families, exactly the sort of person whom the Anglo-Bengalee Company wanted for a medical officer. But Jobling was far too knowing to connect himself with the company in any closer ties than as a paid (and well-paid) functionary, or to allow his connection to be misunderstood abroad, if he could help it. Hence he always stated the case to an inquiring patient, after this manner:

"Why, my dear sir, with regard to the Anglo-Bengalee, my information, you see, is limited: very limited. I am the medical officer, in consideration of a certain monthly payment. The labourer is worthy of his hire; *Bis dat qui citò dat*"— ("Classical scholar, Jobling!" thinks the patient, "well-read

25

man!")—"and I receive it regularly. Therefore I am bound, so far as my own knowledge goes, to speak well of the establishment." ("Nothing can be fairer than Jobling's conduct," thinks the patient, who has just paid Jobling's bill himself.) "If you put any question to me, my dear friend," says the doctor, "touching the responsibility or capital of the company, there I am at fault; for I have no head for figures, and not being a shareholder, am delicate of showing any curiosity whatever on the subject. Delicacy— your amiable lady will agree with me I am sure—should be one of the first characteristics of a medical man." ("Nothing can be finer or more gentlemanly than Jobling's feeling," thinks the patient.) "Very good, my dear sir, so the matter stands. You don't know Mr. Montague? I'm sorry for it. A remarkably handsome man, and quite the gentleman in every respect. Property, I am told, in India. House and everything belonging to him, beautiful. Costly furniture on the most elegant and lavish scale. And pictures, which, even in an anatomical point of view, are per—fection. In case you should ever think of doing anything with the company, I'll pass you, you may depend upon it. I can conscientiously report you a healthy subject. If I understand any man's constitution, it is yours; and this little indisposition has done him more good, ma'am," says the doctor, turning to the patient's wife, "than if he had swallowed the contents of half the nonsensical bottles in my surgery. For they *are* nonsense—to tell the honest truth, one half of them *are* nonsense—compared with such a constitution as his!" ("Jobling is the most friendly creature I ever met with in my life," thinks the patient; "and upon my word and honour, I'll consider of it!")

"Commission to you, doctor, on four new policies, and a loan this morning, eh?" said Crimple, looking, when they had finished lunch, over some papers brought in by the porter. "Well done!"

"Jobling, my dear friend," said Tigg, "long life to you."

THE PORTER PRESENTS A CARD

"No, no. Nonsense. Upon my word I've no right to draw the commission," said the doctor, "I haven't really. It's picking your pocket. I don't recommend anybody here. I only say what I know. My patients ask me what I know, and I tell 'em what I know. Nothing else. Caution is my weak side, that's the truth; and always was from a boy. That is," said the doctor, filling his glass, "caution in behalf of other people. Whether I would repose confidence in this company myself, if I had not been paying money elsewhere for many years—that's quite another question."

He tried to look as if there were no doubt about it; but feeling that he did it but indifferently, changed the theme, and praised the wine.

"Talking of wine," said the doctor, "reminds me of one of the finest glasses of light old port I ever drank in my life; and that was at a funeral. You have not seen anything of— of *that* party, Mr. Montague, have you?" handing him a card.

"He is not buried, I hope?" said Tigg, as he took it. "The honour of his company is not requested if he is."

"Ha, ha!" laughed the doctor. "No; not quite. He was honourably connected with that very occasion though."

"Oh!" said Tigg, smoothing his moustache, as he cast his eyes upon the name. "I recollect. No. He has not been here."

The words were on his lips, when Bullamy entered, and presented a card to the Medical Officer.

"Talk of the what's his name," observed the doctor rising.

"And he's sure to appear, eh?" said Tigg.

"Why, no, Mr. Montague, no," returned the doctor. "We will not say that in the present case, for this gentleman is very far from it."

"So much the better," retorted Tigg. "So much the more adaptable to the Anglo-Bengalee. Bullamy, clear the table and take the things out by the other door. Mr. Crimple, business."

"Shall I introduce him?" asked Jobling.

"I shall be eternally delighted," answered Tigg, kissing his hand and smiling sweetly.

The doctor disappeared into the outer office, and immediately returned with Jonas Chuzzlewit.

"Mr. Montague," said Jobling. "Allow me. My friend Mr. Chuzzlewit. My dear friend—our chairman. Now do you know," he added, checking himself with infinite policy, and looking round with a smile: "that's a very singular instance of the force of example. It really is a very remarkable instance of the force of example. I say *our* chairman. Why do I say our chairman? Because he is not *my* chairman, you know. I have no connection with the company, farther than giving them, for a certain fee and reward, my poor opinion as a medical man, precisely as I may give it any day to Jack Noakes or Tom Styles. Then why do I say our chairman? Simply because I hear the phrase constantly repeated about me. Such is the involuntary operation of the mental faculty in the imitative biped man. Mr. Crimple, I believe you never take snuff? Injudicious. You should."

Pending these remarks on the part of the doctor, and the lengthened and sonorous pinch with which he followed them up, Jonas took a seat at the board: as ungainly a man as ever he has been within the reader's knowledge. It is too common with all of us, but it is especially in the nature of a mean mind, to be overawed by fine clothes and fine furniture. They had a very decided influence on Jonas.

"Now you two gentlemen have business to discuss, I know," said the doctor, "and your time is precious. So is mine; for several lives are waiting for me in the next room, and I have a round of visits to make after—after I have taken 'em. Having had the happiness to introduce you to each other, I may go about my business. Good bye. But allow me, Mr. Montague, before I go, to say this of my friend who sits beside you: That gentleman has done more, sir," rapping his snuff-box solemnly, "to reconcile me to human nature, than any man alive or dead. Good bye!"

A RECRUIT INTRODUCED

With these words Jobling bolted abruptly out of the room, and proceeded in his own official department, to impress the lives in waiting with a sense of his keen conscientiousness in the discharge of his duty, and the great difficulty of getting into the Anglo-Bengalee; by feeling their pulses, looking at their tongues, listening at their ribs, poking them in the chest, and so forth; though, if he didn't well know beforehand that whatever kind of lives they were, the Anglo-Bengalee would accept them readily, he was far from being the Jobling that his friend considered him; and was not the original Jobling, but a spurious imitation.

Mr. Crimple also departed on the business of the morning; and Jonas Chuzzlewit and Tigg were left alone.

"I learn from our friend," said Tigg, drawing his chair towards Jonas with a winning ease of manner, "that you have been thinking—"

"Oh! Ecod then he'd no right to say so," cried Jonas, interrupting. "I didn't tell *him* my thoughts. If he took it into his head that I was coming here for such or such a purpose, why, that's his look-out. I don't stand committed by that."

Jonas said this offensively enough; for over and above the habitual distrust of his character, it was in his nature to seek to revenge himself on the fine clothes and the fine furniture, in exact proportion as he had been unable to withstand their influence.

"If I come here to ask a question or two, and get a document or two to consider of, I don't bind myself to anything. Let's understand that, you know," said Jonas.

"My dear fellow!" cried Tigg, clapping him on the shoulder, "I applaud your frankness. If men like you and I speak openly at first, all possible misunderstanding is avoided. Why should I disguise what you know so well, but what the crowd never dream of? We companies are all birds of prey: mere birds of prey. The only question is, whether, in serving our own turn, we can serve yours too: whether in

29

double-lining our own nest, we can put a single lining into yours. Oh, you're in our secret. You're behind the scenes. We'll make a merit of dealing plainly with you, when we know we can't help it."

It was remarked, on the first introduction of Mr. Jonas into these pages, that there is a simplicity of cunning no less than a simplicity of innocence, and that in all matters involving a faith in knavery, he was the most credulous of men. If Mr. Tigg had preferred any claim to high and honourable dealing, Jonas would have suspected him though he had been a very model of probity; but when he gave utterance to Jonas's own thoughts of everything and everybody, Jonas began to feel that he was a pleasant fellow, and one to be talked to freely.

He changed his position in the chair; not for a less awkward, but for a more boastful attitude; and smiling in his miserable conceit, rejoined:

" You an't a bad man of business, Mr. Montague. You know how to set about it, I *will* say."

" Tut, tut," said Tigg, nodding confidentially, and showing his white teeth: " we are not children, Mr. Chuzzlewit; we are grown men, I hope."

Jonas assented, and said after a short silence, first spreading out his legs, and sticking one arm akimbo to show how perfectly at home he was,

" The truth is— "

" Don't say, the truth," interposed Tigg, with another grin. " It's so like humbug."

Greatly charmed by this, Jonas began again.

" The long and the short of it, is— "

" Better," muttered Tigg. " Much better!"

" —That I didn't consider myself very well used by one or two of the old companies in some negotiations I have had with 'em. Once had, I mean. They started objections they had no right to start, and put questions they had no right to put, and carried things much too high for my taste."

As he made these observations he cast down his eyes, and

looked curiously at the carpet. Mr. Tigg looked curiously at him.

He made so long a pause, that Tigg came to the rescue, and said, in his pleasantest manner:

"Take a glass of wine."

"No, no," returned Jonas, with a cunning shake of the head; "none of that, thankee. No wine over business. All very well for you, but it wouldn't do for me."

"What an old hand you are, Mr. Chuzzlewit!" said Tigg, leaning back in his chair, and leering at him through his half-shut eyes.

Jonas shook his head again, as much as to say, "You're right there;" and then resumed, jocosely:

"Not such an old hand, either, but that I've been and got married. That's rather green, you'll say. Perhaps it is, especially as she's young. But one never knows what may happen to these women, so I'm thinking of insuring her life. It is but fair, you know, that a man should secure some consolation in case of meeting with such a loss."

"If anything *can* console him under such heart-breaking circumstances," murmured Tigg, with his eyes shut up as before.

"Exactly," returned Jonas; "if anything can. Now, supposing I did it here, I should do it cheap, I know, and easy, without bothering her about it; which I'd much rather not do, for it's just in a woman's way to take it into her head, if you talk to her about such things, that she's going to die directly."

"So it is," cried Tigg, kissing his hand in honour of the sex. "You're quite right. Sweet, silly, fluttering little simpletons!"

"Well," said Jonas, "on that account, you know, and because offence has been given me in other quarters, I wouldn't mind patronising this Company. But I want to know what sort of security there is for the Company's going on. That's the—"

31

"Not the truth?" cried Tigg, holding up his jewelled hand. "Don't use that Sunday School expression, please!"

"The long and the short of it," said Jonas. "The long and the short of it is, what's the security?"

"The paid-up capital, my dear sir," said Tigg, referring to some papers on the table, "is, at this present moment— "

"Oh! I understand all about paid-up capitals, you know," said Jonas.

"You do?" cried Tigg, stopping short.

"I should hope so."

He turned the papers down again, and moving nearer to him, said in his ear:

"I know you do. I know you do. Look at me!"

It was not much in Jonas's way to look straight at anybody; but thus requested, he made shift to take a tolerable survey of the chairman's features. The chairman fell back a little, to give him the better opportunity

"You know me?" he inquired, elevating his eyebrows. "You recollect? You've seen me before?"

"Why, I thought I remembered your face when I first came in," said Jonas, gazing at it: "but I couldn't call to mind where I had seen it. No. I don't remember, even now. Was it in the street?"

"Was it in Pecksniff's parlour?" said Tigg.

"In Pecksniff's parlour!" echoed Jonas, fetching a long breath. "You don't mean when— "

"Yes," cried Tigg, "when there was a very charming and delightful little family party, at which yourself and your respected father assisted."

"Well, never mind *him*," said Jonas. "He's dead, and there's no help for it."

"Dead, is he!" cried Tigg. "Venerable old gentleman, is he dead! You're very like him."

Jonas received this compliment with anything but a good grace; perhaps because of his own private sentiments in reference to the personal appearance of his deceased parent;

perhaps because he was not best pleased to find that Montague and Tigg were one. That gentleman perceived it, and tapping him familiarly on the sleeve, beckoned him to the window. From this moment, Mr. Montague's jocularity and flow of spirits were remarkable.

"Do you find me at all changed since that time?" he asked. "Speak plainly."

Jonas looked hard at his waistcoat and jewels; and said, "Rather, ecod!"

"Was I at all seedy in those days?" asked Montague.

"Precious seedy," said Jonas.

Mr. Montague pointed down into the street, where Bailey and the cab were in attendance.

"Neat: perhaps dashing. Do you know whose it is?"

"No."

"Mine. Do you like this room?"

"It must have cost a lot of money," said Jonas.

"You're right. Mine too. Why don't you"—he whispered this, and nudged him in the side with his elbow—"why don't you take premiums, instead of paying 'em? That's what a man like you should do. Join us!"

Jonas stared at him in amazement.

"Is that a crowded street?" asked Montague, calling his attention to the multitude without.

"Very," said Jonas, only glancing at it, and immediately afterwards looking at him again.

"There are printed calculations," said his companion, "which will tell you pretty nearly how many people will pass up and down that thoroughfare in the course of a day. *I* can tell you how many of 'em will come in here, merely because they find this office here; knowing no more about it than they do of the Pyramids. Ha, ha! Join us. You shall come in cheap."

Jonas looked at him harder and harder.

"I can tell you," said Tigg in his ear, "how many of 'em will buy annuities, effect insurances, bring us their money in a hundred shapes and ways, force it upon us, trust us as if we were the Mint; yet know no more about us than you do of that crossing-sweeper at the corner. Not so much. Ha, ha!"

Jonas gradually broke into a smile.

"Yah!" said Montague, giving him a pleasant thrust in the breast; "you're too deep for us, you dog, or I wouldn't have told you. Dine with me to-morrow, in Pall Mall!"

"I will," said Jonas.

"Done!" cried Montague. "Wait a bit. Take these papers with you, and look 'em over. See," he said, snatching some printed forms from the table. "B is a little tradesman, clerk, parson, artist, author, any common thing you like."

"Yes," said Jonas, looking greedily over his shoulder. "Well!"

"B wants a loan. Say fifty or a hundred pound; perhaps more; no matter. B proposes self and two securities. B is accepted. Two securities give a bond. B assures his own life for double the amount, and brings two friends' lives also —just to patronise the office. Ha, ha, ha! Is that a good notion?"

"Ecod, that's a capital notion!" cried Jonas. "But does he really do it?"

"Do it!" repeated the chairman. "B's hard-up, my good fellow, and will do anything. Don't you see? It's my idea."

"It does you honour. I'm blest if it don't," said Jonas.

"I think it does," replied the chairman, "and I'm proud to hear you say so. B pays the highest lawful interest—"

"That an't much," interrupted Jonas.

"Right! quite right!" retorted Tigg. "And hard it is upon the part of the law that it should be so confoundedly down upon us unfortunate victims; when it takes such amazing good interest for itself from all its clients. But charity begins at home, and justice begins next door. Well! The law being hard upon us, we're not exactly soft upon B; for besides charging B the regular interest, we get B's

34

premium, and B's friends' premiums, and we charge B for the bond, and, whether we accept him or not, we charge B for 'inquiries' (we keep a man, at a pound a week, to make 'em), and we charge B a trifle for the secretary; and, in short, my good fellow, we stick it into B, up hill and down dale, and make a devilish comfortable little property out of him. Ha, ha, ha! I drive B, in point of fact," said Tigg, pointing to the cabriolet, "and a thorough-bred horse he is. Ha, ha, ha!"

Jonas enjoyed this joke very much indeed. It was quite in his peculiar vein of humour.

"Then," said Tigg Montague, "we grant annuities on the very lowest and most advantageous terms, known in the money market; and the old ladies and gentlemen down in the country, buy 'em. Ha, ha, ha! And we pay 'em too—perhaps. Ha, ha, ha!"

"But there's responsibility in that," said Jonas, looking doubtful.

"I take it all myself," said Tigg Montague. "Here I am responsible for everything. The only responsible person in the establishment! Ha, ha, ha! Then there are the Life Assurances without loans: the common policies. Very profitable, very comfortable. Money down, you know; repeated every year; capital fun!"

"But when they begin to fall in," observed Jonas. "It's all very well, while the office is young, but when the policies begin to die; that's what I am thinking of."

"At the first start, my dear fellow," said Montague, "to show you how correct your judgment is, we had a couple of unlucky deaths that brought us down to a grand piano."

"Brought you down where?" cried Jonas.

"I give you my sacred word of honour," said Tigg Montague, "that I raised money on every other individual piece of property, and was left alone in the world with a grand piano. And it was an upright-grand too, so that I couldn't even sit upon it. But, my dear fellow, we got over it. We granted a great many new policies that week (liberal allowance to solicitors, by the bye), and got over it in no time. Whenever they should chance to fall in heavily, as you very justly observe they may, one of these days; then—" he finished the sentence in so low a whisper, that only one disconnected word was audible, and that imperfectly. But it sounded like "Bolt."

"Why, you're as bold as brass!" said Jonas, in the utmost admiration.

"A man can well afford to be as bold as brass, my good fellow, when he gets gold in exchange!" cried the chairman, with a laugh that shook him from head to foot. "You'll dine with me to-morrow?"

"At what time?" asked Jonas.

"Seven. Here's my card. Take the documents. I see you'll join us!"

"I don't know about that," said Jonas. "There's a good deal to be looked into first."

"You shall look," said Montague, slapping him on the back, "into anything and everything you please. But you'll join us, I am convinced. You were made for it. Bullamy!"

Obedient to the summons and the little bell, the waistcoat appeared. Being charged to show Jonas out, it went before; and the voice within it cried, as usual, "By your leave there, by your leave! Gentleman from the board-room, by your leave!"

Mr. Montague being left alone, pondered for some moments, and then said, raising his voice,

"Is Nadgett in the office there?"

"Here he is, sir." And he promptly entered: shutting the board-room door after him, as carefully as if he were about to plot a murder.

He was the man at a pound a week who made the inquiries. It was no virtue or merit in Nadgett that he transacted all his Anglo-Bengalee business secretly and in the closest confidence; for he was born to be a secret. He was a short, dried-up, withered, old man, who seemed to have secreted his very blood; for nobody would have given him credit for the possession of six ounces of it in his whole body. How he lived was a secret; where he lived was a secret; and even what he was, was a secret. In his musty old pocket-book he carried contradictory cards, in some of which he called himself a coal-merchant, in others a wine-merchant, in others a commission-agent, in others a collector, in others an accountant: as if he really didn't know the secret himself. He was always keeping appointments in the City, and the other man never seemed to come. He would sit on 'Change for hours, looking at everybody who walked in and out, and would do the like at Garraway's, and in other business coffee-houses, in some of which he would be occasionally seen drying a very damp pocket-handkerchief before the fire, and still looking over his shoulder for the man who never appeared. He was mildewed, threadbare, shabby; always had flue upon his legs and back; and kept his linen so secret by buttoning up and wrapping over, that he might have had none—perhaps he hadn't. He carried one stained beaver glove, which he dangled before him by the forefinger as he walked or sat; but even its fellow was a secret. Some people said he had been a bankrupt, others that he had gone an infant into an ancient Chancery suit which was still depending, but it was all a secret. He carried bits of sealing-wax and a hieroglyphical old copper seal in his pocket, and often secretly indited letters in corner boxes of the trysting-places before mentioned; but they never appeared to go to anybody, for he would put them into a secret place in his coat, and deliver them to himself weeks afterwards, very much to his own surprise, quite yellow. He was that sort of man that if he had died worth a million of money, or had died worth twopence halfpenny, everybody would have been perfectly satisfied, and would have said it was just as they expected. And yet he belonged to a class; a race peculiar to the City; who are secrets as profound to one another, as they are to the rest of mankind.

" Mr. Nadgett," said Montague, copying Jonas Chuzzlewit's address upon a piece of paper, from the card which was still lying on the table, " any information about this name, I shall be glad to have myself. Don't you mind what it is. Any you can scrape together, bring me. Bring it *to me*, Mr. Nadgett."

Nadgett put on his spectacles, and read the name attentively; then looked at the chairman over his glasses, and bowed ; then took them off, and put them in their case ; and then put the case in his pocket. When he had done so, he looked, without his spectacles, at the paper as it lay before him, and at the same time produced his pocket-book from somewhere about the middle of his spine. Large as it was, it was very full of documents, but he found a place for this one ; and having clasped it carefully, passed it by a kind of solemn legerdemain into the same region as before.

He withdrew with another bow and without a word ; opening the door no wider than was sufficient for his passage out ; and shutting it as carefully as before. The chairman of the board employed the rest of the morning in affixing his sign-manual of gracious acceptance to various new proposals of annuity-purchase and assurance. The Company was looking up, for they flowed in gaily.

CHAPTER XXVIII

THERE were many powerful reasons for Jonas Chuzzlewit being strongly prepossessed in favour of the scheme which its great originator had so boldly laid open to him; but three among them stood prominently forward. Firstly, there was money to be made by it. Secondly, the money had the peculiar charm of being sagaciously obtained at other people's cost. Thirdly, it involved much outward show of homage and distinction: a board being an awful institution in its own sphere, and a director a mighty man. " To make a swingeing profit, have a lot of chaps to order about, and get into regular good society by one and the same means, and them so easy to one's hand, ain't such a bad look out," thought Jonas. The latter considerations were only second to his avarice; for, conscious that there was nothing in his person, conduct, character, or accomplishments, to command respect, he was greedy of power, and was, in his heart, as much a tyrant as any laurelled conqueror on record.

But he determined to proceed with cunning and caution, and to be very keen in his observation of the gentility of Mr. Montague's private establishment. For it no more occurred to this shallow knave that Montague wanted him to be so, or he wouldn't have invited him while his decision was yet in abeyance, than the possibility of that genius being able to overreach him in any way, pierced through his self-conceit by the inlet of a needle's point. He had said, in the outset, that Jonas was too sharp for him; and Jonas, who would have been sharp enough to believe him in nothing else, though he had solemnly sworn it, believed him in that, instantly.

It was with a faltering hand, and yet with an imbecile attempt at a swagger, that he knocked at his new friend's door in Pall Mall when the appointed hour arrived. Mr. Bailey quickly answered to the summons. He was not proud, and was kindly disposed to take notice of Jonas; but Jonas had forgotten him.

" Mr. Montague at home ? "

" I should hope he wos at home, and waiting dinner, too," said Bailey, with the ease of an old acquaintance. " Will you take your hat up along with you, or leave it here ? "

Mr. Jonas preferred leaving it there.

" The hold name, I suppose ? " said Bailey, with a grin.

Mr. Jonas stared at him, in mute indignation.

" What, don't you remember hold mother Todgers's ? " said Mr. Bailey, with his favourite action of the knees and boots. " Don't you remember my taking your name up to the young ladies, when you come a courting there ? A reg'lar scaly old shop, warn't it ? Times is changed, ain't they ? I say, how you've growed ! "

Without pausing for any acknowledgment of this compliment, he ushered the visitor up stairs; and having announced him, retired with a private wink.

The lower story of the house was occupied by a wealthy tradesman, but Mr. Montague had all the upper portion, and splendid lodging it was. The room in which he received Jonas was a spacious and elegant apartment, furnished with extreme magnificence: decorated with pictures, copies from the antique in alabaster and marble, china vases, lofty mirrors, crimson hangings of the richest silk, gilded carvings, luxurious couches, glistening cabinets inlaid with precious woods: costly toys of every sort in negligent abundance. The only guests besides Jonas were the doctor, the resident

Director, and two other gentlemen, whom Montague presented in due form.

"My dear friend, I am delighted to see you. Jobling you know, I believe?"

"I think so," said the doctor pleasantly, as he stepped out of the circle to shake hands. "I trust I have that honour. I hope so. My dear sir, I see you well. Quite well? *That's* well!"

"Mr. Wolf," said Montague, as soon as the doctor would allow him to introduce the two others, "Mr. Chuzzlewit. Mr. Pip, Mr. Chuzzlewit."

Both gentlemen were exceedingly happy to have the honour of making Mr. Chuzzlewit's acquaintance. The doctor drew Jonas a little apart, and whispered behind his hand:

"Men of the world, my dear sir—men of the world. Hem! Mr. Wolf—literary character—you needn't mention it—remarkably clever weekly paper—oh, remarkably clever! Mr. Pip—theatrical man—capital man to know—oh, capital man!"

"Well!" said Wolf, folding his arms and resuming a conversation which the arrival of Jonas had interrupted. "And what did Lord Nobley say to that?"

"Why," returned Pip, with an oath. "He didn't know what to say. Damme, sir, if he wasn't as mute as a poker. But you know what a good fellow Nobley is!"

"The best fellow in the world!" cried Wolf. "It was only last week that Nobley said to me, 'By Gad, Wolf, I've got a living to bestow, and if you had but been brought up at the University, strike me blind if I wouldn't have made a parson of you!'"

"Just like him," said Pip with another oath. "And he'd have done it!"

"Not a doubt of it," said Wolf. "But you were going to tell us?—"

"Oh, yes!" cried Pip. "To be sure. So I was. At first

he was dumb—sewn up, dead, sir—but after a minute he said to the Duke, 'Here's Pip. Ask Pip. Pip's our mutual friend. Ask Pip. He knows.' 'Damme!' said the Duke, 'I appeal to Pip then. Come, Pip. Bandy or not bandy? Speak out!' 'Bandy, your Grace, by the Lord Harry!' said I. 'Ha, ha!' laughed the Duke. 'To be sure she is. Bravo, Pip. Well said, Pip. I wish I may die if you're not a trump, Pip. Pop me down among your fashionable visitors whenever I'm in town, Pip.' And so I do, to this day."

The conclusion of this story gave immense satisfaction, which was in no degree lessened by the announcement of dinner. Jonas repaired to the dining-room, along with his distinguished host, and took his seat at the board between that individual and his friend the doctor. The rest fell into their places like men who were well accustomed to the house; and dinner was done full justice to, by all parties.

It was as good a one as money (or credit, no matter which) could produce. The dishes, wines, and fruits were of the choicest kind. Everything was elegantly served. The plate was gorgeous. Mr. Jonas was in the midst of a calculation of the value of this item alone, when his host disturbed him.

" A glass of wine ? "

"Oh!" said Jonas, who had had several glasses already. "As much of that, as you like! It's too good to refuse."

"Well said, Mr. Chuzzlewit!" cried Wolf.

"Tom Gag, upon my soul!" said Pip.

"Positively, you know, that's—ha, ha, ha!" observed the doctor, laying down his knife and fork for one instant, and then going to work again, pell-mell—"that's epigrammatic; quite!"

"You're tolerably comfortable, I hope?" said Tigg, apart to Jonas.

"Oh! You needn't trouble your head about *me*," he replied. "Famous!"

"I thought it best not to have a party," said Tigg. "You feel that?"

"Why, what do you call this?" retorted Jonas. "You don't mean to say you do this every day, do you?"

"My dear fellow," said Montague, shrugging his shoulders, "every day of my life, when I dine at home. This is my common style. It was of no use having anything uncommon for you. You'd have seen through it. 'You'll have a party?' said Crimple. 'No, I won't,' I said; 'he shall take us in the rough!'"

"And pretty smooth too, ecod!" said Jonas, glancing round the table. "This don't cost a trifle."

"Why, to be candid with you, it does not," returned the other. "But I like this sort of thing. It's the way I spend my money."

Jonas thrust his tongue into his cheek, and said, "Was it?"

"When you join us, you won't get rid of your share of the profits in the same way?" said Tigg.

"Quite different," retorted Jonas.

"Well, and you're right," said Tigg, with friendly candour. "You needn't. It's not necessary. One of a Company must do it to hold the connexion together; but, as I take a pleasure in it, that's my department. You don't mind dining expensively at another man's expense, I hope?"

"Not a bit," said Jonas.

"Then I hope you'll often dine with me?"

"Ah!" said Jonas, "I don't mind. On the contrary."

"And I'll never attempt to talk business to you over wine, I take my oath," said Tigg. "Oh deep, deep, deep of you this morning! I must tell 'em that. They're the very men to enjoy it. Pip, my good fellow, I've a splendid little trait to tell you of my friend Chuzzlewit, who is the deepest dog I know. I give you my sacred word of honour he is the deepest dog I know, Pip!"

Pip swore a frightful oath that he was sure of it already; and the anecdote, being told, was received with loud applause, as an incontestable proof of Mr. Jonas's greatness. Pip, in

a natural spirit of emulation, then related some instances of
his own depth; and Wolf, not to be left behind-hand, recited
the leading points of one or two vastly humorous articles he
was then preparing. These lucubrations, being of what he
called "a warm complexion," were highly approved; and all
the company agreed that they were full of point.

"Men of the world, my dear sir," Jobling whispered to
Jonas; "thorough men of the world! To a professional
person like myself, it's quite refreshing to come into this kind
of society. It's not only agreeable—and nothing *can* be more
agreeable—but it's philosophically improving. It's character,
my dear sir; character!"

It is so pleasant to find real merit appreciated, whatever
its particular walk in life may be, that the general harmony
of the company was doubtless much promoted by their knowing that the two men of the world were held in great esteem
by the upper classes of society, and by the gallant defenders
of their country in the army and navy, but particularly the
former. The least of their stories had a colonel in it; lords
were as plentiful as oaths; and even the Blood Royal ran in
the muddy channel of their personal recollections.

"Mr. Chuzzlewit didn't know him, I'm afraid," said Wolf,
in reference to a certain personage of illustrious descent, who
had previously figured in a reminiscence.

"No," said Tigg. "But we must bring him into contact
with this sort of fellows."

"He was very fond of literature," observed Wolf.

"Was he?" said Tigg.

"Oh, yes; he took my paper regularly for many years.
Do you know he said some good things now and then? He
asked a certain Viscount, who's a friend of mine—Pip knows
him—'What's the editor's name, what's the editor's name?'
'Wolf.' 'Wolf, eh? Sharp biter, Wolf. We must keep the
Wolf from the door, as the proverb says.' It was very well.
And being complimentary, I printed it."

"But the Viscount's the boy!" cried Pip, who invented a

44

new oath for the introduction of everything he said. "The Viscount's the boy! He came into our place one night to take Her home; rather slued, but not much; and said, 'Where's Pip? I want to see Pip. Produce Pip!'—'What's the row, my lord?'—'Shakspeare's an infernal humbug, Pip! What's the good of Shakspeare, Pip? I never read him. What the devil is it all about, Pip? There's a lot of feet in Shakspeare's verse, but there ain't any legs worth mentioning in Shakspeare's plays, are there, Pip? Juliet, Desdemona, Lady Macbeth, and all the rest of 'em, whatever their names are, might as well have no legs at all, for anything the audience know about it, Pip. Why, in that respect they're all Miss Biffins to the audience, Pip. I'll tell you what it is. What the people call dramatic poetry is a collection of sermons. Do I go to the theatre to be lectured? No, Pip. If I wanted that, I'd go to church. What's the legitimate object of the drama, Pip? Human nature. What are legs? Human nature. Then let us have plenty of leg pieces, Pip, and I'll stand by you, my buck!' And I am proud to say," added Pip, "that he *did* stand by me, handsomely."

The conversation now becoming general, Mr. Jonas's opinion was requested on this subject; and as it was in full accordance with the sentiments of Mr. Pip, that gentleman was extremely gratified. Indeed, both himself and Wolf had so much in common with Jonas, that they became very amicable; and between their increasing friendship and the fumes of wine, Jonas grew talkative.

It does not follow in the case of such a person that the more talkative he becomes, the more agreeable he is; on the contrary, his merits show to most advantage, perhaps, in silence. Having no means, as he thought, of putting himself on an equality with the rest, but by the assertion of that depth and sharpness on which he had been complimented, Jonas exhibited that faculty to the utmost; and was so deep and sharp that he lost himself in his own profundity, and cut his fingers with his own edge-tools.

It was especially in his way and character to exhibit his quality at his entertainer's expense; and while he drank of his sparkling wines, and partook of his monstrous profusion, to ridicule the extravagance which had set such costly fare before him. Even at such a wanton board, and in such more than doubtful company, this might have proved a disagreeable experiment, but that Tigg and Crimple, studying to understand their man thoroughly, gave him what license he chose: knowing that the more he took, the better for their purpose. And thus while the blundering cheat—gull that he was, for all his cunning—thought himself rolled up hedgehog fashion, with his sharpest points towards them, he was, in fact, betraying all his vulnerable parts to their unwinking watchfulness.

Whether the two gentlemen who contributed so much to the doctor's philosophical knowledge (by the way, the doctor slipped off quietly, after swallowing his usual amount of wine) had had their cue distinctly from the host, or took it from what they saw and heard, they acted their parts very well. They solicited the honour of Jonas's better acquaintance; trusted that they would have the pleasure of introducing him into that elevated society in which he was so well qualified to shine; and informed him, in the most friendly manner, that the advantages of their respective establishments were entirely at his control. In a word, they said "Be one of us!" And Jonas said he was infinitely obliged to them, and he would be: adding within himself, that so long as they "stood treat," there was nothing he would like better.

After coffee, which was served in the drawing-room, there was a short interval (mainly sustained by Pip and Wolf) of conversation; rather highly spiced and strongly seasoned. When it flagged, Jonas took it up and showed considerable humour in appraising the furniture; inquiring whether such an article was paid for; what it had originally cost; and the like. In all of this, he was, as he considered, desperately hard on Montague, and very demonstrative of his own brilliant parts.

Some Champagne Punch gave a new though temporary fillip to the entertainments of the evening. For after leading to some noisy proceedings, which were not intelligible, it ended in the unsteady departure of the two gentlemen of the world, and the slumber of Mr. Jonas upon one of the sofas.

As he could not be made to understand where he was, Mr. Bailey received orders to call a hackney-coach, and take him home: which that young gentleman roused himself from an uneasy sleep in the hall, to do. It being now almost three o'clock in the morning.

"Is he hooked, do you think?" whispered Crimple, as himself and partner stood in a distant part of the room observing him as he lay.

"Ay!" said Tigg, in the same tone. "With a strong iron, perhaps. Has Nadgett been here to-night?"

"Yes. I went out to him. Hearing you had company, he went away."

"Why did he do that?"

"He said he would come back early in the morning, before you were out of bed."

"Tell them to be sure and send him up to my bedside. Hush! Here's the boy! Now Mr. Bailey, take this gentleman home, and see him safely in. Hallo here! Why Chuzzlewit, halloa!"

They got him upright with some difficulty, and assisted him down stairs, where they put his hat upon his head, and tumbled him into the coach. Mr. Bailey, having shut him in, mounted the box beside the coachman, and smoked his cigar with an air of particular satisfaction; the undertaking in which he was engaged having a free and sporting character about it, which was quite congenial to his taste.

Arriving in due time at the house in the City, Mr. Bailey jumped down, and expressed the lively nature of his feelings in a knock: the like of which had probably not been heard in that quarter since the great fire of London. Going out into the road to observe the effect of this feat, he saw that a dim light, previously visible at an upper window, had been already removed and was travelling down stairs. To obtain a foreknowledge of the bearer of this taper, Mr. Bailey skipped back to the door again, and put his eye to the keyhole.

It was the merry one herself. But sadly, strangely altered! So careworn and dejected, so faltering and full of fear; so fallen, humbled, broken; that to have seen her, quiet in her coffin, would have been a less surprise.

She set the light upon a bracket in the hall, and laid her hand upon her heart; upon her eyes; upon her burning head. Then she came on towards the door, with such a wild and hurried step, that Mr. Bailey lost his self-possession, and still had his eye where the keyhole had been, when she opened it.

"Aha!" said Mr. Bailey, with an effort. "There you are, are you? What's the matter? Ain't you well, though?"

In the midst of her astonishment as she recognised him in his altered dress, so much of her old smile came back to her face that Bailey was glad. But next moment he was sorry again, for he saw tears standing in her poor dim eyes.

"Don't be frightened," said Bailey. "There ain't nothing the matter. I've brought home Mr. Chuzzlewit. He ain't ill. He's only a little swipey you know." Mr. Bailey reeled in his boots, to express intoxication.

"Have you come from Mrs. Todgers's?" asked Merry, trembling.

"Todgers's, bless you! No!" cried Mr. Bailey. "I haven't got nothing to do with Todgers's. I cut that connexion long ago. He's been a dining with my governor at the West-end. Didn't you know he was a coming to see us?"

"No," she said, faintly.

"Oh yes! We're heavy swells too, and so I tell you. Don't you come out, a catching cold in your head. I'll wake him!" Mr. Bailey expressing in his demeanour a perfect confidence that he could carry him in with ease, if necessary, opened the coach door, let down the steps, and giving Jonas a shake, cried "We've got home, my flower! Tumble up then!"

He was so far recovered as to be able to respond to this appeal, and to come stumbling out of the coach in a heap, to the great hazard of Mr. Bailey's person. When he got upon the pavement, Mr. Bailey first butted at him in front, and then dexterously propped him up behind; and having steadied him by these means, he assisted him into the house.

"You go up first with the light," said Bailey to Mrs. Jonas, "and we'll foller. Don't tremble so. He won't hurt you. When *I*'ve had a drop too much, I'm full of good natur myself."

She went on before; and her husband and Bailey, by dint of tumbling over each other, and knocking themselves about, got at last into the sitting-room above stairs, where Jonas staggered into a seat.

"There!" said Mr. Bailey. "He's all right now. You ain't got nothing to cry for, bless you! He's righter than a trivet!"

The ill-favoured brute, with dress awry, and sodden face, and rumpled hair, sat blinking and drooping, and rolling his idiotic eyes about, until, becoming conscious by degrees, he recognised his wife, and shook his fist at her.

"Ah!" cried Mr. Bailey, squaring his arms with a sudden emotion. "What, you're wicious, are you? Would you though! You'd better not!"

"Pray, go away!" said Merry. "Bailey, my good boy, go home. Jonas!" she said; timidly laying her hand upon his shoulder, and bending her head down, over him; "Jonas!"

"Look at her!" cried Jonas, pushing her off with his extended arm. "Look here! Look at her! Here's a bargain for a man!"

"Dear Jonas!"

"Dear Devil!" he replied, with a fierce gesture. "You're a pretty clog to be tied to a man for life, you mewling, white-faced cat! Get out of my sight!"

"I know you don't mean it, Jonas. You wouldn't say it if you were sober."

With affected gaiety she gave Bailey a piece of money, and again implored him to be gone. Her entreaty was so earnest, that the boy had not the heart to stay there. But he stopped at the bottom of the stairs, and listened.

"I wouldn't say it if I was sober!" retorted Jonas. "You know better. Have I never said it when I was sober?"

"Often, indeed!" she answered through her tears.

"Hark ye!" cried Jonas, stamping his foot upon the ground. "You made me bear your pretty humours once, and ecod I'll make you bear mine now. I always promised myself I would. I married you that I might. I'll know who's master, and who's slave!"

"Heaven knows I am obedient!" said the sobbing girl. "Much more so than I ever thought to be!"

Jonas laughed in his drunken exultation. "What! you're finding it out, are you! Patience, and you will in time! Griffins have claws, my girl. There's not a pretty slight you ever put upon me, nor a pretty trick you ever played me, nor a pretty insolence you ever showed me, that I won't pay back a hundred-fold. What else did I marry you for? *You*, too!" he said, with coarse contempt.

It might have softened him to hear her turn a little fragment of a song he used to say he liked; trying, with a heart so full, to win him back.

"Oho!" he said, "you're deaf, are you? You don't hear me, eh? So much the better for you. I hate you. I hate myself, for having been fool enough to strap a pack upon my back for the pleasure of treading on it whenever I choose. Why, things have opened to me, now, so that I might marry almost where I liked. But I wouldn't; I'd keep single. I ought to be single, among the friends *I* know. Instead of that, here I am, tied like a log to you. Pah! Why do you show your pale face when I come home? Am I never to forget you?"

"How late it is!" she said cheerfully: opening the shutter after an interval of silence. "Broad day, Jonas!"

"Broad day or black night, what do *I* care!" was the kind rejoinder.

"The night passed quickly, too. I don't mind sitting up, at all."

"Sit up for me again, if you dare!" growled Jonas.

"I was reading," she proceeded, "all night long. I began when you went out, and read till you came home again. The strangest story, Jonas! And true, the book says. I'll tell it you to-morrow."

"True, was it?" said Jonas, doggedly.

"So the book says."

"Was there anything in it, about a man's being determined to conquer his wife, break her spirit, bend her temper, crush all her humours like so many nut-shells—kill her, for aught I know?" said Jonas.

"No. Not a word," she answered quickly.

"Ah!" he returned. "That'll be a true story though, before long; for all the book says nothing about it. It's a lying book, I see. A fit book for a lying reader. But you're deaf. I forgot that."

There was another interval of silence; and the boy was stealing away, when he heard her footstep on the floor, and stopped. She went up to him, as it seemed, and spoke lovingly: saying that she would defer to him in everything, and would consult his wishes and obey them, and they might be very happy if he would be gentle with her. He answered with an imprecation, and—

Not with a blow? Yes. Stern truth against the base-souled villain: with a blow.

No angry cries; no loud reproaches. Even her weeping and her sobs were stifled by her clinging round him. She

51

only said, repeating it in agony of heart, How could he, could he, could he! And lost utterance in tears.

Oh woman, God beloved in old Jerusalem! The best among us need deal lightly with thy faults, if only for the punishment thy nature will endure, in bearing heavy evidence against us, on the Day of Judgment!

CHAPTER XXIX

IN WHICH SOME PEOPLE ARE PRECOCIOUS, OTHERS PROFESSIONAL, AND OTHERS MYSTERIOUS : ALL IN THEIR SEVERAL WAYS.

It may have been the restless remembrance of what he had seen and heard overnight, or it may have been no deeper mental operation than the discovery that he had nothing to do, which caused Mr. Bailey, on the following afternoon, to feel particularly disposed for agreeable society, and prompted him to pay a visit to his friend Poll Sweedlepipe.

On the little bell giving clamorous notice of a visitor's approach (for Mr. Bailey came in at the door with a lunge, to get as much sound out of the bell as possible), Poll Sweedlepipe desisted from the contemplation of a favourite owl, and gave his young friend hearty welcome.

"Why, you look smarter by day," said Poll, "than you do by candle-light. I never see such a tight young dasher."

"Reether so, Polly. How's our fair friend Sairah ?"

"Oh, she's pretty well," said Poll. "She's at home."

"There's the remains of a fine woman about Sairah, Poll," observed Mr. Bailey, with genteel indifference.

"Oh !" thought Poll, "he's old. He must be very old !"

"Too much crumb, you know," said Mr. Bailey ; "too fat, Poll. But there's many worse at her time of life."

"The very owl's a opening his eyes !" thought Poll. "I don't wonder at it, in a bird of his opinions."

He happened to have been sharpening his razors, which

were lying open in a row, while a huge strop dangled from the wall. Glancing at these preparations, Mr. Bailey stroked his chin, and a thought appeared to occur to him.

"Poll," he said, "I ain't as neat as I could wish about the gills. Being here, I may as well have a shave, and get trimmed close."

The barber stood aghast; but Mr. Bailey divested himself of his neck-cloth, and sat down in the easy shaving chair with all the dignity and confidence in life. There was no resisting his manner. The evidence of sight and touch became as nothing. His chin was as smooth as a new-laid egg or a scraped Dutch cheese; but Poll Sweedlepipe wouldn't have ventured to deny, on affidavit, that he had the beard of a Jewish rabbi.

"Go *with* the grain, Poll, all round, please," said Mr. Bailey, screwing up his face for the reception of the lather. "You may do wot you like with the bits of whisker. I don't care for 'em."

The meek little barber stood gazing at him with the brush and soap-dish in his hand, stirring them round and round in a ludicrous uncertainty, as if he were disabled by some fascination from beginning. At last he made a dash at Mr. Bailey's cheek. Then he stopped again, as if the ghost of a beard had suddenly receded from his touch; but receiving mild encouragement from Mr. Bailey, in the form of an adjuration to "Go in and win," he lathered him bountifully. Mr. Bailey smiled through the suds in his satisfaction.

"Gently over the stones, Poll. Go a tip-toe over the pimples!"

Poll Sweedlepipe obeyed, and scraped the lather off again with particular care. Mr. Bailey squinted at every successive dab, as it was deposited on a cloth on his left shoulder, and seemed, with a microscopic eye, to detect some bristles in it; for he murmured more than once, "Reether redder than I could wish, Poll." The operation being concluded, Poll fell back and stared at him again, while Mr. Bailey, wiping his

Easy Shaving

face on the jack-towel, remarked, " that arter late hours nothing freshened up a man so much as a easy shave."

He was in the act of tying his cravat at the glass, without his coat, and Poll had wiped his razor, ready for the next customer, when Mrs. Gamp, coming down stairs, looked in at the shop-door to give the barber neighbourly good day. Feeling for her unfortunate situation, in having conceived a regard for himself which it was not in the nature of things that he could return, Mr. Bailey hastened to soothe her with words of kindness.

" Hallo ! " he said, " Sairah ! I needn't ask you how you've been this long time, for you're in full bloom. All a blowin' and a growin'; ain't she, Polly ? "

" Why, drat the Bragian boldness of that boy ! " cried Mrs. Gamp, though not displeased. " What a imperent young sparrow it is ! I wouldn't be that creetur's mother not for fifty pound ! "

Mr. Bailey regarded this as a delicate confession of her attachment, and a hint that no pecuniary gain could recompense her for its being rendered hopeless. He felt flattered. Disinterested affection is always flattering.

" Ah, dear ! " moaned Mrs. Gamp, sinking into the shaving chair, " That there blessed Bull, Mr. Sweedlepipe, has done his wery best to conker me. Of all the trying inwalieges in this walley of the shadder, that one beats 'em black and blue."

It was the practice of Mrs. Gamp and her friends in the profession, to say this of all the easy customers; as having at once the effect of discouraging competitors for office, and accounting for the necessity of high living on the part of the nurses.

" Talk of constitooshun ! " Mrs. Gamp observed. " A person's constitooshun need be made of Bricks to stand it. Mrs. Harris jestly says to me, but t'other day, ' Oh ! Sairey Gamp,' she says, ' how is it done ? ' ' Mrs. Harris, ma'am,' I says to her, ' we gives no trust ourselves, and puts a deal o' trust elsevere ; these is our religious feelins, and we finds 'em answer.' 'Sairey,' says Mrs. Harris, ' sech is life. Vich likeways is the hend of all things ! ' "

The barber gave a soft murmur, as much as to say that Mrs. Harris's remark, though perhaps not quite so intelligible as could be desired from such an authority, did equal honour to her head and to her heart.

" And here," continued Mrs. Gamp, " and here am I a goin twenty mile in distant, on as wentersome a chance as ever any one as monthlied ever run, I do believe. Says Mrs. Harris, with a woman's and a mother's art a beatin in her human breast, she says to me, ' You're not a goin, Sairey, Lord forgive you ! ' 'Why am I not a going, Mrs. Harris ? ' I replies. ' Mrs. Gill,' I says, ' wos never wrong with six ; and is it likely, ma'am—I ast you as a mother—that she will begin to be unreg'lar now ? Often and often have I heerd him say,' I says to Mrs. Harris, meaning Mr. Gill, ' that he would back his wife agen Moore's almanack, to name the very day and hour, for ninepence farden. *Is* it likely, ma'am,' I says, ' as she will fail this once ? ' Says Mrs. Harris, ' No, ma'am, not in the course of nater. But,' she says, the tears a fillin in her eyes, ' you knows much betterer than me, with your experienge, how little puts us out. A Punch's show,' she says, ' a chimbley sweep, a newfundlandog, or a drunkin man a comin round the corner sharp, may do it.' So it may, Mr. Sweedlepipes," said Mrs. Gamp, " there's no deniging of it ; and though my books is clear for a full week, I takes a anxious art along with me, I do assure you, sir."

" You're so full of zeal, you see ! " said Poll. " You worrit yourself so."

" Worrit myself ! " cried Mrs. Gamp, raising her hands and turning up her eyes. " You speak truth in that, sir, if you never speaks no more 'twixt this and when two Sundays jines together. I feels the sufferins of other people more than I feels my own, though no one mayn't suppoge it. The families I've had," said Mrs. Gamp, " if all was knowd, and credit done where credit's doo, would take a week to chris'en at Saint Polge's fontin!"

"Where's the patient goin?' asked Sweedlepipe.

"Into Har'fordshire, which is his native air. But native airs nor native graces neither," Mrs. Gamp observed, "won't bring *him* round."

"So bad as that?" inquired the wistful barber. "Indeed!"

Mrs. Gamp shook her head mysteriously, and pursed up her lips. "There's fevers of the mind," she said, "as well as body. You may take your slime drafts till you flies into the air with efferwescence; but you won't cure that."

"Ah!" said the barber, opening his eyes, and putting on his raven aspect, "Lor!"

"No. You may make yourself as light as any gash balloon," said Mrs. Gamp. "But talk, when you're wrong in your head and when you're in your sleep, of certain things; and you'll be heavy in your mind."

"Of what kind of things now?" inquired Poll, greedily biting his nails in his great interest. "Ghosts?"

Mrs. Gamp, who perhaps had been already tempted further than she had intended to go, by the barber's stimulating curiosity, gave a sniff of uncommon significance, and said, it didn't signify.

"I'm a going down with my patient in the coach this arternoon," she proceeded. "I'm a going to stop with him a day or so, till he gets a country nuss (drat them country nusses, much the orkard hussies knows about their bis'ness); and then I'm a comin' back; and that's my trouble, Mr. Sweedlepipes. But I hope that everythink 'll only go on right and comfortable as long as I'm away; perwisin which, as Mrs. Harris says, Mrs. Gill is welcome to choose her own time: all times of the day and night bein' equally the same to me."

During the progress of the foregoing remarks, which Mrs. Gamp had addressed exclusively to the barber, Mr. Bailey had been tying his cravat, getting on his coat, and making hideous faces at himself in the glass. Being now personally addressed by Mrs. Gamp, he turned round, and mingled in the conversation.

"You ain't been in the City, I suppose, sir, since we was all three there together," said Mrs. Gamp, "at Mr. Chuzzlewit's?"

"Yes I have, Sairah. I was there, last night."

"Last night!" cried the barber.

"Yes, Poll, reether so. You can call it this morning if you like to be particular. He dined with us."

"Who does that young Limb mean by 'hus?'" said Mrs. Gamp, with most impatient emphasis.

"Me and my Governor, Sairah. He dined at our house. We wos very merry, Sairah. So much so, that I was obliged to see him home in a hackney coach at three o'clock in the morning." It was on the tip of the boy's tongue to relate what had followed; but remembering how easily it might be carried to his master's ears, and the repeated cautions he had had from Mr. Crimple "not to chatter," he checked himself: adding only, "She was sitting up, expecting him."

"And all things considered," said Mrs. Gamp sharply, "she might have know'd better than to go a tiring herself out, by doin' anythink of the sort. Did they seem pretty pleasant together, sir?"

"Oh, yes," answered Bailey, "pleasant enough."

"I'm glad on it," said Mrs. Gamp, with a second sniff of significance.

"They haven't been married so long," observed Poll, rubbing his hands, "that they need be anything but pleasant yet awhile."

"No," said Mrs. Gamp, with a third significant signal.

"Especially," pursued the barber, "when the gentleman bears such a character as you gave him."

"I speak as I find, Mr. Sweedlepipes," said Mrs. Gamp. "Forbid it should be otherways! But we never knows wot's hidden in each other's hearts; and if we had glass winders there, we'd need keep the shetters up, some on us, I do assure you!"

"But you don't mean to say," Poll Sweedlepipe began.

"No," said Mrs. Gamp, cutting him very short, "I don't. Don't think I do. The torters of the Imposition shouldn't make me own I did. All I says is," added the good woman, rising and folding her shawl about her, "that the Bull's a waitin', and the precious moments is a flyin' fast."

The little barber having in his eager curiosity a great desire to see Mrs. Gamp's patient, proposed to Mr. Bailey that they should accompany her to the Bull, and witness the departure of the coach. That young gentleman assenting, they all went out together.

Arriving at the tavern, Mrs. Gamp (who was full-dressed for the journey, in her latest suit of mourning) left her friends to entertain themselves in the yard, while she ascended to the sick room, where her fellow-labourer Mrs. Prig was dressing the invalid.

He was so wasted, that it seemed as if his bones would rattle when they moved him. His cheeks were sunken, and his eyes unnaturally large. He lay back in the easy-chair like one more dead than living; and rolled his languid eyes towards the door when Mrs. Gamp appeared, as painfully as if their weight alone were burdensome to move.

"And how are we by this time?" Mrs. Gamp observed. "We looks charming."

"We looks a deal charminger than we are, then," returned Mrs. Prig, a little chafed in her temper. "We got out of bed back'ards, I think, for we're as cross as two sticks. I never see sich a man. He wouldn't have been washed, if he'd had his own way."

"She put the soap in my mouth," said the unfortunate patient, feebly.

"Couldn't you keep it shut then?" retorted Mrs. Prig. "Who do you think's to wash one feater, and miss another, and wear one's eyes out with all manner of fine-work of that description, for half-a-crown a day! If you wants to be tittivated, you must pay accordin."

"Oh dear me!" cried the patient, "oh dear, dear!"

"There!" said Mrs. Prig, "that's the way he's been a conducting of himself, Sarah, ever since I got him out of bed, if you'll believe it."

"Instead of being grateful," Mrs. Gamp observed, "for all our little ways. Oh, fie for shame, sir, fie for shame!"

Here Mrs. Prig seized the patient by the chin, and began to rasp his unhappy head with a hair-brush.

"I suppose you don't like that, neither!" she observed, stopping to look at him.

It was just possible that he didn't, for the brush was a specimen of the hardest kind of instrument producible by modern art; and his very eye-lids were red with the friction. Mrs. Prig was gratified to observe the correctness of her supposition, and said triumphantly, "she know'd as much."

When his hair was smoothed down comfortably into his eyes, Mrs. Prig and Mrs. Gamp put on his neckerchief: adjusting his shirt-collar with great nicety, so that the starched points should also invade those organs, and afflict them with an artificial ophthalmia. His waistcoat and coat were next arranged: and as every button was wrenched into a wrong button-hole, and the order of his boots was reversed, he presented on the whole rather a melancholy appearance.

"I don't think it's right," said the poor weak invalid. "I feel as if I was in somebody else's clothes. I'm all on one side; and you've made one of my legs shorter than the other. There's a bottle in my pocket too. What do you make me sit upon a bottle for?"

"Deuce take the man!" cried Mrs. Gamp, drawing it forth. "If he ain't been and got my night-bottle here. I made a little cupboard of his coat when it hung behind the door, and quite forgot it, Betsey. You'll find a ingun or two, and a little tea and sugar in his t'other pocket, my dear, if you'll just be good enough to take 'em out."

Betsey produced the property in question, together with some other articles of general chandlery; and Mrs. Gamp transferred them to her own pocket, which was a species of nankeen pannier. Refreshment then arrived in the form of chops and strong ale, for the ladies, and a basin of beef-tea for the patient: which refection was barely at an end when John Westlock appeared.

"Up and dressed!" cried John, sitting down beside him. "That's brave. How do you feel?"

"Much better. But very weak."

"No wonder. You have had a hard bout of it. But country air, and change of scene," said John, "will make another man of you! Why, Mrs. Gamp," he added, laughing, as he kindly arranged the sick man's garments, "you have odd notions of a gentleman's dress!"

"Mr. Lewsome an't a easy gent to get into his clothes, sir," Mrs. Gamp replied with dignity; "as me and Betsey Prig can certify afore the Lord Mayor and Uncommon Counsellors, if needful!"

John at that moment was standing close in front of the sick man, in the act of releasing him from the torture of the collars before mentioned, when he said in a whisper:

"Mr. Westlock! I don't wish to be overheard. I have something very particular and strange to say to you; something that has been a dreadful weight on my mind, through this long illness."

Quick in all his motions, John was turning round to desire the women to leave the room: when the sick man held him by the sleeve.

"Not now. I've not the strength. I've not the courage. May I tell it when I have? May I write it, if I find that easier and better?"

"May you!" cried John. "Why, Lewsome, what is this!"

"Don't ask me what it is. It's unnatural and cruel. Frightful to think of. Frightful to tell. Frightful to know. Frightful to have helped in. Let me kiss your hand for all your goodness to me. Be kinder still, and don't ask me what it is!"

At first, John gazed at him, in great surprise; but remembering how very much reduced he was, and how recently his brain had been on fire with fever, believed that he was labouring under some imaginary horror, or despondent fancy. For farther information on this point, he took an opportunity of drawing Mrs. Gamp aside, while Betsey Prig was wrapping him in cloaks and shawls, and asked her whether he was quite collected in his mind.

"Oh bless you, no!" said Mrs. Gamp. "He hates his nusses to this hour. They always does it, sir. It's a certain sign. If you could have heerd the poor dear soul a findin' fault with me and Betsey Prig, not half an hour ago, you would have wondered how it is we don't get fretted to the tomb."

This almost confirmed John in his suspicion; so, not taking what had passed into any serious account, he resumed his former cheerful manner, and assisted by Mrs. Gamp and Betsey Prig, conducted Lewsome down stairs to the coach: just then upon the point of starting.

Poll Sweedlepipe was at the door with his arms tight folded and his eyes wide open, and looked on with absorbing interest, while the sick man was slowly moved into the vehicle. His bony hands and haggard face impressed Poll wonderfully; and he informed Mr. Bailey, in confidence, that he wouldn't have missed seeing him for a pound. Mr. Bailey, who was of a different constitution, remarked, that he would have stayed away for five shillings.

It was a troublesome matter to adjust Mrs. Gamp's luggage to her satisfaction; for every package belonging to that lady had the inconvenient property of requiring to be put in a boot by itself, and to have no other luggage near it, on pain of actions at law for heavy damages against the proprietors of the coach. The umbrella with the circular patch was particularly hard to be got rid of, and several times thrust out its battered brass nozzle from improper crevices and chinks, to the great terror of the other passengers. Indeed, in her intense anxiety to find a haven of refuge for this chattel, Mrs. Gamp so often moved it, in the course of five minutes, that it seemed not one umbrella but fifty. At length it was lost, or said to be ; and for the next five minutes she was face to face with the coachman, go wherever he might, protesting that it should be " made good," though she took the question to the House of Commons.

At last, her bundle, and her pattens, and her basket, and everything else, being disposed of, she took a friendly leave of Poll and Mr. Bailey, dropped a curtsey to John Westlock, and parted as from a cherished member of the sisterhood with Betsey Prig.

" Wishin' you lots of sickness, my darling creetur," Mrs. Gamp observed, " and good places. It won't be long, I hope, afore we works together, off and on, again, Betsey ; and may our next meetin' be at a large family's, where they all takes it reg'lar, one from another, turn and turn about, and has it business-like."

" I don't care how soon it is," said Mrs. Prig ; " nor how many weeks it lasts."

Mrs. Gamp with a reply in a congenial spirit was backing to the coach, when she came in contact with a lady and gentleman who were passing along the footway.

" Take care, take care here ! " cried the gentleman. " Halloo ! My dear ! Why, it's Mrs. Gamp ! "

" What, Mr. Mould ! " exclaimed the nurse. " And Mrs. Mould ! who would have thought as we should ever have a meetin' here, I'm sure ! "

" Going out of town, Mrs. Gamp ? " cried Mould. " That's unusual, isn't it ? "

" It *is* unusual, sir," said Mrs. Gamp. " But only for a day or two at most. The gent," she whispered, " as I spoke about."

" What, in the coach ! " cried Mould. " The one you thought of recommending ? Very odd. My dear, this will

63

interest you. The gentleman that Mrs. Gamp thought likely to suit us, is in the coach, my love."

Mrs. Mould was greatly interested.

"Here, my dear. You can stand upon the door-step," said Mould, "and take a look at him. Ha! There he is. Where's my glass? Oh! all right. I've got it. Do you see him, my dear?"

"Quite plain," said Mrs. Mould.

"Upon my life you know, this is a very singular circumstance," said Mould, quite delighted. "This is the sort of thing, my dear, I wouldn't have missed on any account. It tickles one. It's interesting. It's almost a little play, you know. Ah! There he is! To be sure. Looks poorly, Mrs. M., don't he?"

Mrs. Mould assented.

"He's coming our way, perhaps, after all," said Mould. "Who knows! I feel as if I ought to show him some little attention, really. He don't seem a stranger to me. I'm very much inclined to move my hat, my dear."

"He's looking hard this way," said Mrs. Mould.

"Then I will!" cried Mould. "How d'ye do, sir? I wish you good day. Ha! He bows too. Very gentlemanly. Mrs. Gamp has the cards in her pocket, I have no doubt. This is very singular, my dear—and very pleasant. I am not superstitious, but it really seems as if one was destined to pay him those little melancholy civilities which belong to our peculiar line of business. There can be no kind of objection to your kissing your hand to him, my dear."

Mrs. Mould did so.

"Ha!" said Mould. "He's evidently gratified. Poor fellow! I'm quite glad you did it, my love. Bye bye, Mrs. Gamp!" waving his hand. "There he goes; there he goes!"

So he did; for the coach rolled off as the words were spoken. Mr. and Mrs. Mould, in high good humour, went their merry way. Mr. Bailey retired with Poll Sweedlepipe as soon as possible; but some little time elapsed before he could remove his friend from the ground, owing to the impression wrought upon the barber's nerves by Mrs. Prig, whom he pronounced, in admiration of her beard, to be a woman of transcendent charms.

When the light cloud of bustle hanging round the coach was thus dispersed, Nadgett was seen in the darkest box of the Bull coffee-room, looking wistfully up at the clock—as if the man who never appeared were a little behind his time.

CHAPTER XXX

PROVES THAT CHANGES MAY BE RUNG IN THE BEST-REGULATED
FAMILIES, AND THAT MR. PECKSNIFF WAS A SPECIAL HAND
AT A TRIPLE-BOB-MAJOR.

As the surgeon's first care after amputating a limb is to take
up the arteries the cruel knife has severed, so it is the duty
of this history, which in its remorseless course has cut from
the Pecksniffian trunk its right arm, Mercy, to look to the
parent stem, and see how in all its various ramifications it
got on without her.

And first of Mr. Pecksniff, it may be observed, that having
provided for his youngest daughter that choicest of blessings,
a tender and indulgent husband; and having gratified the
dearest wish of his parental heart by establishing her in life
so happily; he renewed his youth, and spreading the plumage
of his own bright conscience, felt himself equal to all kinds
of flights. It is customary with fathers in stage-plays, after
giving their daughters to the men of their hearts, to congratulate themselves on having no other business on their
hands but to die immediately: though it is rarely found
that they are in a hurry to do it. Mr. Pecksniff, being a
father of a more sage and practical class, appeared to think
that his immediate business was to live; and having deprived
himself of one comfort, to surround himself with others.

But however much inclined the good man was, to be jocose
and playful, and in the garden of his fancy to disport himself

66

(if one may say so), like an architectural kitten, he had one impediment constantly opposed to him. The gentle Cherry, stung by a sense of slight and injury, which far from softening down or wearing out, rankled and festered in her heart, was in flat rebellion. She waged fierce war against her dear Papa; she led her parent what is usually called, for want of a better figure of speech, the life of a dog. But never did that dog live, in kennel, stable-yard, or house, whose life was half as hard as Mr. Pecksniff's with his gentle child.

The father and daughter were sitting at their breakfast. Tom had retired, and they were alone. Mr. Pecksniff frowned at first; but having cleared his brow, looked stealthily at his child. Her nose was very red indeed, and screwed up tight, with hostile preparation.

"Cherry," cried Mr. Pecksniff, "what is amiss between us? My child, why are we disunited?"

Miss Pecksniff's answer was scarcely a response to this gush of affection, for it was simply, "Bother, Pa!"

"Bother!" repeated Mr. Pecksniff, in a tone of anguish.

"Oh! 'tis too late, Pa," said his daughter, calmly, "to talk to me like this. I know what it means, and what its value is."

"This is hard!" cried Mr. Pecksniff, addressing his breakfast-cup. "This is very hard! She is my child. I carried her in my arms, when she wore shapeless worsted shoes—I might say, mufflers—many years ago!"

"You needn't taunt me with that, Pa," retorted Cherry, with a spiteful look. "I am not so many years older than my sister, either, though she *is* married to your friend!"

"Ah, human nature, human nature! Poor human nature!" said Mr. Pecksniff, shaking his head at human nature, as if he didn't belong to it. "To think that this discord should arise from such a cause! oh dear, oh dear!"

"From such a cause indeed!" cried Cherry. "State the real cause, Pa, or I'll state it myself. Mind! I will!"

Perhaps the energy with which she said this was infectious.

However that may be, Mr. Pecksniff changed his tone and the expression of his face, for one of anger if not downright violence, when he said:

"You will! you have. You did yesterday. You do always. You have no decency; you make no secret of your temper; you have exposed yourself to Mr. Chuzzlewit a hundred times."

"Myself!" cried Cherry, with a bitter smile. "Oh indeed! I don't mind that."

"Me too, then," said Mr. Pecksniff.

His daughter answered with a scornful laugh.

"And since we have come to an explanation, Charity," said Mr. Pecksniff, rolling his head portentously, "let me tell you that I won't allow it. None of your nonsense, Miss! I won't permit it to be done."

"I shall do," said Charity, rocking her chair backwards and forwards, and raising her voice to a high pitch, "I shall do, Pa, what I please and what I have done. I am not going to be crushed in everything, depend upon it. I've been more shamefully used than anybody ever was in this world," here she began to cry and sob, "and may expect the worse treatment from you, I know. But I don't care for that. No I don't!"

Mr. Pecksniff was made so desperate by the loud tone in which she spoke, that, after looking about him in frantic uncertainty for some means of softening it, he rose and shook her until the ornamental bow of hair upon her head nodded like a plume. She was so very much astonished by this assault, that it really had the desired effect.

"I'll do it again!" cried Mr. Pecksniff as he resumed his seat, and fetched his breath, "if you dare to talk in that loud manner. How do you mean about being shamefully used? If Mr. Jonas chose your sister in preference to you, who could help it, I should wish to know? What have *I* to do with it?"

"Wasn't I made a convenience of? Wern't my feelings

trifled with? Didn't he address himself to me first?" sobbed Cherry, clasping her hands; "and oh good gracious, that I should live to be shook!"

"You'll live to be shaken again," returned her parent, "if you drive me to that means of maintaining the decorum of this humble roof. You surprise me. I wonder you have not more spirit. If Mr. Jonas didn't care for you, how could you wish to have him?"

"*I* wish to have him!" exclaimed Cherry. "*I* wish to have him, Pa!"

"Then what are you making all this piece of work for," retorted her father, "if you didn't wish to have him?"

"Because I was treated with duplicity," said Cherry; "and because my own sister and my own father conspired against me. I am not angry with *her*," said Cherry, looking much more angry than ever. "I pity her. I'm sorry for her. I know the fate that's in store for her, with that Wretch."

"Mr. Jonas will survive your calling him a wretch, my child, I dare say," said Mr. Pecksniff, with returning resignation; "but call him what you like and make an end of it."

"Not an end, Pa," said Charity. "No, not an end. That's not the only point on which we're not agreed. I won't submit to it. It's better you should know that, at once. No; I won't submit to it indeed, Pa! I am not quite a fool, and I am not blind. All I have got to say is, I won't submit to it."

Whatever she meant, she shook Mr. Pecksniff now; for his lame attempt to seem composed, was melancholy in the last degree. His anger changed to meekness, and his words were mild and fawning.

"My dear," he said; "if in the short excitement of an angry moment I resorted to an unjustifiable means of suppressing a little outbreak calculated to injure you as well as myself—it's possible I may have done so; perhaps I did—I ask your pardon. A father asking pardon of his child," said Mr. Pecksniff, "is, I believe, a spectacle to soften the most rugged nature."

But it didn't at all soften Miss Pecksniff: perhaps because her nature was not rugged enough. On the contrary, she persisted in saying, over and over again, that she wasn't quite a fool, and wasn't blind, and wouldn't submit to it.

"You labour under some mistake, my child!" said Mr. Pecksniff: "but I will not ask you what it is; I don't desire to know. No, pray!" he added, holding out his hand and colouring again, "let us avoid the subject, my dear, whatever it is!"

"It's quite right that the subject should be avoided between us, sir," said Cherry. "But I wish to be able to avoid it altogether, and consequently must beg you to provide me with a home."

Mr. Pecksniff looked about the room, and said "A home, my child!"

"Another home, Papa," said Cherry with increasing stateliness. "Place me at Mrs. Todgers's or somewhere, on an independent footing; but I will not live here, if such is to be the case."

It is possible that Miss Pecksniff saw in Mrs. Todgers's a vision of enthusiastic men, pining to fall, in adoration, at her feet. It is possible that Mr. Pecksniff, in his new-born juvenility, saw in the suggestion of that same establishment, an easy means of relieving himself from an irksome charge in the way of temper and watchfulness. It is undoubtedly a fact that in the attentive ears of Mr. Pecksniff, the proposition did not sound quite like the dismal knell of all his hopes.

But he was a man of great feeling, and acute sensibility; and he squeezed his pocket-handkerchief against his eyes with both hands—as such men always do: especially when they are observed. "One of my birds," Mr. Pecksniff said, "has left me for the stranger's breast; the other would take wing to Todgers's! Well, well, what am I? I don't know what I am, exactly. Never mind!"

Even this remark, made more pathetic perhaps by his breaking down in the middle of it, had no effect upon Charity. She was grim, rigid, and inflexible.

"But I have ever," said Mr. Pecksniff, "sacrificed my children's happiness to my own—I mean my own happiness to my children's—and I will not begin to regulate my life by other rules of conduct now. If you can be happier at Mrs. Todgers's than in your father's house, my dear, go to Mrs. Todgers's! Do not think of me, my girl!" said Mr. Pecksniff with emotion : " I shall get on pretty well, no doubt."

Miss Charity, who knew he had a secret pleasure in the contemplation of the proposed change, suppressed her own, and went on to negotiate the terms. His views upon this subject were at first so very limited that another difference, involving possibly another shaking, threatened to ensue ; but by degrees they came to something like an understanding, and the storm blew over. Indeed, Miss Charity's idea was so agreeable to both, that it would have been strange if they had not come to an amicable agreement. It was soon arranged between them that the project should be tried, and that immediately ; and that Cherry's not being well and needing change of scene, and wishing to be near her sister, should form the excuse for her departure to Mr. Chuzzlewit and Mary, to both of whom she had pleaded indisposition for some time past. These premises agreed on, Mr. Pecksniff gave her his blessing, with all the dignity of a self-denying man who had made a hard sacrifice, but comforted himself with the reflection that virtue is its own reward. Thus they were reconciled for the first time since that not easily forgiven night, when Mr. Jonas, repudiating the elder, had confessed his passion for the younger sister, and Mr. Pecksniff had abetted him on moral grounds.

But how happened it—in the name of an unexpected addition to that small family, the Seven Wonders of the World, whatever and wherever they may be, how happened it—that Mr. Pecksniff and his daughter were about to part?

How happened it that their mutual relations were so greatly altered? Why was Miss Pecksniff so clamorous to have it understood that she was neither blind nor foolish, and she wouldn't bear it? It is not possible that Mr. Pecksniff had any thoughts of marrying again! or that his daughter with the sharp eye of a single woman, fathomed his design.

Let us inquire into this.

Mr. Pecksniff, as a man without reproach, from whom the breath of slander passed like common breath from any other polished surface, could afford to do what common men could not. He knew the purity of his own motives; and when he had a motive worked at it as only a very good man (or a very bad one) can. Did he set before himself any strong and palpable motives for taking a second wife? Yes: and not one or two of 'them, but a combination of very many.

Old Martin Chuzzlewit had gradually undergone an important change. Even upon the night when he made such an ill-timed arrival at Mr. Pecksniff's house, he was comparatively subdued and easy to deal with. This Mr. Pecksniff attributed, at the time, to the effect his brother's death had had upon him. But from that hour his character seemed to have modified by regular degrees, and to have softened down into a dull indifference for almost every one but Mr. Pecksniff. His looks were much the same as ever, but his mind was singularly altered. It was not that this or that passion stood out in brighter or in dimmer hues; but that the colour of the whole man was faded. As one trait disappeared, no other trait sprung up to take its place. His senses dwindled too. He was less keen of sight; was deaf sometimes; took little notice of what passed before him; and would be profoundly taciturn for days together. The process of this alteration was so easy, that almost as soon as it began to be observed it was complete. But Mr. Pecksniff saw it first, and having Anthony Chuzzlewit fresh in his recollection, saw in his brother Martin the same process of decay.

To a gentleman of Mr. Pecksniff's tenderness, this was a

very mournful sight. He could not but foresee the probability of his respected relative being made the victim of designing persons, and of his riches falling into worthless hands. It gave him so much pain that he resolved to secure the property to himself; to keep bad testamentary suitors at a distance; to wall up the old gentleman, as it were, for his own use. By little and little, therefore, he began to try whether Mr. Chuzzlewit gave any promise of becoming an instrument in his hands, and finding that he did, and indeed that he was very supple in his plastic fingers, he made it the business of his life, kind soul! to establish an ascendancy over him: and every little test he durst apply meeting with a success beyond his hopes, he began to think he heard old Martin's cash already chinking in his own unworldly pockets.

But when Mr. Pecksniff pondered on this subject (as, in his zealous way, he often did), and thought with an uplifted heart of the train of circumstances which had delivered the old gentleman into his hands for the confusion of evil-doers and the triumph of a righteous nature, he always felt that Mary Graham was his stumbling-block. Let the old man say what he would, Mr. Pecksniff knew he had a strong affection for her. He knew that he showed it in a thousand little ways; that he liked to have her near him, and was never quite at ease when she was absent long. That he had ever really sworn to leave her nothing in his will, Mr. Pecksniff greatly doubted. That even if he had, there were many ways by which he could evade the oath and satisfy his conscience, Mr. Pecksniff knew. That her unprotected state was no light burden on the old man's mind, he also knew, for Mr. Chuzzlewit had plainly told him so. "Then," said Mr. Pecksniff, "what if I married her! What," repeated Mr. Pecksniff, sticking up his hair and glancing at his bust by Spoker: "What if, making sure of his approval first—he is nearly imbecile, poor gentleman—I married her!"

Mr. Pecksniff had a lively sense of the Beautiful: especially in women. His manner towards the sex was remarkable for its insinuating character. It is recorded of him in another part of these pages, that he embraced Mrs. Todgers on the smallest provocation: and it was a way he had: it was a part of the gentle placidity of his disposition. Before any thought of matrimony was in his mind, he had bestowed on Mary many little tokens of his spiritual admiration. They had been indignantly received, but that was nothing. True, as the idea expanded within him, these had become too ardent to escape the piercing eye of Cherry, who read his scheme at once; but he had always felt the power of Mary's charms. So Interest and Inclination made a pair, and drew the curricle of Mr. Pecksniff's plan.

As to any thought of revenging himself on young Martin for his insolent expressions when they parted, and of shutting him out still more effectually from any hope of reconciliation with his grandfather, Mr. Pecksniff was much too meek and forgiving to be suspected of harbouring it. As to being refused by Mary, Mr. Pecksniff was quite satisfied that in her position she could never hold out if he and Mr. Chuzzlewit were both against her. As to consulting the wishes of her heart in such a case, it formed no part of Mr. Pecksniff's moral code; for he knew what a good man he was, and what a blessing he must be to anybody. His daughter having broken the ice, and the murder being out between them, Mr. Pecksniff had now only to pursue his design as cleverly as he could, and by the craftiest approaches.

" Well, my good sir," said Mr. Pecksniff, meeting old Martin in the garden, for it was his habit to walk in and out by that way, as the fancy took him: "and how is my dear friend this delicious morning ? "

" Do you mean me ? " asked the old man.

" Ah ! " said Mr. Pecksniff, "one of his deaf days, I see. Could I mean any one else, my dear sir ? "

" You might have meant Mary," said the old man.

" Indeed I might. Quite true. I might speak of her as a dear, dear friend, I hope ? " observed Mr. Pecksniff.

"I hope so," returned old Martin. "I think she deserves it."

"Think!" cried Pecksniff, "Think, Mr. Chuzzlewit!"

"You are speaking I know," returned Martin, "but I don't catch what you say. Speak up!"

"He's getting deafer than a flint," said Pecksniff. "I was saying, my dear sir, that I am afraid I must make up my mind to part with Cherry."

"What has *she* been doing?" asked the old man.

"He puts the most ridiculous questions I ever heard!" muttered Mr. Pecksniff. "He's a child to-day." After which he added, in a mild roar: "She hasn't been doing anything, my dear friend."

"What are you going to part with her for?" demanded Martin.

"She hasn't her health by any means," said Mr. Pecksniff. "She misses her sister, my dear sir; they doated on each other from the cradle. And I think of giving her a run in London for a change. A good long run, sir, if I find she likes it."

"Quite right," cried Martin. "It's judicious."

"I am glad to hear you say so. I hope you mean to bear me company in this dull part, while she's away?" said Mr. Pecksniff.

"I have no intention of removing from it," was Martin's answer.

"Then why," said Mr. Pecksniff, taking the old man's arm in his, and walking slowly on: "Why, my good sir, can't you come and stay with me? I am sure I could surround you with more comforts, lowly as is my cot, than you can obtain at a village house of entertainment. And pardon me, Mr. Chuzzlewit, pardon me if I say that such a place as the Dragon, however well-conducted (and, as far as I know, Mrs. Lupin is one of the worthiest creatures in this county), is hardly a home for Miss Graham."

Martin mused a moment: and then said as he shook him by the hand,

"No. You're quite right; it is not."

"The very sight of skittles," Mr. Pecksniff eloquently pursued, "is far from being congenial to a delicate mind."

"It's an amusement of the vulgar," said old Martin, "certainly."

"Of the very vulgar," Mr. Pecksniff answered. "Then why not bring Miss Graham here, sir? Here is the house. Here am I alone in it, for Thomas Pinch I do not count as any one. Our lovely friend shall occupy my daughter's chamber! you shall choose your own; we shall not quarrel I hope!"

"We are not likely to do that," said Martin.

Mr. Pecksniff pressed his hand. "We understand each other, my dear sir, I see!—I can wind him," he thought, with exultation, "round my little finger!"

"You leave the recompense to me?" said the old man, after a minute's silence.

"Oh! do not speak of recompense!" cried Pecksniff.

"I say," repeated Martin, with a glimmer of his old obstinacy, "you leave the recompense to me. Do you?"

"Since you desire it, my good sir."

"I always desire it," said the old man. "You know I always desire it. I wish to pay as I go, even when I buy of you. Not that I do not leave a balance to be settled one day, Pecksniff."

The architect was too much overcome to speak. He tried to drop a tear upon his patron's hand, but couldn't find one in his dry distillery.

"May that day be very distant!" was his pious exclamation. "Ah sir! If I could say how deep an interest I have in you and yours! I allude to our beautiful young friend."

"True," he answered. "True. She need have some one interested in her. I did her wrong to train her as I did. Orphan though she was, she would have found some one to protect her whom she might have loved again. When she was a child, I pleased myself with the thought that in gratifying my whim of placing her between me and false-hearted

76

knaves, I had done her a kindness. Now she is a woman, I have no such comfort. She has no protector but herself. I have put her at such odds with the world, that any dog may bark or fawn upon her at his pleasure. Indeed she stands in need of delicate consideration. Yes ; indeed she does ! "

" If her position could be altered and defined, sir ? " Mr. Pecksniff hinted.

" How can that be done ? Should I make a seamstress of her, or a governess ? "

" Heaven forbid ! " said Mr. Pecksniff. " My dear sir, there are other ways. There are indeed. But I am much excited and embarrassed at present, and would rather not pursue the subject. I scarcely know what I mean. Permit me to resume it at another time."

" You are not unwell ? " asked Martin anxiously.

" No, no ! " cried Pecksniff. " No. Permit me to resume it at another time. I'll walk a little. Bless you ! "

Old Martin blessed him in return, and squeezed his hand. As he turned away, and slowly walked towards the house, Mr. Pecksniff stood gazing after him : being pretty well recovered from his late emotion, which, in any other man, one might have thought had been assumed as a machinery for feeling Martin's pulse. The change in the old man found such a slight expression in his figure, that Mr. Pecksniff, looking after him, could not help saying to himself :

" And I can wind him round my little finger ! Only think!"

Old Martin happening to turn his head, saluted him affectionately. Mr. Pecksniff returned the gesture.

" Why the time was," said Mr. Pecksniff ; " and not long ago, when he wouldn't look at me ! How soothing is this change. Such is the delicate texture of the human heart ; so complicated is the process of its being softened ! Externally he looks the same, and I can wind him round my little finger. Only think ! "

In sober truth, there did appear to be nothing on which Mr. Pecksniff might not have ventured with Martin Chuzzlewit ;

for whatever Mr. Pecksniff said or did was right, and whatever he advised was done. Martin had escaped so many snares from needy fortune-hunters, and had withered in the shell of his suspicion and distrust for so many years, but to become the good man's tool and plaything. With the happiness of this conviction painted on his face, the architect went forth upon his morning walk.

The summer weather in his bosom was reflected in the breast of Nature. Through deep green vistas where the boughs arched over-head, and showed the sunlight flashing in the beautiful perspective; through dewy fern from which the startled hares leaped up, and fled at his approach; by mantled pools, and fallen trees, and down in hollow places, rustling among last year's leaves whose scent woke memory of the past; the placid Pecksniff strolled. By meadow gates and hedges fragrant with wild roses; and by thatched-roofed cottages whose inmates humbly bowed before him as a man both good and wise; the worthy Pecksniff walked in tranquil meditation. The bee passed onward, humming of the work he had to do; the idle gnats for ever going round and round in one contracting and expanding ring, yet always going on as fast as he, danced merrily before him; the colour of the long grass came and went, as if the light clouds made it timid as they floated through the distant air. The birds, so many Pecksniff consciences, sang gaily upon every branch; and Mr. Pecksniff paid *his* homage to the day by ruminating on his projects as he walked along.

Chancing to trip, in his abstraction, over the spreading root of an old tree, he raised his pious eyes to take a survey of the ground before him. It startled him to see the embodied image of his thoughts not far ahead. Mary herself. And alone.

At first Mr. Pecksniff stopped as if with the intention of avoiding her; but his next impulse was, to advance, which he did at a brisk pace; carolling as he went, so sweetly and with so much innocence, that he only wanted feathers and wings to be a bird.

Hearing notes behind her, not belonging to the songsters of the grove, she looked round. Mr. Pecksniff kissed his hand, and was at her side immediately.

"Communing with nature?" said Mr. Pecksniff. "So am I."

She said the morning was so beautiful that she had walked further than she intended, and would return. Mr. Pecksniff said it was exactly his case, and he would return with her.

"Take my arm, sweet girl," said Mr. Pecksniff.

Mary declined it, and walked so very fast that he remonstrated. "You were loitering when I came upon you," Mr. Pecksniff said. "Why be so cruel as to hurry now! You would not shun me, would you?"

"Yes, I would," she answered, turning her glowing cheek indignantly upon him, "you know I would. Release me, Mr. Pecksniff. Your touch is disagreeable to me."

His touch! What? That chaste patriarchal touch which Mrs. Todgers—surely a discreet lady—had endured, not only without complaint, but with apparent satisfaction! This was positively wrong. Mr. Pecksniff was sorry to hear her say it.

"If you have not observed," said Mary, "that it is so, pray take assurance from my lips, and not, as you are a gentleman, continue to offend me."

"Well, well!" said Mr. Pecksniff, mildly, "I feel that I might consider this becoming in a daughter of my own, and why should I object to it in one so beautiful! It's harsh. It cuts me to the soul," said Mr. Pecksniff: "but I cannot quarrel with you, Mary."

She tried to say she was sorry to hear it, but burst into tears. Mr. Pecksniff now repeated the Todgers' performance on a comfortable scale, as if he intended it to last some time; and in his disengaged hand, catching hers, employed himself in separating the fingers with his own, and sometimes kissing them, as he pursued the conversation thus:

"I am glad we met. I am very glad we met. I am able now to ease my bosom of a heavy load, and speak to you in confidence. Mary," said Mr. Pecksniff in his tenderest tones:

indeed, they were so very tender that he almost squeaked:
"My soul! I love you!"

A fantastic thing, that maiden affection! She made
believe to shudder.

"I love you," said Mr. Pecksniff, "my gentle life, with a
devotion which is quite surprising, even to myself. I did
suppose that the sensation was buried in the silent tomb of
a lady, only second to you in qualities of the mind and form:
but I find I am mistaken."

She tried to disengage her hand, but might as well have
tried to free herself from the embrace of an affectionate boa-
constrictor: if anything so wily may be brought into com-
parison with Pecksniff.

"Although I am a widower," said Mr. Pecksniff, examining
the rings upon her fingers, and tracing the course of one
delicate blue vein with his fat thumb, "a widower with two
daughters, still I am not encumbered, my love. One of
them, as you know, is married. The other, by her own
desire, but with a view, I will confess—why not?—to my
altering my condition, is about to leave her father's house.
I have a character, I hope. People are pleased to speak well
of me, I think. My person and manner are not absolutely
those of a monster, I trust. Ah, naughty Hand!" said Mr.
Pecksniff, apostrophising the reluctant prize, "why did you
take me prisoner! Go, go!"

He slapped the hand to punish it; but relenting, folded it
in his waistcoat, to comfort it again.

"Blessed in each other, and in the society of our venerable
friend, my darling," said Mr. Pecksniff, "we shall be happy.
When he is wafted to a haven of rest, we will console each
other. My pretty primrose, what do you say?"

"It is possible," Mary answered, in a hurried manner,
"that I ought to feel grateful for this mark of your confidence. I cannot say that I do, but I am willing to suppose
you may deserve my thanks. Take them; and pray leave
me, Mr. Pecksniff."

The good man smiled a greasy smile; and drew her closer to him.

"Pray, pray release me, Mr. Pecksniff. I cannot listen to your proposal. I cannot receive it. There are many to whom it may be acceptable, but it is not so to me. As an act of kindness and an act of pity, leave me!"

Mr. Pecksniff walked on with his arm round her waist, and her hand in his, as contentedly as if they had been all in all to each other, and were joined in the bonds of truest love.

"If you force me by your superior strength," said Mary, who finding that good words had not the least effect upon him, made no further effort to suppress her indignation: "if you force me by your superior strength to accompany you back, and to be the subject of your insolence upon the way, you cannot constrain the expression of my thoughts. I hold you in the deepest abhorrence. I know your real nature and despise it."

"No, no," said Mr. Pecksniff, sweetly. "No, no, no!"

"By what arts or unhappy chances you have gained your influence over Mr. Chuzzlewit, I do not know," said Mary: "it may be strong enough to soften even this, but he shall know of this, trust me, sir."

Mr. Pecksniff raised his heavy eyelids languidly, and let them fall again. It was saying with perfect coolness, "Aye, aye! Indeed!"

"Is it not enough," said Mary, "that you warp and change his nature, adapt his every prejudice to your bad ends, and harden a heart naturally kind by shutting out the truth and allowing none but false and distorted views to reach it; is it not enough that you have the power of doing this, and that you exercise it, but must you also be so coarse, so cruel, and so cowardly to me?"

Still Mr. Pecksniff led her calmly on, and looked as mild as any lamb that ever pastured in the fields.

"Will nothing move you, sir?" cried Mary.

"My dear," observed Mr. Pecksniff, with a placid leer, "a

habit of self-examination, and the practice of—shall I say of virtue?"

"Of hypocrisy," said Mary.

"No, no," resumed Mr. Pecksniff, chafing the captive hand reproachfully, "of virtue—have enabled me to set such guards upon myself, that it is really difficult to ruffle me. It is a curious fact, but it is difficult, do you know, for any one to ruffle me. And did she think," said Mr. Pecksniff, with a playful tightening of his grasp, "that *she* could! How little did she know his heart!"

Little, indeed! Her mind was so strangely constituted that she would have preferred the caresses of a toad, an adder, or a serpent: nay, the hug of a bear: to the endearments of Mr. Pecksniff.

"Come, come," said that good gentleman, "a word or two will set this matter right, and establish a pleasant understanding between us. I am not angry, my love."

"*You* angry!"

"No," said Mr. Pecksniff, "I am not. I say so. Neither are you."

There was a beating heart beneath his hand that told another story though.

"I am sure you are not," said Mr. Pecksniff: "and I will tell you why. There are two Martin Chuzzlewits, my dear; and your carrying your anger to one might have a serious effect—who knows!—upon the other. You wouldn't wish to hurt him, would you!"

She trembled violently, and looked at him with such a proud disdain that he turned his eyes away. No doubt lest he should be offended with her in spite of his better self.

"A passive quarrel, my love," said Mr. Pecksniff, "may be changed into an active one, remember. It would be sad to blight even a disinherited young man in his already blighted prospects: but how easy to do it. Ah, how easy! *Have* I influence with our venerable friend, do you think? Well, perhaps I have. Perhaps I have."

He raised his eyes to hers; and nodded with an air of banter that was charming.

"No," he continued, thoughtfully. "Upon the whole, my sweet, if I were you, I'd keep my secret to myself. I am not at all sure: very far from it: that it would surprise our friend in any way, for he and I have had some conversation together only this morning, and he is anxious, very anxious, to establish you in some more settled manner. But whether he was surprised or not surprised, the consequence of your imparting it might be the same. Martin, junior, might suffer severely. I'd have compassion on Martin, junior, do you know?" said Mr. Pecksniff, with a persuasive smile. "Yes. He don't deserve it, but I would."

She wept so bitterly now, and was so much distressed, that he thought it prudent to unclasp her waist, and hold her only by the hand.

"As to our own share in the precious little mystery," said Mr. Pecksniff, "we will keep it to ourselves, and talk of it between ourselves, and you shall think it over. You will consent, my love; you will consent, I know. Whatever you may think; you will. I seem to remember to have heard: I really don't know where, or how:" he added, with bewitching frankness, "that you and Martin, junior, when you were children, had a sort of childish fondness for each other. When we are married, you shall have the satisfaction of thinking that it didn't last, to ruin him, but passed away, to do him good; for we'll see then, what we can do to put some trifling help in Martin, junior's way. *Have* I any influence with our venerable friend? Well! Perhaps I have. Perhaps I have."

The outlet from the wood in which these tender passages occurred, was close to Mr. Pecksniff's house. They were now so near it that he stopped, and holding up her little finger, said in playful accents, as a parting fancy:

"Shall I bite it?"

Receiving no reply he kissed it instead; and then stooping

down, inclined his flabby face to hers (he had a flabby face, although he *was* a good man), and with a blessing, which from such a source was quite enough to set her up in life, and prosper her for that time forth, permitted her to leave him.

Gallantry in its true sense is supposed to ennoble and dignify a man; and love has shed refinements on innumerable Cymons. But Mr. Pecksniff: perhaps because to one of his exalted nature these were mere grossnesses: certainly did not appear to any unusual advantage, now that he was left alone. On the contrary, he seemed to be shrunk and reduced; to be trying to hide himself within himself; and to be wretched at not having the power to do it. His shoes looked too large; his sleeve looked too long; his hair looked too limp; his features looked too mean; his exposed throat looked as if a halter would have done it good. For a minute or two, in fact, he was hot, and pale, and mean, and shy, and slinking, and consequently not at all Pecksniffian. But after that, he recovered himself, and went home with as beneficent an air as if he had been the High Priest of the summer weather.

" I have arranged to go, Papa," said Charity, " to-morrow."

" So soon, my child ! "

" I can't go too soon," said Charity, " under the circumstances. I have written to Mrs. Todgers to propose an arrangement, and have requested her to meet me at the coach, at all events. You'll be quite your own master, now, Mr. Pinch ! "

Mr. Pecksniff had just gone out of the room, and Tom had just come into it.

" My own master ! " repeated Tom.

" Yes, you'll have nobody to interfere with you," said Charity. " At least I hope you won't. Hem ! It's a changing world."

" What ! are *you* going to be married, Miss Pecksniff ? " asked Tom in great surprise.

84

"Not exactly," faltered Cherry. "I haven't made up my mind to be. I believe I could be, if I choose, Mr. Pinch."

"Of course you could!" said Tom. And he said it in perfect good faith. He believed it from the bottom of his heart.

"No," said Cherry, "*I* am not going to be married. Nobody is, that I know of. Hem! But I am not going to live with Papa. I have my reasons, but it's all a secret. I shall always feel very kindly towards you, I assure you, for the boldness you showed that night. As to you and me, Mr. Pinch, *we* part the best friends possible!"

Tom thanked her for her confidence, and for her friendship, but there was a mystery in the former which perfectly bewildered him. In his extravagant devotion to the family, he had felt the loss of Merry more than any one but those who knew that for all the slights he underwent he thought his own demerits were to blame, could possibly have understood. He had scarcely reconciled himself to that, when here was Charity about to leave them. She had grown up, as it were, under Tom's eye. The sisters were a part of Pecksniff, and a part of Tom; items in Pecksniff's goodness, and in Tom's service. He couldn't bear it: not two hours' sleep had Tom that night, through dwelling in his bed upon these dreadful changes.

When morning dawned, he thought he must have dreamed this piece of ambiguity; but no, on going down stairs he found them packing trunks and cording boxes, and making other preparations for Miss Charity's departure, which lasted all day long. In good time for the evening-coach, Miss Charity deposited her housekeeping keys with much ceremony upon the parlour table: took a gracious leave of all the house; and quitted her paternal roof—a blessing, for which the Pecksniffian servant was observed by some profane persons to be particularly active in the thanksgiving at church next Sunday.

THE closing words of the last chapter, lead naturally to the
commencement of this, its successor; for it has to do with a
church. With the church so often mentioned heretofore, in
which Tom Pinch played the organ for nothing.

One sultry afternoon, about a week after Miss Charity's
departure for London, Mr. Pecksniff being out walking by
himself, took it into his head to stray into the churchyard.
As he was lingering among the tombstones, endeavouring to
extract an available sentiment or two from the epitaphs—for
he never lost an opportunity of making up a few moral
crackers, to be let off as occasion served—Tom Pinch began
to practise. Tom could run down to the church and do so
whenever he had time to spare; for it was a simple little
organ, provided with wind by the action of the musician's
feet; and he was independent, even of a bellows-blower.
Though if Tom had wanted one at any time, there was not
a man or boy in all the village, and away to the turnpike
(tollman included), but would have blown away for him till
he was black in the face.

Mr. Pecksniff had no objection to music; not the least.
He was tolerant of everything; he often said so. He considered it a vagabond kind of trifling, in general, just suited
to Tom's capacity. But in regard to Tom's performance

upon this same organ, he was remarkably lenient, singularly amiable; for when Tom played it on Sundays, Mr. Pecksniff in his unbounded sympathy felt as if he played it himself, and were a benefactor to the congregation. So whenever it was impossible to devise any other means of taking the value of Tom's wages out of him, Mr. Pecksniff gave him leave to cultivate this instrument. For which mark of his consideration, Tom was very grateful.

The afternoon was remarkably warm, and Mr. Pecksniff had been strolling a long way. He had not what may be called a fine ear for music, but he knew when it had a tranquillising influence on his soul; and that was the case now, for it sounded to him like a melodious snore. He approached the church, and looking through the diamond lattice of a window near the porch, saw Tom, with the curtains in the loft drawn back, playing away with great expression and tenderness.

The church had an inviting air of coolness. The old oak roof supported by cross-beams, the hoary walls, the marble tablets, and the cracked stone pavement, were refreshing to look at. There were leaves of ivy tapping gently at the opposite windows; and the sun poured in through only one: leaving the body of the church in tempting shade. But the most tempting spot of all, was one red-curtained and soft-cushioned pew, wherein the official dignitaries of the place (of whom Mr. Pecksniff was the head and chief) enshrined themselves on Sundays. Mr. Pecksniff's seat was in the corner: a remarkably comfortable corner; where his very large Prayer-Book was at that minute making the most of its quarto self upon the desk. He determined to go in and rest.

He entered very softly; in part because it was a church; in part because his tread was always soft; in part because Tom played a solemn tune; in part because he thought he would surprise him when he stopped. Unbolting the door of the high pew of state, he glided in and shut it after him;

then sitting in his usual place, and stretching out his legs upon the hassocks, he composed himself to listen to the music.

It is an unaccountable circumstance that he should have felt drowsy there, where the force of association might surely have been enough to keep him wide awake; but he did. He had not been in the snug little corner five minutes before he began to nod. He had not recovered himself one minute before he began to nod again. In the very act of opening his eyes indolently, he nodded again. In the very act of shutting them, he nodded again. So he fell out of one nod into another until at last he ceased to nod at all, and was as fast as the church itself.

He had a consciousness of the organ, long after he fell asleep, though as to its being an organ he had no more idea of that, than he had of its being a Bull. After a while he began to have at intervals the same dreamy impressions of voices; and awakening to an indolent curiosity upon the subject, opened his eyes.

He was so indolent, that after glancing at the hassocks and the pew, he was already half-way off to sleep again, when it occurred to him that there really were voices in the church: low voices, talking earnestly hard by: while the echoes seemed to mutter responses. He roused himself, and listened.

Before he had listened half a dozen seconds, he became as broad awake as ever he had been in all his life. With eyes, and ears, and mouth, wide open, he moved himself a very little with the utmost caution, and gathering the curtain in his hand, peeped out.

Tom Pinch and Mary. Of course. He had recognised their voices, and already knew the topic they discussed. Looking like the small end of a guillotined man, with his chin on a level with the top of the pew, so that he might duck down immediately in case of either of them turning round, he listened. Listened with such concentrated eagerness, that his very hair and shirt-collar stood bristling up to help him.

"No," cried Tom. "No letters have ever reached me, except that one from New York. But don't be uneasy on that account, for it's very likely they have gone away to some far-off place, where the posts are neither regular nor frequent. He said in that very letter that it might be so, even in that city to which they thought of travelling—Eden, you know."

"It is a great weight upon my mind," said Mary.

"Oh, but you mustn't let it be," said Tom. "There's a true saying that nothing travels so fast as ill news; and if the slightest harm had happened to Martin, you may be sure you would have heard of it long ago. I have often wished to say this to you," Tom continued with an embarrassment that became him very well, "but you have never given me an opportunity."

"I have sometimes been almost afraid," said Mary, "that you might suppose I hesitated to confide in you, Mr. Pinch."

"No," Tom stammered, "I—I am not aware that I ever supposed that. I am sure that if I have, I have checked the thought directly, as an injustice to you. I feel the delicacy of your situation in having to confide in me at all," said Tom, "but I would risk my life to save you from one day's uneasiness: indeed I would!"

Poor Tom!

"I have dreaded sometimes," Tom continued, "that I might have displeased you by—by having the boldness to try and anticipate your wishes now and then. At other times I have fancied that your kindness prompted you to keep aloof from me."

"Indeed!"

"It was very foolish: very presumptuous and ridiculous: to think so," Tom pursued: "but I feared you might suppose it possible that I—I—should admire you too much for my own peace; and so denied yourself the slight assistance you would otherwise have accepted from me. If such an idea has ever presented itself to you," faltered Tom, "pray dismiss

89

it. I am easily made happy : and I shall live contented here long after you and Martin have forgotten me. I am a poor, shy, awkward creature : not at all a man of the world : and you should think no more of me, bless you, than if I were an old friar ! "

If friars bear such hearts as thine, Tom, let friars multiply ; though they have no such rule in all their stern arithmetic.

" Dear Mr. Pinch ! " said Mary, giving him her hand ; " I cannot tell you how your kindness moves me. I have never wronged you by the lightest doubt, and have never for an instant ceased to feel that you were all ; much more than all ; that Martin found you. Without the silent care and friendship I have experienced from you, my life here would have been unhappy. But you have been a good angel to me ; filling me with gratitude of heart, hope, and courage."

" I am as little like an angel, I am afraid," replied Tom, shaking his head, " as any stone cherubim among the gravestones ; and I don't think there are many real angels of *that* pattern. But I should like to know (if you will tell me) why you have been so very silent about Martin."

" Because I have been afraid," said Mary, " of injuring you."

" Of injuring me ! " cried Tom.

" Of doing you an injury with your employer."

The gentleman in question dived.

" With Pecksniff ! " rejoined Tom, with cheerful confidence. " Oh dear, he'd never think of us ! He's the best of men. The more at ease you were, the happier he would be. Oh dear, you needn't be afraid of Pecksniff. He is not a spy."

Many a man in Mr. Pecksniff's place, if he could have dived through the floor of the pew of state and come out at Calcutta or any inhabited region on the other side of the earth, would have done it instantly. Mr. Pecksniff sat down upon a hassock, and listening more attentively than ever, smiled.

Mary seemed to have expressed some dissent in the meanwhile, for Tom went on to say, with honest energy :

"Well, I don't know how it is, but it always happens, whenever I express myself in this way, to anybody almost, that I find they won't do justice to Pecksniff. It is one of the most extraordinary circumstances that ever came within my knowledge, but it is so. There's John Westlock, who used to be a pupil here, one of the best-hearted young men in the world, in all other matters: I really believe John would have Pecksniff flogged at the cart's tail if he could. And John is not a solitary case, for every pupil we have had in my time has gone away with the same inveterate hatred of him. There was Mark Tapley, too, quite in another station of life," said Tom: "the mockery he used to make of Pecksniff when he was at the Dragon was shocking. Martin too: Martin was worse than any of 'em. But I forgot. He prepared you to dislike Pecksniff, of course. So you came with a prejudice, you know, Miss Graham, and are not a fair witness."

Tom triumphed very much in this discovery, and rubbed his hands with great satisfaction.

"Mr. Pinch," said Mary, "you mistake him."

"No, no!" cried Tom. "*You* mistake him. But," he added, with a rapid change in his tone, "what is the matter? Miss Graham, what is the matter?"

Mr. Pecksniff brought up to the top of the pew, by slow degrees, his hair, his forehead, his eyebrow, his eye. She was sitting on a bench beside the door with her hands before her face; and Tom was bending over her.

"What is the matter!" cried Tom. "Have I said anything to hurt you? Has any one said anything to hurt you? Don't cry. Pray tell me what it is. I cannot bear to see you so distressed. Mercy on us, I never was so surprised and grieved in all my life!"

Mr. Pecksniff kept his eye in the same place. He could have moved it now for nothing short of a gimlet or a red-hot wire.

"I wouldn't have told you, Mr. Pinch," said Mary, "if I

could have helped it; but your delusion is so absorbing, and it is so necessary that we should be upon our guard; that you should not be compromised; and to that end that you should know by whom I am beset; that no alternative is left me. I came here purposely to tell you, but I think I should have wanted courage if you had not chanced to lead me so directly to the object of my coming."

Tom gazed at her steadfastly, and seemed to say, "What else?" But he said not a word.

"That person whom you think the best of men," said Mary, looking up, and speaking with a quivering lip and flashing eye:

"Lord bless me!" muttered Tom, staggering back. "Wait a moment. That person whom I think the best of men! You mean Pecksniff, of course. Yes, I see you mean Pecksniff. Good gracious me, don't speak without authority. What has he done? If he is not the best of men, what is he?"

"The worst. The falsest, craftiest, meanest, cruellest, most sordid, most shameless," said the trembling girl—trembling with her indignation.

Tom sat down on a seat, and clasped his hands.

"What is he," said Mary, "who receiving me in his house as his guest; his unwilling guest: knowing my history, and how defenceless and alone I am, presumes before his daughters to affront me so, that if I had a brother but a child, who saw it, he would instinctively have helped me?"

"He is a scoundrel!" exclaimed Tom. "Whoever he may be, he is a scoundrel."

Mr. Pecksniff dived again.

"What is he," said Mary, "who, when my only friend: a dear and kind one, too: was in full health of mind, humbled himself before him, but was spurned away (for he knew him then) like a dog. Who, in his forgiving spirit, now that that friend is sunk into a failing state, can crawl about him again, and use the influence he basely gains for every base

92

and wicked purpose, and not for one—not one—that's true or good?"

"I say he is a scoundrel!" answered Tom.

"But what is he: oh Mr. Pinch, what *is* he: who, thinking he could compass these designs the better if I were his wife, assails me with the coward's argument that if I marry him, Martin, on whom I have brought so much misfortune, shall be restored to something of his former hopes; and if I do not, shall be plunged in deeper ruin? What is he who makes my very constancy to one I love with all my heart a torture to myself and wrong to him; who makes me, do what I will, the instrument to hurt a head I would heap blessings on! What is he who, winding all these cruel snares about me, explains their purpose to me, with a smooth tongue and a smiling face, in the broad light of day: dragging me on, the while, in his embrace, and holding to his lips a hand," pursued the agitated girl, extending it, "which I would have struck off, if with it I could lose the shame and degradation of his touch?"

"I say," cried Tom, in great excitement, "he is a scoundrel and a villain! I don't care who he is, I say he is a double-dyed and most intolerable villain!"

Covering her face with her hands again, as if the passion which had sustained her through these disclosures lost itself in an overwhelming sense of shame and grief, she abandoned herself to tears.

Any sight of distress was sure to move the tenderness of Tom, but this especially. Tears and sobs from her, were arrows in his heart. He tried to comfort her; sat down beside her; expended all his store of homely eloquence; and spoke in words of praise and hope of Martin. Ay, though he loved her from his soul with such a self-denying love as woman seldom wins: he spoke from first to last of Martin. Not the wealth of the rich Indies would have tempted Tom to shirk one mention of her lover's name.

When she was more composed, she impressed upon Tom

that this man she had described, was Pecksniff in his real colours; and word by word and phrase by phrase, as well as she remembered it, related what had passed between them in the wood: which was no doubt a source of high gratification to that gentleman himself, who in his desire to see and his dread of being seen, was constantly diving down into the state pew, and coming up again like the intelligent house-holder in Punch's Show, who avoids being knocked on the head with a cudgel. When she had concluded her account, and had besought Tom to be very distant and unconscious in his manner towards her after this explanation, and had thanked him very much, they parted on the alarm of foot-steps in the burial-ground; and Tom was left alone in the church again.

And now the full agitation and misery of the disclosure, came rushing upon Tom indeed. The star of his whole life from boyhood, had become, in a moment, putrid vapour. It was not that Pecksniff, Tom's Pecksniff, had ceased to exist, but that he never had existed. In his death Tom would have had the comfort of remembering what he used to be, but in this discovery, he had the anguish of recollecting what he never was. For as Tom's blindness in this matter had been total and not partial, so was his restored sight. *His* Pecksniff could never have worked the wickedness of which he had just now heard, but any other Pecksniff could; and the Pecksniff who could do that, could do anything, and no doubt had been doing anything and everything except the right thing, all through his career. From the lofty height on which poor Tom had placed his idol it was tumbled down headlong, and

> Not all the king's horses, nor all the king's men,
> Could have set Mr. Pecksniff up again.

Legions of Titans couldn't have got him out of the mud; and serve him right! But it was not he who suffered; it was Tom. His compass was broken, his chart destroyed, his

chronometer had stopped, his masts were gone by the board ;
his anchor was adrift, ten thousand leagues away.

Mr. Pecksniff watched him with a lively interest, for he
divined the purpose of Tom's ruminations, and was curious
to see how he conducted himself. For some time, Tom
wandered up and down the aisle like a man demented,
stopping occasionally to lean against a pew and think it
over ; then he stood staring at a blank old monument
bordered tastefully with skulls and cross-bones, as if it were
the finest work of Art he had ever seen, although at other
times he held it in unspeakable contempt ; then he sat down ;
then walked to and fro again ; then went wandering up into
the organ-loft, and touched the keys. But their minstrelsy
was changed, their music gone ; and sounding one long
melancholy chord, Tom drooped his head upon his hands
and gave it up as hopeless.

"I wouldn't have cared," said Tom Pinch, rising from his
stool, and looking down into the church as if he had been
the Clergyman, "I wouldn't have cared for anything he
might have done to Me, for I have tried his patience often,
and have lived upon his sufferance, and have never been the
help to him that others could have been. I wouldn't have
minded, Pecksniff," Tom continued, little thinking who heard
him, "if you had done Me any wrong ; I could have found
plenty of excuses for that ; and though you might have hurt
me, could have still gone on respecting you. But why did
you ever fall so low as this in my esteem ! Oh Pecksniff,
Pecksniff, there is nothing I would not have given, to have
had you deserve my old opinion of you ; nothing !"

Mr. Pecksniff sat upon the hassock pulling up his shirt-collar,
while Tom, touched to the quick, delivered this apostrophe.
After a pause he heard Tom coming down the stairs, jingling
the church keys ; and bringing his eye to the top of the pew
again, saw him go slowly out, and lock the door.

Mr. Pecksniff durst not issue from his place of concealment ;
for through the windows of the church, he saw Tom passing

on among the graves, and sometimes stopping at a stone, and leaning there, as if he were a mourner who had lost a friend. Even when he had left the churchyard, Mr. Pecksniff still remained shut up: not being at all secure but that in his restless state of mind Tom might come wandering back. At length he issued forth, and walked with a pleasant countenance into the vestry; where he knew there was a window near the ground, by which he could release himself by merely stepping out.

He was in a curious frame of mind, Mr. Pecksniff: being in no hurry to go, but rather inclining to a dilatory trifling with the time, which prompted him to open the vestry cupboard, and look at himself in the parson's little glass that hung within the door. Seeing that his hair was rumpled, he took the liberty of borrowing the canonical brush and arranging it. He also took the liberty of opening another cupboard; but he shut it up again quickly, being rather startled by the sight of a black and a white surplice dangling against the wall; which had very much the appearance of two curates who had committed suicide by hanging themselves. Remembering that he had seen in the first cupboard a port-wine bottle and some biscuits, he peeped into it again, and helped himself with much deliberation: cogitating all the time though, in a very deep and weighty manner, as if his thoughts were otherwise employed.

He soon made up his mind, if it had ever been in doubt; and putting back the bottle and biscuits, opened the casement. He got out into the churchyard without any difficulty; shut the window after him; and walked straight home.

"Is Mr. Pinch in-doors?" asked Mr. Pecksniff of his serving-maid.

"Just come in, sir."

"Just come in, eh?" repeated Mr. Pecksniff, cheerfully. "And gone up stairs, I suppose?"

"Yes, sir. Gone up stairs. Shall I call him, sir?"

"No," said Mr. Pecksniff, "no. You needn't call him, Jane. Thank you, Jane. How are your relations, Jane?"

"Pretty well, I thank you, sir."

"I am glad to hear it. Let them know I asked about them, Jane. Is Mr. Chuzzlewit in the way, Jane?"

"Yes, sir. He's in the parlour, reading."

"He's in the parlour, reading, is he, Jane?" said Mr. Pecksniff. "Very well. Then I think I'll go and see him, Jane."

Never had Mr. Pecksniff been beheld in a more pleasant humour!

But when he walked into the parlour where the old man was engaged as Jane had said; with pen and ink and paper on a table close at hand (for Mr. Pecksniff was always very particular to have him well supplied with writing materials); he became less cheerful. He was not angry, he was not vindictive, he was not cross, he was not moody, but he was grieved: he was sorely grieved. As he sat down by the old man's side, two tears: not tears like those with which recording angels blot their entries out, but drops so precious that they use them for their ink: stole down his meritorious cheeks.

"What is the matter?" asked old Martin. "Pecksniff, what ails you, man?"

"I am sorry to interrupt you, my dear sir, and I am still more sorry for the cause. My good, my worthy friend, I am deceived."

"You are deceived!"

"Ah!" cried Mr. Pecksniff, in an agony, "deceived in the tenderest point Cruelly deceived in that quarter, sir, in which I placed the most unbounded confidence. Deceived, Mr. Chuzzlewit, by Thomas Pinch."

"Oh! bad, bad, bad!" said Martin, laying down his book. "Very bad! I hope not. Are you certain?"

"Certain, my good sir! My eyes and ears are witnesses. I wouldn't have believed it otherwise. I wouldn't have believed

97

it, Mr. Chuzzlewit, if a Fiery Serpent had proclaimed it from the top of Salisbury Cathedral. I would have said," cried Mr. Pecksniff, "that the Serpent lied. Such was my faith in Thomas Pinch, that I would have cast the falsehood back into the Serpent's teeth, and would have taken Thomas to my heart. But I am not a Serpent, sir, myself, I grieve to say, and no excuse or hope is left me."

Martin was greatly disturbed to see him so much agitated, and to hear such unexpected news. He begged him to compose himself, and asked upon what subject Mr. Pinch's treachery had been developed.

"That is almost the worst of all, sir," Mr. Pecksniff answered. "On a subject nearly concerning *you*. Oh! is it not enough," said Mr. Pecksniff, looking upward, "that these blows must fall on me, but must they also hit my friends!"

"You alarm me," cried the old man, changing colour. "I am not so strong as I was. You terrify me, Pecksniff!"

"Cheer up, my noble sir," said Mr. Pecksniff, taking courage, "and we will do what is required of us. You shall know all, sir, and shall be righted. But first excuse me, sir, ex-cuse me. I have a duty to discharge, which I owe to society."

He rang the bell, and Jane appeared. "Send Mr. Pinch here, if you please, Jane."

Tom came. Constrained and altered in his manner, downcast and dejected, visibly confused; not liking to look Pecksniff in the face.

The honest man bestowed a glance on Mr. Chuzzlewit, as who should say "You see!" and addressed himself to Tom in these terms:

"Mr. Pinch, I have left the vestry-window unfastened. Will you do me the favour to go and secure it; then bring the keys of the sacred edifice to me!"

"The vestry-window, sir?" cried Tom.

"You understand me, Mr. Pinch, I think," returned his

patron. "Yes, Mr. Pinch, the vestry-window. I grieve to say that sleeping in the church after a fatiguing ramble, I overheard just now some fragments," he emphasised that word, "of a dialogue between two parties; and one of them locking the church when he went out, I was obliged to leave it myself by the vestry-window. Do me the favour to secure that vestry-window, Mr. Pinch, and then come back to me."

No physiognomist that ever dwelt on earth could have construed Tom's face when he heard these words. Wonder was in it, and a mild look of reproach, but certainly no fear or guilt, although a host of strong emotions struggled to display themselves. He bowed, and without saying one word, good or bad, withdrew.

"Pecksniff," cried Martin, in a tremble, "what does all this mean? You are not going to do anything in haste, you may regret!"

"No, my good sir," said Mr. Pecksniff, firmly, "No. But I have a duty to discharge which I owe to society; and it shall be discharged, my friend, at any cost!"

Oh late-remembered, much-forgotten, mouthing, braggart duty, always owed, and seldom paid in any other coin than punishment and wrath, when will mankind begin to know thee! When will men acknowledge thee in thy neglected cradle, and thy stunted youth, and not begin their recognition in thy sinful manhood and thy desolate old age! Oh ermined Judge whose duty to society is, now, to doom the ragged criminal to punishment and death, hadst thou never, Man, a duty to discharge in barring up the hundred open gates that wooed him to the felon's dock, and throwing but ajar the portals to a decent life! Oh prelate, prelate, whose duty to society it is to mourn in melancholy phrase the sad degeneracy of these bad times in which thy lot of honours has been cast, did nothing go before thy elevation to the lofty seat, from which thou dealest out thy homilies to other tarriers for dead men's shoes, whose duty to society has not begun! Oh magistrate, so rare a country gentleman and

99

brave a squire, had you no duty to society, before the ricks were blazing and the mob were mad; or did it spring up, armed and booted from the earth, a corps of yeomanry, full-grown!

Mr. Pecksniff's duty to society could not be paid till Tom came back. The interval which preceded the return of that young man, he occupied in a close conference with his friend; so that when Tom did arrive, he found the two quite ready to receive him. Mary was in her own room above, whither Mr. Pecksniff, always considerate, had besought old Martin to entreat her to remain some half-hour longer, that her feelings might be spared.

When Tom came back, he found old Martin sitting by the window, and Mr. Pecksniff in an imposing attitude at the table. On one side of him was his pocket-handkerchief; and on the other, a little heap (a very little heap) of gold and silver, and odd pence. Tom saw, at a glance, that it was his own salary for the current quarter.

"Have you fastened the vestry-window, Mr. Pinch?" said Pecksniff.

"Yes, sir."

"Thank you. Put down the keys if you please, Mr. Pinch."

Tom placed them on the table. He held the bunch by the key of the organ-loft (though it was one of the smallest), and looked hard at it as he laid it down. It had been an old, old friend of Tom's; a kind companion to him, many and many a day.

"Mr. Pinch," said Pecksniff, shaking his head: "Oh Mr. Pinch! I wonder you can look me in the face!"

Tom did it though; and notwithstanding that he has been described as stooping generally, he stood as upright then as man could stand.

"Mr. Pinch," said Pecksniff, taking up his handkerchief, as if he felt that he should want it soon, "I will not dwell upon the past. I will spare you, and I will spare myself, that pain at least."

Tom's was not a very bright eye, but it was a very expressive one when he looked at Mr. Pecksniff, and said:

"Thank you, sir. I am very glad you will not refer to the past."

"The present is enough," said Mr. Pecksniff, dropping a penny, "and the sooner *that* is past, the better. Mr. Pinch, I will not dismiss you without a word of explanation. Even such a course would be quite justifiable under the circumstances; but it might wear an appearance of hurry, and I will not do it; for I am," said Mr. Pecksniff, knocking down another penny, "perfectly self-possessed. Therefore I will say to you, what I have already said to Mr. Chuzzlewit."

Tom glanced at the old gentleman, who nodded now and then as approving of Mr. Pecksniff's sentences and sentiments, but interposed between them in no other way.

"From fragments of a conversation which I overheard in the church, just now, Mr. Pinch," said Pecksniff, "between yourself and Miss Graham—I say fragments, because I was slumbering at a considerable distance from you, when I was roused by your voices—and from what I saw, I ascertained (I would have given a great deal not to have ascertained, Mr. Pinch) that you, forgetful of all ties of duty and of honour, sir; regardless of the sacred laws of hospitality, to which you were pledged as an inmate of this house; have presumed to address Miss Graham with un-returned professions of attachment and proposals of love."

Tom looked at him steadily.

"Do you deny it, sir?" asked Mr. Pecksniff, dropping one pound two and fourpence, and making a great business of picking it up again.

"No, sir," replied Tom. "I do not."

"You do not," said Mr. Pecksniff, glancing at the old gentleman. "Oblige me by counting this money, Mr. Pinch, and putting your name to this receipt. You do not?"

No, Tom did not. He scorned to deny it. He saw that

Mr. Pecksniff having overheard his own disgrace, cared not a jot for sinking lower yet in his contempt. He saw that he had devised this fiction as the readiest means of getting rid of him at once, but that it must end in that any way. He saw that Mr. Pecksniff reckoned on his not denying it, because his doing so and explaining, would incense the old man more than ever against Martin, and against Mary: while Pecksniff himself would only have been mistaken in his "fragments." Deny it! No.

"You find the amount correct, do you, Mr. Pinch?" said Pecksniff.

"Quite correct, sir," answered Tom.

"A person is waiting in the kitchen," said Mr. Pecksniff, "to carry your luggage wherever you please. We part, Mr. Pinch, at once, and are strangers from this time."

Something without a name; compassion, sorrow, old tenderness, mistaken gratitude, habit: none of these, and yet all of them; smote upon Tom's gentle heart, at parting. There was no such soul as Pecksniff's in that carcase; and yet, though his speaking out had not involved the compromise of one he loved, he couldn't have denounced the very shape and figure of the man. Not even then.

"I will not say," cried Mr. Pecksniff, shedding tears, "what a blow this is. I will not say how much it tries me; how it works upon my nature; how it grates upon my feelings. I do not care for that. I can endure as well as another man. But what I have to hope, and what you have to hope, Mr. Pinch (otherwise a great responsibility rests upon you), is, that this deception may not alter my ideas of humanity; that it may not impair my freshness, or contract, if I may use the expression, my Pinions. I hope it will not; I don't think it will. It may be a comfort to you, if not now, at some future time, to know, that I shall endeavour not to think the worse of my fellow-creatures in general, for what has passed between us. Farewell!"

Tom had meant to spare him one little puncturation with

a lancet, which he had it in his power to administer, but he changed his mind on hearing this, and said :

" I think you left something in the church, sir."

"Thank you, Mr. Pinch," said Pecksniff. " I am not aware that I did."

"This is your double eye-glass, I believe ? " said Tom.

" Oh ! " cried Pecksniff, with some degree of confusion. " I am obliged to you.' Put it down, if you please."

" I found it," said Tom, slowly, " when I went to bolt the vestry-window, in the pew."

So he had. Mr. Pecksniff had taken it off when he was bobbing up and down, lest it should strike against the panelling : and had forgotten it. Going back to the church with his mind full of having been watched, and wondering very much from what part, Tom's attention was caught by the door of the state pew standing open. Looking into it he found the glass. And thus he knew, and by returning it gave Mr. Pecksniff the information that he knew, where the listener had been ; and that instead of overhearing fragments of the conversation, he must have rejoiced in every word of it.

" I am glad he's gone," said Martin, drawing a long breath when Tom had left the room.

" It *is* a relief," assented Mr. Pecksniff. " It is a great relief. But having discharged—I hope with tolerable firmness —the duty which I owed to society, I will now, my dear sir, if you will give me leave, retire to shed a few tears in the back garden, as an humble individual."

Tom went up stairs : cleared his shelf of books : packed them up with his music and an old fiddle in his trunk ; got out his clothes (they were not so many that they made his head ache) ; put them on the top of his books ; and went into the workroom for his case of instruments. There was a ragged stool there, with the horsehair all sticking out of the top like a wig : a very Beast of a stool in itself : on which he had taken up his daily seat, year after year, during the whole period of his service. They had grown older and shabbier in company. Pupils had served their time; seasons had come and gone; Tom and the worn-out stool had held together through it all. That part of the room was traditionally called "Tom's Corner." It had been assigned to him at first because of its being situated in a strong draught, and a great way from the fire; and he had occupied it ever since. There were portraits of him on the walls, with all his weak points monstrously portrayed. Diabolical sentiments, foreign to his character, were represented as issuing from his mouth in fat balloons. Every pupil had added something, even unto fancy portraits of his father with one eye, and of his mother with a disproportionate nose, and especially of his sister; who always being presented as extremely beautiful, made full amends to Tom for any other joke. Under less uncommon circumstances, it would have cut Tom to the heart to leave these things, and think that he saw them for the last time; but it didn't now. There was no Pecksniff; there never had been a Pecksniff; and all his other griefs were swallowed up in that.

So when he returned into the bedroom, and, having fastened his box and a carpet-bag, put on his walking gaiters, and his great-coat, and his hat, and taken his stick in his hand, looked round it for the last time. Early on summer mornings, and by the light of private candle-ends on winter nights, he had read himself half blind in this same room. He had tried in this same room to learn the fiddle under the bedclothes, but yielding to objections from the other pupils, had reluctantly abandoned the design. At any other time he would have parted from it with a pang, thinking of all he had learned there, of the many hours he had passed there; for the love of his very dreams. But there was no Pecksniff; there never had been a Pecksniff, and the unreality of Pecksniff extended itself to the chamber, in which, sitting on one particular bed, the thing supposed to be that Great Abstraction had often preached morality with such effect, that Tom

104

Mr. Pecksniff discharges a Duty which he owes to Society

had felt a moisture in his eyes, while hanging breathless on the words.

The man engaged to bear his box—Tom knew him well; a Dragon man—came stamping up the stairs, and made a roughish bow to Tom (to whom in common times he would have nodded with a grin), as though he were aware of what had happened, and wished him to perceive it made no difference to *him*. It was clumsily done; he was a mere waterer of horses; but Tom liked the man for it, and felt it more than going away.

Tom would have helped him with the box, but he made no more of it, though it was a heavy one, than an elephant would have made of a castle: just swinging it on his back and bowling down stairs as if, being naturally a heavy sort of fellow, he could carry a box infinitely better than he could go alone. Tom took the carpet-bag, and went down stairs along with him. At the outer door stood Jane, crying with all her might; and on the steps was Mrs. Lupin, sobbing bitterly, and putting out her hand for Tom to shake.

"You're coming to the Dragon, Mr. Pinch?"

"No," said Tom, "no. I shall walk to Salisbury to-night. I couldn't stay here. For goodness' sake, don't make me so unhappy, Mrs. Lupin."

"But you'll come to the Dragon, Mr. Pinch. If it's only for to-night. To see me, you know: not as a traveller."

"God bless my soul!" said Tom, wiping his eyes. "The kindness of people is enough to break one's heart! I mean to go to Salisbury to-night, my dear good creature. If you'll take care of my box for me, till I write for it, I shall consider it the greatest kindness you can do me."

"I wish," cried Mrs. Lupin, "there were twenty boxes, Mr. Pinch, that I might have 'em all."

"Thank'ee," said Tom. "It's like you. Good bye. Good bye."

There were several people, young and old, standing about the door, some of whom cried with Mrs. Lupin; while others tried to keep up a stout heart, as Tom did; and others were absorbed in admiration of Mr. Pecksniff—a man who could build a church, as one may say, by squinting at a sheet of paper; and others were divided between that feeling, and sympathy with Tom. Mr. Pecksniff had appeared on the top of the steps, simultaneously with his old pupil, and while Tom was talking with Mrs. Lupin kept his hand stretched out, as though he said "Go forth!" When Tom went forth, and had turned the corner, Mr. Pecksniff shook his head, shut his eyes, and heaving a deep sigh, shut the door. On which, the best of Tom's supporters said he must have done some dreadful deed, or such a man as Mr. Pecksniff never could have felt like that. If it had been a common quarrel (they observed) he would have said something, but when he didn't, Mr. Pinch must have shocked him dreadfully.

Tom was out of hearing of their shrewd opinions, and plodded on as steadily as he could go, until he came within sight of the turnpike where the tollman's family had cried out "Mr. Pinch!" that frosty morning when he went to meet young Martin. He had got through the village, and this toll-bar was his last trial; but when the infant toll-takers came screeching out, he had half a mind to run for it, and make a bolt across the country.

"Why deary Mr. Pinch! oh deary sir!" cried the tollman's wife. "What an unlikely time for you to be a going this way with a bag!"

"I am going to Salisbury," said Tom.

"Why, goodness, where's the gig then?" cried the tollman's wife, looking down the road, as if she thought Tom might have been upset without observing it.

"I haven't got it," said Tom. "I—" he couldn't evade it; he felt she would have him in the next question, if he got over this one. "I have left Mr. Pecksniff."

The tollman—a crusty customer, always smoking solitary pipes in a Windsor chair, inside, set artfully between two little windows that looked up and down the road, so that when he saw anything coming up, he might hug himself on having toll to take, and when he saw it going down, might hug himself on having taken it—the tollman was out in an instant.

" Left, Mr. Pecksniff ! " cried the tollman.

" Yes," said Tom, " left him."

The tollman looked at his wife, uncertain whether to ask her if she had anything to suggest, or to order her to mind the children. Astonishment making him surly, he preferred the latter, and sent her into the toll-house, with a flea in her ear.

" You left Mr. Pecksniff ! " cried the tollman, folding his arms, and spreading his legs. " I should as soon have thought of his head leaving him."

" Ay ! " said Tom, " so should I, yesterday. Good night!"

If a heavy drove of oxen hadn't come by, immediately, the tollman would have gone down to the village straight, to inquire into it. As things turned out, he smoked another pipe, and took his wife into his confidence. But their united sagacity could make nothing of it, and they went to bed—metaphorically—in the dark. But several times that night, when a waggon or other vehicle came through, and the driver asked the tollkeeper " What news ? " he looked at the man by the light of his lantern, to assure himself that he had an interest in the subject, and then said, wrapping his watch-coat round his legs:

" You've heerd of Mr. Pecksniff down yonder ? "

" Ah ! sure-ly ! "

" And of his young man Mr. Pinch p'raps ? "

" Ah ! "

" They've parted."

After every one of these disclosures, the tollman plunged into his house again, and was seen no more, while the other side went on, in great amazement.

But this was long after Tom was abed, and Tom was now with his face towards Salisbury, doing his best to get there.

The evening was beautiful at first, but it became cloudy and dull at sunset, and the rain fell heavily soon afterwards. For ten long miles he plodded on, wet through, until at last the lights appeared, and he came into the welcome precincts of the city.

He went to the inn where he had waited for Martin, and briefly answering their inquiries after Mr. Pecksniff, ordered a bed. He had no heart for tea or supper, meat or drink of any kind, but sat by himself before an empty table in the public room while the bed was getting ready, revolving in his mind all that had happened that eventful day, and wondering what he could or should do for the future. It was a great relief when the chambermaid came in, and said the bed was ready.

It was a low four-poster shelving downward in the centre like a trough, and the room was crowded with impracticable tables and exploded chests of drawers, full of damp linen. A graphic representation in oil of a remarkably fat ox hung over the fireplace, and the portrait of some former landlord (who might have been the ox's brother, he was so like him) stared roundly in, at the foot of the bed. A variety of queer smells were partially quenched in the prevailing scent of very old lavender; and the window had not been opened for such a long space of time, that it pleaded immemorial usage, and wouldn't come open now.

These were trifles in themselves, but they added to the strangeness of the place, and did not induce Tom to forget his new position. Pecksniff had gone out of the world—had never been in it—and it was as much as Tom could do to say his prayers without him. But he felt happier afterwards, and went to sleep, and dreamed about him as he Never Was.

CHAPTER XXXII

EARLY on the day next after that on which she bade adieu
to the halls of her youth and the scenes of her childhood,
Miss Pecksniff, arriving safely at the coach-office in London,
was there received, and conducted to her peaceful home
beneath the shadow of the Monument, by Mrs. Todgers.
M. Todgers looked a little worn by cares of gravy and other
such solicitudes arising out of her establishment, but displayed her usual earnestness and warmth of manner.

"And how, my sweet Miss Pecksniff," said she, "how is
your princely pa?"

Miss Pecksniff signified (in confidence) that he contemplated
the introduction of a princely ma; and repeated the sentiment
that she wasn't blind, and wasn't quite a fool, and wouldn't
bear it.

Mrs. Todgers was more shocked by the intelligence than
any one could have expected. She was quite bitter. She
said there was no truth in man, and that the warmer he
expressed himself, as a general principle, the falser and more
treacherous he was. She foresaw with astonishing clearness
that the object of Mr. Pecksniff's attachment was designing,
worthless, and wicked; and receiving from Charity the fullest
confirmation of these views, protested with tears in her eyes
that she loved Miss Pecksniff like a sister, and felt her injuries
as if they were her own.

"Your real darling sister, I have not seen her more than once since her marriage," said Mrs. Todgers, "and then I thought her looking poorly. My sweet Miss Pecksniff, I always thought that you was to be the lady?"

"Oh dear no!" cried Cherry, shaking her head. "Oh no, Mrs. Todgers. Thank you. No! not for any consideration he could offer."

"I dare say you are right," said Mrs. Todgers with a sigh. "I feared it all along. But the misery we have had from that match, here among ourselves, in this house, my dear Miss Pecksniff, nobody would believe."

"Lor, Mrs. Todgers!"

"Awful, awful!" repeated Mrs. Todgers, with strong emphasis. "You recollect our youngest gentleman, my dear?"

"Of course I do," said Cherry.

"You might have observed," said Mrs. Todgers, "how he used to watch your sister; and that a kind of stony dumbness came over him whenever she was in company?"

"I am sure I never saw anything of the sort," said Cherry, in a peevish manner. "What nonsense, Mrs. Todgers!"

"My dear," returned that lady in a hollow voice, "I have seen him, again and again, sitting over his pie at dinner, with his spoon a perfect fixture in his mouth, looking at your sister. I have seen him standing in a corner of our drawing-room, gazing at her, in such a lonely, melancholy state, that he was more like a Pump than a man, and might have drawed tears."

"I never saw it!" cried Cherry; "that's all I can say."

"But when the marriage took place," said Mrs. Todgers, proceeding with her subject, "when it was in the paper, and was read out here at breakfast, I thought he had taken leave of his senses, I did indeed. The violence of that young man, my dear Miss Pecksniff; the frightful opinions he expressed upon the subject of self-destruction; the extraordinary actions he performed with his tea; the clenching way in which he bit his bread and butter; the manner in which he taunted

110

Mr. Jinkins; all combined to form a picture never to be forgotten."

"It's a pity he didn't destroy himself, I think," observed Miss Pecksniff.

"Himself!" said Mrs. Todgers, "it took another turn at night. He was for destroying other people then. There was a little chaffing going on—I hope you don't consider that a low expression, Miss Pecksniff; it is always in our gentlemen's mouths—a little chaffing going on, my dear, among 'em, all in good nature, when suddenly he rose up, foaming with his fury, and but for being held by three, would have had Mr. Jinkins's life with a boot-jack."

Miss Pecksniff's face expressed supreme indifference.

"And now," said Mrs. Todgers, "now he is the meekest of men. You can almost bring the tears into his eyes by look-ing at him. He sits with me the whole day long on Sundays, talking in such a dismal way that I find it next to impossible to keep my spirits up equal to the accommodation of the boarders. His only comfort is in female society. He takes me half-price to the play, to an extent which I sometimes fear is beyond his means; and I see the tears a standing in his eyes during the whole performance—particularly if it is anything of a comic nature. The turn I experienced only yesterday," said Mrs. Todgers, putting her hand to her side, "when the housemaid threw his bedside carpet out of the window of his room, while I was sitting here, no one can imagine. I thought it was him, and that he had done it at last!"

The contempt with which Miss Charity received this pathetic account of the state to which the youngest gentleman in company was reduced, did not say much for her power of sympathising with that unfortunate character. She treated it with great levity, and went on to inform herself, then and afterwards, whether any other changes had occurred in the commercial boarding-house.

Mr. Bailey was gone, and had been succeeded (such is the

decay of human greatness!) by an old woman whose name was reported to be Tamaroo—which seemed an impossibility. Indeed it appeared in the fulness of time that the jocular boarders had appropriated the word from an English ballad, in which it is supposed to express the bold and fiery nature of a certain hackney-coachman; and that it was bestowed upon Mr. Bailey's successor by reason of her having nothing fiery about her, except an occasional attack of that fire which is called St. Anthony's. This ancient female had been engaged, in fulfilment of a vow, registered by Mrs. Todgers, that no more boys should darken the commercial doors; and she was chiefly remarkable for a total absence of all comprehension upon every subject whatever. She was a perfect Tomb for messages and small parcels; and when despatched to the Post-office with letters, had been frequently seen endeavouring to insinuate them into casual chinks in private doors, under the delusion that any door with a hole in it would answer the purpose. She was a very little old woman, and always wore a very coarse apron with a bib before and a loop behind, together with bandages on her wrists, which appeared to be afflicted with an everlasting sprain. She was on all occasions chary of opening the street-door, and ardent to shut it again; and she waited at table in a bonnet.

This was the only great change over and above the change which had fallen on the youngest gentleman. As for him, he more than corroborated the account of Mrs. Todgers: possessing greater sensibility than even she had given him credit for. He entertained some terrible notions of Destiny, among other matters, and talked much about people's "Missions:" upon which he seemed to have some private information not generally attainable, as he knew it had been poor Merry's mission to crush him in the bud. He was very frail, and tearful; for being aware that a shepherd's mission was to pipe to his flocks, and that a boatswain's mission was to pipe all hands, and that one man's mission was to be a paid piper, and another man's mission was to pay the piper, so he had got it into his head that his own peculiar mission was to pipe his eye. Which he did perpetually.

He often informed Mrs. Todgers that the sun had set upon him; that the billows had rolled over him; that the Car of Juggernaut had crushed him; and also that the deadly Upas tree of Java had blighted him. His name was Moddle.

Towards this most unhappy Moddle, Miss Pecksniff conducted herself at first with distant haughtiness, being in no humour to be entertained with dirges in honour of her married sister. The poor young gentleman was additionally crushed by this, and remonstrated with Mrs. Todgers on the subject.

" Even she turns from me, Mrs. Todgers," said Moddle.

" Then why don't you try and be a little bit more cheerful, sir ? " retorted Mrs. Todgers.

" Cheerful, Mrs. Todgers ! cheerful ! " cried the youngest gentleman : " when she reminds me of days for ever fled, Mrs. Todgers ! "

" Then you had better avoid her for a short time, if she does," said Mrs. Todgers, " and come to know her again, by degrees. That's my advice."

" But I can't avoid her," replied Moddle. " I haven't strength of mind to do it. Oh, Mrs. Todgers, if you knew what a comfort her nose is to me ! "

" Her nose, sir ! " Mrs. Todgers cried.

" Her profile, in general," said the youngest gentleman, " but particularly her nose. It's so like ; " here he yielded to a burst of grief ; " it's so like hers who is Another's, Mrs. Todgers ! "

The observant matron did not fail to report this conversation to Charity, who laughed at the time, but treated Mr. Moddle that very evening with increased consideration, and presented her side-face to him as much as possible. Mr. Moddle was not less sentimental than usual ; was rather more so, if anything ; but he sat and stared at her with glistening eyes, and seemed grateful.

" Well, sir ! " said the lady of the Boarding-House next day.
" You held up your head last night. You're coming round,
I think."

" Only because she's so like her who is Another's, Mrs.
Todgers," rejoined the youth. " When she talks, and when
she smiles, I think I'm looking on HER brow again, Mrs.
Todgers."

This was likewise carried to Charity, who talked and smiled
next evening in her most engaging manner, and rallying Mr.
Moddle on the lowness of his spirits, challenged him to play a
rubber at cribbage. Mr. Moddle taking up the gauntlet, they
played several rubbers for sixpences, and Charity won them
all. This may have been partially attributable to the gallantry
of the youngest gentleman, but it was certainly referable to
the state of his feelings also : for his eyes being frequently
dimmed by tears, he thought that aces were tens, and knaves
queens, which at times occasioned some confusion in his
play.

On the seventh night of cribbage, when Mrs. Todgers,
sitting by, proposed that instead of gambling they should play
for " love," Mr. Moddle was seen to change colour. On the
fourteenth night, he kissed Miss Pecksniff's snuffers, in the
passage, when she went up stairs to bed : meaning to have
kissed her hand, but missing it.

In short, Mr. Moddle began to be impressed with the idea
that Miss Pecksniff's mission was to comfort him ; and Miss
Pecksniff began to speculate on the probability of its being
her mission to become ultimately Mrs. Moddle. He was a
young gentleman (Miss Pecksniff was not a very young lady)
with rising prospects, and " almost " enough to live on. Really
it looked very well.

Besides, besides, he had been regarded as devoted to Merry.
Merry had joked about him, and had once spoken of it to her
sister as a conquest. He was better looking, better shaped,
better spoken, better tempered, better mannered than Jonas.
He was easy to manage, could be made to consult the humours

Mr. Moddle is both particular and peculiar in his Attentions

of his Betrothed, and could be shown off like a lamb when Jonas was a bear. There was the rub!

In the meantime the cribbage went on, and Mrs. Todgers went off; for the youngest gentleman, dropping her society, began to take Miss Pecksniff to the play. He also began, as Mrs. Todgers said, to slip home "in his dinner-times," and to get away from "the office" at unholy seasons; and twice, as he informed Mrs. Todgers himself, he received anonymous letters, inclosing cards from Furniture Warehouses —clearly the act of that ungentlemanly ruffian Jinkins: only he hadn't evidence enough to call him out upon. All of which, so Mrs. Todgers told Miss Pecksniff, spoke as plain English as the shining sun.

"My dear Miss Pecksniff, you may depend upon it," said Mrs. Todgers, "that he is burning to propose."

"My goodness me, why don't he then?" cried Cherry.

"Men are so much more timid than we think 'em, my dear," returned Mrs. Todgers. "They baulk themselves continually. I saw the words on Todgers's lips for months and months and months, before he said 'em."

Miss Pecksniff submitted that Todgers might not have been a fair specimen.

"Oh yes he was. Oh bless you, yes my dear. I was very particular in those days, I assure you," said Mrs. Todgers, bridling. "No, no. You give Mr. Moddle a little encouragement, Miss Pecksniff, if you wish him to speak; and he'll speak fast enough, depend upon it."

"I am sure I don't know what encouragement he would have, Mrs. Todgers," returned Charity. "He walks with me, and plays cards with me, and he comes and sits alone with me."

"Quite right," said Mrs. Todgers. "That's indispensable, my dear."

"And he sits very close to me."

"Also quite correct," said Mrs. Todgers.

"And he looks at me."

"To be sure he does," said Mrs. Todgers.

"And he has his arm upon the back of the chair or sofa, or whatever it is—behind me, you know."

"*I* should think so," said Mrs. Todgers.

"And then he begins to cry!

Mrs. Todgers admitted that he might do better than that; and might undoubtedly profit by the recollection of the great Lord Nelson's signal at the battle of Trafalgar. Still, she said, he would come round, or, not to mince the matter, would be brought round, if Miss Pecksniff took up a decided position, and plainly showed him that it must be done.

Determining to regulate her conduct by this opinion, the young lady received Mr. Moddle, on the earliest subsequent occasion, with an air of constraint: and gradually leading him to inquire, in a dejected manner, why she was so changed, confessed to him that she felt it necessary for their mutual peace and happiness to take a decided step. They had been much together lately, she observed, much together, and had tasted the sweets of a genuine reciprocity of sentiment. She never could forget him, nor could she ever cease to think of him with feelings of the liveliest friendship; but people had begun to talk, the thing had been observed, and it was necessary that they should be nothing more to each other, than any gentleman and lady in society usually are. She was glad she had had the resolution to say thus much before her feelings had been tried too far; they had been greatly tried, she would admit; but though she was weak and silly, she would soon get the better of it, she hoped.

Moddle, who had by this time become in the last degree maudlin, and wept abundantly, inferred from the foregoing avowal, that it was his mission to communicate to others the blight which had fallen on himself; and that, being a kind of unintentional Vampire, he had had Miss Pecksniff assigned to him by the Fates, as Victim Number One. Miss Pecksniff controverting this opinion as sinful, Moddle was goaded on to ask whether she could be contented with a blighted heart;

116

and it appearing on further examination that she could be, plighted his dismal troth, which was accepted and returned.

He bore his good fortune with the utmost moderation. Instead of being triumphant, he shed more tears than he had ever been known to shed before: and, sobbing, said:

"Oh! what a day this has been! I can't go back to the office this afternoon. Oh, what a trying day this has been, Good Gracious!"

CHAPTER XXXIII

FURTHER PROCEEDINGS IN EDEN, AND A PROCEEDING OUT OF IT.
MARTIN MAKES A DISCOVERY OF SOME IMPORTANCE

FROM Mr. Moddle to Eden is an easy and natural transition.
Mr. Moddle, living in the atmosphere of Miss Pecksniff's
love, dwelt (if he had but known it) in a terrestrial Paradise.
The thriving city of Eden was also a terrestrial Paradise,
upon the showing of its proprietors. The beautiful Miss
Pecksniff might have been poetically described as a something
too good for man in his fallen and degraded state. That
was exactly the character of the thriving city of Eden, as
poetically heightened by Zephaniah Scadder, General Choke,
and other worthies: part and parcel of the talons of that
great American Eagle, which is always airing itself sky-high
in purest æther, and never, no never, never, tumbles down
with draggled wings into the mud.

When Mark Tapley, leaving Martin in the architectural
and surveying offices, had effectually strengthened and encouraged his own spirits by the contemplation of their joint
misfortunes, he proceeded, with new cheerfulness, in search
of help: congratulating himself, as he went along, on the
enviable position to which he had at last attained.

"I used to think, sometimes," said Mr. Tapley, "as a
desolate island would suit me, but I should only have had
myself to provide for there, and being naterally a easy man
to manage, there wouldn't have been much credit in *that*.

118

Now here I've got my partner to take care on, and he's something like the sort of man for the purpose. I want a man as is always a sliding off his legs when he ought to be on 'em. I want a man as is so low down in the school of life that he's always a making figures of one in his copy-book, and can't get no further. I want a man as is his own great-coat and cloak, and is always a wrapping himself up in himself. And I have got him too," said Mr. Tapley, after a moment's silence. "What a happiness!"

He paused to look round, uncertain to which of the log-houses he should repair.

"I don't know which to take," he observed; "that's the truth. They're equally prepossessing outside, and equally commodious, no doubt, within; being fitted up with every convenience that a Alligator, in a state of natur', could possibly require. Let me see! The citizen as turned out last night, lives under water, in the right-handed dog-kennel at the corner. I don't want to trouble him if I can help it, poor man, for he is a melancholy object; a reg'lar Settler in every respect. There's a house with a winder, but I am afraid of their being proud. I don't know whether a door ain't too aristocratic; but here goes for the first one!"

He went up to the nearest cabin, and knocked with his hand. Being desired to enter, he complied.

"Neighbour," said Mark: "for I *am* a neighbour, though you don't know me; I've come a begging. Hallo! hal—lo! ——Am I a-bed, and dreaming!"

He made this exclamation on hearing his own name pronounced, and finding himself clasped about the skirts by two little boys, whose faces he had often washed, and whose suppers he had often cooked, on board of that noble, and fast-sailing line-of-packet ship, the Screw.

"My eyes is wrong!" said Mark. "I don't believe 'em. That ain't my fellow-passenger yonder, a nursing her little girl, who, I am sorry to see, is so delicate; and that ain't her husband as come to New York to fetch her. Nor these," he added, looking down upon the boys, "ain't them two young shavers as was so familiar to me; though they are uncommon like 'em. That I must confess."

The woman shed tears, in very joy to see him; the man shook both his hands, and would not let them go; the two boys hugged his legs; the sick child, in the mother's arms, stretched out her burning little fingers, and muttered, in her hoarse, dry throat, his well-remembered name.

It was the same family, sure enough. Altered by the salubrious air of Eden. But the same.

"This is a new sort of a morning call," said Mark, drawing a long breath. "It strikes one all of a heap. Wait a little bit! I'm a coming round, fast. That'll do! These gentlemen ain't my friends. Are they on the visiting list of the house?"

The inquiry referred to certain gaunt pigs, who had walked in after him, and were much interested in the heels of the family. As they did not belong to the mansion, they were expelled by the two little boys.

"I ain't superstitious about toads," said Mark, looking round the room, "but if you could prevail upon the two or three I see in company, to step out at the same time, my young friends, I think they'd find the open air refreshing. Not that I at all object to 'em. A very handsome animal is a toad," said Mr. Tapley, sitting down upon a stool: "very spotted; very like a partickler style of old gentleman about the throat; very bright-eyed, very cool, and very slippy. But one sees 'em to the best advantage out of doors perhaps."

While pretending, with such talk as this, to be perfectly at his ease, and to be the most indifferent and careless of men, Mark Tapley had an eye on all around him. The wan and meagre aspect of the family, the changed looks of the poor mother, the fevered child she held in her lap, the air of great despondency and little hope on everything, were plain to him, and made a deep impression on his mind. He saw it all as clearly and as quickly, as with his bodily eyes he saw the rough shelves supported by pegs driven between the logs, of which the house was made; the flour-cask in the corner, serving also for a table; the blankets, spades, and other articles against the walls; the damp that blotched the ground; or the crop of vegetable rottenness in every crevice of the hut.

"How is it that you have come here?" asked the man, when their first expressions of surprise were over.

"Why, we come by the steamer last night," replied Mark. "Our intention is to make our fortuns with punctuality and dispatch; and to retire upon our property as soon as ever it's realised. But how are you all? You're looking noble!"

"We are but sickly now," said the poor woman, bending over her child. "But we shall do better when we are seasoned to the place."

"There are some here," thought Mark, "whose seasoning will last for ever."

But he said cheerfully, "Do better! To be sure you will. We shall all do better. What we've got to do is, to keep up our spirits, and be neighbourly. We shall come all right in the end, never fear. That reminds me, by the bye, that my partner's all wrong just at present; and that I looked in, to beg for him. I wish you'd come, and give me your opinion of him, master."

That must have been a very unreasonable request on the part of Mark Tapley, with which, in their gratitude for his kind offices on board the ship, they would not have complied instantly. The man rose to accompany him without a moment's delay. Before they went, Mark took the sick child in his arms, and tried to comfort the mother; but the hand of death was on it then, he saw.

They found Martin in the house, lying wrapped up in his blanket on the ground. He was, to all appearance, very ill indeed, and shook and shivered horribly: not as people do from cold, but in a frightful kind of spasm or convulsion,

that racked his whole body. Mark's friend pronounced his
disease an aggravated kind of fever, accompanied with ague;
which was very common in those parts, and which he predicted
would be worse to-morrow, and for many more to-morrows.
He had had it himself off and on, he said, for a couple of
years or so; but he was thankful that, while so many he had
known had died about him, he had escaped with life.

"And with not too much of that," thought Mark, surveying his emaciated form. "Eden for ever!"

They had some medicine in their chest; and this man of
sad experience showed Mark how and when to administer it,
and how he could best alleviate the sufferings of Martin.
His attentions did not stop there; for he was backwards and
forwards constantly, and rendered Mark good service in all
his brisk attempts to make their situation more endurable.
Hope or comfort for the future he could not bestow. The
season was a sickly one; the settlement a grave. His child
died that night; and Mark, keeping the secret from Martin,
helped to bury it, beneath a tree, next day.

With all his various duties of attendance upon Martin
(who became the more exacting in his claims, the worse he
grew), Mark worked out of doors, early and late; and with
the assistance of his friend and others, laboured to do something with their land. Not that he had the least strength
of heart or hope, or steady purpose in so doing, beyond the
habitual cheerfulness of his disposition, and his amazing power
of self-sustainment; for within himself, he looked on their
condition as beyond all hope, and, in his own words, "came
out strong" in consequence.

"As to coming out as strong as I could wish, sir," he
confided to Martin in a leisure moment; that is to say, one
evening, while he was washing the linen of the establishment,
after a hard day's work, "that I give up. It's a piece of
good fortune as never is to happen to me, I see!"

"Would you wish for circumstances stronger than these?"
Martin retorted with a groan, from underneath his blanket.

Mr. Tapley is recognised by some Fellow-Citizens of Eden

" Why, only see how easy they might have been stronger, sir," said Mark, "if it wasn't for the envy of that uncommon fortun of mine, which is always after me, and tripping me up. The night we landed here, I thought things did look pretty jolly. I won't deny it. I thought they did look pretty jolly."

" How do they look now ? " groaned Martin.

" Ah ! " said Mark, " Ah to be sure. That's the question. How do they look now ! On the very first morning of my going out, what do I do ? Stumble on a family I know, who are constantly assisting of us in all sorts of ways, from that time to this ! That won't do, you know : that ain't what I'd a right to expect. If I had stumbled on a serpent, and got bit; or stumbled on a first-rate patriot, and got bowie-knifed ; or stumbled on a lot of Sympathisers with inverted shirt-collars, and got made a lion of ; I might have distinguished myself, and earned some credit. As it is, the great object of my voyage is knocked on the head. So it would be, wherever I went. How do you feel to-night, sir ? "

" Worse than ever," said poor Martin.

"That's something," returned Mark, "but not enough. Nothing but being very bad myself, and jolly to the last, will ever do me justice."

" In Heaven's name, don't talk of that," said Martin, with a thrill of terror. " What should I do, Mark, if you were taken ill ! "

Mr. Tapley's spirits appeared to be stimulated by this remark, although it was not a very flattering one. He proceeded with his washing in a brighter mood ; and observed " that his glass was a-rising."

" There's one good thing in this place, sir," said Mr. Tapley, scrubbing away at the linen, " as disposes me to be jolly ; and that is, that it's a reg'lar little United States in itself. There's two or three American settlers left ; and they coolly comes over one, even here, sir, as if it was the wholesomest and loveliest spot in the world. But they're like the cock that went and hid himself to save his life, and was found out by the noise he made. They can't help crowing. They was born to do it, and do it they must, whatever comes of it."

Glancing from his work out at the door as he said these words, Mark's eyes encountered a lean person in a blue frock and a straw hat, with a short black pipe in his mouth, and a great hickory stick, studded all over with knots, in his hand; who smoking and chewing as he came along, and spitting frequently, recorded his progress by a train of decomposed tobacco on the ground.

"Here's one on 'em," cried Mark, "Hannibal Chollop."

"Don't let him in," said Martin, feebly.

"He won't want any letting in," replied Mark. "He'll come in, sir." Which turned out to be quite true, for he did. His face was almost as hard and knobby as his stick; and so were his hands. His head was like an old black hearth-broom. He sat down on the chest with his hat on; and crossing his legs and looking up at Mark, said without removing his pipe:

"Well, Mr. Co! and how do you git along, sir?"

It may be necessary to observe that Mr. Tapley had gravely introduced himself to all strangers, by that name.

"Pretty well, sir; pretty well," said Mark.

"If this ain't Mr. Chuzzlewit, ain't it!" exclaimed the visitor. "How do *you* git along, sir?"

Martin shook his head, and drew the blanket over it involuntarily; for he felt that Hannibal was going to spit; and his eye, as the song says, was upon him.

"You need not regard me, sir," observed Mr. Chollop, complacently. "I am fever-proof, and likewise agur."

"Mine was a more selfish motive," said Martin, looking out again. "I was afraid you were going to——"

"I can calc'late my distance, sir," returned Mr. Chollop, "to an inch."

With a proof of which happy faculty he immediately favoured him.

124

"I re-quire, sir," said Hannibal, "two foot clear in a circ'lar di-rection, and can engage my-self toe keep within it. I *have* gone ten foot, in a circ'lar di-rection, but that was for a wager."

"I hope you won it, sir," said Mark.

"Well, sir, I realised the stakes," said Chollop. "Yes, sir."

He was silent for a time, during which he was actively engaged in the formation of a magic circle round the chest on which he sat. When it was completed, he began to talk again.

"How do you like our country, sir?" he inquired, looking at Martin.

"Not at all," was the invalid's reply.

Chollop continued to smoke without the least appearance of emotion, until he felt disposed to speak again. That time at length arriving, he took his pipe from his mouth, and said:

"I am not surprised to hear you say so. It re-quires An elevation, and A preparation of the intellect. The mind of man must be prepared for Freedom, Mr. Co."

He addressed himself to Mark: because he saw that Martin, who wished him to go, being already half-mad with feverish irritation, which the droning voice of this new horror rendered almost insupportable, had closed his eyes, and turned on his uneasy bed.

"A little bodily preparation wouldn't be amiss, either, would it, sir," said Mark, "in the case of a blessed old swamp like this?"

"Do you con-sider this a swamp, sir?" inquired Chollop gravely.

"Why yes, sir," returned Mark. "I haven't a doubt about it, myself."

"The sentiment is quite Europian," said the major, "and does not surprise me: what would your English millions say to such a swamp in England, sir?"

"They'd say it was an uncommon nasty one, I should

think," said Mark; "and that they would rather be inoculated for fever in some other way."

"Europian!" remarked Chollop, with sardonic pity. "Quite Europian!"

And there he sat. Silent and cool, as if the house were his; smoking away like a factory chimney.

Mr. Chollop was, of course, one of the most remarkable men in the country; but he really was a notorious person besides. He was usually described by his friends, in the South and West, as " a splendid sample of our na-tive raw material, sir," and was much esteemed for his devotion to rational Liberty; for the better propagation whereof he usually carried a brace of revolving pistols in his coat pocket, with seven barrels a-piece. He also carried, amongst other trinkets, a sword-stick, which he called his "Tickler;" and a great knife, which (for he was a man of a pleasant turn of humour) he called "Ripper," in allusion to its usefulness as a means of ventilating the stomach of any adversary in a close contest. He had used these weapons with distinguished effect in several instances, all duly chronicled in the news-papers; and was greatly beloved for the gallant manner in which he had "jobbed out" the eye of one gentleman, as he was in the act of knocking at his own street-door.

Mr. Chollop was a man of a roving disposition; and, in any less advanced community, might have been mistaken for a violent vagabond. But his fine qualities being perfectly understood and appreciated in those regions where his lot was cast, and where he had many kindred spirits to consort with, he may be regarded as having been born under a for-tunate star, which is not lways the case with a man so much before the age in which he lives. Preferring, with a view to the gratification of his tickling and ripping fancies, to dwell upon the outskirts of society, and in the more remote towns and cities, he was in the habit of emigrating from place to place, and establishing in each some business—usually a newspaper— which he presently sold: for the most part closing the bargain by challenging, stabbing, pistolling, or gouging, the new editor, before he had quite taken possession of the property.

He had come to Eden on a speculation of this kind, but had abandoned it, and was about to leave. He always introduced himself to strangers as a worshipper of Freedom; was the consistent advocate of Lynch law, and slavery; and invariably recommended, both in print and speech, the "tarring and feathering" of any unpopular person who differed from himself. He called this "planting the standard of civilisation in the wilder gardens of My country."

There is little doubt that Chollop would have planted this standard in Eden at Mark's expense, in return for his plainness of speech (for the genuine Freedom is dumb, save when she vaunts herself), but for the utter desolation and decay prevailing in the settlement, and his own approaching departure from it. As it was, he contented himself with showing Mark one of the revolving-pistols, and asking him what he thought of that weapon.

"It ain't long since I shot a man down with that, sir, in the State of Illin*oy*," observed Chollop.

"Did you, indeed!" said Mark, without the smallest agitation. "Very free of you. And very independent!"

"I shot him down, sir," pursued Chollop, "for asserting in the Spartan Portico, a tri-weekly journal, that the ancient Athenians went a-head of the present Locofoco Ticket."

"And what's that?" asked Mark.

"Europian not to know," said Chollop, smoking placidly. "Europian quite!"

After a short devotion to the interests of the magic circle, he resumed the conversation by observing:

"You won't half feel yourself at home in Eden, now?"

"No," said Mark, "I don't."

"You miss the imposts of your country. You miss the house dues?" observed Chollop.

"And the houses—rather," said Mark.

"No window dues here, sir," observed Chollop.

127

"And no windows to put 'em on," said Mark.

"No stakes, no dungeons, no blocks, no racks, no scaffolds, no thumbscrews, no pikes, no pillories," said Chollop.

"Nothing but rewolwers and bowie-knives," returned Mark. "And what are they? Not worth mentioning!"

The man who had met them on the night of their arrival came crawling up at this juncture, and looked in at the door.

"Well, sir," said Chollop. "How do *you* git along?"

He had considerable difficulty in getting along at all, and said as much in reply.

"Mr. Co. And me, sir," observed Chollop, "are disputating a piece. He ought to be slicked up pretty smart, to disputate between the Old World and the New, I do expect?"

"Well!" returned the miserable shadow. "So he had."

"I was merely observing, sir," said Mark, addressing this new visitor, "that I looked upon the city in which we have the honour to live, as being swampy. What's your sentiments?"

"I opinionate it's moist perhaps, at certain times," returned the man.

"But not as moist as England, sir?" cried Chollop, with a fierce expression in his face.

"Oh! Not as moist as England; let alone its Institutions," said the man.

"I should hope there ain't a swamp in all Americay, as don't whip *that* small island into mush and molasses," observed Chollop, decisively. "You bought slick, straight, and right away, of Scadder, sir?" to Mark.

He answered in the affirmative. Mr. Chollop winked at the other citizen.

"Scadder is a smart man, sir? He is a rising man? He is a man as will come up'ards, right side up, sir?" Mr. Chollop winked again at the other citizen.

"He should have his right side very high up, if I had my way," said Mark. "As high up as the top of a good tall gallows, perhaps."

Mr. Chollop was so delighted at the smartness of his excellent countryman having been too much for the Britisher, and at the Britisher's resenting it, that he could contain himself no longer, and broke forth in a shout of delight. But the strangest exposition of this ruling passion was in the other: the pestilence-stricken, broken, miserable shadow of a man: who derived so much entertainment from the circumstance, that he seemed to forget his own ruin in thinking of it, and laughed outright when he said "that Scadder was a smart man, and had draw'd a lot of British capital that way, as sure as sun-up."

After a full enjoyment of this joke, Mr. Hannibal Chollop sat smoking and improving the circle, without making any attempts either to converse, or to take leave; apparently labouring under the not uncommon delusion, that for a free and enlightened citizen of the United States to convert another man's house into a spittoon for two or three hours together, was a delicate attention, full of interest and politeness, of which nobody could ever tire. At last he rose.

"I am a going easy," he observed.

Mark entreated him to take particular care of himself.

"Afore I go," he said sternly, "I have got a leetle word to say to you. You are darnnation 'cute you are."

Mark thanked him for the compliment.

"But you are much too 'cute to last. I can't con-ceive of any spotted Painter in the bush, as ever was so riddled through and through as you will be, I bet."

"What for?" asked Mark.

"We must be cracked-up, sir," retorted Chollop, in a tone of menace. "You are not now in A despotic land. We are a model to the airth, and must be jist cracked-up, I tell you."

"What, I speak too free, do I?" cried Mark.

"I have draw'd upon A man, and fired upon A man for less," said Chollop, frowning. "I have know'd strong men obleeged to make themselves uncommon skase for less. I

129

have know'd men Lynched for less, and beaten into punkin'-sarse for less, by an enlightened people. We are the intellect and virtue of the airth, the cream Of human natur', and the flower Of moral force. Our backs is easy ris. We must be cracked-up, or they rises, and we snarls. We shows our teeth, I tell you, fierce. You'd better crack us up, you had ! "

After the delivery of this caution, Mr. Chollop departed; with Ripper, Tickler, and the revolvers, all ready for action on the shortest notice.

" Come out from under the blanket, sir," said Mark, " he's gone. What's this ! " he added softly : kneeling down to look into his partner's face, and taking his hot hand. " What's come of all that chattering and swaggering ? He's wandering in his mind to-night, and don't know me ! "

Martin indeed was dangerously ill; very near his death. He lay in that state many days, during which time Mark's poor friends, regardless of themselves, attended him. Mark, fatigued in mind and body ; working all the day and sitting up at night; worn with hard living and the unaccustomed toil of his new life; surrounded by dismal and discouraging circumstances of every kind ; never complained or yielded in the least degree. If ever he had thought Martin selfish or inconsiderate, or had deemed him energetic only by fits and starts, and then too passive for their desperate fortunes, he now forgot it all. He remembered nothing but the better qualities of his fellow-wanderer, and was devoted to him, heart and hand.

Many weeks elapsed before Martin was strong enough to move about with the help of a stick and Mark's arm ; and even then his recovery, for want of wholesome air and proper nourishment, was very slow. He was yet in a feeble and weak condition, when the misfortune he had so much dreaded fell upon them. Mark was taken ill.

Mark fought against it; but the malady fought harder, and his efforts were in vain.

FLOORED, BUT JOLLY!

"Floored for the present, sir," he said one morning, sinking back upon his bed: "but jolly!"

Floored indeed, and by a heavy blow! As any one but Martin might have known beforehand.

If Mark's friends had been kind to Martin (and they had been very), they were twenty times kinder to Mark. And now it was Martin's turn to work, and sit beside the bed and watch, and listen through the long, long nights, to every sound in the gloomy wilderness; and hear poor Mr. Tapley, in his wandering fancy, playing at skittles in the Dragon, making love-remonstrances to Mrs. Lupin, getting his sea-legs on board the Screw, travelling with old Tom Pinch on English roads, and burning stumps of trees in Eden, all at once.

But whenever Martin gave him drink or medicine, or tended him in any way, or came into the house returning from some drudgery without, the patient Mr. Tapley brightened up, and cried: "I'm jolly, sir: I'm jolly!"

Now, when Martin began to think of this, and to look at Mark as he lay there; never reproaching him by so much as an expression of regret; never murmuring; always striving to be manful and staunch; he began to think, how was it that this man who had had so few advantages, was so much better than he who had had so many? And attendance upon a sick bed, but especially the sick bed of one whom we have been accustomed to see in full activity and vigour, being a great breeder of reflection, he began to ask himself in what they differed.

He was assisted in coming to a conclusion on this head by the frequent presence of Mark's friend, their fellow-passenger across the ocean: which suggested to him that in regard to having aided her, for example, they had differed very much. Somehow he coupled Tom Pinch with this train of reflection; and thinking that Tom would be very likely to have struck up the same sort of acquaintance under similar circumstances, began to think in what respects two people so extremely different were like each other, and were unlike him. At first sight there was nothing very distressing in these meditations, but they did undoubtedly distress him for all that.

Martin's nature was a frank and generous one; but he had been bred up in his grandfather's house; and it will usually be found that the meaner domestic vices propagate themselves to be their own antagonists. Selfishness does this especially; so do suspicion, cunning, stealth, and covetous propensities. Martin had unconsciously reasoned as a child, "My guardian takes so much thought of himself, that unless I do the like by *myself*, I shall be forgotten." So he had grown selfish.

But he had never known it. If any one had taxed him with the vice, he would have indignantly repelled the accusation, and conceived himself unworthily aspersed. He never would have known it, but that being newly risen from a bed of dangerous sickness, to watch by such another couch, he felt how nearly Self had dropped into the grave, and what a poor dependent, miserable thing it was.

It was natural for him to reflect—he had months to do it in—upon his own escape, and Mark's extremity. This led him to consider which of them could be the better spared, and why? Then the curtain slowly rose a very little way; and Self, Self, Self, was shown below.

He asked himself, besides, when dreading Mark's decease (as all men do and must, at such a time), whether he had done his duty by him, and had deserved and made a good response to his fidelity and zeal. No. Short as their companionship had been, he felt in many, many instances, that there was blame against himself; and still inquiring why, the curtain slowly rose a little more, and Self, Self, Self, dilated on the scene.

It was long before he fixed the knowledge of himself so firmly in his mind that he could thoroughly discern the truth; but in the hideous solitude of that most hideous place, with Hope so far removed, Ambition quenched, and Death beside him rattling at the very door, reflection came, as in a plague-beleaguered town ; and so he felt and knew the failing of his life, and saw distinctly what an ugly spot it was.

Eden was a hard school to learn so hard a lesson in ; but there were teachers in the swamp and thicket, and the pestilential air, who had a searching method of their own.

He made a solemn resolution that when his strength returned he would not dispute the point or resist the conviction, but would look upon it as an established fact, that selfishness was in his breast, and must be rooted out. He was so doubtful (and with justice) of his own character, that he determined not to say one word of vain regret or good resolve to Mark, but steadily to keep his purpose before his own eyes solely : and there was not a jot of pride in this ; nothing but humility and steadfastness : the best armour he could wear. So low had Eden brought him down. So high had Eden raised him up.

After a long and lingering illness (in certain forlorn stages of which, when too far gone to speak, he had feebly written "jolly !" on a slate), Mark showed some symptoms of returning health. They came and went, and flickered for a time ; but he began to mend at last decidedly ; and after that, continued to improve from day to day.

As soon as he was well enough to talk without fatigue, Martin consulted him upon a project he had in his mind, and which a few months back he would have carried into execution without troubling anybody's head but his own.

" Ours is a desperate case," said Martin. " Plainly. The place is deserted ; its failure must have become known ; and selling what we have bought to any one, for anything, is hopeless, even if it were honest. We left home on a mad enterprise, and have failed. The only hope left us : the only one end for which we have now to try, is to quit this settlement for ever, and get back to England. Anyhow ! by any means ! Only to get back there, Mark."

" That's all, sir," returned Mr. Tapley, with a significant stress upon the words : " only that ! "

133

" Now, upon this side of the water," said Martin, " we have but one friend who can help us, and that is Mr. Bevan."

" I thought of him when you was ill," said Mark.

" But for the time that would be lost, I would even write to my grandfather," Martin went on to say, " and implore him for money to free us from this trap into which we were so cruelly decoyed. Shall I try Mr. Bevan first ? "

" He's a very pleasant sort of a gentleman," said Mark. " I think so."

" The few goods we brought here, and in which we spent our money, would produce something if sold," resumed Martin ; " and whatever they realise shall be paid him instantly. But they can't be sold here."

" There's nobody but corpses to buy 'em," said Mr. Tapley, shaking his head with a rueful air, " and pigs."

" Shall I tell him so, and only ask him for money enough to enable us by the cheapest means to reach New York, or any port from which we may hope to get a passage home, by serving in any capacity ? Explaining to him at the same time how I am connected, and that I will endeavour to repay him, even through my grandfather, immediately on our arrival in England ? "

" Why to be sure," said Mark : " he can only say no, and he may say yes. If you don't mind trying him, sir— "

" Mind ! " exclaimed Martin. " I am to blame for coming here, and I would do anything to get away. I grieve to think of the past. If I had taken your opinion sooner, Mark, we never should have been here, I am certain."

Mr. Tapley was very much surprised at this admission, but protested, with great vehemence, that they would have been there all the same ; and that he had set his heart upon coming to Eden, from the first word he had ever heard of it.

Martin then read him a letter to Mr. Bevan, which he had already prepared. It was frankly and ingenuously written, and described their situation without the least concealment ; plainly stated the miseries they had undergone ; and preferred their request in modest but straightforward terms. Mark highly commended it; and they determined to despatch it by the next steamboat going the right way, that might call to take in wood at Eden,—where there was plenty of wood to spare. Not knowing how to address Mr. Bevan at his own place of abode, Martin superscribed it to the care of the memorable Mr. Norris of New York, and wrote upon the cover an entreaty that it might be forwarded without delay.

More than a week elapsed before a boat appeared; but at length they were awakened very early one morning by the high-pressure snorting of the "Esau Slodge;" named after one of the most remarkable men in the country, who had been very eminent somewhere. Hurrying down to the landing-place, they got it safe on board; and waiting anxiously to see the boat depart, stopped up the gangway : an instance of neglect which caused the "Capting" of the Esau Slodge to "wish he might be sifted fine as flour, and whittled small as chips; that if they didn't come off that there fixing right smart too, he'd spill 'em in the drink :" whereby the Capting metaphorically said he'd throw them in the river.

They were not likely to receive an answer for eight or ten weeks at the earliest. In the meantime they devoted such strength as they had, to the attempted improvement of their land; to clearing some of it, and preparing it for useful purposes. Monstrously defective as their farming was, still it was better than their neighbours'; for Mark had some practical knowledge of such matters, and Martin learned of him; whereas the other settlers who remained upon the putrid swamp (a mere handful, and those withered by disease), appeared to have wandered there with the idea that husbandry was the natural gift of all mankind. They helped each other after their own manner in these struggles, and in all others; but they worked as hopelessly and sadly as a gang of convicts in a penal settlement.

Often at night when Mark and Martin were alone, and

lying down to sleep, they spoke of home, familiar places, houses, roads, and people whom they knew; sometimes in the lively hope of seeing them again, and sometimes with a sorrowful tranquillity, as if that hope were dead. It was a source of great amazement to Mark Tapley to find, pervading all these conversations, a singular alteration in Martin.

"I don't know what to make of him," he thought one night, "he ain't what I supposed. He don't think of himself half as much. I'll try him again. Asleep, sir?"

"No, Mark."

"Thinking of home, sir?"

"Yes, Mark."

"So was I, sir. I was wondering how Mr. Pinch and Mr. Pecksniff gets on now."

"Poor Tom!" said Martin, thoughtfully.

"Weak-minded man, sir," observed Mr. Tapley. "Plays the organ for nothing, sir. Takes no care of himself?"

"I wish he took a little more, indeed," said Martin. "Though I don't know why I should. We shouldn't like him half as well, perhaps."

"He gets put upon, sir," hinted Mark.

"Yes," said Martin, after a short silence. "*I* know that, Mark."

He spoke so regretfully, that his partner abandoned the theme, and was silent for a short time, until he had thought of another.

"Ah, sir!" said Mark, with a sigh. "Dear me! You've ventured a good deal for a young lady's love!"

"I tell you what. I'm not so sure of that, Mark," was the reply; so hastily and energetically spoken, that Martin sat up in his bed to give it. "I begin to be far from clear upon it. You may depend upon it, she is very unhappy. She has sacrificed her peace of mind; she has endangered her interests very much; she can't run away from those who are jealous of her, and opposed to her, as I have done. She has to endure, Mark: to endure without the possibility of action, poor girl!

I begin to think she has more to bear than ever I have had. Upon my soul I do ! "

Mr. Tapley opened his eyes wide, in the dark ; but did not interrupt.

" And I'll tell you a secret, Mark," said Martin, " since we *are* upon this subject. That ring—"

" Which ring, sir ? " Mark inquired ; opening his eyes still wider.

" That ring she gave me when we parted, Mark. She bought it ; bought it ; knowing I was poor and proud (Heaven help me ! Proud !) and wanted money."

" Who says so, sir ? " asked Mark.

" I say so. I know it. I thought of it, my good fellow, hundreds of times, while you were lying ill. And like a beast, I took it from her hand, and wore it on my own, and never dreamed of this even at the moment when I parted with it, when some faint glimmering of the truth might surely have possessed me ! But it's late," said Martin, checking himself, " and you are weak and tired, I know. You only talk to cheer me up. Good night ! God bless you, Mark ! "

" God bless you, sir ! But I'm reg'larly defrauded," thought Mr. Tapley, turning round, with a happy face. " It's a swindle. I never entered for this sort of service. There'll be no credit in being jolly with *him !* "

The time wore on, and other steamboats coming from the point on which their hopes were fixed, arrived to take in wood ; but still no answer to the letter. Rain, heat, foul slime, and noxious vapour, with all the ills and filthy things they bred, prevailed. The earth, the air, the vegetation, and the water that they drank, all teemed with deadly properties. Their fellow-passenger had lost two children long before ; and buried now her last. Such things are much too common to be widely known or cared for. Smart citizens grow rich, and friendless victims smart and die, and are forgotten. That is all.

At last, a boat came panting up the ugly river, and stopped

at Eden. Mark was waiting at the wood hut, when it came, and had a letter handed to him from on board. He bore it off to Martin. They looked at one another, trembling.

"It feels heavy," faltered Martin. And opening it, a little roll of dollar-notes fell out upon the ground.

What either of them said, or did, or felt, at first, neither of them knew. All Mark could ever tell was, that he was at the river's bank again out of breath, before the boat had gone, inquiring when it would retrace its track, and put in there.

The answer was, in ten or twelve days: notwithstanding which, they began to get their goods together and to tie them up, that very night. When this stage of excitement was passed, each of them believed (they found this out, in talking of it afterwards) that he would surely die before the boat returned.

They lived, however, and it came, after the lapse of three long crawling weeks. At sunrise, on an autumn day, they stood upon her deck.

"Courage! We shall meet again!" cried Martin, waving his hand to two thin figures on the bank. "In the Old World!"

"Or in the next one," added Mark below his breath. "To see them standing side by side, so quiet, is a'most the worst of all!"

They looked at one another, as the vessel moved away, and then looked backward at the spot from which it hurried fast. The log-house, with the open door, and drooping trees about it; the stagnant morning mist, and red sun, dimly seen beyond; the vapour rising up from land and river; the quick stream making the loathsome banks it washed more flat and dull: how often they returned in dreams! How often it was happiness to wake, and find them Shadows that had vanished!

CHAPTER XXXIV

AMONG the passengers on board the steamboat, there was a
faint gentleman sitting on a low camp-stool, with his legs on
a high barrel of flour, as if he were looking at the prospect
with his ankles; who attracted their attention speedily.

He had straight black hair, parted up the middle of his
head and hanging down upon his coat; a little fringe of hair
upon his chin; wore no neckcloth; a white hat; a suit of
black, long in the sleeves, and short in the legs; soiled brown
stockings, and laced shoes. His complexion, naturally muddy,
was rendered muddier by too strict an economy of soap and
water; and the same observation will apply to the washable
part of his attire, which he might have changed with comfort
to himself, and gratification to his friends. He was about
five and thirty; was crushed and jammed up in a heap, under
the shade of a large green cotton umbrella; and ruminated
over his tobacco-plug like a cow.

He was not singular, to be sure, in these respects; for every
gentleman on board appeared to have had a difference with
his laundress, and to have left off washing himself in early
youth. Every gentleman, too, was perfectly stopped up with
tight plugging, and was dislocated in the greater part of his
joints. But about this gentleman there was a peculiar air of
sagacity and wisdom, which convinced Martin that he was no
common character; and this turned out to be the case.

"How do you do, sir?" said a voice in Martin's ear.

"How do you do, sir?" said Martin.

It was a tall thin gentleman who spoke to him, with a carpet-cap on, and a long loose coat of green baize, ornamented about the pockets with black velvet.

"You air from Europe, sir?"

"I am," said Martin.

"You air fortunate, sir."

Martin thought so too: but he soon discovered that the gentleman and he attached different meanings to this remark.

"You air fortunate, sir, in having an opportunity of beholding our Elijah Pogram, sir."

"Your Elijahpogram!" said Martin, thinking it was all one word, and a building of some sort.

"Yes, sir."

Martin tried to look as if he understood him, but he couldn't make it out.

"Yes, sir," repeated the gentleman. "Our Elijah Pogram, sir, is, at this minute, identically settin' by the en-gine biler."

The gentleman under the umbrella put his right forefinger to his eyebrow, as if he were revolving schemes of state.

"That is Elijah Pogram, is it?" said Martin.

"Yes, sir," replied the other. "That is Elijah Pogram."

"Dear me!" said Martin. "I am astonished." But he had not the least idea who this Elijah Pogram was; having never heard the name in all his life.

"If the biler of this vessel was Toe bust, sir," said his new acquaintance, "and Toe bust now, this would be a fesrival day in the calendar of despotism; pretty nigh equallin', sir, in its effects upon the human race, our Fourth of glorious July. Yes, sir, that is the Honourable Elijah Pogram, Member of Congress; one of the master-minds of our country, sir. There is a brow, sir, there!"

"Quite remarkable," said Martin.

"Yes, sir. Our own immortal Chiggle, sir, is said to have observed, when he made the celebrated Pogram statter in marble, which rose so much con-test and preju-dice in Europe, that the brow was more than mortal. This was before the Pogram Defiance, and was, therefore, a pre-diction, cruel smart."

"What is the Pogram Defiance?" asked Martin, thinking, perhaps, it was the sign of a public-house.

"An o-ration, sir," returned his friend.

"Oh! to be sure," cried Martin. "What am I thinking of! It defied—"

"It defied the world, sir," said the other, gravely. "Defied the world in general to com-pete with our country upon any hook; and devellop'd our internal resources for making war upon the universal airth. You would like to know Elijah Pogram, sir?"

"If you please," said Martin.

"Mr. Pogram," said the stranger—Mr. Pogram having over-heard every word of the dialogue—"this is a gentleman from Europe, sir: from England, sir. But gen'rous ene-mies may meet upon the neutral sile of private life, I think."

The languid Mr. Pogram shook hands with Martin, like a clock-work figure that was just running down. But he made amends by chewing like one that was just wound up.

"Mr. Pogram," said the introducer, "is a public servant, sir. When Congress is recessed, he makes himself acquainted with those free United States, of which he is the gifted son."

It occurred to Martin, that if the Honourable Elijah Pogram had stayed at home, and sent his shoes upon a tour, they would have answered the same purpose; for they were the only part of him in a situation to see anything.

In course of time, however, Mr. Pogram rose; and having ejected certain plugging consequences which would have im-peded his articulation, took up a position where there was something to lean against, and began to talk to Martin: shading himself with the green umbrella all the time.

As he began with the words, "How do you like—?" Martin took him up and said:

"The country, I presume?"

141

"Yes, sir," said Elijah Pogram. A knot of passengers gathered round to hear what followed: and Martin heard his friend say, as he whispered to another friend, and rubbed his hands, "Pogram will smash him into sky-blue fits I know!"

"Why," said Martin, after a moment's hesitation, "I have learned by experience, that you take an unfair advantage of a stranger, when you ask that question. You don't mean it to be answered, except in one way. Now, I don't choose to answer it in that way, for I cannot honestly answer it in that way. And therefore, I would rather not answer it at all."

But Mr. Pogram was going to make a great speech in the next session about foreign relations, and was going to write strong articles on the subject; and as he greatly favoured the free and independent custom (a very harmless and agreeable one) of procuring information of any sort in any kind of confidence, and afterwards perverting it publicly in any manner that happened to suit him, he had determined to get at Martin's opinions somehow or other. For, if he could have got nothing out of him, he would have had to invent it for him, and that would have been laborious. He made a mental note of his answer, and went in again.

"You are from Eden, sir? How did you like Eden?"

Martin said what he thought of that part of the country, in pretty strong terms.

"It is strange," said Pogram, looking round upon the group, "this hatred of our country, and her Institutions! This national antipathy is deeply rooted in the British mind!"

"Good Heaven, sir," cried Martin. "Is the Eden Land Corporation, with Mr. Scadder at its head, and all the misery it has worked, at its door, an Institution of America? A part of any form of government that ever was known or heard of?"

"I con-sider the cause of this to be," said Pogram, looking round again and taking himself up where Martin had interrupted him, "partly jealousy and pre-judice, and partly the nat'ral unfitness of the British people to appreciate the ex-alted

142

Institutions of our native land. I expect, sir," turning to Martin again, "that a gentleman named Chollop happened in upon you during your lo-cation in the town of Eden?"

"Yes," answered Martin; "but my friend can answer this better than I can, for I was very ill at the time. Mark! The gentleman is speaking of Mr. Chollop."

"Oh. Yes, sir. Yes. *I* see him," observed Mark.

"A splendid example of our na-tive raw material, sir?" said Pogram, interrogatively.

"Indeed, sir!" cried Mark.

The Honourable Elijah Pogram glanced at his friends as though he would have said, "Observe this! See what follows!" and they rendered tribute to the Pogram genius, by a gentle murmur.

"Our fellow-countryman is a model of a man, quite fresh from Natur's mould!" said Pogram, with enthusiasm. "He is a true-born child of this free hemisphere! Verdant as the mountains of our country; bright and flowing as our mineral Licks; unspiled by withering conventionalities as air our broad and boundless Perearers! Rough he may be. So air our Barrs. Wild he may be. So air our Buffalers. But he is a child of Natur', and a child of Freedom; and his boastful answer to the Despot and the Tyrant is, that his bright home is in the Settin Sun."

Part of this referred to Chollop, and part to a Western postmaster, who, being a public defaulter not very long before (a character not at all uncommon in America), had been removed from office; and on whose behalf Mr. Pogram (he voted for Pogram) had thundered the last sentence from his seat in Congress, at the head of an unpopular President. It told brilliantly; for the bystanders were delighted, and one of them said to Martin, "that he guessed he had now seen something of the eloquential aspect of our country, and was chawed up pritty small."

Mr. Pogram waited until his hearers were calm again, before he said to Mark:

143

"You do not seem to coincide, sir?"

"Why," said Mark, "I didn't like him much; and that's the truth, sir. I thought he was a bully; and I didn't admire his carryin' them murderous little persuaders, and being so ready to use 'em."

"It's singler!" said Pogram, lifting his umbrella high enough to look all round from under it. "It's strange! You observe the settled opposition to our Institutions which pervades the British mind!"

"What an extraordinary people you are!" cried Martin. "Are Mr. Chollop and the class he represents, an Institution here? Are pistols with revolving barrels, sword-sticks, bowie-knives, and such things, Institutions on which you pride yourselves? Are bloody duels, brutal combats, savage assaults, shooting down and stabbing in the streets, your Institutions.! Why, I shall hear next, that Dishonour and Fraud are among the Institutions of the great republic!"

The moment the words passed his lips, the Honourable Elijah Pogram looked round again.

"This morbid hatred of our Institutions," he observed, "is quite a study for the psychological observer. He's alludin' to Repudiation now!"

"Oh! You may make anything an Institution if you like," said Martin, laughing, "and I confess you had me there, for you certainly have made that, one. But the greater part of these things are one Institution with us, and we call it by the generic name of Old Bailey!"

The bell being rung for dinner at this moment, everybody ran away into the cabin, whither the Honourable Elijah Pogram fled with such precipitation that he forgot his umbrella was up, and fixed it so tightly in the cabin door that it could neither be let down nor got out. For a minute or so this accident created a perfect rebellion among the hungry passengers behind, who, seeing the dishes, and hearing the knives and forks at work, well knew what would happen unless they got there instantly, and were nearly mad: while several virtuous

144

A CALM PHILOSOPHER

citizens at the table were in deadly peril of choking themselves in their unnatural efforts to get rid of all the meat before these others came.

They carried the umbrella by storm, however, and rushed in at the breach. The Honourable Elijah Pogram and Martin found themselves, after a severe struggle, side by side, as they might have come together in the pit of a London theatre; and for four whole minutes afterwards, Pogram was snapping up great blocks of everything he could get hold of, like a raven. When he had taken this unusually protracted dinner, he began to talk to Martin; and begged him not to have the least delicacy in speaking with perfect freedom to him, for he was a calm philosopher. Which Martin was extremely glad to hear; for he had begun to speculate on Elijah being a disciple of that other school of republican philosophy, whose noble sentiments are carved with knives upon a pupil's body, and written, not with pen and ink, but tar and feathers.

"What do you think of my countrymen who are present, sir?" inquired Elijah Pogram.

"Oh! very pleasant," said Martin.

They were a very pleasant party. No man had spoken a word; every one had been intent, as usual, on his own private gorging; and the greater part of the company were decidedly dirty feeders.

The Honourable Elijah Pogram looked at Martin as if he thought "You don't mean that, I know!" and he was soon confirmed in this opinion.

Sitting opposite to them was a gentleman in a high state of tobacco, who wore quite a little beard, composed of the overflowings of that weed, as they had dried about his mouth and chin: so common an ornament that it would scarcely have attracted Martin's observation, but that this good citizen, burning to assert his equality against all comers, sucked his knife for some moments, and made a cut with it at the butter, just as Martin was in the act of taking some. There was a juiciness about the deed that might have sickened a scavenger.

When Elijah Pogram (to whom this was an every-day incident) saw that Martin put the plate away, and took no butter, he was quite delighted, and said,

"Well! The morbid hatred of you British to the Institutions of our country is as-tonishing!"

"Upon my life!" cried Martin, in his turn. "This is the most wonderful community that ever existed. A man deliberately makes a hog of himself, and *that's* an Institution!"

"We have no time to ac-quire forms, sir," said Elijah Pogram.

"Acquire!" cried Martin. "But it's not a question of acquiring anything. It's a question of losing the natural politeness of a savage, and that instinctive good breeding which admonishes one man not to offend and disgust another. Don't you think that man over the way, for instance, naturally knows better, but considers it a very fine and independent thing to be a brute in small matters?"

"He is a na-tive of our country, and is nat'rally bright and spry, of course," said Mr. Pogram.

"Now, observe what this comes to, Mr. Pogram," pursued Martin. "The mass of your countrymen begin by stubbornly neglecting little social observances, which have nothing to do with gentility, custom, usage, government, or country, but are acts of common, decent, natural, human politeness. You abet them in this, by resenting all attacks upon their social offences as if they were a beautiful national feature. From disregarding small obligations they come in regular course to disregard great ones; and so refuse to pay their debts. What they may do, or what they may refuse to do next, I don't know; but any man may see if he will, that it will be something following in natural succession, and a part of one great growth, which is rotten at the root."

The mind of Mr. Pogram was too philosophical to see this; so they went on deck again, where, resuming his former post, he chewed until he was in a lethargic state, amounting to insensibility.

DISAPPOINTMENT OF CAPTAIN KEDGICK

After a weary voyage of several days, they came again to that same wharf where Mark had been so nearly left behind, on the night of starting for Eden. Captain Kedgick, the landlord, was standing there, and was greatly surprised to see them coming from the boat.

"Why, what the 'tarnal!" cried the Captain. "Well! I do admire at this, I do!"

"We can stay at your house until to-morrow, Captain, I suppose?" said Martin.

"I reckon you can stay there for a twelvemonth if you like," retorted Kedgick coolly. "But our people won't best like your coming back."

"Won't like it, Captain Kedgick!" said Martin.

"They did ex-pect you was a-going to settle," Kedgick answered, as he shook his head. "They've been took in, you can't deny!"

"What do you mean?" cried Martin.

"You didn't ought to have received 'em," said the Captain. "No, you didn't!"

"My good friend," returned Martin, "did I want to receive them? Was it any act of mine? Didn't you tell me they would rile up, and that I should be flayed like a wild cat—and threaten all kinds of vengeance, if I didn't receive them?"

"I don't know about that," returned the Captain. "But when our people's frills is out, they're starched up pretty stiff, I tell you!"

With that, he fell into the rear to walk with Mark, while Martin and Elijah Pogram went on to the National.

"We've come back alive, you see!" said Mark.

"It ain't the thing I did expect," the Captain grumbled. "A man ain't got no right to be a public man, unless he meets the public views. Our fashionable people wouldn't have attended his le-vee, if they had know'd it."

Nothing mollified the Captain, who persisted in taking it very ill that they had not both died in Eden. The boarders at the National felt strongly on the subject too; but it happened by good fortune that they had not much time to think about this grievance, for it was suddenly determined to pounce upon the Honourable Elijah Pogram, and give *him* a le-vee forthwith.

As the general evening meal of the house was over before the arrival of the boat, Martin, Mark, and Pogram, were taking tea and fixings at the public table by themselves, when the deputation entered, to announce this honour: consisting of six gentlemen boarders, and a very shrill boy.

"Sir!" said the spokesman.

"Mr. Pogram!" cried the shrill boy.

The spokesman thus reminded of the shrill boy's presence, introduced him. "Doctor Ginery Dunkle, sir. A gentleman of great poetical elements. He has recently jined us here, sir, and is an acquisition to us, sir, I do assure you. Yes, sir. Mr. Jodd, sir. Mr. Izzard, sir. Mr. Julius Bib. sir."

"Julius Washington Merryweather Bib," said the gentleman himself *to* himself.

"I beg your pardon, sir. Excuse, me. Mr. Julius Washington Merryweather Bib, sir; a gentleman in the lumber line, sir, and much esteemed. Colonel Groper, sir. Pro-fessor Piper, sir. My own name, sir, is Oscar Buffum."

Each man took one slide forward as he was named; butted at the Honourable Elijah Pogram with his head; shook hands, and slid back again. The introductions being completed, the spokesman resumed.

"Sir!"

"Mr. Pogram!" cried the shrill boy.

"Perhaps," said the spokesman, with a hopeless look, "you will be so good, Dr. Ginery Dunkle, as to charge yourself with the execution of our little office, sir?"

As there was nothing the shrill boy desired more, he immediately stepped forward.

"Mr. Pogram! Sir! A handful Of your fellow-citizens, sir, hearing Of your arrival at the National Hotel, and feeling the patriotic character Of your public services, wish, sir, to have the gratification Of beholding you, and mixing with you, sir; and unbending with you, sir, in those moments which—"

"Air," suggested Buffum.

"Which air so peculiarly the lot, sir, Of our great and happy country."

"Hear!" cried Colonel Groper, in a loud voice. "Good! Hear him! Good!"

"And therefore, sir," pursued the Doctor, "they request; as A mark Of their respect; the honour of your company at a little le-Vee, sir, in the ladies' ordinary, at eight o'clock."

Mr. Pogram bowed, and said:

"Fellow-countrymen!"

"Good!" cried the Colonel. "Hear him! Good!"

Mr. Pogram bowed to the Colonel individually, and then resumed:

"Your approbation of My labours in the common cause, goes to My heart. At all times and in all places; in the ladies' ordinary, My friends, and in the Battle Field—"

"Good, very good! Hear him! Hear him!" said the Colonel.

"The name Of Pogram will be proud to jine you. And may it, My friends, be written on My tomb, 'He was a member of the Con-gress of our common country, and was ac-Tive in his trust.'"

"The Com-mittee, sir," said the shrill boy, "will wait upon you at five minutes afore eight. I take My leave, sir!"

Mr. Pogram shook hands with him, and everybody else, once more; and when they came back again at five minutes before eight, they said, one by one, in a melancholy voice, "How do you do, sir?" and shook hands with Mr. Pogram all over again, as if he had been abroad for a twelvemonth in the meantime, and they met, now, at a funeral.

But by this time Mr. Pogram had freshened himself up, and had composed his hair and features after the Pogram statue, so that any one with half an eye might cry out, "There he is! as he delivered the Defiance!" The Committee were embellished also; and when they entered the ladies' ordinary in a body, there was much clapping of hands from ladies and gentlemen, accompanied by cries of " Pogram ! Pogram ! " and some standing up on chairs to see him.

The object of the popular caress looked round the room as he walked up it, and smiled: at the same time observing to the shrill boy, that he knew something of the beauty of the daughters of their common country, but had never seen it in such lustre and perfection as at that moment. Which the shrill boy put in the paper next day; to Elijah Pogram's great surprise.

" We will re-quest you, sir, if you please," said Buffum, laying hands on Mr. Pogram as if he were taking his measure for a coat, " to stand up with your back agin the wall right in the furthest corner, that there may be more room for our fellow cit-izens. If you could set your back right slap agin that curtain-peg, sir, keeping your left leg everlastingly behind the stove, we should be fixed quite slick."

Mr. Pogram did as he was told, and wedged himself into such a little corner, that the Pogram statue wouldn't have known him.

The entertainments of the evening then began. Gentlemen brought ladies up, and brought themselves up, and brought each other up; and asked Elijah Pogram what he thought of this political question, and what he thought of that; and looked at him, and looked at one another, and seemed very unhappy indeed. The ladies on the chairs looked at Elijah Pogram through their glasses, and said audibly, "I wish he'd speak. Why don't he speak? Oh, do ask him to speak ! " And Elijah Pogram looked sometimes at the ladies and some-times elsewhere, delivering senatorial opinions, as he was asked for them. But the great end and object of the meeting seemed to be, not to let Elijah Pogram out of the corner on any account: so there they kept him, hard and fast.

A great bustle at the door, in the course of the evening, announced the arrival of some remarkable person ; and immediately afterwards an elderly gentleman, much excited, was seen to precipitate himself upon the crowd, and battle his way towards the Honourable Elijah Pogram. Martin, who had found a snug place of observation in a distant corner, where he stood with Mark beside him (for he did not so often forget him now as formerly, though he still did sometimes), thought he knew this gentleman, but had no doubt of it, when he cried as loud as he could, with his eyes starting out of his head:

"Sir, Mrs. Hominy!"

"Lord bless that woman, Mark. She has turned up again!"

"Here she comes, sir," answered Mr. Tapley. "Pogram knows her. A public character! Always got her eye upon her country, sir! If that there lady's husband is of my opinion, what a jolly old gentleman he must be!"

A lane was made; and Mrs. Hominy, with the aristocratic stalk, the pocket handkerchief, the clasped hands, and the classical cap, came slowly up it, in a procession of one. Mr. Pogram testified emotions of delight on seeing her, and a general hush prevailed. For it was known that when a woman like Mrs. Hominy encountered a man like Pogram, something interesting must be said.

Their first salutations were exchanged in a voice too low to reach the impatient ears of the throng; but they soon became audible, for Mrs. Hominy felt her position, and knew what was expected of her.

Mrs. H. was hard upon him at first; and put him through a rigid catechism in reference to a certain vote he had given, which she had found it necessary, as the mother of the modern Gracchi, to deprecate in a line by itself, set up expressly for the purpose in German text. But Mr. Pogram evading it by a well-timed allusion to the star-spangled banner, which, it appeared, had the remarkable peculiarity of flouting the breeze whenever it was hoisted where the wind blew, she forgave him. They now enlarged on certain questions of tariff, commercial treaty, boundary, importation and exportation, with great effect. And Mrs. Hominy not only talked, as the saying is, like a book, but actually did talk her own books, word for word.

"My! what is this?" cried Mrs. Hominy, opening a little note which was handed her by her excited gentleman-usher. "Do tell! oh, well, now! on'y think!"

And then she read aloud, as follows:

"Two literary ladies present their compliments to the mother of the modern Gracchi, and claim her kind introduction, as their talented countrywoman, to the honourable (and distinguished) Elijah Pogram, whom the two L.L.'s have often contemplated in the speaking marble of the soul-subduing Chiggle. On a verbal intimation from the mother of the M.G., that she will comply with the request of the two L.L.'s, they will have the immediate pleasure of joining the galaxy assembled to do honour to the patriotic conduct of a Pogram. It may be another bond of union between the two L.L.'s and the mother of the M.G. to observe, that the two L.L.'s are Transcendental."

Mrs. Hominy promptly rose, and proceeded to the door, whence she returned, after a minute's interval, with the two L.L.'s, whom she led, through the lane in the crowd, with all that stateliness of department which was so remarkably her own, up to the great Elijah Pogram. It was (as the shrill boy cried out in an ecstasy) quite the Last Scene from Coriolanus.

One of the L.L.'s wore a brown wig of uncommon size. Sticking on the forehead of the other, by invisible means, was a massive cameo, in size and shape like the raspberry tart which is ordinarily sold for a penny, representing on its front the Capitol at Washington.

"Miss Toppit, and Miss Codger!" said Mrs. Hominy.

"Codger's the lady so often mentioned in the English newspapers, I should think, sir," whispered Mark. "The oldest inhabitant as never remembers anything."

"To be presented to a Pogram," said Miss Codger, "by a Hominy, indeed, a thrilling moment is it in its impressiveness on what we call our feelings. But why we call them so, or why impressed they are, or if impressed they are at all, or if at all we are, or if there really is, oh gasping one! a Pogram or a Hominy, or any active principle to which we give those titles, is a topic, Spirit searching, light abandoned, much too vast to enter on, at this unlooked-for crisis."

"Mind and matter," said the lady in the wig, "glide swift into the vortex of immensity. Howls the sublime, and softly sleeps the calm Ideal, in the whispering chambers of Imagination. To hear it, sweet it is. But then, outlaughs the stern philosopher, and saith to the Grotesque, 'What ho! arrest for me that Agency. Go, bring it here!' And so the vision fadeth."

After this, they both took Mr. Pogram by the hand, and pressed it to their lips, as a patriotic palm. That homage paid, the mother of the modern Gracchi called for chairs, and the three literary ladies went to work in earnest, to bring poor Pogram out, and make him show himself in all his brilliant colours.

How Pogram got out of his depth instantly, and how the three L.L.'s were never in theirs, is a piece of history not worth recording. Suffice it, that being all four out of their depths, and all unable to swim, they splashed up words in all directions, and floundered about famously. On the whole, it was considered to have been the severest mental exercise ever heard in the National Hotel. Tears stood in the shrill boy's eyes several times; and the whole company observed that their heads ached with the effort—as well they might.

When it at last became necessary to release Elijah Pogram from the corner, and the Committee saw him safely back again to the next room, they were fervent in their admiration.

"Which," said Mr. Buffum, "must have vent, or it will bust. Toe you, Mr. Pogram, I am grateful. Toe-wards you, sir, I am inspired with lofty veneration, and with deep e-mo-tion. The sentiment Toe which I would propose to give ex-pression, sir, is this: 'May you ever be as firm, sir, as your marble statter! May it ever be as great a terror 'Toe its ene-mies as you.'"

There is some reason to suppose that it was rather terrible to its friends; being a statue of the Elevated or Goblin School, in which the Honourable Elijah Pogram was represented as in a very high wind, with his hair all standing on end, and his nostrils blown wide open. But Mr. Pogram thanked his friend and countryman for the aspiration to which he had given utterance, and the Committee, after another solemn shaking of hands, retired to bed, except the Doctor; who immediately repaired to the newspaper-office, and there wrote a short poem suggested by the events of the evening, beginning with fourteen stars, and headed, "A Fragment. Suggested by witnessing the Honourable Elijah Pogram engaged in a philosophical disputation with three of Columbia's fairest daughters. By Doctor Ginery Dunkle. Of Troy."

If Pogram was as glad to get to bed as Martin was, he must have been well rewarded for his labours. They started off again next day (Martin and Mark previously disposing of their goods to the storekeepers of whom they had purchased them, for anything they would bring), and were fellow-travellers to within a short distance of New York. When Pogram was about to leave them he grew thoughtful, and after pondering for some time, took Martin aside.

"We air going to part, sir," said Pogram.

"Pray don't distress yourself," said Martin; "we must bear it."

"It ain't that, sir," returned Pogram, "not at all. But I should wish you to accept a copy of My oration."

"Thank you," said Martin, "you are very good. I shall be most happy."

"It ain't quite that, sir, neither," resumed Pogram: "air you bold enough to introduce a copy into your country?"

"Certainly," said Martin. "Why not?"

"Its sentiments air strong, sir," hinted Pogram, darkly.

154

"That makes no difference," said Martin. "I'll take a dozen if you like."

"No, sir," retorted Pogram. "Not A dozen. That is more than I require. If you are content to run the hazard, sir, here is one for your Lord Chancellor," producing it, "and one for Your principal Secretary of State. I should wish them to see it, sir, as expressing what my opinions air. That they may not plead ignorance at a future time. But don't get into danger, sir, on my account!"

"There is not the least danger, I assure you," said Martin. So he put the pamphlets in his pocket, and they parted.

Mr. Bevan had written in his letter that, at a certain time, which fell out happily just then, he would be at a certain hotel in the city, anxiously expecting to see them. To this place they repaired without a moment's delay. They had the satisfaction of finding him within; and of being received by their good friend, with his own warmth and heartiness.

"I am truly sorry and ashamed," said Martin, "to have begged of you. But look at us. See what we are, and judge to what we are reduced!"

"So far from claiming to have done you any service," returned the other, "I reproach myself with having been, unwittingly, the original cause of your misfortunes. I no more supposed you would go to Eden on such representations as you received; or, indeed, that you would do anything but be dispossessed, by the readiest means, of your idea that fortunes were so easily made here; than I thought of going to Eden myself."

"The fact is, I closed with the thing in a mad and sanguine manner," said Martin, "and the less said about it the better for me. Mark, here, hadn't a voice in the matter."

"Well! But he hadn't a voice in any other matter, had he?" returned Mr. Bevan: laughing with an air that showed his understanding of Mark and Martin too.

"Not a very powerful one, I am afraid," said Martin with

a blush. "But live and learn, Mr. Bevan! Nearly die and learn : and we learn the quicker.'

"Now," said their friend, "about your plans. You mean to return home at once?"

"Oh, I think so," returned Martin hastily, for he turned pale at the thought of any other suggestion. "That is your opinion too, I hope?"

"Unquestionably. For I don't know why you ever came here; though it's not such an unusual case, I am sorry to say, that we need go any farther into that. You don't know that the ship in which you came over with our friend General Fladdock, is in port, of course?"

"Indeed!" said Martin.

"Yes. And is advertised to sail to-morrow."

This was tempting news, but tantalising too : for Martin knew that his getting any employment on board a ship of that class was hopeless. The money in his pocket would not pay one-fourth of the sum he had already borrowed, and if it had been enough for their passage-money, he could hardly have resolved to spend it. He explained this to Mr. Bevan, and stated what their project was.

"Why, that's as wild as Eden every bit," returned his friend. "You must take your passage like a Christian; at least, as like a Christian as a fore-cabin passenger can; and owe me a few more dollars than you intend. If Mark will go down to the ship and see what passengers there are, and finds that you can go in her without being actually suffocated, my advice is, go! You and I will look about us in the meantime (we won't call at the Norris's unless you like), and we will all three dine together, in the afternoon."

Martin had nothing to express but gratitude, and so it was arranged. But he went out of the room after Mark, and advised him to take their passage in the Screw, though they lay upon the bare deck; which Mr. Tapley, who needed no entreaty on the subject, readily promised to do.

When he and Martin met again, and were alone, he was in

high spirits, and evidently had something to communicate, in which he gloried very much.

"I've done Mr. Bevan, sir," said Mark.

"Done Mr. Bevan!" repeated Martin.

"The cook of the Screw went and got married yesterday, sir," said Mr. Tapley.

Martin looked at him for farther explanation.

"And when I got on board, and the word was passed that it was me," said Mark, "the mate he comes and asks me whether I'd engage to take this said cook's place upon the passage home. 'For you're used to it,' he says: 'you were always a cooking for everybody on your passage out.' And so I was," said Mark, "although I never cooked before, I'll take my oath."

"What did you say?" demanded Martin.

"Say!" cried Mark. "That I'd take anything I could get. 'If that's so,' says the mate, 'why, bring a glass of rum;' which they brought according. And my wages, sir," said Mark in high glee, "pays your passage; and, I've put the rolling-pin in your berth to take it (it's the easy one up in the corner); and there we are, Rule Britannia, and Britons strike home!"

"There never was such a good fellow as you are!" cried Martin, seizing him by the hand. "But what do you mean by 'doing' Mr. Bevan, Mark?"

"Why, don't you see?" said Mark. "We don't tell him, you know. We take his money, but we don't spend it, and we don't keep it. What we do is, write him a little note, explaining this engagement, and roll it up, and leave it at the bar, to be given to him after we are gone. Don't you see?"

Martin's delight in this idea was not inferior to Mark's. It was all done as he proposed. They passed a cheerful evening; slept at the hotel; left the letter as arranged; and went off to the ship betimes next morning, with such light hearts, as the weight of their past miseries engendered.

"Good bye! a hundred thousand times good bye!" said Martin to their friend. "How shall I remember all your kindness! How shall I ever thank you!"

"If you ever become a rich man, or a powerful one," returned his friend, "you shall try to make your Government more careful of its subjects when they roam abroad to live. Tell it what you know of emigration in your own case, and impress upon it how much suffering may be prevented with a little pains!"

Cheerily, lads, cheerily! Anchor weighed. Ship in full sail. Her sturdy bowsprit pointing true to England. America a cloud upon the sea behind them!

"Why, Cook? what are you thinking of so steadily?" said Martin.

"Why, I was a thinking, sir," returned Mark, "that if I was a painter and was called upon to paint the American Eagle, how should I do it?"

"Paint it as like an Eagle as you could, I suppose."

"No," said Mark. "That wouldn't do for me, sir. I should want to draw it like a Bat, for its short-sightedness; like a Bantam, for its bragging; like a Magpie, for its honesty; like a Peacock, for its vanity; like a Ostrich, for its putting its head in the mud, and thinking nobody sees it—"

"And like a Phœnix, for its power of springing from the ashes of its faults and vices, and soaring up anew into the sky!" said Martin. "Well, Mark. Let us hope so."

CHAPTER XXXV

ARRIVING IN ENGLAND, MARTIN WITNESSES A CEREMONY, FROM
WHICH HE DERIVES THE CHEERING INFORMATION THAT HE
HAS NOT BEEN FORGOTTEN IN HIS ABSENCE.

It was mid-day, and high water in the English port for which the Screw was bound, when, borne in gallantly upon the fulness of the tide, she let go her anchor in the river.

Bright as the scene was; fresh, and full of motion; airy, free, and sparkling; it was nothing to the life and exultation in the breasts of the two travellers, at sight of the old churches, roofs, and darkened chimney stacks of Home. The distant roar, that swelled up hoarsely from the busy streets, was music in their ears; the lines of people gazing from the wharves, were friends held dear; the canopy of smoke that overhung the town was brighter and more beautiful to them, than if the richest silks of Persia had been waving in the air. And though the water going on its glistening track, turned, ever and again, aside to dance and sparkle round great ships, and heave them up; and leaped from off the blades of oars, a shower of diving diamonds; and wantoned with the idle boats, and swiftly passed, in many a sportive chase, through obdurate old iron rings, set deep into the stone-work of the quays; not even it was half so buoyant, and so restless, as their fluttering hearts, when yearning to set foot, once more, on native ground.

A year had passed, since those same spires and roofs had

159

faded from their eyes. It seemed, to them, a dozen years. Some trifling changes, here and there, they called to mind; and wondered that they were so few and slight. In health and fortune, prospect and resource, they came back poorer men than they had gone away. But it was home. And though home is a name, a word, it is a strong one; stronger than magician ever spoke, or spirit answered to, in strongest conjuration.

Being set ashore, with very little money in their pockets, and no definite plan of operation in their heads, they sought out a cheap tavern, where they regaled upon a smoking steak, and certain flowing mugs of beer, as only men just landed from the sea can revel in the generous dainties of the earth. When they had feasted, as two grateful-tempered giants might have done, they stirred the fire, drew back the glowing curtain from the window, and making each a sofa for himself, by union of the great unwieldy chairs, gazed blissfully into the street.

Even the street was made a fairy street, by being half hidden in an atmosphere of steak, and strong, stout, stand-up English beer. For, on the window-glass hung such a mist, that Mr. Tapley was obliged to rise and wipe it with his handkerchief, before the passengers appeared like common mortals. And even then, a spiral little cloud went curling up from their two glasses of hot grog, which nearly hid them from each other.

It was one of those unaccountable little rooms which are never seen anywhere but in a tavern, and are supposed to have got into taverns by reason of the facilities afforded to the architect for getting drunk while engaged in their construction. It had more corners in it than the brain of an obstinate man; was full of mad closets, into which nothing could be put that was not specially invented and made for that purpose; had mysterious shelvings and bulk-heads, and indications of staircases in the ceiling; and was elaborately provided with a bell that rung in the room itself, about two feet from the handle, and had no connection whatever with any other part of the establishment. It was a little below the pavement, and abutted close upon it ; so that passengers grated against the window-panes with their buttons, and scraped it with their baskets ; and fearful boys suddenly coming between a thoughtful guest and the light, derided him, or put out their tongues as if he were a physician ; or made white knobs on the ends of their noses by flattening the same against the glass, and vanished awfully, like spectres.

Martin and Mark sat looking at the people as they passed, debating every now and then, what their first step should be.

" We want to see Miss Mary, of course," said Mark.

" Of course," said Martin. " But I don't know where she is. Not having had the heart to write in our distress—you yourself thought silence most advisable—and consequently, never having heard from her since we left New York the first time, I don't know where she is, my good fellow."

" My opinion is, sir," returned Mark, " that what we've got to do, is to travel straight to the Dragon. There's no need for you to go there, where you're known, unless you like. You may stop ten mile short of it. I'll go on. Mrs. Lupin will tell me all the news. Mr. Pinch will give me every information that we want : and right glad Mr. Pinch will be to do it. My proposal is : To set off walking this afternoon. To stop when we are tired. To get a lift when we can. To walk when we can't. To do it at once, and do it cheap."

" Unless we do it cheap, we shall have some difficulty in doing it at all," said Martin, pulling out the bank, and telling it over in his hand.

" The greater reason for losing no time, sir," replied Mark. " Whereas, when you've seen the young lady ; and know what state of mind the old gentleman's in, and all about it ; then you'll know what to do next."

" No doubt," said Martin. " You are quite right."

They were raising their glasses to their lips, when their hands stopped midway, and their gaze was arrested by a figure which slowly, very slowly, and reflectively, passed the window at that moment.

Mr. Pecksniff. Placid, calm, but proud. Honestly proud. Dressed with peculiar care, smiling with even more than usual blandness, pondering on the beauties of his art with a mild abstraction from all sordid thoughts, and gently travelling across the disc, as if he were a figure in a magic lantern.

As Mr. Pecksniff passed, a person coming in the opposite direction stopped to look after him with great interest and respect: almost with veneration; and the landlord bouncing out of the house, as if he had seen him too, joined this person, and spoke to him, and shook his head gravely, and looked after Mr. Pecksniff likewise.

Martin and Mark sat staring at each other, as if they could not believe it; but there stood the landlord, and the other man still. In spite of the indignation with which this glimpse of Mr. Pecksniff had inspired him, Martin could not help laughing heartily. Neither could Mark.

"We must inquire into this!" said Martin. "Ask the landlord in, Mark."

Mr. Tapley retired for that purpose, and immediately returned with their large-headed host in safe convoy.

"Pray, landlord!" said Martin, "who is that gentleman who passed just now, and whom you were looking after?"

The landlord poked the fire as if, in his desire to make the most of his answer, he had become indifferent even to the price of coals; and putting his hands in his pockets, said, after inflating himself to give still further effect to his reply:

"That, gentlemen, is the great Mr. Pecksniff! The celebrated architect, gentlemen!"

He looked from one to the other while he said it, as if he were ready to assist the first man who might be overcome by the intelligence.

"The great Mr. Pecksniff, the celebrated architect, gentlemen," said the landlord, "has come down here, to help to lay the first stone of a new and splendid public building."

"Is it to be built from his designs?" asked Martin.

"The great Mr. Pecksniff, the celebrated architect, gentlemen," returned the landlord, who seemed to have an unspeakable delight in the repetition of these words, "carried off the First Premium, and will erect the building."

"Who lays the stone?" asked Martin.

"Our member has come down express," returned the landlord. "No scrubs would do for no such a purpose. Nothing less would satisfy our Directors than our member in the House of Commons, who is returned upon the Gentlemanly Interest."

"Which interest is that?" asked Martin.

"What, don't you know!" returned the landlord.

It was quite clear the landlord didn't. They always told him at election time, that it was the Gentlemanly side, and he immediately put on his top-boots, and voted for it.

"When does the ceremony take place?" asked Martin.

"This day," replied the landlord. Then pulling out his watch, he added, impressively, "almost this minute."

Martin hastily inquired whether there was any possibility of getting in to witness it; and finding that there would be no objection to the admittance of any decent person, unless indeed the ground were full, hurried off with Mark, as hard as they could go.

They were fortunate enough to squeeze themselves into a famous corner on the ground, where they could see all that passed, without much dread of being beheld by Mr. Pecksniff in return. They were not a minute too soon, for as they were in the act of congratulating each other, a great noise was heard at some distance, and everybody looked towards the gate. Several ladies prepared their pocket handkerchiefs for waving; and a stray teacher belonging to the charity school being much cheered by mistake, was immensely groaned at when detected.

"Perhaps he has Tom Pinch with him," Martin whispered Mr. Tapley.

"It would be rather too much of a treat for him, wouldn't it, sir?" whispered Mr. Tapley in return.

There was no time to discuss the probabilities either way, for the charity school, in clean linen, came filing in two and two, so much to the self-approval of all the people present who didn't subscribe to it, that many of them shed tears. A band of music followed, led by a conscientious drummer who never left off. Then came a great many gentlemen with wands in their hands, and bows on their breasts, whose share in the proceedings did not appear to be distinctly laid down, and who trod upon each other, and blocked up the entry for a considerable period. These were followed by the Mayor and Corporation, all clustering round the member for the Gentlemanly Interest; who had the great Mr. Pecksniff, the celebrated architect, on his right hand, and conversed with him familiarly as they came along. Then the ladies waved their handkerchiefs, and the gentlemen their hats, and the charity children shrieked, and the member for the Gentlemanly Interest bowed.

Silence being restored, the member for the Gentlemanly Interest rubbed his hands, and wagged his head, and looked about him pleasantly; and there was nothing this member did, at which some lady or other did not burst into an ecstatic waving of her pocket handkerchief. When he looked up at the stone, they said how graceful! when he peeped into the hole, they said how condescending! when he chatted with the Mayor, they said how easy! when he folded his arms they cried with one accord, how statesman-like!

Mr. Pecksniff was observed too; closely. When he talked to the Mayor, they said, Oh really, what a courtly man he was! When he laid his hand upon the mason's shoulder, giving him directions, how pleasant his demeanour to the working classes: just the sort of man who made their toil a pleasure to them, poor dear souls!

But now a silver trowel was brought; and when the member for the Gentlemanly Interest, tucking up his coat-sleeve, did a little sleight-of-hand with the mortar, the air was rent, so loud was the applause. The workman-like manner in which he did it was amazing. No one could conceive where such a gentlemanly creature could have picked the knowledge up.

When he had made a kind of dirt-pie under the direction of the mason, they brought a little vase containing coins, the which the member for the Gentlemanly Interest jingled, as if he were going to conjure. Whereat they said how droll, how cheerful, what a flow of spirits! This put into its place, an ancient scholar read the inscription, which was in Latin: not in English: that would never do. It gave great satisfaction; especially every time there was a good long substantive in the third declension, ablative case, with an adjective to match; at which periods the assembly became very tender, and were much affected.

And now the stone was lowered down into its place, amidst the shouting of the concourse. When it was firmly fixed, the member for the Gentlemanly Interest struck upon it thrice with the handle of the trowel, as if inquiring, with a touch of humour, whether anybody was at home. Mr. Pecksniff then unrolled his Plans (prodigious plans they were), and people gathered round to look at and admire them.

Martin, who had been fretting himself—quite unnecessarily, as Mark thought—during the whole of these proceedings, could no longer restrain his impatience; but stepping forward among several others, looked straight over the shoulder of the unconscious Mr. Pecksniff, at the designs and plans he had unrolled. He returned to Mark, boiling with rage.

" Why, what's the matter, sir ? " cried Mark.

" Matter ! This is *my* building."

" Your building, sir ! " said Mark.

" My grammar-school. I invented it. I did it all. He has only put four windows in, the villain, and spoilt it ! "

Mark could hardly believe it at first, but being assured that it was really so, actually held him to prevent his interference foolishly, until his temporary heat was past. In the meantime, the member addressed the company on the gratifying deed which he had just performed.

He said that since he had sat in Parliament to represent the Gentlemanly Interest of that town; and he might add, the Lady Interest he hoped, besides (pocket handkerchiefs); it had been his pleasant duty to come among them, and to raise his voice on their behalf in Another Place (pocket handkerchiefs and laughter), often. But he had never come among them, and had never raised his voice, with half such pure, such deep, such unalloyed delight, as now. "The present occasion," he said, "will ever be memorable to me: not only for the reasons I have assigned, but because it has afforded me an opportunity of becoming personally known to a gentleman—"

Here he pointed the trowel at Mr. Pecksniff, who was greeted with vociferous cheering, and laid his hand upon his heart.

"To a gentleman who, I am happy to believe, will reap both distinction and profit from this field: whose fame had previously penetrated to me—as to whose ears has it not !— but whose intellectual countenance I never had the distinguished honour to behold until this day, and whose intellectual conversation I had never before the improving pleasure to enjoy."

Everybody seemed very glad of this, and applauded more than ever.

"But I hope my Honourable Friend," said the Gentlemanly member—of course he added 'if he will allow me to call him so,' and of course Mr. Pecksniff bowed—"will give me many opportunities of cultivating the knowledge of him; and that I may have the extraordinary gratification of reflecting in after time that I laid on this day two first stones, both belonging to structures which shall last my life ! "

Great cheering again. All this time, Martin was cursing Mr. Pecksniff up hill and down dale.

"My friends ! " said Mr. Pecksniff, in reply. "My duty is to build, not speak; to act, not talk; to deal with marble,

Martin is much gratified by an Imposing Ceremony

stone, and brick: not language. I am very much affected. God bless you!"

This address, pumped out apparently from Mr. Pecksniff's very heart, brought the enthusiasm to its highest pitch. The pocket handkerchiefs were waved again; the charity children were admonished to grow up Pecksniffs, every boy among them; the Corporation, gentlemen with wands, member for the Gentlemanly Interest, all cheered for Mr. Pecksniff. Three cheers for Mr. Pecksniff! Three more for Mr. Pecksniff! Three more for Mr. Pecksniff, gentlemen, if you please! One more, gentlemen, for Mr. Pecksniff, and let it be a good one to finish with!

In short, Mr. Pecksniff was supposed to have done a great work, and was very kindly, courteously, and generously rewarded. When the procession moved away, and Martin and Mark were left almost alone upon the ground, his merits and a desire to acknowledge them, formed the common topic. He was only second to the Gentlemanly member.

"Compare that fellow's situation to-day with ours!" said Martin, bitterly.

"Lord bless you, sir!" cried Mark, "what's the use? Some architects are clever at making foundations, and some architects are clever at building on 'em when they're made. But it'll all come right in the end, sir; it'll all come right!"

"And in the meantime—" began Martin.

"In the meantime, as you say, sir, we have a deal to do, and far to go. So sharp's the word, and Jolly!"

"You are the best master in the world, Mark," said Martin, "and I will not be a bad scholar if I can help it, I am resolved! So come! Best foot foremost, old fellow!"

CHAPTER XXXVI

Oh! what a different town Salisbury was in Tom Pinch's eyes to be sure, when the substantial Pecksniff of his heart melted away into an idle dream! He possessed the same faith in the wonderful shops, the same intensified appreciation of the mystery and wickedness of the place; made the same exalted estimate of its wealth, population, and resources; and yet it was not the old city nor anything like it. He walked into the market while they were getting breakfast ready for him at the Inn: and though it was the same market as of old, crowded by the same buyers and sellers; brisk with the same business; noisy with the same confusion of tongues and cluttering of fowls in coops; fair with the same display of rolls of butter, newly made, set forth in linen cloths of dazzling whiteness; green with the same fresh show of dewy vegetables; dainty with the same array in higglers' baskets of small shaving-glasses, laces, braces, trouser-straps, and hardware; savoury with the same unstinted show of delicate pigs' feet, and pies made precious by the pork that once had walked upon them: still it was strangely changed to Tom. For, in the centre of the market-place, he missed a statue he had set up there, as in all other places of his personal resort; and it looked cold and bare without that ornament.

The change lay no deeper than this, for Tom was far from

being sage enough to know, that, having been disappointed in one man, it would have been a strictly rational and eminently wise proceeding to have revenged himself upon mankind in general, by mistrusting them one and all. Indeed this piece of justice, though it is upheld by the authority of divers profound poets and honourable men, bears a nearer resemblance to the justice of that good Vizier in the Thousand-and-one Nights, who issues orders for the destruction of all the Porters in Bagdad because one of that unfortunate fraternity is supposed to have misconducted himself, than to any logical, not to say Christian system of conduct, known to the world in later times.

Tom had so long been used to steep the Pecksniff of his fancy in his tea, and spread him out upon his toast, and take him as a relish with his beer, that he made but a poor breakfast on the first morning after his expulsion. Nor did he much improve his appetite for dinner by seriously considering his own affairs, and taking counsel thereon with his friend the organist's assistant.

The organist's assistant gave it as his decided opinion that whatever Tom did, he must go to London; for there was no place like it. Which may be true in the main, though hardly, perhaps, in itself, a sufficient reason for Tom's going there.

But Tom had thought of London before, and had coupled with it thoughts of his sister, and of his old friend John Westlock, whose advice he naturally felt disposed to seek in this important crisis of his fortunes. To London, therefore, he resolved to go; and he went away to the coach-office at once, to secure his place. The coach being already full, he was obliged to postpone his departure until the next night; but even this circumstance had its bright side as well as its dark one, for though it threatened to reduce his poor purse with unexpected country-charges, it afforded him an opportunity of writing to Mrs. Lupin and appointing his box to be brought to the old finger-post at the old time; which would enable him to take that treasure with him to the metropolis, and save the expense of its carriage. "So," said Tom, comforting himself, "it's very nearly as broad as it's long."

And it cannot be denied that, when he had made up his mind to even this extent, he felt an unaccustomed sense of freedom—a vague and indistinct impression of holiday-making —which was very luxurious. He had his moments of depression and anxiety, and they were, with good reason, pretty numerous; but still, it was wonderfully pleasant to reflect that he was his own master, and could plan and scheme for himself. It was startling, thrilling, vast, difficult to understand; it was a stupendous truth, teeming with responsibility and self-distrust; but, in spite of all his cares, it gave a curious relish to the viands at the Inn, and interposed a dreamy haze between him and his prospects, in which they sometimes showed to magical advantage.

In this unsettled state of mind, Tom went once more to bed in the low four-poster, to the same immoveable surprise of the effigies of the former landlord and the fat ox; and in this condition, passed the whole of the succeeding day. When the coach came round at last, with "London" blazoned in letters of gold upon the boot, it gave Tom such a turn, that he was half disposed to run away. But he didn't do it; for he took his seat upon the box instead, and looking down upon the four grays, felt as if he were another gray himself, or, at all events, a part of the turn-out; and was quite confused by the novelty and splendour of his situation.

And really it might have confused a less modest man than Tom to find himself sitting next that coachman; for of all the swells that ever flourished a whip, professionally, he might have been elected emperor. He didn't handle his gloves like another man, but put them on—even when he was standing on the pavement, quite detached from the coach—as if the four grays were, somehow or other, at the ends of the fingers. It was the same with his hat. He did things with his hat, which nothing but an unlimited knowledge of horses and the wildest freedom of the road, could ever have made him perfect in. Valuable little parcels were brought to him with particular instructions, and he pitched them into this hat, and stuck it on again; as if the laws of gravity did not admit of such an event as its being knocked off or blown off, and nothing like an accident could befall it. The guard, too! Seventy breezy miles a-day were written in his very whiskers. His manners were a canter; his conversation a round trot. He was a fast coach upon a down-hill turnpike road; he was all pace. A waggon couldn't have moved slowly, with that guard and his key-bugle on the top of it.

These were all foreshadowings of London, Tom thought, as he sat upon the box, and looked about him. Such a coachman, and such a guard, never could have existed between Salisbury and any other place. The coach was none of your steady-going, yokel coaches, but a swaggering, rakish, dissipated London coach; up all night, and lying by all day, and leading a devil of a life. It cared no more for Salisbury than if it had been a hamlet. It rattled noisily through the best streets, defied the Cathedral, took the worst corners sharpest, went cutting in everywhere, making everything get out of its way; and spun along the open country-road, blowing a lively defiance out of its key-bugle, as its last glad parting legacy.

It was a charming evening. Mild and bright. And even with the weight upon his mind which arose out of the immensity and uncertainty of London, Tom could not resist the captivating sense of rapid motion through the pleasant air. The four grays skimmed along, as if they liked it quite as well as Tom did; the bugle was in as high spirits as the grays; the coachman chimed in sometimes with his voice; the wheels hummed cheerfully in unison; the brass work on the harness was an orchestra of little bells; and thus, as they went clinking, jingling, rattling smoothly on, the whole concern, from the buckles of the leaders' coupling-reins, to the handle of the hind boot, was one great instrument of music.

Yoho, past hedges, gates, and trees; past cottages and barns, and people going home from work. Yoho, past donkey-chaises, drawn aside into the ditch, and empty carts with rampant horses, whipped up at a bound upon the little watercourse, and held by struggling carters close to the five-barred gate, until the coach had passed the narrow turning in the road. Yoho, by churches dropped down by themselves in quiet nooks, with rustic burial-grounds about them, where the graves are green, and daisies sleep—for it is evening—on the bosoms of the dead. Yoho, past streams, in which the cattle cool their feet, and where the rushes grow; past paddock-fences, farms, and rick-yards; past last year's stacks, cut, slice by slice, away, and showing, in the waning light, like ruined gables, old and brown. Yoho, down the pebbly dip, and through the merry water-splash, and up at a canter to the level road again. Yoho! Yoho!

Was the box there, when they came up to the old finger-post? The box! Was Mrs. Lupin herself? Had she turned out magnificently as a hostess should, in her own chaise-cart, and was she sitting in a mahogany chair, driving her own horse Dragon (who ought to have been called Dumpling), and look-ing lovely? Did the stage-coach pull up beside her, shaving her very wheel, and even while the guard helped her man up with the trunk, did he send the glad echoes of his bugle career-ing down the chimneys of the distant Pecksniff, as if the coach expressed its exultation in the rescue of Tom Pinch?

"This is kind indeed!" said Tom, bending down to shake hands with her. "I didn't mean to give you this trouble."

"Trouble, Mr. Pinch!" cried the hostess of the Dragon.

"Well! It's a pleasure to you, I know," said Tom, squeezing her hand heartily. "Is there any news?"

The hostess shook her head.

"Say you saw me," said Tom, "and that I was very bold and cheerful, and not a bit down-hearted; and that I entreated her to be the same, for all is certain to come right at last. Good bye!"

"You'll write when you get settled, Mr. Pinch?" said Mrs. Lupin.

THE LANDLADY'S BASKET

"When I get settled!" cried Tom, with an involuntary opening of his eyes. "Oh, yes, I'll write when I get settled. Perhaps I had better write before, because I may find that it takes a little time to settle myself: not having too much money, and having only one friend. I shall give your love to the friend, by the way. You were always great with Mr. Westlock, you know. Good bye!"

"Good bye!" said Mrs. Lupin, hastily producing a basket with a long bottle sticking out of it. "Take this. Good bye!"

"Do you want me to carry it to London for you?" cried Tom. She was already turning the chaise-cart round.

"No, no," said Mrs. Lupin. "It's only a little something for refreshment on the road. Sit fast, Jack. Drive on, sir. All right! Good bye!"

She was a quarter of a mile off, before Tom collected himself; and then he was waving his hand lustily; and so was she.

"And that's the last of the old finger-post," thought Tom, straining his eyes, "where I have so often stood to see this very coach go by, and where I have parted with so many companions! I used to compare this coach to some great monster that appeared at certain times to bear my friends away into the world. And now it's bearing me away, to seek my fortune, Heaven knows where and how!"

It made Tom melancholy to picture himself walking up the lane and back to Pecksniff's as of old; and being melancholy, he looked downwards at the basket on his knee, which he had for the moment forgotten.

"She is the kindest and most considerate creature in the world," thought Tom. "Now I *know* that she particularly told that man of hers not to look at me, on purpose to prevent my throwing him a shilling! I had it ready for him all the time, and he never once looked towards me; whereas that man naturally, (for I know him very well), would have done nothing but grin and stare. Upon my word, the kindness of people perfectly melts me."

Here he caught the coachman's eye. The coachman winked. "Remarkable fine woman for her time of life," said the coachman.

"I quite agree with you," returned Tom. "So she is."

"Finer than many a young 'un, I mean to say," observed the coachman. "Eh?"

"Than many a young one," Tom assented.

"I don't care for 'em myself when they're too young," remarked the coachman.

This was a matter of taste, which Tom did not feel himself called upon to discuss.

"You'll seldom find 'em possessing correct opinions about refreshment, for instance, when they're too young, you know," said the coachman: "a woman must have arrived at maturity, before her mind's equal to coming provided with a basket like that."

"Perhaps you would like to know what it contains?" said Tom, smiling.

As the coachman only laughed, and as Tom was curious himself, he unpacked it, and put the articles, one by one, upon the footboard. A cold roast fowl, a packet of ham in slices, a crusty loaf, a piece of cheese, a paper of biscuits, half a dozen apples, a knife, some butter, a screw of salt, and a bottle of old sherry. There was a letter besides, which Tom put in his pocket.

The coachman was so earnest in his approval of Mrs. Lupin's provident habits, and congratulated Tom so warmly on his good fortune, that Tom felt it necessary, for the lady's sake, to explain that the basket was a strictly Platonic basket, and had merely been presented to him in the way of friendship. When he had made the statement with perfect gravity; for he felt it incumbent on him to disabuse the mind of this lax rover of any incorrect impressions on the subject; he signified that he would be happy to share the gifts with him, and proposed that they should attack the basket in a spirit of good fellowship at any time in the course of the night which the

174

Mr. Pinch departs to seek his Fortune

coachman's experience and knowledge of the road might suggest, as being best adapted to the purpose. From this time they chatted so pleasantly together, that although Tom knew infinitely more of unicorns than horses, the coachman informed his friend the guard, at the end of the next stage, "that rum as the box-seat looked, he was as good a one to go, in pint of conversation, as ever he'd wish to sit by."

Yoho, among the gathering shades; making of no account the deep reflections of the trees, but scampering on through light and darkness, all the same, as if the light of London fifty miles away, were quite enough to travel by, and some to spare. Yoho, beside the village-green, where cricket-players linger yet, and every little indentation made in the fresh grass by bat or wicket, ball or player's foot, sheds out its perfume on the night. Away with four fresh horses from the Bald-faced Stag, where topers congregate about the door admiring; and the last team with traces hanging loose, go roaming off towards the pond, until observed and shouted after by a dozen throats, while volunteering boys pursue them. Now, with a clattering of hoofs and striking out of fiery sparks, across the old stone bridge, and down again into the shadowy road, and through the open gate, and far away, away, into the wold. Yoho!

Yoho, behind there, stop that bugle for a moment! Come creeping over to the front, along the coach-roof, guard, and make one at this basket! Not that we slacken in our pace the while, not we: we rather put the bits of blood upon their metal, for the greater glory of the snack. Ah! It is long since this bottle of old wine was brought into contact with the mellow breath of night, you may depend, and rare good stuff it is to wet a bugler's whistle with. Only try it. Don't be afraid of turning up your finger, Bill, another pull! Now, take your breath, and try the bugle, Bill. There's music! There's a tone! "Over the hills and far away," indeed. Yoho! The skittish mare is all alive to-night. Yoho! Yoho!

See the bright moon! High up before we know it: making the earth reflect the objects on its breast like water. Hedges,

trees, low cottages, church steeples, blighted stumps and flourishing young slips, have all grown vain upon the sudden, and
mean to contemplate their own fair images till morning. The
poplars yonder rustle that their quivering leaves may see
themselves upon the ground. Not so the oak; trembling does
not become *him*; and he watches himself in his stout old burly
steadfastness, without the motion of a twig. The moss-grown
gate, ill-poised upon its creaking hinges, crippled and decayed,
swings to and fro before its glass, like some fantastic dowager;
while our own ghostly likeness travels on, Yoho! Yoho!
through ditch and brake, upon the ploughed land and the
smooth, along the steep hill-side and steeper wall, as if it were
a phantom-Hunter.

Clouds too! And a mist upon the Hollow! Not a dull
fog that hides it, but a light airy gauze-like mist, which in
our eyes of modest admiration gives a new charm to the
beauties it is spread before: as real gauze has done ere now,
and would again, so please you, though we were the Pope.
Yoho! Why now we travel like the Moon herself. Hiding
this minute in a grove of trees; next minute in a patch of
vapour; emerging now upon our broad clear course; withdraw-
ing now, but always dashing on, our journey is a counterpart
of hers. Yoho! A match against the Moon!

The beauty of the night is hardly felt, when Day comes
leaping up. Yoho! Two stages, and the country roads are
almost changed to a continuous street. Yoho, past market-
gardens, rows of houses, villas, crescents, terraces, and squares;
past waggons, coaches, carts; past early workmen, late stragglers, drunken men, and sober carriers of loads; past brick
and mortar in its every shape; and in among the rattling pavements, where a jaunty-seat upon a coach is not so easy to
preserve! Yoho, down countless turnings, and through countless mazy ways, until an old Inn-yard is gained, and Tom Pinch,
getting down, quite stunned and giddy, is in London!

"Five minutes before the time, too!" said the driver, as
he received his fee of Tom.

JOHN WESTLOCK'S CHAMBERS

"Upon my word," said Tom, "I should not have minded very much, if we had been five hours after it; for at this early hour I don't know where to go, or what to do with myself."

"Don't they expect you then?" inquired the driver.

"Who?" said Tom.

"Why, them," returned the driver.

His mind was so clearly running on the assumption of Tom's having come to town to see an extensive circle of anxious relations and friends, that it would have been pretty hard work to undeceive him. Tom did not try. He cheerfully evaded the subject, and going into the Inn, fell fast asleep before a fire in one of the public rooms opening from the yard. When he awoke, the people in the house were all astir, so he washed and dressed himself; to his great refreshment after the journey; and, it being by that time eight o'clock, went forth at once to see his old friend John.

John Westlock lived in Furnival's Inn, High Holborn, which was within a quarter of an hour's walk of Tom's starting-point, but seemed a long way off, by reason of his going two or three miles out of the straight road to make a short cut. When at last he arrived outside John's door, two stories up, he stood faltering with his hand upon the knocker, and trembled from head to foot. For he was rendered very nervous by the thought of having to relate what had fallen out between himself and Pecksniff; and he had a misgiving that John would exult fearfully in the disclosure.

"But it must be made," thought Tom, "sooner or later; and I had better get it over."

Rat tat.

"I am afraid that's not a London knock," thought Tom. "It didn't sound bold. Perhaps that's the reason why nobody answers the door."

It is quite certain that nobody came, and that Tom stood looking at the knocker: wondering whereabouts in the neighbourhood a certain gentleman resided, who was roaring out to somebody "Come in!" with all his might.

"Bless my soul!" thought Tom at last. "Perhaps he lives here, and is calling to me. I never thought of that. Can I open the door from the outside, I wonder. Yes, to be sure I can."

To be sure he could, by turning the handle: and to be sure when he did turn it the same voice came rushing out, crying "Why don't you come in? Come in, do you hear? What are you standing there for?"—quite violently.

Tom stepped from the little passage into the room from which these sounds proceeded, and had barely caught a glimpse of a gentleman in a dressing-gown and slippers (with his boots beside him ready to put on), sitting at his breakfast with a newspaper in his hand, when the said gentleman, at the imminent hazard of oversetting his tea-table, made a plunge at Tom, and hugged him.

"Why, Tom, my boy!" cried the gentleman. "Tom!"

"How glad I am to see you, Mr. Westlock!" said Tom Pinch, shaking both his hands, and trembling more than ever. "How kind you are!"

"Mr. Westlock!" repeated John, "what do you mean by that, Pinch? You have not forgotten my Christian name, I suppose?"

"No, John, no. I have not forgotten it," said Thomas Pinch. "Good gracious me, how kind you are!"

"I never saw such a fellow in all my life!" cried John. "What do you mean by saying *that* over and over again? What did you expect me to be, I wonder! Here, sit down, Tom, and be a reasonable creature. How are you, my boy? I am delighted to see you!"

"And I am delighted to see *you*," said Tom.

"It's mutual, of course," returned John. "It always was, I hope. If I had known you had been coming, Tom, I would have had something for breakfast. I would rather have such a surprise than the best breakfast in the world, myself; but yours is another case, and I have no doubt you are as hungry as a hunter. You must make out as well as you can, Tom, and we'll recompense ourselves at dinner-time. You take sugar

I know: I recollect the sugar at Pecksniff's. Ha, ha, ha! How *is* Pecksniff? When did you come to town? *Do* begin at something or other, Tom. There are only scraps here, but they are not at all bad. Boar's Head potted. Try it, Tom. Make a beginning whatever you do. What an old Blade you are! I am delighted to see you."

While he delivered himself of these words in a state of great commotion, John was constantly running backwards and forwards to and from the closet, bringing out all sorts of things in pots, scooping extraordinary quantities of tea out of the caddy, dropping French rolls into his boots, pouring hot water over the butter, and making a variety of similar mistakes without disconcerting himself in the least.

"There!" said John, sitting down for the fiftieth time, and instantly starting up again to make some other addition to the breakfast. "Now we are as well off as we are likely to be till dinner. And now let us have the news, Tom. Imprimis, how's Pecksniff?"

"I don't know how he is," was Tom's grave answer.

John Westlock put the teapot down, and looked at him, in astonishment.

"I don't know how he is," said Thomas Pinch; "and saving that I wish him no ill, I don't care. I have left him, John. I have left him for ever."

"Voluntarily?"

"Why no, for he dismissed me. But I had first found out that I was mistaken in him; and I could not have remained with him under any circumstances. I grieve to say that you were right in your estimate of his character. It may be a ridiculous weakness, John, but it has been very painful and bitter to me to find this out, I do assure you."

Tom had no need to direct that appealing look towards his friend, in mild and gentle deprecation of his answering with a laugh. John Westlock would as soon have thought of striking him down upon the floor.

"It was all a dream of mine," said Tom, "and it is over.

I'll tell you how it happened, at some other time. Bear with my folly, John. I do not, just now, like to think or speak about it."

"I swear to you, Tom," returned his friend, with great earnestness of manner, after remaining silent for a few moments, "that when I see, as I do now, how deeply you feel this, I don't know whether to be glad or sorry that you have made the discovery at last. I reproach myself with the thought that I ever jested on the subject; I ought to have known better."

"My dear friend," said Tom, extending his hand, "it is very generous and gallant in you to receive me and my disclosure in this spirit; it makes me blush to think that I should have felt a moment's uneasiness as I came along. You can't think what a weight is lifted off my mind," said Tom, taking up his knife and fork again, and looking very cheerful. I shall punish the Boar's Head dreadfully."

The host, thus reminded of his duties, instantly betook himself to piling up all kinds of irreconcilable and contradictory viands in Tom's plate, and a very capital breakfast Tom made, and very much the better for it, Tom felt.

"That's all right," said John, after contemplating his visitor's proceedings, with infinite satisfaction. "Now, about our plans. You are going to stay with me, of course. Where's your box?"

"It's at the Inn," said Tom. "I didn't intend—— "

"Never mind what you didn't intend," John Westlock interposed. "What you *did* intend is more to the purpose. You intended, in coming here, to ask my advice, did you not, Tom?"

"Certainly."

"And to take it when I gave it to you?"

"Yes," rejoined Tom, smiling, "if it were good advice, which, being yours, I have no doubt it will be."

"Very well. Then don't be an obstinate old humbug in the outset, Tom, or I shall shut up shop and dispense none of that invaluable commodity. You are on a visit to me. I wish I had an organ for you, Tom!"

"So do the gentlemen down stairs, and the gentlemen overhead, I have no doubt," was Tom's reply.

"Let me see. In the first place, you will wish to see your sister this morning," pursued his friend, "and of course you will like to go there alone. I'll walk part of the way with you; and see about a little business of my own, and meet you here again in the afternoon. Put that in your pocket, Tom. It's only the key of the door. If you come home first, you'll want it."

"Really," said Tom, "quartering one's self upon a friend in this way——"

"Why, there are two keys," interposed John Westlock. "I can't open the door with them both at once, can I? What a ridiculous fellow you are, Tom! Nothing particular you'd like for dinner, is there?"

"Oh dear no," said Tom.

"Very well, then you may as well leave it to me. Have a glass of cherry brandy, Tom?"

"Not a drop! What remarkable chambers these are!" said Pinch, "there's everything in 'em!"

"Bless your soul, Tom, nothing but a few little bachelor contrivances! the sort of impromptu arrangements that might have suggested themselves to Philip Quarll or Robinson Crusoe: that's all. What do you say? Shall we walk?"

"By all means," cried Tom. "As soon as you like."

Accordingly, John Westlock took the French rolls out of his boots, and put his boots on, and dressed himself: giving Tom the paper to read in the meanwhile. When he returned, equipped for walking, he found Tom in a brown study, with the paper in his hand.

"Dreaming, Tom?"

"No," said Mr. Pinch, "No. I have been looking over the advertising sheet, thinking there might be something in it, which would be likely to suit me. But, as I often think, the strange thing seems to be that nobody is suited. Here are all kinds of employers wanting all sorts of servants, and all sorts of servants wanting all kinds of employers, and they never seem to come together. Here is a gentleman in a public office in a position of temporary difficulty, who wants to borrow five hundred pounds; and in the very next advertisement here is another gentleman who has got exactly that sum to lend. But he'll never lend it to him, John, you'll find! Here is a lady possessing a moderate independence, who wants to board and lodge with a quiet, cheerful family; and here is a family describing themselves in those very words, ' a quiet, cheerful family,' who want exactly such a lady to come and live with them. But she'll never go, John! Neither do any of these single gentlemen who want an airy bed-room, with the occasional use of a parlour, ever appear to come to terms with these other people who live in a rural situation, remarkable for its bracing atmosphere, within five minutes' walk of the Royal Exchange. Even those letters of the alphabet, who are always running away from their friends and being entreated at the tops of columns to come back, never *do* come back, if we may judge from the number of times they are asked to do it, and don't. It really seems," said Tom, relinquishing the paper, with a thoughtful sigh, " as if people had the same gratification in printing their complaints as in making them known by word of mouth; as if they found it a comfort and consolation to proclaim 'I want such and such a thing, and I can't get it, and I don't expect I ever shall!'"

John Westlock laughed at the idea, and they went out together. So many years had passed since Tom was last in London, and he had known so little of it then, that his interest in all he saw was very great. He was particularly anxious, among other notorious localities, to have those streets pointed out to him which were appropriated to the slaughter of countrymen; and was quite disappointed to find, after a half-an-hour's walking, that he hadn't had his pocket picked. But on John Westlock's inventing a pickpocket for his gratification, and pointing out a highly respectable stranger as one of that fraternity, he was much delighted.

His friend accompanied him to within a short distance of Camberwell, and having put him beyond the possibility of mistaking the wealthy brass-and-copper founder's, left him to make his visit. Arriving before the great bell-handle, Tom gave it a gentle pull. The porter appeared.

"Pray does Miss Pinch live here?" said Tom.

"Miss Pinch is Governess here," replied the porter.

At the same time he looked at Tom from head to foot, as if he would have said, "You are a nice man, *you* are; where did *you* come from?"

"It's the same young lady," said Tom. "It's quite right. Is she at home?"

"I don't know, I'm sure," rejoined the porter.

"Do you think you could have the goodness to ascertain?" said Tom. He had quite a delicacy in offering the suggestion, for the possibility of such a step did not appear to present itself to the porter's mind at all.

The fact was that the porter in answering the gate-bell had, according to usage, rung the house-bell (for it is as well to do these things in the Baronial style while you are about it), and that there the functions of his office had ceased. Being hired to open and shut the gate, and not to explain himself to strangers, he left this little incident to be developed by the footman with the tags, who, at this juncture, called out from the door steps:

"Hollo, there! wot are you up to? This way, young man!"

"Oh!" said Tom, hurrying towards him. "I didn't observe that there was anybody else. Pray is Miss Pinch at home?"

"She's *in*," replied the footman. As much as to say to Tom: "But if you think she has anything to do with the proprietorship of this place, you had better abandon that idea."

"I wish to see her if you please," said Tom.

The footman, being a lively young man, happened to have his attention caught at that moment by the flight of a pigeon, in which he took so warm an interest, that his gaze was rivetted on the bird until it was quite out of sight. He then invited Tom to come in, and showed him into a parlour.

"Hany neem?" said the young man, pausing languidly at the door.

It was a good thought: because without providing the stranger, in case he should happen to be of a warm temper, with a sufficient excuse for knocking him down, it implied this young man's estimate of his quality, and relieved his breast of the oppressive burden of rating him in secret as a nameless and obscure individual.

"Say her brother, if you please," said Tom.

"Mother?" drawled the footman.

"Brother," repeated Tom, slightly raising his voice. "And if you will say, in the first instance, a gentleman, and then say her brother, I shall be obliged to you, as she does not expect me, or know I am in London, and I do not wish to startle her."

The young man's interest in Tom's observations had ceased long before this time, but he kindly waited until now; when, shutting the door, he withdrew.

"Dear me!" said Tom. "This is very disrespectful and uncivil behaviour. I hope these are new servants here, and that Ruth is very differently treated."

His cogitations were interrupted by the sound of voices in the adjoining room. They seemed to be engaged in high dispute, or in indignant reprimand of some offender; and gathering strength occasionally, broke out into a perfect whirlwind. It was in one of these gusts, as it appeared to Tom, that the footman announced him; for an abrupt and unnatural calm took place, and then a dead silence. He was standing before the window, wondering what domestic quarrel might have caused these sounds, and hoping Ruth had nothing to do with it, when the door opened, and his sister ran into his arms.

"Why, bless my soul!" said Tom, looking at her with great pride, when they had tenderly embraced each other, "how altered you are, Ruth! I should scarcely have known you, my love, if I had seen you anywhere else, I declare! You are so improved," said Tom, with inexpressible delight: "you are so womanly; you are so—positively, you know, you are so handsome!"

"If *you* think so, Tom—"

"Oh, but everybody must think so, you know," said Tom, gently smoothing down her hair. "It's a matter of fact; not opinion. But what's the matter?" said Tom, looking at her more intently, "how flushed you are! and you have been crying."

"No, I have not, Tom."

"Nonsense," said her brother stoutly. "That's a story. Don't tell me! I know better. What is it, dear? I'm not with Mr. Pecksniff now; I am going to try and settle myself in London; and if you are not happy here (as I very much fear you are not, for I begin to think you have been deceiving me with the kindest and most affectionate intention) you shall not remain here."

Oh! Tom's blood was rising; mind that! Perhaps the Boar's Head had something to do with it, but certainly the footman had. So had the sight of his pretty sister—a great deal to do with it. Tom could bear a good deal himself, but he was proud of her, and pride is a sensitive thing. He began to think, "there are more Pecksniffs than one, perhaps," and by all the pins and needles that run up and down in angry veins, Tom was in a most unusual tingle all at once!

"We will talk about it, Tom," said Ruth, giving him another kiss to pacify him. "I am afraid I cannot stay here."

"Cannot!" replied Tom. "Why then, you shall not, my

love. Heyday! You are not an object of charity! Upon my word!"

Tom was stopped in these exclamations by the footman, who brought a message from his master, importing that he wished to speak with him before he went, and with Miss Pinch also.

"Show the way," said Tom. "I'll wait upon him at once."

Accordingly they entered the adjoining room from which the noise of altercation had proceeded; and there they found a middle-aged gentleman, with a pompous voice and manner, and a middle-aged lady, with what may be termed an excise-able face, or one in which starch and vinegar were decidedly employed. There was likewise present that eldest pupil of Miss Pinch, whom Mrs. Todgers, on a previous occasion, had called a syrup, and who was now weeping and sobbing spitefully.

"My brother, sir," said Ruth Pinch, timidly presenting Tom

"Oh!" cried the gentleman, surveying Tom attentively. "You really are Miss Pinch's brother, I presume? You will excuse my asking. I don't observe any resemblance."

"Miss Pinch has a brother, I know," observed the lady.

"Miss Pinch is always talking about her brother, when she ought to be engaged upon my education," sobbed the pupil.

"Sophia! Hold your tongue!" observed the gentleman. "Sit down, if you please," addressing Tom.

Tom sat down, looking from one face to another, in mute surprise.

"Remain here, if you please, Miss Pinch," pursued the gentleman, looking slightly over his shoulder.

Tom interrupted him here, by rising to place a chair for his sister. Having done which he sat down again.

"I am glad you chance to have called to see your sister to-day, sir," resumed the brass-and-copper founder. "For although I do not approve, as a principle, of any young person engaged in my family in the capacity of a governess, receiving visitors, it happens in this case to be well-timed. I am sorry to inform you that we are not at all satisfied with your sister."

"We are very much *dis*satisfied with her," observed the lady.

"I'd never say another lesson to Miss Pinch if I was to be beat to death for it!" sobbed the pupil.

"Sophia!" cried her father. "Hold your tongue!"

"Will you allow me to inquire what your ground of dissatisfaction is?" asked Tom.

"Yes," said the gentleman, "I will. I don't recognise it as a right; but I will. Your sister has not the slightest innate power of commanding respect. It has been a constant source of difference between us. Although she has been in this family for some time, and although the young lady who is now present, has almost, as it were, grown up under her tuition, that young lady has no respect for her. Miss Pinch has been perfectly unable to command my daughter's respect, or to win my daughter's confidence. Now," said the gentleman, allowing the palm of his hand to fall gravely down upon the table: "I maintain that there is something radically wrong in that! You, as her brother, may be disposed to deny it—"

"I beg your pardon, sir," said Tom. "I am not at all disposed to deny it. I am sure that there is something radically wrong: radically monstrous: in that."

"Good Heavens!" cried the gentleman, looking round the room with dignity, "what do I find to be the case! what results obtrude themselves upon me as flowing from this weakness of character on the part of Miss Pinch! What are my feelings as a father, when, after my desire (repeatedly expressed to Miss Pinch, as I think she will not venture to deny) that my daughter should be choice in her expressions, genteel in her deportment, as becomes her station in life, and politely distant to her inferiors in society, I find her, only this very morning, addressing Miss Pinch herself as a beggar!"

187

"A beggarly thing," observed the lady, in correction.

"Which is worse," said the gentleman, triumphantly; "which is worse. A beggarly thing. A low, coarse, despicable expression!"

"Most despicable," cried Tom. "I am glad to find that there is a just appreciation of it here."

"So just, sir," said the gentleman, lowering his voice to be the more impressive. "So just, that, but for my knowing Miss Pinch to be an unprotected young person, an orphan, and without friends, I would, as I assured Miss Pinch, upon my veracity and personal character, a few minutes ago, I would have severed the connection between us at that moment and from that time."

"Bless my soul, sir!" cried Tom, rising from his seat; for he was now unable to contain himself any longer; "don't allow such considerations as those to influence you, pray. They don't exist, sir. She is not unprotected. She is ready to depart this instant. Ruth, my dear, get your bonnet on!"

"Oh, a pretty family!" cried the lady. "Oh, he's her brother! There's no doubt about that!"

"As little doubt, madam," said Tom; "as that the young lady yonder is the child of your teaching, and not my sister's. Ruth, my dear, get your bonnet on!"

"When you say, young man," interposed the brass-and-copper founder, haughtily, "with that impertinence which is natural to you, and which I therefore do not condescend to notice further, that the young lady, my eldest daughter, has been educated by any one but Miss Pinch, you—I needn't proceed. You comprehend me fully. I have no doubt you are used to it."

"Sir!" cried Tom, after regarding him in silence for some little time. "If you do not understand what I mean, I will tell you. If you do understand what I mean, I beg you not to repeat that mode of expressing yourself in answer to it. My meaning is, that no man can expect his children to respect what he degrades."

188

"Ha, ha, ha!" laughed the gentleman. "Cant! cant! The common cant!"

"The common story, sir!" said Tom; "the story of a common mind. Your governess cannot win the confidence and respect of your children, forsooth! Let her begin by winning yours, and see what happens then."

"Miss Pinch is getting her bonnet on, I trust, my dear?" said the gentleman.

"I trust she is," said Tom, forestalling the reply. "I have no doubt she is. In the meantime I address myself to you, sir. You made your statement to me, sir; you required to see me for that purpose; and I have a right to answer it. I am not loud or turbulent," said Tom, which was quite true, "though I can scarcely say as much for you, in your manner of addressing yourself to me. And I wish, on my sister's behalf, to state the simple truth."

"You may state anything you like, young man," returned the gentleman, affecting to yawn. "My dear, Miss Pinch's money."

"When you tell me," resumed Tom, who was not the less indignant for keeping himself quiet, "that my sister has no innate power of commanding the respect of your children, I must tell you it is not so; and that she has. She is as well bred, as well taught, as well qualified by nature to command respect, as any hirer of a governess you know. But when you place her at a disadvantage in reference to every servant in your house, how can you suppose, if you have the gift of common sense, that she is not in a tenfold worse position in reference to your daughters?"

"Pretty well! Upon my word," exclaimed the gentleman, "this is pretty well!"

"It is very ill, sir," said Tom. "It is very bad and mean, and wrong and cruel. Respect! I believe young people are quick enough to observe and imitate; and why or how should they respect whom no one else respects, and everybody slights? And very partial they must grow—oh, very partial!—to

189

their studies, when they see to what a pass proficiency in those same tasks has brought their governess! Respect! Put anything the most deserving of respect before your daughters in the light in which you place her, and you will bring it down as low, no matter what it is!"

"You speak with extreme impertinence, young man," observed the gentleman.

"I speak without passion, but with extreme indignation and contempt for such a course of treatment, and for all who practise it," said Tom. "Why, how can you, as an honest gentleman, profess displeasure or surprise, at your daughter telling my sister she is something beggarly and humble, when you are for ever telling her the same thing yourself in fifty plain, out-speaking ways, though not in words; and when your very porter and footman make the same delicate announcement to all comers? As to your suspicion and distrust of her: even of her word; if she is not above their reach, you have no right to employ her."

"No right!" cried the brass-and-copper founder.

"Distinctly not," Tom answered. "If you imagine that the payment of an annual sum of money gives it to you, you immensely exaggerate its power and value. Your money is the least part of your bargain in such a case. You may be punctual in that to half a second on the clock, and yet be Bankrupt. I have nothing more to say," said Tom, much flushed and flustered, now that it was over, "except to crave permission to stand in your garden until my sister is ready."

Not waiting to obtain it, Tom walked out.

Before he had well begun to cool, his sister joined him. She was crying; and Tom could not bear that any one about the house should see her doing that.

"They will think you are sorry to go," said Tom. "You are not sorry to go?"

"No, Tom, no. I have been anxious to go for a very long time."

"Very well, then! Don't cry!" said Tom.

"I am so sorry for *you*, dear," sobbed Tom's sister.

"But you ought to be glad on my account," said Tom. "I shall be twice as happy with you for a companion. Hold up your head. There! Now we go out as we ought. Not blustering, you know, but firm and confident in ourselves."

The idea of Tom and his sister blustering, under any circumstances, was a splendid absurdity. But Tom was very far from feeling it to be so, in his excitement; and passed out at the gate with such severe determination written in his face that the porter hardly knew him again.

It was not until they had walked some short distance, and Tom found himself getting cooler and more collected, that he was quite restored to himself by an inquiry from his sister, who said in her pleasant little voice:

"Where are we going, Tom?"

"Dear me!" said Tom, stopping, "I don't know."

"Don't you—don't you live anywhere, dear?" asked Tom's sister, looking wistfully in his face.

"No," said Tom. "Not at present. Not exactly. I only arrived this morning. We must have some lodgings."

He didn't tell her that he had been going to stay with his friend John, and could on no account think of billeting two inmates upon him, of whom one was a young lady; for he knew that would make her uncomfortable, and would cause her to regard herself as being an inconvenience to him. Neither did he like to leave her anywhere while he called on John, and told him of this change in his arrangements; for he was delicate of seeming to encroach upon the generous and hospitable nature of his friend. Therefore he said again, "We must have some lodgings, of course;" and said it as stoutly as if he had been a perfect Directory and Guide-Book to all the lodgings in London.

"Where shall we go and look for 'em?" said Tom. "What do you think?"

Tom's sister was not much wiser on such a topic than he was. So she squeezed her little purse into his coat-pocket, and folding the little hand with which she did so on the other little hand with which she clasped his arm, said nothing.

"It ought to be a cheap neighbourhood," said Tom, "and not too far from London. Let me see. Should you think Islington a good place?"

"I should think it was an excellent place, Tom."

"It used to be called Merry Islington, once upon a time," said Tom. "Perhaps it's merry now; if so, it's all the better. Eh?"

"If it's not too dear," said Tom's sister.

"Of course, if it's not too dear," assented Tom. "Well, where *is* Islington? We can't do better than go there, I should think. Let's go."

Tom's sister would have gone anywhere with him; so they walked off, arm in arm, as comfortably as possible. Finding, presently, that Islington was not in that neighbourhood, Tom made inquiries respecting a public conveyance thither: which they soon obtained. As they rode along they were very full of conversation indeed, Tom relating what had happened to him, and Tom's sister relating what had happened to her, and both finding a great deal more to say than time to say it in: for they had only just begun to talk, in comparison with what they had to tell each other, when they reached their journey's end.

"Now," said Tom, "we must first look out for some very unpretending streets, and then look out for bills in the windows."

So they walked off again, quite as happily as if they had just stepped out of a snug little house of their own, to look for lodgings on account of somebody else. Tom's simplicity was unabated, Heaven knows; but now that he had somebody to rely upon him, he was stimulated to rely a little more upon himself, and was, in his own opinion, quite a desperate fellow.

After roaming up and down for hours, looking at some scores of lodgings, they began to find it rather fatiguing, especially as they saw none which were at all adapted to their purpose. At length, however, in a singular little old-fashioned house, up a blind street, they discovered two small bed-rooms and a triangular parlour, which promised to suit them well enough. Their desiring to take possession immediately was a suspicious circumstance, but even this was surmounted by the payment of their first week's rent, and a reference to John Westlock, Esquire, Furnival's Inn, High Holborn.

Ah! It was a goodly sight, when this important point was settled, to behold Tom and his sister trotting round to the baker's, and the butcher's, and the grocer's, with a kind of dreadful delight in the unaccustomed cares of housekeeping; taking secret counsel together as they gave their small orders, and distracted by the least suggestion on the part of the shopkeeper! When they got back to the triangular parlour, and Tom's sister, bustling to and fro, busy about a thousand pleasant nothings, stopped every now and then to give old Tom a kiss, or smile upon him, Tom rubbed his hands as if all Islington were his.

It was late in the afternoon now, though, and high time for Tom to keep his appointment. So, after agreeing with his sister that in consideration of not having dined, they would venture on the extravagance of chops for supper, at nine, he walked out again to narrate these marvellous occurrences to John.

"I am quite a family man all at once," thought Tom. "If I can only get something to do, how comfortable Ruth and I may be! Ah, that if! But it's of no use to despond. I can but do that, when I have tried everything and failed; and even then it won't serve me much. Upon my word," thought Tom, quickening his pace, "I don't know what John will think has become of me. He'll begin to be afraid I have strayed into one of those streets where the countrymen are murdered; and that I have been made meat pies of, or some such horrible thing."

CHAPTER XXXVII

TOM PINCH, GOING ASTRAY, FINDS THAT HE IS NOT THE ONLY PERSON IN THAT PREDICAMENT. HE RETALIATES UPON A FALLEN FOE

TOM's evil genius did not lead him into the dens of any of those preparers of cannibalic pastry, who are represented in many standard country legends, as doing a lively retail business in the Metropolis; nor did it mark him out as the prey of ring-droppers, pea and thimble-riggers, duffers, touters, or any of those bloodless sharpers, who are, perhaps, a little better known to the Police. He fell into conversation with no gentleman, who took him into a public-house, where there happened to be another gentleman, who swore he had more money than any gentleman, and very soon proved he had more money than one gentleman, by taking his away from him : neither did he fall into any other of the numerous man-traps which are set up, without notice, in the public grounds of this city. But he lost his way. He very soon did that; and in trying to find it again, he lost it more and more.

Now, Tom, in his guileless distrust of London, thought himself very knowing in coming to the determination that he would not ask to be directed to Furnival's Inn, if he could help it; unless, indeed, he should happen to find himself near the Mint, or the Bank of England; in which case, he would step in, and ask a civil question or two, confiding in the perfect respectability of the concern. So on he went, looking

194

up all the streets he came near, and going up half of them; and thus, by dint of not being true to Goswell Street, and filing off into Aldermanbury, and bewildering himself in Barbican, and being constant to the wrong point of the compass in London Wall, and then getting himself crosswise into Thames Street, by an instinct that would have been marvellous if he had had the least desire or reason to go there, he found himself, at last, hard by the Monument.

The Man in the Monument was quite as mysterious a being to Tom as the Man in the Moon. It immediately occurred to him that the lonely creature who held himself aloof from all mankind in that pillar like some old hermit, was the very man of whom to ask his way. Cold, he might be; little sympathy he had, perhaps, with human passion—the column seemed too tall for that; but if Truth didn't live in the base of the Monument, notwithstanding Pope's couplet about the outside of it, where in London (thought Tom) was she likely to be found!

Coming close below the pillar, it was a great encouragement to Tom to find that the Man in the Monument had simple tastes; that stony and artificial as his residence was, he still preserved some rustic recollections; that he liked plants, hung up bird-cages, was not wholly cut off from fresh groundsel, and kept young trees in tubs. The Man in the Monument, himself, was sitting outside the door—his own door: the Monument-door: what a grand idea!—and was actually yawning, as if there were no Monument to stop his mouth, and give him a perpetual interest in his own existence.

Tom was advancing towards this remarkable creature, to inquire the way to Furnival's Inn, when two people came to see the Monument. They were a gentleman and a lady; and the gentleman said, "How much a-piece?"

The Man in the Monument replied, "A Tanner."

It seemed a low expression, compared with the Monument.

The gentleman put a shilling into his hand, and the Man in the Monument opened a dark little door. When the gentleman and lady had passed out of view, he shut it again, and came slowly back to his chair.

He sat down and laughed.

"They don't know what a many steps there is!" he said. "It's worth twice the money to stop here. Oh, my eye!"

The Man in the Monument was a Cynic; a worldly man! Tom couldn't ask his way of *him*. He was prepared to put no confidence in anything he said.

"My Gracious!" cried a well-known voice behind Mr. Pinch. "Why, to be sure it is!"

At the same time he was poked in the back by a parasol. Turning round to inquire into this salute, he beheld the eldest daughter of his late patron.

"Miss Pecksniff!" said Tom.

"Why, my goodness, Mr. Pinch!" cried Cherry. "What are you doing here?"

"I have rather wandered from my way," said Tom. "I—"

"I hope you have run away," said Charity. "It would be quite spirited and proper if you had, when my Papa so far forgets himself."

"I have left him," returned Tom. "But it was perfectly understood on both sides. It was not done clandestinely."

"Is he married?" asked Cherry, with a spasmodic shake of her chin.

"No, not yet," said Tom, colouring: "to tell you the truth, I don't think he is likely to be, if—if Miss Graham is the object of his passion."

"Tcha, Mr. Pinch!" cried Charity, with sharp impatience, "you're very easily deceived. You don't know the arts of which such a creature is capable. Oh! it's a wicked world."

"You are not married?" Tom hinted, to divert the conversation.

"N—no!" said Cherry, tracing out one particular paving stone in Monument Yard with the end of her parasol. "I— but really it's quite impossible to explain. Won't you walk in?"

"You live here, then?" said Tom.

"Yes," returned Miss Pecksniff, pointing with her parasol to Todgers's: "I reside with this lady, *at present.*"

The great stress on the two last words suggested to Tom that he was expected to say something in reference to them. So he said:

"Only at present! Are you going home again, soon?"

"No, Mr. Pinch," returned Charity. "No, thank you. No! A mother-in-law who is younger than—I mean to say, who is as nearly as possible about the same age as one's self, would not quite suit my spirit. Not quite!" said Cherry, with a spiteful shiver.

"I thought from your saying at present"—Tom observed.

"Really upon my word! I had no idea you would press me so very closely on the subject, Mr. Pinch," said Charity, blushing, "or I should not have been so foolish as to allude to—Oh really!—won't you walk in?"

Tom mentioned, to excuse himself, that he had an appointment in Furnival's Inn, and that coming from Islington he had taken a few wrong turnings, and arrived at the Monument instead. Miss Pecksniff simpered very much when he asked her if she knew the way to Furnival's Inn, and at length found courage to reply:

"A gentleman who is a friend of mine, or at least who is not exactly a friend so much as a sort of acquaintance—Oh, upon my word, I hardly know what I say, Mr. Pinch; you mustn't suppose there is any engagement between us; or at least if there is, that it is at all a settled thing as yet—is going to Furnival's Inn immediately, I believe upon a little business, and I am sure he would be very glad to accompany you, so as to prevent your going wrong again. You had better walk in. You will very likely find my sister Merry here," she said, with a curious toss of her head, and anything but an agreeable smile.

"Then, I think, I'll endeavour to find my way alone," said Tom: "for I fear she would not be very glad to see me.

That unfortunate occurrence, in relation to which you and I had some amicable words together, in private, is not likely to have impressed her with any friendly feeling towards me. Though it really was not my fault."

"She has never heard of that, you may depend," said Cherry, gathering up the corners of her mouth, and nodding at Tom. "I am far from sure that she would bear you any mighty ill will for it, if she had."

"You don't say so?" cried Tom, who was really concerned by this insinuation.

"I say nothing," said Charity. "If I had not already known what shocking things treachery and deceit are in themselves, Mr. Pinch, I might perhaps have learnt it from the success they meet with — from the success they meet with." Here she smiled as before. "But I don't say anything. On the contrary, I should scorn it. You had better walk in!"

There was something hidden here, which piqued Tom's interest and troubled his tender heart. When, in a moment's irresolution, he looked at Charity, he could not but observe a struggle in her face between a sense of triumph and a sense of shame; nor could he but remark how, meeting even his eyes, which she cared so little for, she turned away her own, for all the splenetic defiance in her manner.

An uneasy thought entered Tom's head; a shadowy misgiving that the altered relations between himself and Pecksniff, were somehow to involve an altered knowledge on his part of other people, and were to give him an insight into much of which he had had no previous suspicion. And yet he put no definite construction upon Charity's proceedings. He certainly had no idea that as he had been the audience and spectator of her mortification, she grasped with eager delight at any opportunity of reproaching her sister with his presence in *her* far deeper misery; for he knew nothing of it, and only pictured that sister as the same giddy, careless, trivial creature she always had been, with the same slight estimation of himself which she had never been at the least pains to conceal. In short, he had merely a confused impression that Miss Pecksniff was not quite sisterly or kind; and being curious to set it right, accompanied her, as she desired.

The house-door being opened, she went in before Tom, requesting him to follow her; and led the way to the parlour door.

"Oh, Merry!" she said, looking in, "I am so glad you have not gone home. Who do you think I have met in the street, and brought to see you! Mr. Pinch! There. Now you *are* surprised, I am sure!"

Not more surprised than Tom was, when he looked upon her. Not so much. Not half so much.

"Mr. Pinch has left Papa, my dear," said Cherry, "and his prospects are quite flourishing. I have promised that Augustus, who is going that way, shall escort him to the place he wants. Augustus, my child, where are you?"

With these words Miss Pecksniff screamed her way out of the parlour, calling on Augustus Moddle to appear; and left Tom Pinch alone with her sister.

If she had always been his kindest friend; if she had treated him through all his servitude with such consideration as was never yet received by struggling man; if she had lightened every moment of those many years, and had ever spared and never wounded him; his honest heart could not have swelled before her with a deeper pity, or a purer freedom from all base remembrance than it did then.

"My gracious me! You are really the last person in the world I should have thought of seeing, I am sure!"

Tom was sorry to hear her speaking in her old manner. He had not expected that. Yet he did not feel it a contradiction that he should be sorry to see her so unlike her old self, and sorry at the same time to hear her speaking in her old manner. The two things seemed quite natural.

"I wonder you find any gratification in coming to see me. I can't think what put it in your head. I never had much in seeing you. There was no love lost between us, Mr. Pinch, at any time, I think."

Her bonnet lay beside her on the sofa, and she was very busy with the ribbons as she spoke. Much too busy to be conscious of the work her fingers did.

"We never quarrelled," said Tom.—Tom was right in that, for one person can no more quarrel without an adversary, than one person can play at chess, or fight a duel. "I hoped you would be glad to shake hands with an old friend. Don't let us rake up byegones," said Tom. "If I ever offended you, forgive me."

She looked at him for a moment; dropped her bonnet from her hands; spread them before her altered face and burst into tears.

"Oh, Mr. Pinch!" she said, "although I never used you well, I did believe your nature was forgiving. I did not think you could be cruel."

She spoke as little like her old self now, for certain, as Tom could possibly have wished. But she seemed to be appealing to him reproachfully, and he did not understand her.

"I seldom showed it—never—I know that. But I had that belief in you, that if I had been asked to name the person in the world least likely to retort upon me, I would have named you, confidently."

"Would have named me!" Tom repeated.

"Yes," she said with energy, "and I have often thought so."

After a moment's reflection, Tom sat himself upon a chair beside her.

"Do you believe," said Tom, "oh, can you think, that what I said just now, I said with any but the true and plain intention which my words professed? I mean it, in the spirit and the letter. If I ever offended you, forgive me; I may have done so, many times. You never injured or offended me. How, then, could I possibly retort, if even I were stern and bad enough to wish to do it!"

After a little while she thanked him, through her tears and

sobs, and told him she had never been at once so sorry and so comforted, since she left home. Still she wept bitterly; and it was the greater pain to Tom to see her weeping, from her standing in especial need, just then, of sympathy and tenderness.

"Come, come!" said Tom, "you used to be as cheerful as the day was long."

"Ah! used!" she cried, in such a tone as rent Tom's heart.

"And will be again," said Tom.

"No, never more. No, never, never more. If you should talk with old Mr. Chuzzlewit, at any time," she added, looking hurriedly into his face—"I sometimes thought he liked you, but suppressed it—will you promise me to tell him that you saw me here, and that I said I bore in mind the time we talked together in the churchyard?"

Tom promised that he would.

"Many times since then, when I have wished I had been carried there before that day, I have recalled his words. I wish that he should know how true they were, although the least acknowledgment to that effect has never passed my lips, and never will."

Tom promised this, conditionally, too. He did not tell her how improbable it was that he and the old man would ever meet again, because he thought it might disturb her more.

"If he should ever know this, through your means, dear Mr. Pinch," said Mercy, "tell him that I sent the message, not for myself, but that he might be more forbearing and more patient, and more trustful to some other person, in some other time of need. Tell him that if he could know how my heart trembled in the balance that day, and what a very little would have turned the scale, his own would bleed with pity for me."

"Yes, yes," said Tom, "I will."

"When I appeared to him the most unworthy of his help, I was—I know I was, for I have often, often, thought about it since—the most inclined to yield to what he showed me.

Oh! if he had relented but a little more; if he had thrown himself in my way for but one other quarter of an hour; if he had extended his compassion for a vain, unthinking, miserable girl, in but the least degree; he might, and I believe he would, have saved her! Tell him that I don't blame him, but am grateful for the effort that he made; but ask him for the love of God, and youth, and in merciful consideration for the struggle which an ill-advised and unawakened nature makes to hide the strength it thinks its weakness—ask him never, never, to forget this, when he deals with one again!"

Although Tom did not hold the clue to her full meaning, he could guess it pretty nearly. Touched to the quick, he took her hand and said, or meant to say, some words of consolation. She felt and understood them, whether they were spoken or no. He was not quite certain, afterwards, but that she had tried to kneel down at his feet, and bless him.

He found that he was not alone in the room when she had left it. Mrs. Todgers was there, shaking her head. Tom had never seen Mrs. Todgers, it is needless to say, but he had a perception of her being the lady of the house; and he saw some genuine compassion in her eyes, that won his good opinion.

"Ah, sir! You are an old friend, I see," said Mrs. Todgers.

"Yes," said Tom.

"And yet," quoth Mrs. Todgers, shutting the door softly, "she hasn't told you what her troubles are, I'm certain."

Tom was struck by these words, for they were quite true. "Indeed," he said, "she has not."

"And never would," said Mrs. Todgers, "if you saw her daily. She never makes the least complaint to me, or utters a single word of explanation or reproach. But I know," said Mrs. Todgers, drawing in her breath, "*I* know!"

Tom nodded sorrowfully, "so do I."

"I fully believe," said Mrs. Todgers, taking her pocket-handkerchief from the flat reticule, "that nobody can tell one half of what that poor young creature has to undergo. But though she comes here, constantly, to ease her poor full heart without his knowing it; and saying, 'Mrs. Todgers, I am very low to-day; I think that I shall soon be dead,' sits crying in my room until the fit is past; I know no more from her. And, I believe," said Mrs. Todgers, putting back her handkerchief again, "that she considers me a good friend too."

Mrs. Todgers might have said her best friend. Commercial gentlemen and gravy had tried Mrs. Todgers's temper; the main chance — it was such a very small one in her case, that she might have been excused for looking sharp after it, lest it should entirely vanish from her sight—had taken a firm hold on Mrs. Todgers's attention. But in some odd nook in Mrs. Todgers's breast, up a great many steps, and in a corner easy to be overlooked, there was a secret door, with "Woman" written on the spring, which, at a touch from Mercy's hand, had flown wide open, and admitted her for shelter.

When boarding-house accounts are balanced with all other ledgers, and the books of the Recording Angel are made up for ever, perhaps there may be seen an entry to thy credit, lean Mrs. Todgers, which shall make thee beautiful!

She was growing beautiful so rapidly in Tom's eyes; for he saw that she was poor, and that this good had sprung up in her from among the sordid strivings of her life; that she might have been a very Venus in a minute more, if Miss Pecksniff had not entered with her friend.

"Mr. Thomas Pinch!" said Charity, performing the ceremony of introduction with evident pride. "Mr. Moddle. Where's my sister?"

"Gone, Miss Pecksniff," Mrs. Todgers answered. "She had appointed to be home."

"Ah!" said Charity, looking at Tom. "Oh, dear me!"

"She's greatly altered since she's been Anoth—since she's been married, Mrs. Todgers!" observed Moddle.

"My dear Augustus!" said Miss Pecksniff, in a low voice, "I verily believe you have said that fifty thousand times, in my hearing. What a Prose you are!"

This was succeeded by some trifling love passages, which appeared to originate with, if not to be wholly carried on by Miss Pecksniff. At any rate, Mr. Moddle was much slower in his responses than is customary with young lovers, and exhibited a lowness of spirits which was quite oppressive.

He did not improve at all when Tom and he were in the streets, but sighed so dismally that it was dreadful to hear him. As a means of cheering him up, Tom told him that he wished him joy.

"Joy!" cried Moddle. "Ha, ha!"

"What an extraordinary young man!" thought Tom.

"The Scorner has not set his seal upon you. *You* care what becomes of you?" said Moddle.

Tom admitted that it was a subject in which he certainly felt some interest.

"I don't," said Mr. Moddle. "The Elements may have me when they please. I'm ready."

Tom inferred from these, and other expressions of the same nature, that he was jealous. Therefore he allowed him to take his own course; which was such a gloomy one, that he felt a load removed from his mind when they parted company at the gate of Furnival's Inn.

It was now a couple of hours past John Westlock's dinner-time; and he was walking up and down the room, quite anxious for Tom's safety. The table was spread; the wine was carefully decanted; and the dinner smelt delicious.

"Why, Tom, old boy, where on earth have you been? Your box is here. Get your boots off instantly, and sit down!"

"I am sorry to say I can't stay, John," replied Tom Pinch, who was breathless with the haste he had made in running up the stairs.

"Can't stay!"

"If you'll go on with your dinner," said Tom, "I'll tell you my reason the while. I mustn't eat myself, or I shall have no appetite for the chops."

"There are no chops here, my good fellow."

"No. But there are at Islington," said Tom.

John Westlock was perfectly confounded by this reply, and vowed he would not touch a morsel until Tom had explained himself fully. So Tom sat down, and told him all; to which he listened with the greatest interest.

He knew Tom too well, and respected his delicacy too much, to ask him why he had taken these measures without communicating with him first. He quite concurred in the expediency of Tom's immediately returning to his sister, as he knew so little of the place in which he had left her; and good-humouredly proposed to ride back with him in a cab, in which he might convey his box. Tom's proposition that he should sup with them that night, he flatly rejected, but made an appointment with him for the morrow. "And now, Tom," he said, as they rode along, "I have a question to ask you, to which I expect a manly and straightforward answer. Do you want any money? I am pretty sure you do."

"I don't indeed," said Tom.

"I believe you are deceiving me."

"No. With many thanks to you, I am quite in earnest," Tom replied. "My sister has some money, and so have I. If I had nothing else, John, I have a five-pound note, which that good creature, Mrs. Lupin, of the Dragon, handed up to me outside the coach, in a letter, begging me to borrow it; and then drove off as hard as she could go."

"And a blessing on every dimple in her handsome face, say I!" cried John, "though why you should give her the preference over me, I don't know. Never mind. I bide my time, Tom."

"And I hope you'll continue to bide it," returned Tom, gaily. "For I owe you more, already, in a hundred other ways, than I can ever hope to pay."

They parted at the door of Tom's new residence. John Westlock, sitting in the cab, and, catching a glimpse of a blooming little busy creature darting out to kiss Tom and to help him with his box, would not have had the least objection to change places with him.

Well! she *was* a cheerful little thing; and had a quaint, bright quietness about her, that was infinitely pleasant. Surely she was the best sauce for chops ever invented. The potatoes seemed to take a pleasure in sending up their grateful steam before her; the froth upon the pint of porter pouted to attract her notice. But it was all in vain. She saw nothing but Tom. Tom was the first and last thing in the world.

As she sat opposite to Tom at supper, fingering one of Tom's pet tunes upon the table-cloth, and smiling in his face, he had never been so happy in his life.

CHAPTER XXXVIII

In walking from the City with his sentimental friend, Tom Pinch had looked into the face, and brushed against the threadbare sleeve, of Mr. Nadgett, man of mystery to the Anglo-Bengalee Disinterested Loan and Life Assurance Company. Mr. Nadgett naturally passed away from Tom's remembrance as he passed out of his view; for he didn't know him, and had never heard his name.

As there are a vast number of people in the huge metropolis of England who rise up every morning not knowing where their heads will rest at night, so there are a multitude who shooting arrows over houses as their daily business, never know on whom they fall. Mr. Nadgett might have passed Tom Pinch ten thousand times; might even have been quite familiar with his face, his name, pursuits, and character; yet never once have dreamed that Tom had any interest in any act or mystery of his. Tom might have done the like by him, of course. But the same private man out of all the men alive, was in the mind of each at the same moment; was prominently connected, though in a different manner, with the day's adventures of both; and formed, when they passed each other in the street, the one absorbing topic of their thoughts.

Why Tom had Jonas Chuzzlewit in his mind requires no explanation. Why Mr. Nadgett should have had Jonas Chuzzlewit in his, is quite another thing.

207

But, somehow or other, that amiable and worthy orphan had become a part of the mystery of Mr. Nadgett's existence. Mr. Nadgett took an interest in his lightest proceedings; and it never flagged or wavered. He watched him in and out of the Assurance Office, where he was now formally installed as a Director; he dogged his footsteps in the streets; he stood listening when he talked; he sat in coffee-rooms entering his name in the great pocket-book, over and over again; he wrote letters to himself about him constantly; and, when he found them in his pocket, put them in the fire, with such distrust and caution that he would bend down to watch the crumpled tinder while it floated upward, as if his mind misgave him, that the mystery it had contained might come out at the chimney-pot.

And yet all this was quite a secret. Mr. Nadgett kept it to himself, and kept it close. Jonas had no more idea that Mr. Nadgett's eyes were fixed on him, than he had that he was living under the daily inspection and report of a whole order of Jesuits. Indeed Mr. Nadgett's eyes were seldom fixed on any other objects than the ground, the clock, or the fire; but every button on his coat might have been an eye: he saw so much.

The secret manner of the man disarmed suspicion in this wise; suggesting, not that he was watching any one, but that he thought some other man was watching him. He went about so stealthily, and kept himself so wrapped up in himself, that the whole object of his life appeared to be, to avoid notice and preserve his own mystery. Jonas sometimes saw him in the street, hovering in the outer office, waiting at the door for the man who never came, or slinking off with his immoveable face and drooping head, and the one beaver glove dangling before him; but he would as soon have thought of the cross upon the top of St. Paul's Cathedral taking note of what he did, or slowly winding a great net about his feet, as of Nadgett's being engaged in such an occupation.

Mr. Nadgett made a mysterious change about this time

in his mysterious life: for whereas he had, until now, been first seen every morning coming down Cornhill, so exactly like the Nadgett of the day before as to occasion a popular belief that he never went to bed or took his clothes off, he was now first seen in Holborn, coming out of Kingsgate Street; and it was soon discovered that he actually went every morning to a barber's shop in that street to get shaved; and that the barber's name was Sweedlepipe. He seemed to make appointments with the man who never came, to meet him at this barber's; for he would frequently take long spells of waiting in the shop, and would ask for pen and ink, and pull out his pocket-book, and be very busy over it for an hour at a time. Mrs. Gamp and Mr. Sweedlepipe had many deep discoursings on the subject of this mysterious customer; but they usually agreed that he had speculated too much and was keeping out of the way.

He must have appointed the man who never kept his word, to meet him at another new place too; for one day he was found, for the first time, by the waiter at the Mourning Coach-Horse, the House-of-call for Undertakers, down in the City there, making figures with a pipe-stem in the sawdust of a clean spittoon; and declining to call for anything, on the ground of expecting a gentleman presently. As the gentleman was not honourable enough to keep his engagement, he came again next day, with his pocket-book in such a state of distention that he was regarded in the bar as a man of large property. After that, he repeated his visits every day, and had so much writing to do, that he made nothing of emptying a capacious leaden inkstand in two sittings. Although he never talked much, still, by being there among the regular customers, he made their acquaintance; and in course of time became quite intimate with Mr. Tacker, Mr. Mould's foreman; and even with Mr. Mould himself, who openly said he was a long-headed man, a dry one, a salt fish, a deep file, a rasper; and made him the subject of many other flattering encomiums.

At the same time, too, he told the people at the Assurance

Office, in his own mysterious way, that there was something wrong (secretly wrong, of course) in his liver, and that he feared he must put himself under the doctor's hands. He was delivered over to Jobling upon this representation; and though Jobling could not find out where his liver was wrong, wrong Mr. Nadgett said it was; observing that it was his own liver, and he hoped he ought to know. Accordingly, he became Mr. Jobling's patient; and detailing his symptoms in his slow and secret way, was in and out of that gentleman's room a dozen times a-day.

As he pursued all these occupations at once; and all steadily; and all secretly; and never slackened in his watchfulness of everything that Mr. Jonas said and did, and left unsaid and undone; it is not improbable that they were, secretly, essential parts of some great scheme which Mr. Nadgett had on foot.

It was on the morning of this very day on which so much had happened to Tom Pinch, that Nadgett suddenly appeared before Mr. Montague's house in Pall Mall—he always made his appearance as if he had that moment come up a trap —when the clocks were striking nine. He rang the bell in a covert under-handed way, as though it were a treasonable act; and passed in at the door, the moment it was opened wide enough to receive his body. That done, he shut it immediately, with his own hands.

Mr. Bailey, taking up his name without delay, returned with a request that he would follow him into his master's chamber. The chairman of the Anglo-Bengalee Disinterested Loan and Life Assurance Board was dressing, and received him as a business person who was often backwards and forwards, and was received at all times for his business' sake.

" Well, Mr. Nadgett ? "

Mr. Nadgett put his hat upon the ground and coughed. The boy having withdrawn and shut the door, he went to it softly, examined the handle, and returned to within a pace or two of the chair in which Mr. Montague sat.

" Any news, Mr. Nadgett ? "

"I think we have some news at last, sir."

"I am happy to hear it. I began to fear you were off the scent, Mr. Nadgett."

"No, sir. It grows cold occasionally. It will sometimes. We can't help that."

"You are truth itself, Mr. Nadgett. Do you report a great success?"

"That depends upon your judgment and construction of it," was his answer, as he put on his spectacles.

"What do you think of it yourself? Have you pleased yourself?"

Mr. Nadgett rubbed his hands slowly, stroked his chin, looked round the room, and said, "Yes, yes, I think it's a good case. I am disposed to think it's a good case. Will you go into it at once?"

"By all means."

Mr. Nadgett picked out a certain chair from among the rest, and having planted it in a particular spot, as carefully as if he had been going to vault over it, placed another chair in front of it: leaving room for his own legs between them. He then sat down in chair number two, and laid his pocket-book, very carefully, on chair number one. He then untied the pocket-book, and hung the string over the back of chair number one. He then drew both the chairs a little nearer Mr. Montague, and opening the pocket-book spread out its contents. Finally he selected a certain memorandum from the rest, and held it out to his employer, who, during the whole of these preliminary ceremonies, had been making violent efforts to conceal his impatience.

"I wish you wouldn't be so fond of making notes, my excellent friend," said Tigg Montague with a ghastly smile. "I wish you would consent to give me their purport by word of mouth."

"I don't like word of mouth," said Mr. Nadgett gravely. "We never know who's listening."

Mr. Montague was going to retort, when Nadgett handed

him the paper, and said, with quiet exultation in his tone, "We'll begin at the beginning, and take that one first, if you please, sir."

The chairman cast his eyes upon it, coldly, and with a smile which did not render any great homage to the slow and methodical habits of his spy. But he had not read half-a-dozen lines when the expression of his face began to change, and before he had finished the perusal of the paper, it was full of grave and serious attention.

"Number Two," said Mr. Nadgett, handing him another, and receiving back the first. "Read Number Two, sir, if you please. There is more interest as you go on."

Tigg Montague leaned backward in his chair, and cast upon his emissary such a look of vacant wonder (not unmingled with alarm), that Mr. Nadgett considered it necessary to repeat the request he had already twice preferred: with the view of recalling his attention to the point in hand. Profiting by the hint, Mr. Montague went on with Number Two, and afterwards with Numbers Three, and Four, and Five, and so on.

These documents were all in Mr. Nadgett's writing, and were apparently a series of memoranda, jotted down from time to time upon the backs of old letters, or any scrap of paper that came first to hand. Loose straggling scrawls they were, and of very uninviting exterior; but they had weighty purpose in them, if the chairman's face were any index to the character of their contents.

The progress of Mr. Nadgett's secret satisfaction arising out of the effect they made, kept pace with the emotions of the reader. At first, Mr. Nadgett sat with his spectacles low down upon his nose, looking over them at his employer, and nervously rubbing his hands. After a little while, he changed his posture in his chair for one of greater ease, and leisurely perused the next document he held ready, as if an occasional glance at his employer's face were now enough, and all occasion for anxiety or doubt were gone. And finally he rose and looked out of the window, where he stood with a triumphant air, until Tigg Montague had finished.

"And this is the last, Mr. Nadgett!" said that gentleman, drawing a long breath.

"That, sir, is the last."

"You are a wonderful man, Mr. Nadgett!"

"I think it is a pretty good case," he returned as he gathered up his papers. "It cost some trouble, sir."

"The trouble shall be well rewarded, Mr. Nadgett." Nadgett bowed. "There is a deeper impression of Somebody's Hoof here, than I had expected, Mr. Nadgett. I may congratulate myself upon your being such a good hand at a secret."

"Oh! nothing has an interest to me that's not a secret," replied Nadgett, as he tied the string about his pocket-book, and put it up. "It almost takes away any pleasure I may have had in this inquiry even to make it known to you."

"A most invaluable constitution," Tigg retorted. "A great gift for a gentleman employed as you are, Mr. Nadgett. Much better than discretion: though you possess that quality also in an eminent degree. I think I heard a double knock. Will you put your head out of window, and tell me whether there is anybody at the door?"

Mr. Nadgett softly raised the sash, and peered out from the very corner, as a man might· who was looking down into a street from whence a brisk discharge of musketry might be expected at any moment. Drawing in his head with equal caution, he observed, not altering his voice or manner:

"Mr. Jonas Chuzzlewit!"

"I thought so," Tigg retorted.

"Shall I go?"

"I think you had better. Stay though! No! remain here, Mr. Nadgett, if you please."

It was remarkable how pale and flurried he had become in an instant. There was nothing to account for it. His eye had fallen on his razors; but what of them!

Mr. Chuzzlewit was announced.

"Show him up directly, Nadgett! Don't you leave us alone together. Mind you don't, now! By the Lord!" he added in a whisper to himself: "We don't know what may happen."

Saying this, he hurriedly took up a couple of hair-brushes, and began to exercise them on his own head, as if his toilet had not been interrupted. Mr. Nadgett withdrew to the stove, in which there was a small fire for the convenience of heating curling-irons; and taking advantage of so favourable an opportunity for drying his pocket-handkerchief, produced it without loss of time. There he stood, during the whole interview, holding it before the bars, and sometimes, but not often, glancing over his shoulder.

"My dear Chuzzlewit!" cried Montague, as Jonas entered: "you rise with the lark. Though you go to bed with the nightingale, you rise with the lark. You have superhuman energy, my dear Chuzzlewit!"

"Ecod!" said Jonas, with an air of languor and ill-humour, as he took a chair, "I should be very glad not to get up with the lark, if I could help it. But I am a light sleeper; and it's better to be up, than lying awake, counting the dismal old church-clocks, in bed."

"A light sleeper!" cried his friend. "Now, what is a light sleeper? I often hear the expression, but upon my life I have not the least conception what a light sleeper is."

"Hallo!" said Jonas, "Who's that? Oh, old what's-his-name: looking (as usual) as if he wanted to skulk up the chimney."

"Ha, ha! I have no doubt he does."

"Wéll! He's not wanted here, I suppose," said Jonas. "He may go, mayn't he?"

"Oh, let him stay, let him stay!" said Tigg. "He's a mere piece of furniture. He has been making his report, and is waiting for further orders. He has been told," said Tigg, raising his voice, "not to lose sight of certain friends of ours, or to think that he has done with them by any means. He understands his business."

"He need," replied Jonas; "for of all the precious old dummies in appearance that ever I saw, he's about the worst. He's afraid of me, I think."

"It's my belief," said Tigg, "that you are Poison to him. Nadgett! give me that towel!"

He had as little occasion for a towel as Jonas had for a start. But Nadgett brought it quickly; and, having lingered for a moment, fell back upon his old post by the fire.

"You see, my dear fellow," resumed Tigg, "you are too—— What's the matter with your lips? How white they are!"

"I took some vinegar just now," said Jonas. "I had oysters for my breakfast. Where are they white?" he added, muttering an oath, and rubbing them upon his handkerchief. "I don't believe they *are* white."

"Now I look again, they are not," replied his friend. "They are coming right again."

"Say what you were going to say," cried Jonas angrily, "and let my face be! As long as I can show my teeth when I want to (and I can do that pretty well), the colour of my lips is not material."

"Quite true," said Tigg. "I was only going to say that you are too quick and active for our friend. He is too shy to cope with such a man as you, but does his duty well. Oh, very well! But what is a light sleeper?"

"Hang a light sleeper!" exclaimed Jonas pettishly.

"No, no," interrupted Tigg. "No. We'll not do that."

"A light sleeper ain't a heavy one," said Jonas in his sulky way; "don't sleep much, and don't sleep well, and don't sleep sound."

"And dreams," said Tigg, "and cries out in an ugly manner; and when the candle burns down in the night, is in an agony; and all that sort of thing. I see!"

They were silent for a little time. Then Jonas spoke:

"Now we've done with child's talk, I want to have a word

with you. I want to have a word with you before we meet up yonder to-day. I am not satisfied with the state of affairs."

"Not satisfied!" cried Tigg. "The money comes in well."

"The money comes in well enough," retorted Jonas: "but it don't come out well enough. It can't be got at, easily enough. I haven't sufficient power; it is all in your hands. Ecod! what with one of your bye-laws, and another of your bye-laws, and your votes in this capacity, and your votes in that capacity, and your official rights, and your individual rights, and other people's rights who are only you again, there are no rights left for me. Everybody else's rights are my wrongs. What's the use of my having a voice if it's always drowned? I might as well be dumb, and it would be much less aggravating. I'm not agoing to stand that, you know."

"No!" said Tigg in an insinuating tone.

"No!" returned Jonas, "I'm not indeed. I'll play Old Gooseberry with the office, and make you glad to buy me out at a good high figure, if you try any of your tricks with me."

"I give you my honour——," Montague began.

"Oh! confound your honour," interrupted Jonas, who became more coarse and quarrelsome as the other remonstrated, which may have been a part of Mr. Montague's intention: "I want a little more control over the money. You may have all the honour, if you like; I'll never bring you to book for that. But I'm not agoing to stand it, as it is now. If you should take it into your honourable head to go abroad with the bank, I don't see much to prevent you. Well! That won't do. I've had some very good dinners here, but they'd come too dear on such terms: and therefore, that won't do."

"I am unfortunate to find you in this humour," said Tigg, with a remarkable kind of smile: "for I was going to propose to you—for your own advantage; solely for your own advantage—that you should venture a little more with us."

Mr. Nadgett breathes, as usual, an Atmosphere of Mystery

"Was you, by G—?" said Jonas, with a short laugh.

"Yes. And to suggest," pursued Montague, "that surely you have friends; indeed, I know you have; who would answer our purpose admirably, and whom we should be delighted to receive."

"How kind of you! You'd be delighted to receive 'em, would you?" said Jonas, bantering.

"I give you my sacred honour, quite transported. As your friends, observe!"

"Exactly," said Jonas; "as my friends, of course. You'll be very much delighted when you get 'em, I have no doubt. And it'll be all to my advantage, won't it?"

"It will be very much to your advantage," answered Montague, poising a brush in each hand, and looking steadily upon him. "It will be very much to your advantage, I assure you."

"And you can tell me how," said Jonas, "can't you?"

"SHALL I tell you how?" returned the other.

"I think you had better," said Jonas. "Strange things have been done in the Assurance way before now, by strange sorts of men, and I mean to take care of myself."

"Chuzzlewit!" replied Montague, leaning forward, with his arms upon his knees, and looking full into his face. "Strange things have been done, and are done every day; not only in our way, but in a variety of other ways; and no one suspects them. But ours, as you say, my good friend, is a strange way; and we strangely happen, sometimes, to come into the knowledge of very strange events."

He beckoned to Jonas to bring his chair nearer; and looking slightly round, as if to remind him of the presence of Nadgett, whispered in his ear.

From red to white; from white to red again; from red to yellow; then to a cold, dull, awful, sweat-bedabbled blue. In that short whisper, all these changes fell upon the face of Jonas Chuzzlewit; and when at last he laid his hand upon the whisperer's mouth, appalled, lest any syllable of what he said should reach the ears of the third person present, it was as bloodless, and as heavy as the hand of Death.

He drew his chair away, and sat a spectacle of terror, misery, and rage. He was afraid to speak, or look, or move, or sit still. Abject, crouching, and miserable, he was a greater degradation to the form he bore, than if he had been a loathsome wound from head to heel.

His companion leisurely resumed his dressing, and completed it, glancing sometimes with a smile at the transformation he had effected, but never speaking once.

"You'll not object," he said, when he was quite equipped, "to venture further with us, Chuzzlewit, my friend?"

His pale lips faintly stammered out a "No."

"Well said! That's like yourself. Do you know I was thinking yesterday that your father-in-law, relying on your advice as a man of great sagacity in money matters, as no doubt you are, would join us, if the thing were well presented to him. He has money?"

"Yes, he has money."

"Shall I leave Mr. Pecksniff to you? Will you undertake for Mr. Pecksniff?"

"I'll try. I'll do my best."

"A thousand thanks," replied the other, clapping him upon the shoulder. "Shall we walk down stairs? Mr. Nadgett! Follow us, if you please."

They went down in that order. Whatever Jonas felt in reference to Montague; whatever sense he had of being caged, and barred, and trapped, and having fallen down into a pit of deepest ruin; whatever thoughts came crowding on his mind even at that early time, of one terrible chance of escape, of one red glimmer in a sky of blackness; he no more thought that the slinking figure half a dozen stairs behind him was his pursuing Fate, than that the other figure at his side was his Good Angel.

CHAPTER XXXIX

CONTAINING SOME FURTHER PARTICULARS OF THE DOMESTIC
ECONOMY OF THE PINCHES; WITH STRANGE NEWS FROM
THE CITY, NARROWLY CONCERNING TOM

PLEASANT little Ruth! Cheerful, tidy, bustling, quiet little
Ruth! No doll's house ever yielded greater delight to its
young mistress, than little Ruth derived from her glorious
dominion over the triangular parlour and the two small bed-
rooms.

To be Tom's housekeeper. What dignity! Housekeeping,
upon the commonest terms, associated itself with elevated
responsibilities of all sorts and kinds; but housekeeping for
Tom, implied the utmost complication of grave trusts and
mighty charges. Well might she take the keys out of the
little chiffonier which held the tea and sugar; and out of
the two little damp cupboards down by the fire-place, where
the very black beetles got mouldy, and had the shine taken
out of their backs by envious mildew; and jingle them upon
a ring before Tom's eyes when he came down to breakfast!
Well might she, laughing musically, put them up in that
blessed little pocket of hers with a merry pride! For it was
such a grand novelty to be mistress of anything, that if she
had been the most relentless and despotic of all little house-
keepers, she might have pleaded just that much for her excuse,
and have been honourably acquitted.

So far from being despotic, however, there was a coyness

219

about her very way of pouring out the tea, which Tom quite revelled in. And when she asked him what he would like to have for dinner, and faltered out "chops" as a reasonably good suggestion after their last night's successful supper, Tom grew quite facetious and rallied her desperately.

"I don't know, Tom," said his sister, blushing, "I am not quite confident, but I think I could make a beef-steak pudding, if I tried, Tom."

"In the whole catalogue of cookery, there is nothing I should like so much as a beef-steak pudding!" cried Tom: slapping his leg to give the greater force to this reply.

"Yes, dear, that's excellent! But if it should happen not to come quite right the first time," his sister faltered; "if it should happen not to be a pudding exactly, but should turn out a stew, or a soup, or something of that sort, you'll not be vexed, Tom, will you?"

The serious way in which she looked at Tom; the way in which Tom looked at her; and the way in which she gradually broke into a merry laugh at her own expense; would have enchanted you.

"Why," said Tom, "this is capital. It gives us a new, and quite an uncommon interest in the dinner. We put into a lottery for a beef-steak pudding, and it is impossible to say what we may get. We may make some wonderful discovery, perhaps, and produce such a dish as never was known before."

"I shall not be at all surprised if we do, Tom," returned his sister, still laughing merrily, "or if it should prove to be such a dish as we shall not feel very anxious to produce again; but the meat must come out of the saucepan at last, somehow or other, you know. We can't cook it into nothing at all: that's a great comfort. So if you like to venture, *I* will."

"I have not the least doubt," rejoined Tom, "that it will come out an excellent pudding; or at all events, I am sure that I shall think it so. There is naturally something so handy and brisk about you, Ruth, that if you said you could make a bowl of faultless turtle soup, I should believe you."

A BORN HOUSEWIFE

And Tom was right. She was precisely that sort of person. Nobody ought to have been able to resist her coaxing manner; and nobody had any business to try. Yet she never seemed to know it was her manner at all. That was the best of it.

Well! she washed up the breakfast cups, chatting away the whole time, and telling Tom all sorts of anecdotes about the brass-and-copper founder; put everything in its place; made the room as neat as herself;—you must not suppose its shape was half as neat as hers though, or anything like it— and brushed Tom's old hat round and round and round again, until it was as sleek as Mr. Pecksniff. Then she discovered, all in a moment, that Tom's shirt-collar was frayed at the edge; and flying up stairs for a needle and thread, came flying down again with her thimble on, and set it right with wonderful expertness; never once sticking the needle into his face, although she was humming his pet tune from first to last, and beating time with the fingers of her left hand upon his neckcloth. She had no sooner done this, than off she was again; and there she stood once more, as brisk and busy as a bee, tying that compact little chin of hers into an equally compact little bonnet: intent on bustling out to the butcher's, without a minute's loss of time; and inviting Tom to come and see the steak cut, with his own eyes. As to Tom, he was ready to go anywhere; so, off they trotted, arm-in-arm, as nimbly as you please; saying to each other what a quiet street it was to lodge in, and how very cheap, and what an airy situation.

To see the butcher slap the steak, before he laid it on the block, and give his knife a sharpening, was to forget breakfast instantly. It was agreeable, too—it really was—to see him cut it off, so smooth and juicy. There was nothing savage in the act, although the knife was large and keen; it was a piece of art, high art; there was delicacy of touch, clearness of tone, skilful handling of the subject, fine shading. It was the triumph of mind over matter; quite.

Perhaps the greenest cabbage-leaf ever grown in a garden

221

was wrapped about this steak, before it was delivered over to Tom. But the butcher had a sentiment for his business, and knew how to refine upon it. When he saw Tom putting the cabbage-leaf into his pocket awkwardly, he begged to be allowed to do it for him; "for meat," he said with some emotion, "must be humoured, not drove."

Back they went to the lodgings again, after they had bought some eggs, and flour, and such small matters; and Tom sat gravely down to write, at one end of the parlour table, while Ruth prepared to make the pudding, at the other end; for there was nobody in the house but an old woman (the landlord being a mysterious sort of man, who went out early in the morning, and was scarcely ever seen); and saving in mere household drudgery, they waited on themselves.

"What are you writing, Tom?" inquired his sister, laying her hand upon his shoulder.

"Why, you see, my dear," said Tom, leaning back in his chair, and looking up in her face, "I am very anxious of course, to obtain some suitable employment; and before Mr. Westlock comes this afternoon, I think I may as well prepare a little description of myself and my qualifications; such as he could show to any friend of his."

"You had better do the same for me, Tom, also," said his sister, casting down her eyes. "I should dearly like to keep house for you, and take care of you always, Tom; but we are not rich enough for that."

"We are not rich," returned Tom, "certainly; and we may be much poorer. But we will not part, if we can help it. No, no: we will make up our minds, Ruth, that, unless we are so very unfortunate as to render me quite sure that you would be better off away from me than with me, we will battle it out together. I am certain we shall be happier if we can battle it out together. Don't you think we shall?"

"Think, Tom!"

"Oh, tut, tut!" interposed Tom, tenderly. "You mustn't cry."

"No, no; I won't, Tom. But you can't afford it, dear. You can't, indeed."

"We don't know that," said Tom. "How are we to know that, yet awhile, and without trying? Lord bless my soul!" Tom's energy became quite grand. "There is no knowing what may happen, if we try hard. And I am sure we can live contentedly upon a very little—if we can only get it."

"Yes: that I am sure we can, Tom."

"Why, then," said Tom, "we must try for it. My friend, John Westlock, is a capital fellow, and very shrewd and intelligent. I'll take his advice. We'll talk it over with him— both of us together. You'll like John very much, when you come to know him, I am certain. Don't cry, don't cry. *You* make a beef-steak pudding, indeed!" said Tom, giving her a gentle push. "Why, you haven't boldness enough for a dumpling!"

"You *will* call it a pudding, Tom. Mind! I told you not!"

"I may as well call it that, till it proves to be something else," said Tom. "Oh, you are going to work in earnest, are you?"

Aye, aye! That she was. And in such pleasant earnest, moreover, that Tom's attention wandered from his writing every moment. First, she tripped down stairs into the kitchen for the flour, then for the pie-board, then for the eggs, then for the butter, then for a jug of water, then for the rolling-pin, then for a pudding-basin, then for the pepper, then for the salt; making a separate journey for everything, and laughing every time she started off afresh. When all the materials were collected, she was horrified to find she had no apron on, and so ran *up* stairs, by way of variety, to fetch it. She didn't put it on up stairs, but came dancing down with it in her hand; and being one of those little women to whom an apron is a most becoming little vanity, it took an immense time to arrange; having to be carefully smoothed down beneath—Oh, heaven, what a wicked little stomacher!

and to be gathered up into little plaits by the strings before it could be tied, and to be tapped, rebuked, and wheedled, at the pockets, before it would set right, which at last it did, and when it did—but never mind; this is a sober chronicle. And then, there were her cuffs to be tucked up, for fear of flour; and she had a little ring to pull off her finger, which wouldn't come off (foolish little ring!); and during the whole of these preparations she looked demurely every now and then at Tom, from under her dark eye-lashes, as if they were all a part of the pudding and indispensable to its composition.

For the life and soul of him Tom could get no further in his writing than, "A respectable young man, aged thirty-five," and this, notwithstanding the show she made of being super-naturally quiet, and going about on tiptoe, lest she should disturb him: which only served as an additional means of distracting his attention, and keeping it upon her.

"Tom," she said at last, in high glee. "Tom!"

"What now?" said Tom, repeating to himself, "aged thirty-five!"

"Will you look here a moment, please?"

As if he hadn't been looking all the time!

"I am going to begin, Tom. Don't you wonder why I butter the inside of the basin?" said his busy little sister.

"Not more than you do, I dare say," replied Tom, laughing. "For I believe you don't know anything about it."

"What an Infidel you are, Tom! How else do you think it would turn out easily when it was done! For a civil-engineer and land-surveyor not to know that! My goodness, Tom!"

It was wholly out of the question to try to write. Tom lined out "respectable young man, aged thirty-five;" and sat looking on, pen in hand, with one of the most loving smiles imaginable.

Such a busy little woman as she was! So full of self-importance, and trying so hard not to smile, or seem uncertain about anything! It was a perfect treat to Tom to see her with her brows knit, and her rosy lips pursed up, kneading away at the crust, rolling it out, cutting it up into strips, lining the basin with it, shaving it off fine round the rim, chopping up the steak into small pieces, raining down pepper and salt upon them, packing them into the basin, pouring in cold water for gravy, and never venturing to steal a look in his direction, lest her gravity should be disturbed; until, at last, the basin being quite full and only wanting the top crust, she clapped her hands all covered with paste and flour, at Tom, and burst out heartily into such a charming little laugh of triumph, that the pudding need have had no other seasoning to commend it to the taste of any reasonable man on earth.

"Where's the pudding?" said Tom. For he was cutting his jokes, Tom was.

"Where!" she answered, holding it up with both hands. "Look at it!"

"*That* a pudding!" said Tom.

"It will be, you stupid fellow, when it's covered in," returned his sister. Tom still pretending to look incredulous, she gave him a tap on the head with the rolling-pin, and still laughing merrily, had returned to the composition of the top crust, when she started and turned very red. Tom started, too, for following her eyes, he saw John Westlock in the room.

"Why, my goodness, John! How did *you* come in?"

"I beg pardon," said John—"your sister's pardon especially —but I met an old lady at the street door, who requested me to enter here; and as you didn't hear me knock, and the door was open, I made bold to do so. I hardly know," said John, with a smile, "why any of us should be disconcerted at my having accidentally intruded upon such an agreeable domestic occupation, so very agreeably and skilfully pursued; but I must confess that *I* am. Tom, will you kindly come to my relief?"

"Mr. John Westlock," said Tom. "My sister."

"I hope, that as the sister of so old a friend," said John,

laughing, "you will have the goodness to detach your first impressions of me from my unfortunate entrance."

"My sister is not indisposed perhaps to say the same to you on her own behalf," retorted Tom.

John said, of course, that this was quite unnecessary, for he had been transfixed in silent admiration; and he held out his hand to Miss Pinch; who couldn't take it, however, by reason of the flour and paste upon her own. This, which might seem calculated to increase the general confusion and render matters worse, had in reality the best effect in the world, for neither of them could help laughing; and so they both found themselves on easy terms immediately.

"I am delighted to see you," said Tom. "Sit down."

"I can only think of sitting down, on one condition," returned his friend: "and that is, that your sister goes on with the pudding, as if you were still alone."

"That I am sure she will," said Tom. "On one other condition, and that is, that you stay and help us to eat it."

Poor little Ruth was seized with a palpitation of the heart when Tom committed this appalling indiscretion, for she felt that if the dish turned out a failure, she never would be able to hold up her head before John Westlock again. Quite unconscious of her state of mind, John accepted the invitation with all imaginable heartiness; and after a little more pleasantry concerning this same pudding, and the tremendous expectations he made believe to entertain of it, she blushingly resumed her occupation, and he took a chair.

"I am here much earlier than I intended, Tom; but I will tell you what brings me, and I think I can answer for your being glad to hear it. Is that anything you wish to show me?"

"Oh dear no!" cried Tom, who had forgotten the blotted scrap of paper in his hand, until this inquiry brought it to his recollection. "'A respectable young man, aged thirty-five'—The beginning of a description of myself. That's all."

"I don't think you will have occasion to finish it, Tom.

Mr. Pinch and Ruth unconscious of a Visitor

But how is it you never told me you had friends in London ? "

Tom looked at his sister with all his might; and certainly his sister looked with all her might at him.

"Friends in London !" echoed Tom.

"Ah !" said Westlock, " to be sure."

" Have *you* any friends in London, Ruth, my dear ? " asked Tom.

" No, Tom."

" I am very happy to hear that *I* have," said Tom, " but it's news to me. I never knew it. They must be capital people to keep a secret, John."

"You shall judge for yourself," returned the other. " Seriously, Tom, here is the plain state of the case. As I was sitting at breakfast this morning, there comes a knock at my door."

" On which you cried out, very loud, ' Come in !'" suggested Tom.

" So I did. And the person who knocked, not being a respectable young man, aged thirty-five, from the country, came in when he was invited, instead of standing gaping and staring about him on the landing. Well ! When he came in, I found he was a stranger; a grave, business-like, sedate-looking, stranger. ' Mr. Westlock ? ' said he. ' That is my name,' said I. ' The favour of a few words with you ? ' said he. ' Pray be seated, sir,' said I."

Here John stopped for an instant, to glance towards the table, where Tom's sister, listening attentively, was still busy with the basin, which by this time made a noble appearance. Then he resumed :

" The pudding having taken a chair, Tom— "

" What ! " cried Tom.

" Having taken a chair."

" You said a pudding."

" No, no," replied John, colouring rather; " a chair. The idea of a stranger coming into my rooms at half-past eight

227

o'clock in the morning, and taking a pudding! Having taken a chair, Tom, a chair—amazed me by opening the conversation thus: ' I believe you are acquainted, sir, with Mr. Thomas Pinch?'"

"No!" cried Tom.

"His very words, I assure you. I told him I was. Did I know where you were at present residing? Yes. In London? Yes. He had casually heard, in a roundabout way, that you had left your situation with Mr. Pecksniff. Was that the fact? Yes, it was. Did you want another? Yes, you did."

"Certainly," said Tom, nodding his head.

"Just what I impressed upon him. You may rest assured that I set that point beyond the possibility of any mistake, and gave him distinctly to understand that he might make up his mind about it. Very well."

"'Then,' said he, 'I think I can accommodate him.'"

Tom's sister stopped short.

"Lord bless me!" cried Tom. "Ruth, my dear, 'think I can accommodate him.'"

"Of course I begged him," pursued John Westlock, glancing at Tom's sister, who was not less eager in her interest than Tom himself, "to proceed, and said that I would undertake to see you immediately. He replied that he had very little to say, being a man of few words, but such as it was, it was to the purpose: and so, indeed, it turned out: for he immediately went on to tell me that a friend of his was in want of a kind of secretary and librarian; and that although the salary was small, being only a hundred pounds a year, with neither board nor lodging, still the duties were not heavy, and there the post was. Vacant, and ready for your acceptance."

"Good gracious me!" cried Tom; "a hundred pounds a year! My dear John! Ruth, my love! A hundred pounds a year!"

"But the strangest part of the story," resumed John Westlock, laying his hand on Tom's wrist, to bespeak his attention, and repress his ecstasies for the moment: "the strangest part of the story, Miss Pinch, is this. I don't know this man from Adam; neither does this man know Tom."

"He can't," said Tom, in great perplexity, "if he's a Londoner. I don't know any one in London."

"And on my observing," John resumed, still keeping his hand upon Tom's wrist, "that I had no doubt he would excuse the freedom I took, in inquiring who directed him to me; how he came to know of the change which had taken place in my friend's position; and how he came to be acquainted with my friend's peculiar fitness for such an office as he had described; he drily said that he was not at liberty to enter into any explanations."

"Not at liberty to enter into any explanations!" repeated Tom, drawing a long breath.

"'I must be perfectly aware,' he said," John added, "'that to any person who had ever been in Mr. Pecksniff's neighbourhood, Mr. Thomas Pinch and his acquirements were as well known as the Church steeple, or the Blue Dragon.'"

"The Blue Dragon!" repeated Tom, staring alternately at his friend and his sister.

"Aye; think of that! He spoke as familiarly of the Blue Dragon, I give you my word, as if he had been Mark Tapley. I opened my eyes, I can tell you, when he did so; but I could not fancy I had ever seen the man before, although he said with a smile, 'You know the Blue Dragon, Mr. Westlock; you kept it up there, once or twice, yourself.' Kept it up there! So I did. You remember, Tom?"

Tom nodded with great significance, and, falling into a state of deeper perplexity than before, observed that this was the most unaccountable and extraordinary circumstance he had ever heard of in his life.

"Unaccountable?" his friend repeated. "I became afraid of the man. Though it was broad day, and bright sunshine, I was positively afraid of him. I declare I half suspected him to be a supernatural visitor, and not a mortal, until he took out a common-place description of pocket-book, and handed me this card."

"Mr. Fips," said Tom, reading it aloud. "Austin Friars. Austin Friars sounds ghostly, John."

"Fips don't, I think," was John's reply. "But there he lives, Tom, and there he expects us to call this morning. And now you know as much of this strange incident as I do, upon my honour."

Tom's face, between his exultation in the hundred pounds a year, and his wonder at this narration, was only to be equalled by the face of his sister, on which there sat the very best expression of blooming surprise that any painter could have wished to see. What the beef-steak pudding would have come to, if it had not been by this time finished, astrology itself could hardly determine.

"Tom," said Ruth, after a little hesitation, "perhaps Mr. Westlock, in his friendship for you, knows more of this than he chooses to tell."

"No, indeed!" cried John, eagerly. "It is not so, I assure you. I wish it were. I cannot take credit to myself, Miss Pinch, for any such thing. All that I know, or, so far as I can judge, am likely to know, I have told you."

"Couldn't you know more, if you thought proper?" said Ruth, scraping the pie-board industriously.

"No," retorted John. "Indeed, no. It is very ungenerous in you, to be so suspicious of me, when I repose implicit faith in you. I have unbounded confidence in the pudding, Miss Pinch."

She laughed at this, but they soon got back into a serious vein, and discussed the subject with profound gravity. Whatever else was obscure in the business, it appeared to be quite plain that Tom was offered a salary of one hundred pounds a year; and this being the main point, the surrounding obscurity rather set it off than otherwise.

Tom, being in a great flutter, wished to start for Austin Friars instantly, but they waited nearly an hour, by John's advice, before they departed. Tom made himself as spruce as he could before leaving home, and when John Westlock, through the half-opened parlour door, had glimpses of that brave little sister brushing the collar of his coat in the passage, taking up loose stitches in his gloves, and hovering lightly about and about him, touching him up here and there in the height of her quaint, little, old-fashioned tidiness, he called to mind the fancy-portraits of her on the wall of the Pecksniffian work-room, and decided with uncommon indignation that they were gross libels, and not half pretty enough: though, as hath been mentioned in its place, the artists always made those sketches beautiful, and he had drawn at least a score of them with his own hands.

"Tom," he said, as they were walking along, "I begin to think you must be somebody's son."

"I suppose I am," Tom answered in his quiet way.

"But I mean somebody's of consequence."

"Bless your heart," replied Tom, "my poor father was of no consequence, nor my mother either."

"You remember them perfectly, then?"

"Remember them? oh dear yes. My poor mother was the last. She died when Ruth was a mere baby, and then we both became a charge upon the savings of that good old grandmother I used to tell you of. You remember! Oh! There's nothing romantic in our history, John."

"Very well," said John in quiet despair. "Then there is no way of accounting for my visitor of this morning. So we'll not try, Tom."

They did try, notwithstanding, and never left off trying until they got to Austin Friars, where, in a very dark passage on the first floor, oddly situated at the back of a house, across some leads, they found a little blear-eyed glass door up in one corner, with MR. FIPS painted on it in characters which were meant to be transparent. There was also a wicked old sideboard hiding in the gloom hard by, meditating designs upon the ribs of visitors; and an old mat, worn into lattice

231

work, which, being useless as a mat (even if anybody could have seen it, which was impossible), had for many years directed its industry into another channel, and regularly tripped up every one of Mr. Fips's clients.

Mr. Fips, hearing a violent concussion between a human hat and his office door, was apprised, by the usual means of communication, that somebody had come to call upon him, and giving that somebody admission, observed that it was " rather dark."

" Dark indeed," John whispered in Tom Pinch's ear. " Not a bad place to dispose of a countryman in, I should think, Tom."

Tom had been already turning over in his mind the possibility of their having been tempted into that region to furnish forth a pie; but the sight of Mr. Fips, who was small and spare, and looked peaceable, and wore black shorts and powder, dispelled his doubts.

" Walk in," said Mr. Fips.

They walked in. And a mighty yellow-jaundiced little office Mr. Fips had of it : with a great, black, sprawling splash upon the floor in one corner, as if some old clerk had cut his throat there, years ago, and had let out ink instead of blood.

" I have brought my friend Mr. Pinch, sir," said John Westlock.

" Be pleased to sit," said Mr. Fips.

They occupied the two chairs, and Mr. Fips took the office stool, from the stuffing whereof he drew forth a piece of horsehair of immense length, which he put into his mouth with a great appearance of appetite.

He looked at Tom Pinch curiously, but with an entire freedom from any such expression as could be reasonably construed into an unusual display of interest. After a short silence, during which Mr. Fips was so perfectly unembarrassed as to render it manifest that he could have broken it sooner without hesitation, if he had felt inclined to do so, he asked if Mr. Westlock had made his offer fully known to Mr. Pinch.

John answered in the affirmative.

"And you think it worth your while, sir, do you?" Mr. Fips inquired of Tom.

"I think it a piece of great good fortune, sir," said Tom. "I am exceedingly obliged to you for the offer."

"Not to me," said Mr. Fips. "I act upon instructions."

"To your friend, sir, then," said Tom. "To the gentleman with whom I am to engage, and whose confidence I shall endeavour to deserve. When he knows me better, sir, I hope he will not lose his good opinion of me. He will find me punctual and vigilant, and anxious to do what is right. That I think I can answer for, and so," looking towards him, "can Mr. Westlock."

"Most assuredly," said John.

Mr Fips appeared to have some little difficulty in resuming the conversation. To relieve himself, he took up the wafer-stamp, and began stamping capital F's all over his legs.

"The fact is," said Mr. Fips, "that my friend is not, at this present moment, in town."

Tom's countenance fell; for he thought this equivalent to telling him that his appearance did not answer; and that Fips must look out for somebody else.

"When do you think he will be in town, sir?" he asked.

"I can't say; it's impossible to tell. I really have no idea. But," said Fips, taking off a very deep impression of the wafer-stamp upon the calf of his left leg, and looking steadily at Tom, "I don't know that it's a matter of much consequence."

Poor Tom inclined his head deferentially, but appeared to doubt that.

"I say," repeated Mr. Fips, "that I don't know it's a matter of much consequence. The business lies entirely between yourself and me, Mr. Pinch. With reference to your duties, I can set you going; and with reference to your salary, I can pay it. Weekly," said Mr. Fips, putting down the wafer-stamp, and looking at John Westlock and Tom Pinch by turns, "weekly; in this office; at any time between the hours of four and five o'clock in the afternoon." As Mr. Fips said

233

this, he made up his face as if he were going to whistle. But he didn't.

"You are very good," said Tom, whose countenance was now suffused with pleasure: "and nothing can be more satisfactory or straightforward. My attendance will be required—"

"From half-past nine to four o'clock or so, I should say," interrupted Mr. Fips. "About that."

"I did not mean the hours of attendance," retorted Tom, "which are light and easy, I am sure; but the place."

"Oh, the place! The place is in the Temple."

Tom was delighted.

"Perhaps," said Mr. Fips, "you would like to see the place?"

"Oh dear!" cried Tom. "I shall only be too glad to consider myself engaged, if you will allow me; without any further reference to the place."

"You may consider yourself engaged, by all means," said Mr. Fips: "you couldn't meet me at the Temple Gate in Fleet Street, in an hour from this time, I suppose, could you?"

Certainly Tom could.

"Good," said Mr. Fips, rising. "Then I will show you the place; and you can begin your attendance to-morrow morning. In an hour, therefore, I shall see you. You too, Mr. Westlock? Very good. Take care how you go. It's rather dark."

With this remark, which seemed superfluous, he shut them out upon the staircase, and they groped their way into the street again.

The interview had done so little to remove the mystery in which Tom's new engagement was involved, and had done so much to thicken it, that neither could help smiling at the puzzled looks of the other. They agreed, however, that the introduction of Tom to his new office and office companions could hardly fail to throw a light upon the subject; and therefore postponed its further consideration until after the fulfilment of the appointment they had made with Mr. Fips.

IN THE TEMPLE

After looking at John Westlock's chambers, and devoting a few spare minutes to the Boar's Head, they issued forth again to the place of meeting. The time agreed upon had not quite come; but Mr. Fips was already at the Temple Gate, and expressed his satisfaction at their punctuality.

He led the way through sundry lanes and courts, into one more quiet and more gloomy than the rest, and, singling out a certain house, ascended a common staircase: taking from his pocket, as he went, a bunch of rusty keys. Stopping before a door upon an upper story, which had nothing but a yellow smear of paint where custom would have placed the tenant's name, he began to beat the dust out of one of these keys, very deliberately, upon the great broad hand-rail of the balustrade.

"You had better have a little plug made," he said, looking round at Tom, after blowing a shrill whistle into the barrel of the key. "It's the only way of preventing them from getting stopped up. You'll find the lock go the better, too, I dare say, for a little oil."

Tom thanked him; but was too much occupied with his own speculations, and John Westlock's looks, to be very talkative. In the meantime, Mr. Fips opened the door, which yielded to his hand very unwillingly, and with a horribly discordant sound. He took the key out, when he had done so, and gave it to Tom.

"Aye, aye!" said Mr. Fips. "The dust lies rather thick here."

Truly, it did. Mr. Fips might have gone so far as to say, very thick. It had accumulated everywhere; lay deep on everything; and in one part, where a ray of sun shone through a crevice in the shutter and struck upon the opposite wall, it went twirling round and round, like a gigantic squirrel-cage.

Dust was the only thing in the place that had any motion about it. When their conductor admitted the light freely, and lifting up the heavy window-sash, let in the summer air, he showed the mouldering furniture, discoloured wainscoting

235

and ceiling, rusty stove, and ashy hearth, in all their inert neglect. Close to the door, there stood a candlestick, with an extinguisher upon it: as if the last man who had been there, had paused, after securing a retreat, to take a parting look at the dreariness he left behind, and then had shut out light and life together, and closed the place up like a tomb.

There were two rooms on that floor; and in the first or outer one a narrow staircase, leading to two more above. These last were fitted up as bed-chambers. Neither in them, nor in the rooms below, was any scarcity of convenient furniture observable, although the fittings were of a by-gone fashion; but solitude and want of use seemed to have rendered it unfit for any purposes of comfort, and to have given it a grisly, haunted air.

Moveables of every kind lay strewn about, without the least attempt at order, and were intermixed with boxes, hampers, and all sorts of lumber. On all the floors were piles of books, to the amount, perhaps, of some thousands of volumes: these, still in bales: those, wrapped in paper, as they had been purchased: others scattered singly or in heaps: not one upon the shelves which lined the walls. To these, Mr. Fips called Tom's attention.

"Before anything else can be done, we must have them put in order, catalogued, and ranged upon the book-shelves, Mr. Pinch. That will do to begin with, I think, sir."

Tom rubbed his hands in the pleasant anticipation of a task so congenial to his taste, and said:

"An occupation full of interest for me, I assure you. It will occupy me, perhaps, until Mr. —— "

"Until Mr. —— " repeated Fips; as much as to ask Tom what he was stopping for.

"I forgot that you had not mentioned the gentleman's name," said Tom.

"Oh!" cried Mr. Fips, pulling on his glove, "didn't I? No, by-the-bye, I don't think I did. Ah! I dare say he'll be here soon. You will get on very well together, I have no doubt. I wish you success, I am sure. You won't forget to shut the door? It'll lock of itself if you slam it. Half-past nine, you know. Let us say from half-past nine to four, or half-past four, or thereabouts; one day, perhaps, a little earlier, another day, perhaps, a little later, according as you feel disposed, and as you arrange your work. Mr. Fips, Austin Friars, of course you'll remember? And you won't forget to slam the door, if you please?"

He said all this in such a comfortable, easy manner, that Tom could only rub his hands, and nod his head, and smile in acquiescence, which he was still doing, when Mr. Fips walked coolly out.

" Why, he's gone!" cried Tom.

"And what's more, Tom," said John Westlock, seating himself upon a pile of books, and looking up at his aston-ished friend, " he is evidently not coming back again: so here you are, installed. Under rather singular circumstances, Tom!"

It was such an odd affair throughout, and Tom standing there among the books with his hat in one hand and the key in the other, looked so prodigiously confounded, that his friend could not help laughing heartily. Tom himself was tickled: no less by the hilarity of his friend, than by the recollection of the sudden manner in which he had been brought to a stop, in the very height of his urbane conference with Mr. Fips; so, by degrees Tom burst out laughing too; and each making the other laugh more, they fairly roared.

When they had had their laugh out, which did not happen very soon, for, give John an inch that way, and he was sure to take several ells, being a jovial, good-tempered fellow, they looked about them more closely, groping among the lumber for any stray means of enlightenment that might turn up. But no scrap or shred of information could they find. The books were marked with a variety of owners' names, having, no doubt, been bought at sales, and collected here and there at different times; but whether any one of these names belonged

237

to Tom's employer, and, if so, which of them, they had no means whatever of determining. It occurred to John as a very bright thought, to make inquiry at the steward's office, to whom the chambers belonged, or by whom they were held; but he came back no wiser than he went, the answer being, "Mr. Fips, of Austin Friars."

"After all, Tom, I begin to think it lies no deeper than this. Fips is an eccentric man; has some knowledge of Pecksniff; despises him, of course; has heard or seen enough of you to know that you are the man he wants; and engages you in his own whimsical manner."

"But why in his own whimsical manner?" asked Tom.

"Oh! why does any man entertain his own whimsical taste? Why does Mr. Fips wear shorts and powder, and Mr. Fips's next-door neighbour boots and a wig?"

Tom, being in that state of mind in which any explanation is a great relief, adopted this last one (which indeed was quite as feasible as any other) readily, and said he had no doubt of it. Nor was his faith at all shaken by his having said exactly the same thing to each suggestion of his friend's, in turn, and being perfectly ready to say it again if he had any new solution to propose.

As he had not, Tom drew down the window sash, and folded the shutter; and they left the rooms. He closed the door heavily, as Mr. Fips had desired him; tried it, found it all safe, and put the key in his pocket.

They made a pretty wide circuit in going back to Islington, as they had time to spare, and Tom was never tired of looking about him. It was well he had John Westlock for his companion, for most people would have been weary of his perpetual stoppages at shop-windows, and his frequent dashes into the crowded carriage-way at the peril of his life, to get the better view of church steeples, and other public buildings. But John was charmed to see him so much interested, and every time Tom came back with a beaming face from among the wheels of carts and hackney-coaches, wholly unconscious

Mysterious Installation of Mr. Pinch

of the personal congratulations addressed to him by the drivers, John seemed to like him better than before.

There was no flour on Ruth's hands when she received them in the triangular parlour, but there were pleasant smiles upon her face, and a crowd of welcomes shining out of every smile, and gleaming in her bright eyes. By-the-bye, how bright they were! Looking into them for but a moment, when you took her hand, you saw, in each, such a capital miniature of yourself, representing you as such a restless, flashing, eager, brilliant little fellow—

Ah! if you could only have kept them for your own miniature! But, wicked, roving, restless, too impartial eyes, it was enough for any one to stand before them, and straightway, there he danced and sparkled quite as merrily as you!

The table was already spread for dinner; and though it was spread with nothing very choice in the way of glass or linen, and with green-handled knives, and very mountebanks of two-pronged forks, which seemed to be trying how far asunder they could possibly stretch their legs, without converting themselves into double the number of iron toothpicks, it wanted neither damask, silver, gold, nor china: no, nor any other garniture at all. There it was: and, being there, nothing else would have done as well.

The success of that initiative dish: that first experiment of hers in cookery: was so entire, so unalloyed and perfect, that John Westlock and Tom agreed she must have been studying the art in secret for a long time past; and urged her to make a full confession of the fact. They were exceedingly merry over this jest, and many smart things were said concerning it; but John was not as fair in his behaviour as might have been expected, for, after luring Tom Pinch on, for a long time, he suddenly went over to the enemy, and swore to everything his sister said. However, as Tom observed the same night before going to bed, it was only in joke, and John had always been famous for being polite to ladies, even when he was quite a boy. Ruth said, "Oh! indeed!" She didn't say anything else.

It is astonishing how much three people may find to talk about. They scarcely left off talking once. And it was not all lively chat which occupied them; for, when Tom related how he had seen Mr. Pecksniff's daughters, and what a change had fallen on the younger, they were very serious.

John Westlock became quite absorbed in her fortunes; asking many questions of Tom Pinch about her marriage, inquiring whether her husband was the gentleman whom Tom had brought to dine with him at Salisbury; in what degree of relationship they stood towards each other, being different persons; and taking, in short, the greatest interest in the subject. Tom then went into it at full length; he told how Martin had gone abroad, and had not been heard of for a long time; how Dragon Mark had borne him company; how Mr. Pecksniff had got the poor old doting grandfather into his power; and how he basely sought the hand of Mary Graham. But, not a word said Tom of what lay hidden in his heart; his heart, so deep, and true, and full of honour, and yet with so much room for every gentle and unselfish thought: not a word.

Tom, Tom! The man in all this world most confident in his sagacity and shrewdness; the man in all this world most proud of his distrust of other men, and having most to show in gold and silver as the gains belonging to his creed; the meekest favourer of that wise doctrine, Every man for himself, and God for us all (there being high wisdom in the thought that the Eternal Majesty of Heaven ever was, or can be, on the side of selfish lust and love!); shall never find, oh, never find, be sure of that, the time come home to him, when all his wisdom is an idiot's folly, weighed against a simple heart!

Well, well, Tom, it was simple too, though simple in a different way, to be so eager touching that same theatre, of which John said, when tea was done, he had the absolute command, so far as taking parties in without the payment of a sixpence, was concerned; and simpler yet, perhaps, never to suspect that when he went in first, alone, he paid the money! Simple in thee, dear Tom, to laugh and cry so heartily, at such a sorry show, so poorly shown; simple, to be so happy and loquacious trudging home with Ruth; simple, to be so surprised to find that merry present of a cookery-book, awaiting her in the parlour next morning, with the beef-steak-pudding-leaf turned down, and blotted out. There! Let the record stand! Thy quality of soul was simple, simple; quite contemptible, Tom Pinch!

CHAPTER XI

THERE was a ghostly air about these uninhabited chambers
in the Temple, and attending every circumstance of Tom's
employment there, which had a strange charm in it. Every
morning when he shut his door at Islington, he turned his
face towards an atmosphere of unaccountable fascination, as
surely as he turned it to the London smoke; and from that
moment, it thickened round and round him all day long, until
the time arrived for going home again, and leaving it, like a
motionless cloud, behind.

It seemed to Tom, every morning, that he approached this
ghostly mist, and became enveloped in it, by the easiest
succession of degrees imaginable. Passing from the roar and
rattle of the streets into the quiet court-yards of the Temple,
was the first preparation. Every echo of his footsteps sounded
to him like a sound from the old walls and pavements, wanting language to relate the histories of the dim, dismal rooms;
to tell him what lost documents were decaying in forgotten
corners of the shut-up cellars, from whose lattices such mouldy
sighs came breathing forth as he went past; to whisper of
dark bins of rare old wine, bricked up in vaults among the
old foundations of the Halls; or mutter in a lower tone
yet darker legends of the cross-legged knights, whose marble
effigies were in the church. With the first planting of his

242

foot upon the staircase of his dusty office, all these mysteries increased; until, ascending step by step, as Tom ascended, they attained their full growth in the solitary labours of the day.

Every day brought one recurring, never-failing source of speculation. This employer; would he come to-day, and what would he be like? For Tom could not stop short at Mr. Fips; he quite believed that Mr. Fips had spoken truly, when he said he acted for another; and what manner of man that other was, became a full-blown flower of wonder in the garden of Tom's fancy, which never faded or got trodden down.

At one time, he conceived that Mr. Pecksniff, repenting of his falsehood, might, by exertion of his influence with some third person, have devised these means of giving him employment. He found this idea so insupportable after what had taken place between that good man and himself, that he confided it to John Westlock on the very same day; informing John that he would rather ply for hire as a porter, than fall so low in his own esteem as to accept the smallest obligation from the hands of Mr. Pecksniff. But John assured him that he (Tom Pinch) was far from doing justice to the character of Mr. Pecksniff yet, if he supposed that gentleman capable of performing a generous action; and that he might make his mind quite easy on that head until he saw the sun turn green and the moon black, and at the same time distinctly perceived with the naked eye, twelve first-rate comets careering round those planets. In which unusual state of things, he said (and not before), it might become not absolutely lunatic to suspect Mr. Pecksniff of anything so monstrous. In short he laughed the idea down, completely; and Tom, abandoning it, was thrown upon his beam-ends again, for some other solution.

In the meantime Tom attended to his duties daily, and made considerable progress with the books: which were already reduced to some sort of order, and made a great appearance in his fairly-written catalogue. During his business hours, he indulged himself occasionally with snatches of reading; which were often, indeed, a necessary part of his pursuit; and as he usually made bold to carry one of these goblin volumes home at night (always bringing it back again next morning, in case his strange employer should appear and ask what had become of it), he led a happy, quiet, studious kind of life, after his own heart.

But, though the books were never so interesting, and never so full of novelty to Tom, they could not so enchain him, in those mysterious chambers, as to render him unconscious, for a moment, of the lightest sound. Any footstep on the flags without, set him listening attentively, and when it turned into that house, and came up, up, up, the stairs, he always thought with a beating heart, "Now I am coming face to face with him, at last!" But no footstep ever passed the floor immediately below : except his own.

This mystery and loneliness engendered fancies in Tom's mind, the folly of which his common sense could readily discover, but which his common sense was quite unable to keep away, notwithstanding; that quality being with most of us, in such a case, like the old French Police—quick at detection, but very weak as a preventive power. Misgivings, undefined, absurd, inexplicable, that there was some one hiding in the inner room—walking softly overhead, peeping in through the door-chink, doing something stealthy, anywhere where he was not—came over him a hundred times a day, making it pleasant to throw up the sash, and hold communication even with the sparrows who had built in the roof and water-spout, and were twittering about the windows all day long.

He sat with the outer door wide open, at all times, that he might hear the footsteps as they entered, and turned off into the chambers on the lower floor. He formed odd prepossessions too, regarding strangers in the streets ; and would say within himself of such or such a man, who struck him as having anything uncommon in his dress or aspect, "I shouldn't wonder, now, if that were he!" But it never was. And though he actually turned back and followed more than one of these suspected individuals, in a singular belief that they were going to the place he was then upon his way from, he never got any other satisfaction by it, than the satisfaction of knowing it was not the case.

Mr. Fips, of Austin Friars, rather deepened than illumined the obscurity of his position; for, on the first occasion of Tom's waiting on him to receive his weekly pay, he said :

" Oh! by-the-bye, Mr. Pinch, you needn't mention it, if you please ! "

Tom thought he was going to tell him a secret; so he said that he wouldn't on any account, and that Mr. Fips might entirely depend upon him. But as Mr. Fips said " Very good," in reply, and nothing more, Tom prompted him :

" Not on any account," repeated Tom.

Mr. Fips repeated " Very good."

" You were going to say "—Tom hinted.

" Oh dear no ! " cried Fips. " Not at all."—However, seeing Tom confused, he added, " I mean that you needn't mention any particulars about your place of employment, to people generally. You'll find it better not."

" I have not had the pleasure of seeing my employer yet, sir," observed Tom, putting his week's salary in his pocket.

" Haven't you ? " said Fips. " No, I don't suppose you have though."

" I should like to thank him, and to know that what I have done so far, is done to his satisfaction," faltered Tom.

" Quite right," said Mr. Fips, with a yawn. " Highly creditable. Very proper."

Tom hastily resolved to try him on another tack.

" I shall soon have finished with the books," he said. " I hope that will not terminate my engagement, sir, or render me useless ? "

" Oh dear no ! " retorted Fips. " Plenty to do : plen-ty to do ! Be careful how you go. It's rather dark."

This was the very utmost extent of information Tom could ever get out of *him*. So it was dark enough in all conscience: and if Mr. Fips expressed himself with a double meaning, he had good reason for doing so.

But now a circumstance occurred, which helped to divert Tom's thoughts from even this mystery, and to divide them between it and a new channel, which was a very Nile in itself.

The way it came about was this. Having always been an early riser, and having now no organ to engage him in sweet converse every morning, it was his habit to take a long walk before going to the Temple; and naturally inclining, as a stranger, towards those parts of the town which were conspicuous for the life and animation pervading them, he became a great frequenter of the market-places, bridges, quays, and especially the steam-boat wharves; for it was very lively and fresh to see the people hurrying away upon their many schemes of business or pleasure, and it made Tom glad to think that there was that much change and freedom in the monotonous routine of city lives.

In most of these morning excursions Ruth accompanied him. As their landlord was always up and away at his business (whatever that might be, no one seemed to know) at a very early hour, the habits of the people of the house in which they lodged corresponded with their own. Thus, they had often finished their breakfast, and were out in the summer-air, by seven o'clock. After a two hours' stroll they parted at some convenient point: Tom going to the Temple, and his sister returning home, as methodically as you please.

Many and many a pleasant stroll they had in Covent-Garden Market: snuffing up the perfume of the fruits and flowers, wondering at the magnificence of the pine-apples and melons; catching glimpses down side avenues, of rows and rows of old women, seated on inverted baskets shelling peas; looking unutterable things at the fat bundles of asparagus with which the dainty shops were fortified as with a breastwork; and, at the herbalists' doors, gratefully inhaling scents as of veal-stuffing yet uncooked, dreamily mixed up with capsicums, brown-paper, seeds : even with hints of lusty snails and fine young curly leeches. Many and many a pleasant stroll they had among the poultry markets, where ducks and fowls, with necks unnaturally long, lay stretched out in pairs, ready for cooking; where there were speckled eggs in mossy baskets, white country sausages beyond impeachment by surviving cat or dog, or horse or donkey, new cheeses to any wild extent, live birds in coops and cages, looking much too big to be natural, in consequence of those receptacles being much too little; rabbits, alive and dead, innumerable. Many a pleasant stroll they had among the cool, refreshing, silvery fish-stalls, with a kind of moonlight effect about their stock in trade, excepting always for the ruddy lobsters. Many a pleasant stroll among the waggon-loads of fragrant hay, beneath which dogs and tired waggoners lay fast asleep, oblivious of the pieman and the public-house. But, never half so good a stroll, as down among the steam-boats on a bright morning.

There they lay, alongside of each other; hard and fast for ever, to all appearance, but designing to get out somehow, and quite confident of doing it; and in that faith shoals of passengers, and heaps of luggage, were proceeding hurriedly on board. Little steam-boats dashed up and down the stream incessantly. Tiers upon tiers of vessels, scores of masts, laby-rinths of tackle, idle sails, splashing oars, gliding row-boats, lumbering barges, sunken piles, with ugly lodgings for the water-rat within their mud-discoloured nooks; church steeples, warehouses, house-roofs, arches, bridges, men and women, children, casks, cranes, boxes, horses, coaches, idlers, and hard-labourers : there they were, all jumbled up together, any summer morning, far beyond Tom's power of separation.

In the midst of all this turmoil, there was an incessant roar from every packet's funnel, which quite expressed and carried out the uppermost emotion of the scene. They all appeared to be perspiring and bothering themselves, exactly as their passengers did; they never left off fretting and chafing, in their own hoarse manner, once; but were always panting out, without any stops, "Come along do make haste I'm very nervous come along oh good gracious we shall never get there how late you are do make haste I'm off directly come along!" Even when they had left off, and had got safely out into the current, on the smallest provocation they began again: for the bravest packet of them all, being stopped by some entanglement in the river, would immediately begin to fume and pant afresh, "Oh here's a stoppage what's the matter do go on there I'm in a hurry it's done on purpose did you ever oh my goodness *do* go on here!" and so, in a state of mind bordering on distraction, would be last seen drifting slowly through the mist into the summer light beyond, that made it red.

Tom's ship, however; or, at least, the packet-boat in which Tom and his sister took the greatest interest on one particular occasion; was not off yet, by any means; but was at the height of its disorder. The press of passengers was very great; another steam-boat lay on each side of her; the gangways were choked up; distracted women, obviously bound for Gravesend, but turning a deaf ear to all representations that this particular vessel was about to sail for Antwerp, persisted in secreting baskets of refreshments behind bulk-heads and water-casks, and under seats; and very great confusion prevailed.

It was so amusing, that Tom, with Ruth upon his arm, stood looking down from the wharf, as nearly regardless as it was in the nature of flesh and blood to be, of an elderly lady behind him, who had brought a large umbrella with her, and didn't know what to do with it. This tremendous instrument had a hooked handle; and its vicinity was first made known to him by a painful pressure on the windpipe, consequent upon its having caught him round the throat. Soon after disengaging himself with perfect good humour, he had a sensation of the ferule in his back; immediately afterwards, of the hook entangling his ankles; then of the umbrella generally, wandering about his hat, and flapping at it like a great bird ; and, lastly, of a poke or thrust below the ribs, which gave him such exceeding anguish, that he could not refrain from turning round to offer a mild remonstrance.

Upon his turning round, he found the owner of the umbrella struggling on tip-toe, with a countenance expressive of violent animosity, to look down upon the steam-boats; from which he inferred that she had attacked him, standing in the front row, by design, and as her natural enemy.

" What a very ill-natured person you must be ! " said Tom.

The lady cried out fiercely, " Where's the pelisse ! " meaning the constabulary—and went on to say, shaking the handle of the umbrella at Tom, that but for them fellers never being in the way when they was wanted, she'd have given him in charge, she would.

" If they greased their whiskers less, and minded the duties which they're paid so heavy for, a little more," she observed, " no one needn't be drove mad by scrouding so ! "

She had been grievously knocked about, no doubt, for her bonnet was bent into the shape of a cocked hat. Being a fat little woman, too, she was in a state of great exhaustion and intense heat. Instead of pursuing the altercation, therefore, Tom civilly inquired what boat she wanted to go on board of ?

" I suppose," returned the lady, " as nobody but yourself can want to look at a steam package, without wanting to go a boarding of it, can they !   Booby ! "

" Which one do you want to look at then ? " said Tom. " We'll make room for you if we can.   Don't be so ill-tempered."

" No blessed creetur as ever I was with in trying times," returned the lady, somewhat softened, " and they're a many in their numbers, ever brought it as a charge again myself that I was anythin' but mild and equal in my spirits.   Never mind a contradicting of me, if you seems to feel it does you good, ma'am, I often says, for well you know that Sairey may be trusted not to give it back again.   But I will not denige that I am worrited and wexed this day, and with good reagion, Lord forbid!"

By this time, Mrs. Gamp (for it was no other than that experienced practitioner) had, with Tom's assistance, squeezed and worked herself into a small corner between Ruth and the rail; where, after breathing very hard for some little time, and performing a short series of dangerous evolutions with her umbrella, she managed to establish herself pretty comfortably.

"And which of all them smoking monsters is the Ankworks boat, I wonder. Goodness me!" cried Mrs. Gamp.

"What boat did you want?" asked Ruth.

"The Ankworks package," Mrs. Gamp replied. "I will not deceive you, my sweet. Why should I?"

"That is the Antwerp packet in the middle," said Ruth.

"And I wish it was in Jonadge's belly, I do," cried Mrs. Gamp; appearing to confound the prophet with the whale in this miraculous aspiration.

Ruth said nothing in reply; but, as Mrs. Gamp, laying her chin against the cool iron of the rail, continued to look intently at the Antwerp boat, and every now and then to give a little groan, she inquired whether any child of hers was going abroad that morning? Or perhaps her husband, she said kindly.

"Which shows," said Mrs. Gamp, casting up her eyes, "what a little way you've travelled into this wale of life, my dear young creetur! As a good friend of mine has frequent made remark to me, which her name, my love, is Harris, Mrs. Harris through the square and up the steps a turnin' round by the tobacker shop, 'Oh Sairey, Sairey, little do we know wot lays afore us!' 'Mrs. Harris, ma'am,' I says, 'not much, it's true, but more than you suppoge. Our calcilations, ma'am,' I says, 'respectin' wot the number of a family will be, comes most times within one, and oftener than you would suppoge, exact.' 'Sairey,' says Mrs. Harris, in a awful way, 'Tell me wot is my indiwidgle number.' 'No, Mrs. Harris,'

I says to her, 'ex-cuge me, if you please. My own,' I says, 'has fallen out of three-pair backs, and had damp doorsteps settled on their lungs, and one was turned up smilin' in a bedstead, unbeknown. Therefore, ma'am,' I says, ' seek not to proticipate, but take 'em as they come and as they go.' Mine," said Mrs. Gamp, " mine is all gone, my dear young chick. And as to husbands, there's a wooden leg gone like-ways home to its account, which in its constancy of walkin' into wine vaults, and never comin' out again 'till fetched by force, was quite as weak as flesh, if not weaker."

When she had delivered this oration, Mrs. Gamp leaned her chin upon the cool iron again; and looking intently at the Antwerp packet, shook her head and groaned.

" I wouldn't," said Mrs. Gamp, " I wouldn't be a man and have such a think upon my mind!—but nobody as owned the name of man, could do it ! "

Tom and his sister glanced at each other; and Ruth, after a moment's hesitation, asked Mrs. Gamp what troubled her so much.

" My dear," returned that lady, dropping her voice, " you are single, ain't you ? "

Ruth laughed, blushed, and said " Yes."

" Worse luck," proceeded Mrs. Gamp, " for all parties ! But others is married, and in the marriage state; and there is a dear young creetur a comin' down this mornin' to that very package, which is no more fit to trust herself to sea, than nothin' is ! "

She paused here, to look over the deck of the packet in question, and on the steps leading down to it, and on the gangways. Seeming to have thus assured herself that the object of her commiseration had not yet arrived, she raised her eyes gradually up to the top of the escape-pipe, and indignantly apostrophised the vessel :

" Oh drat you ! " said Mrs. Gamp, shaking her umbrella at it, " you're a nice spluttering nisy monster for a delicate young creetur to go and be a passinger by ; ain't you ! *You* never do no harm in that way, do you? With your hammering, and roaring, and hissing, and lamp-iling, you brute! Them Confugion steamers," said Mrs. Gamp, shaking her umbrella again, "has done more to throw us out of our reg'lar work and bring ewents on at times when nobody counted on 'em (especially them screeching railroad ones), than all the other frights that ever was took. I have heerd of one young man, a guard upon a railway, only three years opened—well does Mrs. Harris know him, which indeed he is her own relation by her sister's marriage with a master sawyer —as is godfather at this present time to six-and-twenty blessed little strangers, equally unexpected, and all on 'um named after the Ingeins as was the cause. Ugh!" said Mrs. Gamp, resuming her apostrophe, "one might easy know you was a man's invention, from your disregardlessness of the weakness of our naturs, so one might, you brute!"

It would not have been unnatural to suppose, from the first part of Mrs. Gamp's lamentations, that she was connected with the stage-coaching or post-horsing trade. She had no means of judging of the effect of her concluding remarks upon her young companion; for she interrupted herself at this point, and exclaimed:

"There she identically goes! Poor sweet young creetur, there she goes, like a lamb to the sacrifige! If there's any illness when that wessel gets to sea," said Mrs. Gamp, prophetically, "it's murder, and I'm the witness for the persecution."

She was so very earnest on the subject, that Tom's sister (being as kind as Tom himself) could not help saying something to her in reply.

"Pray which is the lady," she inquired, "in whom you are so much interested?"

"There!" groaned Mrs. Gamp. "There she goes! A crossin' the little wooden bridge at this minute. She's a slippin' on a bit of orange-peel!" tightly clutching her umbrella. "What a turn it give me!"

" Do you mean the lady who is with that man wrapped up from head to foot in a large cloak, so that his face is almost hidden ? "

" Well he may hide it ? " Mrs. Gamp replied. " He's good call to be ashamed of himself. Did you see him a jerking of her wrist, then ? "

" He seems to be hasty with her, indeed."

" Now he's a taking of her down into the close cabin ! " said Mrs. Gamp, impatiently. " What's the man about ! The deuce is in him, I think. Why can't he leave her in the open air ? "

He did not, whatever his reason was, but led her quickly down and disappeared himself, without loosening his cloak, or pausing on the crowded deck one moment longer than was necessary to clear their way to that part of the vessel.

Tom had not heard this little dialogue ; for his attention had been engaged in an unexpected manner. A hand upon his sleeve had caused him to look round, just when Mrs. Gamp concluded her apostrophe to the steam-engine ; and on his right arm, Ruth being on his left, he found their landlord : to his great surprise.

He was not so much surprised at the man's being there, as at his having got close to him so quietly and swiftly ; for another person had been at his elbow one instant before ; and he had not in the meantime been conscious of any change or pressure in the knot of people among whom he stood. He and Ruth had frequently remarked how noiselessly this land-lord of theirs came into and went out of his own house ; but Tom was not the less amazed to see him at his elbow now.

" I beg your pardon, Mr. Pinch," he said in his ear. " I am rather infirm, and out of breath, and my eyes are not very good. I am not as young as I was, sir. You don't see a gentleman in a large cloak down yonder, with a lady on his arm ; a lady in a veil and a black shawl ; do you ? "

If *he* did not, it was curious that in speaking he should have singled out from all the crowd the very people whom he described : and should have glanced hastily from them to Tom, as if he were burning to direct his wandering eyes.

"A gentleman in a large cloak!" said Tom, "and a lady in a black shawl! Let me see!"

"Yes, yes!" replied the other, with keen impatience. "A gentleman muffled up from head to foot—strangely muffled up for such a morning as this—like an invalid, with his hand to his face at this minute, perhaps. No, no, no! not there," he added, following Tom's gaze ; the other way ; in that direction ; down yonder." Again he indicated, but this time in his hurry, with his outstretched finger, the very spot on which the progress of these persons was checked at that moment.

"There are so many people, and so much motion, and so many objects," said Tom, "that I find it difficult to—no, I really don't see a gentleman in a large cloak, and a lady in a black shawl. There's a lady in a red shawl over there!"

"No, no, no!" cried his landlord, pointing eagerly again, "not there. The other way: the other way. Look at the cabin steps. To the left. They must be near the cabin steps. Do you see the cabin steps? There's the bell ringing already! *Do* you see the steps?"

"Stay!" said Tom, "you're right. Look! there they go now. Is that the gentleman you mean? Descending at this minute, with the folds of a great cloak trailing down after him?"

"The very man!" returned the other, not looking at what Tom pointed out, however, but at Tom's own face. "Will you do me a kindness, sir, a great kindness? Will you put that letter in his hand? Only give him that? He expects it. I am charged to do it by my employers, but I am late in finding him, and, not being as young as I have been, should never be able to make my way on board and off the deck again in time. Will you pardon my boldness, and do me that great kindness?"

His hands shook, and his face bespoke the utmost interest and agitation, as he pressed the letter upon Tom, and pointed to its destination, like the Tempter in some grim old carving.

JONAS SUMMONED BACK

To hesitate in the performance of a good-natured or compassionate office, was not in Tom's way. He took the letter; whispered Ruth to wait till he returned, which would be immediately; and ran down the steps with all the expedition he could make. There were so many people going down, so many others coming up, such heavy goods in course of transit to and fro, such a ringing of bells, blowing-off of steam, and shouting of men's voices, that he had much ado to force his way, or keep in mind to which boat he was going. But, he reached the right one with good speed, and, going down the cabin-stairs immediately, descried the object of his search standing at the upper end of the saloon, with his back towards him, reading some notice which was hung against the wall. As Tom advanced to give him the letter, he started, hearing footsteps, and turned round.

What was Tom's astonishment to find in him the man with whom he had had the conflict in the field—poor Mercy's husband. Jonas!

Tom understood him to say, what the devil did he want; but it was not easy to make out what he said; he spoke so indistinctly.

"I want nothing with you for myself," said Tom; "I was asked, a moment since, to give you this letter. You were pointed out to me, but I didn't know you in your strange dress. Take it!"

He did so, opened it, and read the writing on the inside. The contents were evidently very brief; not more perhaps than one line; but they struck upon him like a stone from a sling. He reeled back as he read.

His emotion was so different from any Tom had ever seen before, that he stopped involuntarily. Momentary as his state of indecision was, the bell ceased while he stood there, and a hoarse voice calling down the steps, inquired if there was any one to go ashore?

"Yes," cried Jonas, "I—I am coming. Give me time. Where's that woman! Come back; come back here."

He threw open another door as he spoke, and dragged, rather than led, her forth. She was pale and frightened, and amazed to see her old acquaintance; but had no time to speak, for they were making a great stir above; and Jonas drew her rapidly towards the deck.

"Where are we going? What is the matter?"

"We are going back," said Jonas. "I have changed my mind. I can't go. Don't question me, or I shall be the death of you, or some one else. Stop there! Stop! We're for the shore. Do you hear? We're for the shore!"

He turned, even in the madness of his hurry, and scowling darkly back at Tom, shook his clenched hand at him. There are not many human faces capable of the expression with which he accompanied that gesture.

He dragged her up, and Tom followed them. Across the deck, over the side, along the crazy plank, and up the steps, he dragged her fiercely; not bestowing any look on her, but gazing upwards all the while among the faces on the wharf. Suddenly he turned again, and said to Tom with a tremendous oath:

"Where is he?"

Before Tom, in his indignation and amazement, could return an answer to a question he so little understood, a gentleman approached Tom behind, and saluted Jonas Chuzzlewit by name. He was a gentleman of foreign appearance, with a black moustache and whiskers; and addressed him with a polite composure, strangely different from his own distracted and desperate manner.

"Chuzzlewit, my good fellow!" said the gentleman, raising his hat in compliment to Mrs. Chuzzlewit, "I ask your pardon twenty thousand times. I am most unwilling to interfere between you and a domestic trip of this nature (always so very charming and refreshing, I know, although I have not the happiness to be a domestic man myself, which is the great infelicity of my existence): but the bee-hive, my dear friend, the bee-hive—will you introduce me?"

256

SPOILING THE EXCURSION

"This is Mr. Montague," said Jonas, whom the words appeared to choke.

"The most unhappy and most penitent of men, Mrs. Chuzzlewit," pursued that gentleman, "for having been the means of spoiling this excursion; but as I tell my friend, the bee-hive, the bee-hive. You projected a short little continental trip, my dear friend, of course?"

Jonas maintained a dogged silence.

"May I die," cried Montague, "but I am shocked! Upon my soul I am shocked. But that confounded bee-hive of ours in the city must be paramount to every other consideration, when there is honey to be made; and that is my best excuse. Here is a very singular old female dropping curtseys on my right," said Montague, breaking off in his discourse, and looking at Mrs. Gamp, "who is not a friend of mine. Does anybody know her?"

"Ah! Well they knows me, bless their precious hearts!" said Mrs. Gamp, "not forgettin' your own merry one, sir, and long may it be so! Wishin' as every one," (she delivered this in the form of a toast or sentiment) "was as merry, and as handsome-looking, as a little bird has whispered me a certain gent is, which I will not name for fear I give offence where none is doo! My precious lady," here she stopped short in her merriment, for she had until now affected to be vastly entertained, "you're too pale by half!"

"*You* are here too, are you?" muttered Jonas. "Ecod, there are enough of you."

"I hope, sir," returned Mrs. Gamp, dropping an indignant curtsey, "as no bones is broke by me and Mrs. Harris a walkin' down upon a public wharf. Which was the very words she says to me (although they was the last I ever had to speak) was these: 'Sairey,' she says, 'is it a public wharf?' 'Mrs. Harris,' I makes answer, 'can you doubt it? You have know'd me now, ma'am, eight and thirty year; and did you ever know me go, or wish to go, where I was not made welcome, say the words.' 'No, Sairey,' Mrs. Harris says, 'contrairy quite.' And well she knows it too. I am but a poor woman, but I've been sought arter, sir, though you may not think it. I've been knocked up at all hours of the night, and warned out by a many landlords, in consequence of being mistook for Fire. I goes out working for my bread, 'tis true, but I maintains my indepency, with your kind leave, and which I will till death. I has my feelins as a woman, sir, and I have been a mother likeways; but touch a pipkin as belongs to me, or make the least remarks on what I eats or drinks, and though you was the favouritest young for'ard hussy of a servant-gal as ever come into a house, either you leaves the place, or me. My earnings is not great, sir, but I will not be impoged upon. Bless the babe, and save the mother, is my mortar, sir; but I makes so free as add to that, Don't try no impogician with the Nuss, for she will not abear it!"

Mrs. Gamp concluded by drawing her shawl tightly over herself with both hands, and, as usual, referring to Mrs. Harris for full corroboration of these particulars. She had that peculiar trembling of the head, which, in ladies of her excitable nature, may be taken as a sure indication of their breaking out again very shortly; when Jonas made a timely interposition.

"As you *are* here," he said, "you had better see to her, and take her home. I am otherwise engaged." He said nothing more; but looked at Montague as if to give him notice that he was ready to attend him.

"I am sorry to take you away," said Montague.

Jonas gave him a sinister look, which long lived in Tom's memory, and which he often recalled afterwards.

"I am, upon my life," said Montague. "Why did you make it necessary?"

With the same dark glance as before, Jonas replied, after a moment's silence,

"The necessity is none of my making. You have brought it about yourself."

He said nothing more. He said even this as if he were

bound, and in the other's power, but had a sullen and suppressed devil within him, which he could not quite resist. His very gait, as they walked away together, was like that of a fettered man; but, striving to work out at his clenched hands, knitted brows, and fast-set lips, was the same imprisoned devil still.

They got into a handsome cabriolet, which was waiting for them, and drove away.

The whole of this extraordinary scene had passed so rapidly, and the tumult which prevailed around was so unconscious of any impression from it, that, although Tom had been one of the chief actors, it was like a dream. No one had noticed him after they had left the packet. He had stood behind Jonas, and so near him, that he could not help hearing all that passed. He had stood there, with his sister on his arm, expecting and hoping to have an opportunity of explaining his strange share in this yet stranger business. But Jonas had not raised his eyes from the ground; no one else had even looked towards him; and before he could resolve on any course of action, they were all gone.

He gazed round for his landlord. But he had done that, more than once already, and no such man was to be seen. He was still pursuing this search with his eyes, when he saw a hand beckoning to him from a hackney-coach; and hurrying towards it, found it was Merry's. She addressed him hurriedly, but bent out of the window, that she might not be overheard by her companion, Mrs. Gamp.

"What is it?" she said, "Good Heaven, what is it? Why did he tell me last night to prepare for a long journey, and why have you brought us back like criminals? Dear Mr. Pinch!" she clasped her hands distractedly, "be merciful to us. Whatever this dreadful secret is, be merciful, and God will bless you!"

"If any power of mercy lay with me," cried Tom, "trust me, you shouldn't ask in vain. But I am far more ignorant and weak than you."

She withdrew into the coach again, and he saw the hand waving towards him for a moment; but whether in reproachfulness or incredulity, or misery, or grief, or sad adieu, or what else, he could not, being so hurried, understand. *She* was gone now; and Ruth and he were left to walk away, and wonder.

Had Mr. Nadgett appointed the man who never came, to meet him upon London Bridge that morning? He was certainly looking over the parapet, and down upon the steamboat-wharf at that moment. It could not have been for pleasure; he never took pleasure. No. He must have had some business there.

CHAPTER XLI

THE office of the Anglo-Bengalee Disinterested Loan and
Life Assurance Company being near at hand, and Mr. Montague driving Jonas straight there, they had very little way to
go. But, the journey might have been one of several hours'
duration, without provoking a remark from either: for it was
clear that Jonas did not mean to break the silence which
prevailed between them, and that it was not, as yet, his dear
friend's cue to tempt him into conversation.

He had thrown aside his cloak, as having now no motive
for concealment, and with that garment huddled on his knees,
sat as far removed from his companion as the limited space in
such a carriage would allow. There was a striking difference
in his manner, compared with what it had been, within a few
minutes, when Tom encountered him so unexpectedly on board
the packet, or when the ugly change had fallen on him in Mr.
Montague's dressing-room. He had the aspect of a man found
out, and held at bay; of being baffled, hunted, and beset; but
there was now a dawning and increasing purpose in his face,
which changed it very much. It was gloomy, distrustful,
lowering; pale with anger, and defeat; it still was humbled,
abject, cowardly, and mean; but, let the conflict go on as it
would, there was one strong purpose wrestling with every
emotion of his mind, and casting the whole series down as
they arose.

261

Not prepossessing in appearance at the best of times, it may be readily supposed that he was not so now. He had left deep marks of his front teeth in his nether lip; and those tokens of the agitation he had lately undergone, improved his looks as little as the heavy corrugations in his forehead. But he was self-possessed now; unnaturally self-possessed, indeed, as men quite otherwise than brave are known to be in desperate extremities; and when the carriage stopped, he waited for no invitation, but leapt hardily out, and went up stairs.

The chairman followed him; and closing the board-room door as soon as they had entered, threw himself upon a sofa. Jonas stood before the window, looking down into the street; and leaned against the sash, resting his head upon his arms.

"This is not handsome, Chuzzlewit!" said Montague at length. "Not handsome, upon my soul!"

"What would you have me do?" he answered, looking round abruptly; "what do you expect?"

"Confidence, my good fellow. Some confidence!" said Montague, in an injured tone.

"Ecod! You show great confidence in me," retorted Jonas. "Don't you?"

"Do I not?" said his companion, raising his head, and looking at him, but he had turned again. "Do I not? Have I not confided to you the easy schemes I have formed for our advantage; *our* advantage, mind; not mine alone; and what is my return? Attempted flight!"

"How do you know that? Who said I meant to fly?"

"Who said! Come, come. A foreign boat, my friend, an early hour, a figure wrapped up for disguise! Who said? If you didn't mean to jilt me, why were you there? If you didn't mean to jilt me, why did you come back?"

"I came back," said Jonas, "to avoid disturbance."

"You were wise," rejoined his friend.

Jonas stood quite silent; still looking down into the street, and resting his head upon his arms.

"Now, Chuzzlewit," said Montague, "notwithstanding what

262

has passed, I will be plain with you. Are you attending to me there? I only see your back."

"*I* hear you. Go on!"

"I say that notwithstanding what has passed, I will be plain with you."

"You said that before. And I have told you once, I heard you say it. Go on."

"You are a little chafed, but I can make allowance for that, and am, fortunately, myself in the very best of tempers. Now, let us see how circumstances stand. A day or two ago, I mentioned to you, my dear fellow, that I thought I had discovered—— "

"Will you hold your tongue?" said Jonas, looking fiercely round, and glancing at the door.

"Well, well!" said Montague. "Judicious! Quite correct! My discoveries being published, would be like many other men's discoveries in this honest world; of no further use to me. You see, Chuzzlewit, how ingenuous and frank I am in showing you the weakness of my own position! To return. I make, or think I make, a certain discovery, which I take an early opportunity of mentioning in your ear, in that spirit of confidence which I really hoped did prevail between us, and was reciprocated by you. Perhaps there is something in it; perhaps there is nothing. I have my knowledge and opinion on the subject. You have yours. We will not discuss the question. But, my good fellow, you have been weak; what I wish to point out to you is, that you have been weak. I may desire to turn this little incident to my account (indeed, I do—I'll not deny it), but my account does not lie in probing it, or using it against you."

"What do you call using it against me?" asked Jonas, who had not yet changed his attitude.

"Oh!" said Montague, with a laugh. "We'll not enter into that."

"Using it, to make a beggar of me. Is that the use you mean?"

" No."

" Ecod," muttered Jonas, bitterly. " That's the use in which your account *does* lie. You speak the truth there."

" I wish you to venture (it's a very safe venture) a little more with us, certainly, and to keep quiet," said Montague. " You promised me you would ; and you must. I say it plainly, Chuzzlewit, you MUST. Reason the matter. If you don't, my secret is worthless to me ; and being so, it may as well become the public property as mine : better, for I shall gain some credit, bringing it to light. I want you, besides, to act as a decoy in a case I have already told you of. You don't mind that, I know. You care nothing for the man (you care nothing for any man ; you are too sharp ; so am I, I hope) ; and could bear any loss of his, with pious fortitude. Ha, ha, ha ! You have tried to escape from the first consequence. You cannot escape it, I assure you. I have shown you that, to-day. Now, I am not a moral man, you know. I am not the least in the world affected by anything you may have done ; by any little indiscretion you may have committed ; but I wish to profit by it, if I can ; and to a man of your intelligence I make that free confession. I am not at all singular in that infirmity. Everybody profits by the indiscretion of his neighbour ; and the people in the best repute, the most. Why do you give me this trouble ? It must come to a friendly agreement, or an unfriendly crash. It must. If the former, you are very little hurt. If the latter—well ! you know best what is likely to happen then."

Jonas left the window, and walked up close to him. He did not look him in the face ; it was not his habit to do that ; but he kept his eyes towards him—on his breast, or thereabouts—and was at great pains to speak slowly and distinctly, in reply. Just as a man in a state of conscious drunkenness might be.

" Lying is of no use, now," he said. " I *did* think of getting away this morning, and making better terms with you from a distance."

"To be sure! To be sure!" replied Montague. "Nothing more natural. I foresaw that, and provided against it. But I am afraid I am interrupting you."

"How the devil," pursued Jonas, with a still greater effort, "you made choice of your messenger, and where you found him, I'll not ask you. I owed him one good turn before to-day. If you are so careless of men in general, as you said you were just now, you are quite indifferent to what becomes of such a crop-tailed cur as that, and will leave me to settle my account with him in my own manner."

If he had raised his eyes to his companion's face, he would have seen that Montague was evidently unable to comprehend his meaning. But, continuing to stand before him, with his furtive gaze directed as before, and pausing here, only to moisten his dry lips with his tongue, the fact was lost upon him. It might have struck a close observer that this fixed and steady glance of Jonas's was a part of the alteration which had taken place in his demeanour. He kept it rivetted on one spot, with which his thoughts had manifestly nothing to do; like as a juggler walking on a cord or wire to any dangerous end, holds some object in his sight to steady him, and never wanders from it, lest he trip.

Montague was quick in his rejoinder, though he made it at a venture. There was no difference of opinion between him and his friend on *that* point. Not the least.

"Your great discovery," Jonas proceeded, with a savage sneer that got the better of him for the moment, "may be true, and may be false. Whichever it is, I dare say I'm no worse than other men."

"Not a bit," said Tigg. "Not a bit. We're all alike—or nearly so."

"I want to know this," Jonas went on to say; "is it your own? You'll not wonder at my asking the question."

"My own!" repeated Montague.

"Aye!" returned the other, gruffly. "Is it known to anybody else? Come! Don't waver about that."

265

"No!" said Montague, without the smallest hesitation. "What would it be worth, do you think, unless I had the keeping of it?"

Now, for the first time, Jonas looked at him. After a pause, he put out his hand, and said, with a laugh:

"Come! make things easy to me, and I'm yours. I don't know that I may not be better off here, after all, than if I had gone away this morning. But here I am, and here I'll stay now. Take your oath!"

He cleared his throat, for he was speaking hoarsely, and said in a lighter tone:

"Shall I go to Pecksniff! When? Say when!"

"Immediately!" cried Montague. "He cannot be enticed too soon."

"Ecod!" cried Jonas, with a wild laugh. "There's some fun in catching that old hypocrite. I hate him. Shall I go to-night?"

"Aye! This," said Montague, ecstatically, "is like business! We understand each other now! To-night, my good fellow, by all means."

"Come with me," cried Jonas. "We must make a dash: go down in state, and carry documents, for he's a deep file to deal with, and must be drawn on with an artful hand, or he'll not follow. I know him. As I can't take your lodgings or your dinners down, I must take you. Will you come to-night?"

His friend appeared to hesitate; and neither to have anticipated this proposal, nor to relish it very much.

"We can concert our plans upon the road," said Jonas. "We must not go direct to him, but cross over from some other place, and turn out of our way to see him. I may not want to introduce you, but I must have you on the spot. I know the man, I tell you."

"But, what if the man knows me?" said Montague, shrugging his shoulders.

"He know!" cried Jonas. "Don't you run that risk with

fifty men a day! Would your father know you? Did *I* know you? Ecod! you were another figure when I saw you first. Ha, ha, ha! I see the rents and patches now! No false hair then, no black dye! You were another sort of joker, in those days, you were! You even spoke different, then. You've acted the gentleman so seriously since, that you've taken in yourself. If he should know you, what does it matter? Such a change is a proof of your success. You know that, or you would not have made yourself known to me. Will you come?"

"My good fellow," said Montague, still hesitating, "I can trust you alone."

"Trust me! Ecod, you may trust me now, far enough. I'll try to go away no more—no more!" He stopped, and added in a more sober tone, "I can't get on without you. Will you come?"

"I will," said Montague, "if that's your opinion." And they shook hands upon it.

The boisterous manner which Jonas had exhibited during the latter part of this conversation, and which had gone on rapidly increasing with almost every word he had spoken; from the time when he looked his honourable friend in the face until now; did not now subside, but, remaining at its height, abided by him. Most unusual with him at any period; most inconsistent with his temper and constitution; especially unnatural it would appear in one so darkly circumstanced; it abided by him. It was not like the effect of wine, or any ardent drink, for he was perfectly coherent. It even made him proof against the usual influence of such means of excitement; for, although he drank deeply several times that day, with no reserve or caution, he remained exactly the same man, and his spirits neither rose nor fell in the least observable degree.

Deciding, after some discussion, to travel at night, in order that the day's business might not be broken in upon, they took counsel together in reference to the means. Mr.

Montague being of opinion that four horses were advisable, at all events for the first stage, as throwing a great deal of dust into people's eyes, in more senses than one, a travelling chariot and four lay under orders for nine o'clock. Jonas did not go home : observing, that his being obliged to leave town on business in so great a hurry, would be a good excuse for having turned back so unexpectedly in the morning. So he wrote a note for his portmanteau, and sent it by a messenger, who duly brought his luggage back, with a short note from that other piece of luggage, his wife, expressive of her wish to be allowed to come and see him for a moment. To this request he sent for answer, "she had better;" and one such threatening affirmative being sufficient, in defiance of the English grammar, to express a negative, she kept away.

Mr. Montague, being much engaged in the course of the day, Jonas bestowed his spirits chiefly on the doctor, with whom he lunched in the medical officer's own room. On his way thither, encountering Mr. Nadgett in the outer room, he bantered that stealthy gentleman on always appearing anxious to avoid him, and inquired if he were afraid of him. Mr. Nadgett slyly answered, "No, but he believed it must be his way, as he had been charged with much the same kind of thing before."

Mr. Montague was listening to, or, to speak with greater elegance, he overheard, this dialogue. As soon as Jonas was gone, he beckoned Nadgett to him with the feather of his pen, and whispered in his ear,

"Who gave him my letter this morning?"

"My lodger, sir," said Nadgett, behind the palm of his hand.

"How came that about?"

"I found him on the wharf, sir. Being so much hurried, and you not arrived, it was necessary to do something. It fortunately occurred to me, that if I gave it him myself, I could be of no further use. I should have been blown upon immediately."

"Mr. Nadgett, you are a jewel," said Montague, patting him on the back. "What's your lodger's name?"

"Pinch, sir. Thomas Pinch."

Montague reflected for a little while, and then asked:

"From the country, do you know?"

"From Wiltshire, sir, he told me."

They parted without another word. To see Mr. Nadgett's bow when Montague and he next met, and to see Mr. Montague acknowledge it, anybody might have undertaken to swear that they had never spoken to each other confidentially, in all their lives.

In the meanwhile, Mr. Jonas and the doctor made themselves very comfortable up stairs, over a bottle of the old Madeira, and some sandwiches; for the doctor having been already invited to dine below, at six o'clock, preferred a light repast for lunch. It was advisable, he said, in two points of view: First, as being healthy in itself. Secondly, as being the better preparation for dinner.

"And you are bound for all our sakes to take particular care of your digestion, Mr. Chuzzlewit, my dear sir," said the doctor, smacking his lips after a glass of wine; "for depend upon it, it is worth preserving. It must be in admirable condition, sir; perfect chronometer-work. Otherwise your spirits could not be so remarkable. Your bosom's lord sits lightly on its throne, Mr. Chuzzlewit, as what's-his-name says in the play. I wish he said it in a play which did anything like common justice to our profession, by-the-bye. There is an apothecary in that drama, sir, which is a low thing; vulgar, sir; out of nature altogether."

Mr. Jobling pulled out his shirt-frill of fine linen, as though he would have said, "This is what I call nature in a medical man, sir;" and looked at Jonas for an observation.

Jonas not being in a condition to pursue the subject, took up a case of lancets that was lying on the table, and opened it.

"Ah!" said the doctor, leaning back in his chair, "I always

take 'em out of my pocket before I eat. My pockets are rather tight. Ha, ha, ha!"

Jonas had opened one of the shining little instruments; and was scrutinising it with a look as sharp and eager as its own bright edge.

"Good steel, doctor. Good steel. Eh?"

"Ye-es," replied the doctor, with the faltering modesty of ownership. "One might open a vein pretty dexterously with that, Mr. Chuzzlewit."

"It has opened a good many in its time, I suppose?" said Jonas, looking at it with a growing interest.

"Not a few, my dear sir, not a few. It has been engaged in a—in a pretty good practice, I believe I may say," replied the doctor, coughing as if the matter-of-fact were so very dry and literal that he couldn't help it. In a pretty good practice," repeated the doctor, putting another glass of wine to his lips.

"Now, could you cut a man's throat with such a thing as this?" demanded Jonas.

"Oh certainly, certainly, if you took him in the right place," returned the doctor. "It all depends upon that."

"Where you have your hand now, hey?" cried Jonas, bending forward to look at it.

"Yes," said the doctor; "that's the jugular."

Jonas, in his vivacity, made a sudden sawing in the air, so close behind the doctor's jugular, that he turned quite red. Then Jonas (in the same strange spirit of vivacity) burst into a loud discordant laugh.

"No, no," said the doctor, shaking his head: "edge tools, edge tools; never play with 'em. A very remarkable instance of the skilful use of edge-tools, by the way, occurs to me at this moment. It was a case of murder. I am afraid it was a case of murder, committed by a member of our profession; it was so artistically done."

"Aye!" said Jonas. "How was that?"

"Why, sir," returned Jobling, "the thing lies in a nut-shell. A certain gentleman was found, one morning, in an obscure street, lying in an angle of a doorway—I should rather say, leaning, in an upright position, in the angle of a doorway, and supported consequently *by* the doorway. Upon his waist-coat there was one solitary drop of blood. He was dead, and cold; and had been murdered, sir."

"Only one drop of blood!" said Jonas.

"Sir, that man," replied the doctor, "had been stabbed to the heart. Had been stabbed to the heart with such dexterity, sir, that he had died instantly, and had bled internally. It was supposed that a medical friend of his (to whom suspicion attached) had engaged him in conversation on some pretence; had taken him, very likely, by the button in a conversational manner; had examined his ground at leisure with his other hand; had marked the exact spot; drawn out the instrument, whatever it was, when he was quite prepared; and——"

"And done the trick," suggested Jonas.

"Exactly so," replied the doctor. "It was quite an opera-tion in its way, and very neat. The medical friend never turned up; and, as I tell you, he had the credit of it. Whether he did it or not, I can't say. But, having had the honour to be called in with two or three of my professional brethren on the occasion, and having assisted to make a careful examination of the wound, I have no hesitation in saying that it would have reflected credit on any medical man; and that in an unprofessional person, it could not but be considered, either as an extraordinary work of art, or the result of a still more extraordinary, happy, and favourable conjunction of circum-stances."

His hearer was so much interested in this case, that the doctor went on to elucidate it with the assistance of his own finger and thumb and waistcoat; and at Jonas's request, he took the further trouble of going into a corner of the room, and alternately representing the murdered man and the mur-derer; which he did with great effect. The bottle being emptied and the story done, Jonas was in precisely the same boisterous and unusual state as when they had sat down. If, as Jobling theorised, his good digestion were the cause, he must have been a very ostrich.

At dinner, it was just the same; and after dinner too; though wine was drunk in abundance, and various rich meats eaten. At nine o'clock it was still the same. There being a lamp in the carriage, he swore they would take a pack of cards, and a bottle of wine: and with these things under his cloak, went down to the door.

"Out of the way, Tom Thumb, and get to bed!"

This was the salutation he bestowed on Mr. Bailey, who, booted and wrapped up, stood at the carriage-door to help him in.

"To bed, sir! I'm a going, too," said Bailey.

He alighted quickly, and walked back into the hall, where Montague was lighting a cigar: conducting Mr. Bailey with him, by the collar.

"You are not a going to take this monkey of a boy, are you?"

"Yes," said Montague.

He gave the boy a shake, and threw him roughly aside. There was more of his familiar self in the action, than in anything he had done that day; but he broke out laughing immediately afterwards, and making a thrust at the doctor with his hand, in imitation of his representation of the medical friend, went out to the carriage again, and took his seat. His companion followed immediately. Mr. Bailey climbed into the rumble.

"It will be a stormy night!" exclaimed the doctor, as they started.

CHAPTER XLII

THE Doctor's prognostication in reference to the weather was speedily verified. Although the weather was not a patient of his, and no third party had required him to give an opinion on the case, the quick fulfilment of his prophecy may be taken as an instance of his professional tact; for, unless the threatening aspect of the night had been perfectly plain and unmistakeable, Mr. Jobling would never have compromised his reputation by delivering any sentiments on the subject. He used this principle in Medicine with too much success, to be unmindful of it in his commonest transactions.

It was one of those hot, silent, nights, when people sit at windows, listening for the thunder which they know will shortly break; when they recall dismal tales of hurricanes and earthquakes; and of lonely travellers on open plains, and lonely ships at sea, struck by lightning. Lightning flashed and quivered on the black horizon even now; and hollow murmurings were in the wind, as though it had been blowing where the thunder rolled, and still was charged with its exhausted echoes. But the storm, though gathering swiftly, had not yet come up; and the prevailing stillness was the more solemn, from the dull intelligence that seemed to hover in the air, of noise and conflict afar off.

It was very dark; but in the murky sky there were masses of cloud which shone with a lurid light, like monstrous heaps

273

of copper that had been heated in a furnace, and were growing cold. These had been advancing steadily and slowly, but they were now motionless, or nearly so. As the carriage clattered round the corners of the streets, it passed at every one, a knot of persons, who had come there—many from their houses close at hand, without hats—to look up at that quarter of the sky. And now, a very few large drops of rain began to fall, and thunder rumbled in the distance.

Jonas sat in a corner of the carriage, with his bottle resting on his knee, and gripped as tightly in his hand, as if he would have ground its neck to powder if he could. Instinctively attracted by the night, he had laid aside the pack of cards upon the cushion : and with the same involuntary impulse, so intelligible to both of them as not to occasion a remark on either side, his companion had extinguished the lamp. The front glasses were down; and they sat looking silently out upon the gloomy scene before them.

They were clear of London, or as clear of it as travellers can be, whose way lies on the Western Road, within a stage of that enormous city. Occasionally, they encountered a foot-passenger, hurrying to the nearest place of shelter; or some unwieldy cart proceeding onward at a heavy trot, with the same end in view. Little clusters of such vehicles were gathered round the stable-yard or baiting-place of every way-side tavern ; while their drivers watched the weather from the doors and open windows, or made merry within. Everywhere, the people were disposed to bear each other company, rather than sit alone; so that groups of watchful faces seemed to be looking out upon the night *and them*, from almost every house they passed.

It may appear strange that this should have disturbed Jonas, or rendered him uneasy : but it did. After muttering to himself, and often changing his position, he drew up the blind on his side of the carriage, and turned his shoulder sulkily towards it. But he neither looked at his companion, nor broke the silence which prevailed between them, and which had fallen so suddenly upon himself, by addressing a word to him.

The thunder rolled, the lightning flashed; the rain poured down, like Heaven's wrath. Surrounded at one moment by intolerable light, and at the next by pitchy darkness, they still pressed forward on their journey. Even when they arrived at the end of the stage, and might have tarried, they did not; but ordered horses out, immediately. Nor had this any reference to some five minutes' lull, which at that time seemed to promise a cessation of the storm. They held their course as if they were impelled and driven by its fury. Although they had not exchanged a dozen words, and might have tarried very well, they seemed to feel, by joint consent, that onward they must go.

Louder and louder the deep thunder rolled, as through the myriad halls of some vast temple in the sky; fiercer and brighter became the lightning; more and more heavily the rain poured down. The horses (they were travelling now with a single pair) plunged and started from the rills of quivering fire that seemed to wind along the ground before them; but there these two men sat, and forward they went as if they were led on by an invisible attraction.

The eye, partaking of the quickness of the flashing light, saw in its every gleam a multitude of objects which it could not see at steady noon in fifty times that period. Bells in steeples, with the rope and wheel that moved them; ragged nests of birds in cornices and nooks; faces full of consternation in the tilted waggons that came tearing past: their frightened teams ringing out a warning which the thunder drowned; harrows and ploughs left out in fields; miles upon miles of hedge-divided country, with the distant fringe of trees as obvious as the scarecrow in the beanfield close at hand; in a trembling, vivid, flickering instant, everything was clear and plain: then came a flush of red into the yellow light; a change to blue; a brightness so intense that there was nothing else but light; and then the deepest and profoundest darkness.

The lightning being very crooked and very dazzling, may have presented or assisted a curious optical illusion, which suddenly rose before the startled eyes of Montague in the carriage, and as rapidly disappeared. He thought he saw Jonas with his hand lifted, and the bottle clenched in it like a hammer, making as if he would aim a blow at his head. At the same time he observed (or so believed), an expression in his face: a combination of the unnatural excitement he had shown all day, with a wild hatred and fear: which might have rendered a wolf a less terrible companion.

He uttered an involuntary exclamation, and called to the driver, who brought his horses to a stop with all speed.

It could hardly have been as he supposed, for although he had not taken his eyes off his companion, and had not seen him move, he sat reclining in his corner as before.

"What's the matter?" said Jonas. "Is that your general way of waking out of your sleep?"

"I could swear," returned the other, "that I have not closed my eyes!"

"When you have sworn it," said Jonas, composedly, "we had better go on again, if you have only stopped for that."

He uncorked the bottle with the help of his teeth; and putting it to his lips, took a long draught.

"I wish we had never started on this journey. This is not," said Montague, recoiling instinctively, and speaking in a voice that betrayed his agitation: "this is not a night to travel in."

"Ecod! you're right there," returned Jonas: "and we shouldn't be out in it but for you. If you hadn't kept me waiting all day, we might have been at Salisbury by this time; snug abed and fast asleep. What are we stopping for?"

His companion put his head out of window for a moment, and drawing it in again, observed (as if that were his cause of anxiety), that the boy was drenched to the skin.

"Serve him right," said Jonas. "I'm glad of it. What the devil are we stopping for? Are you going to spread him out to dry?"

276

"I have half a mind to take him inside," observed the other with some hesitation.

"Oh! thankee!" said Jonas. "We don't want any damp boys here; especially a young imp like him. Let him be where he is. He ain't afraid of a little thunder and lightning, I dare say; whoever else is. Go on, driver! We had better have *him* inside perhaps," he muttered with a laugh; "and the horses!"

"Don't go too fast," cried Montague to the postillion; "and take care how you go. You were nearly in the ditch when I called to you."

This was not true; and Jonas bluntly said so, as they moved forward again. Montague took little or no heed of what he said, but repeated that it was not a night for travelling, and showed himself, both then and afterwards, unusually anxious.

From this time, Jonas recovered his former spirits, if such a term may be employed to express the state in which he had left the city. He had his bottle often at his mouth; roared out snatches of songs, without the least regard to time or tune or voice, or anything but loud discordance; and urged his silent friend to be merry with him.

"You're the best company in the world, my good fellow," said Montague with an effort, "and in general irresistible; but to-night—do you hear it?"

"Ecod I hear and see it too," cried Jonas, shading his eyes, for the moment, from the lightning which was flashing, not in any one direction, but all around them. "What of that? It don't change you, nor me, nor our affairs. Chorus, chorus.

> It may lighten and storm,
> Till it hunt the red worm
> From the grass where the gibbet is driven;
> But it can't hurt the dead,
> And it won't save the head
> That is doom'd to be rifled and riven.

That must be a precious old song," he added with an oath, as he stopped short in a kind of wonder at himself. "I haven't heard it since I was a boy, and how it comes into my head now, unless the lightning put it there, I don't know. 'Can't hurt the dead'! No no. 'And won't save the head'! No no. No! Ha ha ha!"

His mirth was of such a savage and extraordinary character, and was, in an inexplicable way, at once so suited to the night, and yet such a coarse intrusion on its terrors, that his fellow-traveller, always a coward, shrunk from him in positive fear. Instead of Jonas being his tool and instrument, their places seemed to be reversed. But there was reason for this too, Montague thought; since the sense of his debasement might naturally inspire such a man with the wish to assert a noisy independence, and in that license to forget his real condition. Being quick enough, in reference to such subjects of contemplation, he was not long in taking this argument into account, and giving it its full weight. But, still, he felt a vague sense of alarm, and was depressed and uneasy.

He was certain he had not been asleep; but his eyes might have deceived him; for, looking at Jonas now in any interval of darkness, he could represent his figure to himself in any attitude his state of mind suggested. On the other hand, he knew full well that Jonas had no reason to love him; and even taking the piece of pantomime which had so impressed his mind to be a real gesture, and not the working of his fancy, the most that could be said of it, was, that it was quite in keeping with the rest of his diabolical fun, and had the same impotent expression of truth in it. "If he could kill me with a wish," thought the swindler, "I should not live long."

He resolved, that when he should have had his use of Jonas, he would restrain him with an iron curb: in the meantime, that he could not do better than leave him to take his own way, and preserve his own peculiar description of good-humour, after his own uncommon manner. It was no great sacrifice to bear with him: "for when all is got that can be got," thought Montague, "I shall decamp across the water, and have the laugh on my side—and the gains."

Such were his reflections from hour to hour; his state of mind being one in which the same thoughts constantly present themselves over and over again in wearisome repetition; while Jonas, who appeared to have dismissed reflection altogether, entertained himself as before. They agreed that they would go to Salisbury, and would cross to Mr. Pecksniff's in the morning; and at the prospect of deluding that worthy gentleman, the spirits of his amiable son-in-law became more boisterous than ever.

As the night wore on, the thunder died away, but still rolled gloomily and mournfully in the distance. The lightning too, though now comparatively harmless, was yet bright and frequent. The rain was quite as violent as it had ever been.

It was their ill-fortune, at about the time of dawn and in the last stage of their journey, to have a restive pair of horses. These animals had been greatly terrified in their stable by the tempest; and coming out into the dreary interval between night and morning, when the glare of the lightning was yet unsubdued by day, and the various objects in their view were presented in indistinct and exaggerated shapes which they would not have worn by night, they gradually became less and less capable of control; until, taking a sudden fright at something by the roadside, they dashed off wildly down a steep hill, flung the driver from his saddle, drew the carriage to the brink of a ditch, stumbled headlong down, and threw it crashing over.

The travellers had opened the carriage door, and had either jumped or fallen out. Jonas was the first to stagger to his feet. He felt sick and weak, and very giddy, and, reeling to a five-barred gate, stood holding by it: looking drowsily about, as the whole landscape swam before his eyes. But, by degrees, he grew more conscious, and presently observed that Montague was lying senseless in the road, within a few feet of the horses.

In an instant, as if his own faint body were suddenly animated by a demon, he ran to the horses' heads; and pulling at their bridles with all his force, set them struggling and plunging with such mad violence as brought their hoofs at every effort nearer to the skull of the prostrate man; and must have led in half a minute to his brains being dashed out on the highway.

As he did this, he fought and contended with them like a man possessed: making them wilder by his cries.

"Whoop!" cried Jonas. "Whoop! again! another! A little more, a little more! Up, ye devils! Hillo!"

As he heard the driver who had risen and was hurrying up, crying to him to desist, his violence increased.

"Hillo! Hillo!" cried Jonas.

"For God's sake!" cried the driver. "The gentleman—in the road—he'll be killed!"

The same shouts and the same struggles were his only answer. But the man darting in at the peril of his own life, saved Montague's, by dragging him through the mire and water out of the reach of present harm. That done, he ran to Jonas; and with the aid of his knife they very shortly disengaged the horses from the broken chariot, and got them, cut and bleeding, on their legs again. The postillion and Jonas had now leisure to look at each other, which they had not had yet.

"Presence of mind, presence of mind!" cried Jonas, throwing up his hands wildly. "What would you have done without me!"

"The other gentleman would have done badly without *me*," returned the man, shaking his head. "You should have moved him first. I gave him up for dead."

"Presence of mind, you croaker, presence of mind!" cried Jonas, with a harsh loud laugh. "Was he struck, do you think?"

They both turned to look at him. Jonas muttered something to himself, when he saw him sitting up beneath the hedge, looking vacantly round.

"What's the matter?" asked Montague. "Is anybody hurt?"

280

Mr. Jonas exhibits his Presence of Mind

"Ecod!" said Jonas, "it don't seem so. There are no bones broke, after all."

They raised him, and he tried to walk. He was a good deal shaken, and trembled very much. But with the exception of a few cuts and bruises this was all the damage he had sustained.

"Cuts and bruises, eh?" said Jonas. "We've all got them. Only cuts and bruises, eh?"

"I wouldn't have given sixpence for the gentleman's head in half a dozen seconds more, for all he's only cut and bruised," observed the post-boy. "If ever you're in an accident of this sort again, sir; which I hope you won't be; never you pull at the bridle of a horse that's down, when there's a man's head in the way. That can't be done twice without there being a dead man in the case; it would have ended in that, this time, as sure as ever you were born, if I hadn't come up just when I did."

Jonas replied by advising him with a curse to hold his tongue, and to go somewhere, whither he was not very likely to go of his own accord. But Montague, who had listened eagerly to every word, himself diverted the subject, by exclaiming: "Where's the boy!"

"Ecod, I forgot that monkey," said Jonas. "What's become of him!" A very brief search settled that question. The unfortunate Mr. Bailey had been thrown sheer over the hedge or the five-barred gate; and was lying in the neighbouring field, to all appearance dead.

"When I said to-night, that I wished I had never started on this journey," cried his master, "I knew it was an ill-fated one. Look at this boy!"

"Is that all?" growled Jonas. "If you call *that* a sign of it—"

"Why, what should I call a sign of it?" asked Montague, hurriedly. "What do you mean?"

"I mean," said Jonas, stooping down over the body, "that I never heard you were his father, or had any particular reason to care much about him. Halloa. Hold up here!"

But the boy was past holding up, or being held up, or giving any other sign of life, than a faint and fitful beating of the heart. After some discussion, the driver mounted the horse which had been least injured, and took the lad in his arms, as well as he could; while Montague and Jonas leading the other horse, and carrying a trunk between them, walked by his side towards Salisbury.

"You'd get there in a few minutes, and be able to send assistance to meet us, if you went forward, post-boy," said Jonas. "Trot on!"

"No, no," cried Montague; "we'll keep together."

"Why, what a chicken you are! You are not afraid of being robbed; are you?" said Jonas.

"I am not afraid of anything," replied the other, whose looks and manner were in flat contradiction to his words. "But we'll keep together."

"You were mighty anxious about the boy, a minute ago," said Jonas. "I suppose you know that he may die in the meantime?"

"Aye, aye. I know. But we'll keep together."

As it was clear that he was not to be moved from this determination, Jonas made no other rejoinder than such as his face expressed; and they proceeded in company. They had three or four good miles to travel; and the way was not made easier by the state of the road, the burden by which they were embarrassed, or their own stiff and sore condition. After a sufficiently long and painful walk, they arrived at the Inn; and having knocked the people up (it being yet very early in the morning), sent out messengers to see to the carriage and its contents, and roused a surgeon from his bed to tend the chief sufferer. All the service he could render, he rendered promptly and skilfully. But he gave it as his opinion that the boy was labouring under a severe concussion of the brain, and that Mr. Bailey's mortal course was run.

If Montague's strong interest in the announcement could have been considered as unselfish in any degree, it might have

been a redeeming trait in a character that had no such linea-
ments to spare. But it was not difficult to see that, for some
unexpressed reason best appreciated by himself, he attached a
strange value to the company and presence of this mere child.
When, after receiving some assistance from the surgeon himself,
he retired to the bed-room prepared for him, and it was broad
day, his mind was still dwelling on this theme.

"I would rather have lost," he said, "a thousand pounds
than lost the boy just now. But I'll return home alone. I
am resolved upon that. Chuzzlewit shall go forward first,
and I will follow in my own time. I'll have no more of this,"
he added, wiping his damp forehead. "Twenty-four hours of
this would turn my hair grey!"

After examining his chamber, and looking under the bed,
and in the cupboards, and even behind the curtains, with
unusual caution (although it was, as has been said, broad day)
he double-locked the door by which he had entered, and
retired to rest. There was another door in the room, but it
was locked on the outer side; and with what place it communicated, he knew not.

His fears or evil conscience reproduced this door in all his
dreams. He dreamed that a dreadful secret was connected
with it: a secret which he knew, and yet did not know, for
although he was heavily responsible for it, and a party to it,
he was harassed even in his vision by a distracting uncertainty
in reference to its import. Incoherently entwined with this
dream was another, which represented it as the hiding-place
of an enemy, a shadow, a phantom; and made it the business
of his life to keep the terrible creature closed up, and prevent
it from forcing its way in upon him. With this view Nadgett,
and he, and a strange man with a bloody smear upon his head
(who told him that he had been his playfellow, and told him,
too, the real name of an old schoolmate, forgotten until then),
worked with iron plates and nails to make the door secure;
but though they worked never so hard, it was all in vain, for
the nails broke, or changed to soft twigs, or what was worse,

to worms, between their fingers; the wood of the door splintered and crumbled, so that even nails would not remain in it; and the iron plates curled up like hot paper. All this time the creature on the other side—whether it was in the shape of man, or beast, he neither knew nor sought to know —was gaining on them. But his greatest terror was when the man with the bloody smear upon his head demanded of him if he knew this creature's name, and said that he would whisper it. At this the dreamer fell upon his knees, his whole blood thrilling with inexplicable fear, and held his ears. But looking at the speaker's lips, he saw that they formed the utterance of the letter "J;" and crying out aloud that the secret was discovered, and they were all lost, he awoke.

Awoke to find Jonas standing at his bedside watching him. And that very door wide open.

As their eyes met, Jonas retreated a few paces, and Montague sprang out of bed.

"Heyday!" said Jonas. "You're all alive this morning."

"Alive!" the other stammered, as he pulled the bell-rope violently: "What are you doing here?"

"It's your room to be sure," said Jonas; "but I'm almost inclined to ask you what *you* are doing here? My room is on the other side of that door. No one told me last night not to open it. I thought it led into a passage, and was coming out to order breakfast. There's—there's no bell in my room."

Montague had in the meantime admitted the man with his hot water and boots, who hearing this, said, yes, there was; and passed into the adjoining room to point it out, at the head of the bed.

"I couldn't find it, then," said Jonas: "it's all the same. Shall I order breakfast?"

Montague answered in the affirmative. When Jonas had retired, whistling, through his own room, he opened the door of communication, to take out the key and fasten it on the inner side. But it was taken out already.

AN EVIL JOURNEY

He dragged a table against the door, and sat down to collect himself, as if his dreams still had some influence upon his mind.

"An evil journey," he repeated several times. "An evil journey. But I'll travel home alone. I'll have no more of this!"

His presentiment, or superstition, that it was an evil journey, did not at all deter him from doing the evil for which the journey was undertaken. With this in view, he dressed himself more carefully than usual to make a favourable impression on Mr. Pecksniff: and, reassured by his own appearance, the beauty of the morning, and the flashing of the wet boughs outside his window in the merry sunshine, was soon sufficiently inspirited to swear a few round oaths, and hum the fag-end of a song.

But he still muttered to himself at intervals, for all that: "I'll travel home alone!"

CHAPTER XLIII

HAS AN INFLUENCE ON THE FORTUNES OF SEVERAL PEOPLE. MR. PECKSNIFF IS EXHIBITED IN THE PLENITUDE OF POWER, AND WIELDS THE SAME WITH FORTITUDE AND MAGNANIMITY

On the night of the storm, Mrs. Lupin, hostess of the Blue Dragon, sat by herself in her little bar. Her solitary condition, or the bad weather, or both united, made Mrs. Lupin thoughtful, not to say sorrowful. As she sat with her chin upon her hand, looking out through a low back lattice, rendered dim in the brightest daytime by clustering vine-leaves, she shook her head very often, and said, "Dear me! Ah, dear, dear me!"

It was a melancholy time, even in the snugness of the Dragon bar. The rich expanse of corn-field, pasture-land, green slope, and gentle undulation, with its sparkling brooks, its many hedgerows, and its clumps of beautiful trees, was black and dreary, from the diamond panes of the lattice away to the far horizon, where the thunder seemed to roll along the hills. The heavy rain beat down the tender branches of vine and jessamine, and trampled on them in its fury; and when the lightning gleamed, it showed the tearful leaves shivering and cowering together at the window, and tapping at it urgently, as if beseeching to be sheltered from the dismal night.

As a mark of her respect for the lightning, Mrs. Lupin had removed her candle to the chimney-piece. Her basket of needlework stood unheeded at her elbow; her supper, spread on a round table not far off, was untasted; and the knives had been removed for fear of attraction. She had sat for a long time with her chin upon her hand, saying to herself at intervals, "Dear me! Ah, dear, dear me!"

She was on the eve of saying so, once more, when the latch of the house-door (closed to keep the rain out), rattled on its well-worn catch, and a traveller came in, who, shutting it after him, and walking straight up to the half-door of the bar, said, rather gruffly:

"A pint of the best old beer here."

He had some reason to be gruff, for if he had passed the day in a waterfall, he could scarcely have been wetter than he was. He was wrapped up to the eyes in a rough blue sailor's coat, and had an oil-skin hat on, from the capacious brim of which, the rain fell trickling down upon his breast, and back, and shoulders. Judging from a certain liveliness of chin—he had so pulled down his hat, and pulled up his collar to defend himself from the weather, that she could only see his chin, and even across that he drew the wet sleeve of his shaggy coat, as she looked at him—Mrs. Lupin set him down for a good-natured fellow, too.

"A bad night!" observed the hostess cheerfully.

The traveller shook himself like a Newfoundland dog, and said it was, rather.

"There's a fire in the kitchen," said Mrs. Lupin, "and very good company there. Hadn't you better go and dry yourself?"

"No, thankee," said the man, glancing towards the kitchen as he spoke; he seemed to know the way.

"It's enough to give you your death of cold," observed the hostess.

"I don't take my death easy," returned the traveller; "or I should most likely have took it afore to-night. Your health, ma'am!"

Mrs. Lupin thanked him; but in the act of lifting the

tankard to his mouth, he changed his mind, and put it down again. Throwing his body back, and looking about him stiffly, as a man does who is wrapped up, and has his hat low down over his eyes, he said,

"What do you call this house? Not the Dragon, do you?"

Mrs. Lupin complacently made answer, "Yes, the Dragon."

"Why, then, you've got a sort of a relation of mine here, ma'am," said the traveller: "a young man of the name of Tapley. What! Mark, my boy!" apostrophising the premises, "have I come upon you at last, old buck!"

This was touching Mrs. Lupin on a tender point. She turned to trim the candle on the chimney-piece, and said, with her back towards the traveller:

"Nobody should be made more welcome at the Dragon, master, than any one who brought me news of Mark. But it's many and many a long day and month since he left here and England. And whether he's alive or dead, poor fellow, Heaven above us only knows!"

She shook her head, and her voice trembled; her hand must have done so too, for the light required a deal of trimming.

"Where did he go, ma'am?" asked the traveller, in a gentler voice.

"He went," said Mrs. Lupin, with increased distress, "to America. He was always tender-hearted and kind, and perhaps at this moment may be lying in prison under sentence of death, for taking pity on some miserable black, and helping the poor runaway creetur to escape. How could he ever go to America! Why didn't he go to some of those countries where the savages eat each other fairly, and give an equal chance to every one!"

Quite subdued by this time, Mrs. Lupin sobbed, and was retiring to a chair to give her grief free vent, when the traveller caught her in his arms, and she uttered a glad cry of recognition.

"Yes, I will!" cried Mark, "another—one more—twenty

288

more! You didn't know me in that hat and coat? I thought you would have known me anywheres! Ten more!"

"So I should have known you, if I could have seen you; but I couldn't, and you spoke so gruff. I didn't think you could speak gruff to me, Mark, at first coming back."

"Fifteen more!" said Mr. Tapley. "How handsome and how young you look! Six more! The last half-dozen warn't a fair one, and must be done over again. Lord bless you, what a treat it is to see you! One more! Well, I never was so jolly. Just a few more, on account of there not being any credit in it!"

When Mr. Tapley stopped in these calculations in simple addition, he did it, not because he was at all tired of the exercise, but because he was out of breath. The pause reminded him of other duties.

"Mr. Martin Chuzzlewit's outside," he said. "I left him under the cart-shed, while I came on to see if there was anybody here. We want to keep quiet to-night, till we know the news from you, and what it's best for us to do."

"There's not a soul in the house, except the kitchen company," returned the hostess. "If they were to know you had come back, Mark, they'd have a bonfire in the street, late as it is."

"But they mustn't know it to-night, my precious soul," said Mark: "so have the house shut, and the kitchen fire made up; and when it's all ready, put a light in the winder, and we'll come in. One more! I long to hear about old friends. You'll tell me all about 'em, won't you: Mr. Pinch, and the butcher's dog down the street, and the terrier over the way, and the wheelwright's, and every one of 'em. When I first caught sight of the church to-night, I thought the steeple would have choked me, I did. One more! Won't you? Not a very little one to finish off with?"

"You have had plenty, I am sure," said the hostess. "Go along with your foreign manners!"

"That ain't foreign, bless you!" cried Mark. "Native as

oysters, that is! One more, because it's native! As a mark of respect for the land we live in! This don't count as between you and me, you understand," said Mr. Tapley. "I ain't a kissing you now, you'll observe. I have been among the patriots: I'm a kissin' my country."

It would have been very unreasonable to complain of the exhibition of his patriotism with which he followed up this explanation, that it was all lukewarm or indifferent. When he had given full expression to his nationality, he hurried off to Martin; while Mrs. Lupin, in a state of great agitation and excitement, prepared for their reception.

The company soon came tumbling out: insisting to each other that the Dragon clock was half an hour too fast, and that the thunder must have affected it. Impatient, wet, and weary though they were, Martin and Mark were overjoyed to see these old faces, and watched them with delighted interest as they departed from the house, and passed close by them.

"There's the old tailor, Mark!" whispered Martin.

"There he goes, sir! A little bandier than he was, I think, sir, ain't he? His figure's so far altered, as it seems to me, that you might wheel a rather larger barrow between his legs as he walks, than you could have done conveniently, when we know'd him. There's Sam a coming out, sir."

"Ah, to be sure!" cried Martin: "Sam, the hostler. I wonder whether that horse of Pecksniff's is alive still?"

"Not a doubt on it, sir," returned Mark. "That's a description of animal, sir, as will go on in a bony way peculiar to himself for a long time, and get into the newspapers at last under the title of 'Sing'lar Tenacity of Life in a Quadruped.' As if he had ever been alive in all his life, worth mentioning! There's the clerk, sir,—wery drunk, as usual."

"I see him!" said Martin, laughing. "But, my life, how wet you are, Mark!"

"*I* am! What do you consider yourself, sir?"

"Oh, not half as bad," said his fellow-traveller, with an air of great vexation. "I told you not to keep on the windy side, Mark, but to let us change and change about. The rain has been beating on you, ever since it began."

"You don't know how it pleases me, sir," said Mark, after a short silence: "if I may make so bold as say so, to hear you a going on in that there uncommon considerate way of yours; which I don't mean to attend to, never, but which, ever since that time when I was floored in Eden, you have showed."

"Ah, Mark!" sighed Martin, "the less we say of that the better. Do I see the light yonder?"

"That's the light!" cried Mark. "Lord bless her, what briskness she possesses! Now for it, sir. Neat wines, good beds, and first-rate entertainment for man or beast."

The kitchen fire burnt clear and red, the table was spread out, the kettle boiled; the slippers were there, the boot-jack too, sheets of ham were there, cooking on the gridiron; half-a-dozen eggs were there, poaching in the frying-pan; a plethoric cherry-brandy bottle was there, winking at a foaming jug of beer upon the table; rare provisions were there, dangling from the rafters as if you had only to open your mouth, and something exquisitely ripe and good would be glad of the excuse for tumbling into it. Mrs. Lupin, who for their sakes had dislodged the very cook, high priestess of the temple, with her own genial hands was dressing their repast.

It was impossible to help it—a ghost must have hugged her. The Atlantic Ocean and the Red Sea being, in that respect, all one, Martin hugged her instantly. Mr. Tapley (as if the idea were quite novel, and had never occurred to him before), followed, with much gravity, on the same side.

"Little did I ever think," said Mrs. Lupin, adjusting her cap and laughing heartily; yes, and blushing too; "often as I have said that Mr. Pecksniff's young gentlemen were the life and soul of the Dragon, and that without them it would be too dull to live in—little did I ever think, I am sure, that any one of them would ever make so free as you, Mr. Martin!

291

And still less that I shouldn't be angry with him, but should be glad with all my heart, to be the first to welcome him home from America, with Mark Tapley, for his—"

"For his friend, Mrs. Lupin," interposed Martin.

"For his friend," said the hostess, evidently gratified by this distinction, but at the same time admonishing Mr. Tapley with a fork to remain at a respectful distance. "Little did I ever think that! But still less, that I should ever have the changes to relate that I shall have to tell you of, when you have done your supper!"

"Good Heaven!" cried Martin, changing colour, "what changes?"

"*She*," said the hostess, "is quite well, and now at Mr. Pecksniff's. Don't be at all alarmed about her. She is everything you could wish. It's of no use mincing matters, or making secrets, is it?" added Mrs. Lupin. "I know all about it, you see!"

"My good creature," returned Martin, "you are exactly the person who ought to know all about it. I am delighted to think you *do* know all about it. But what changes do you hint at? Has any death occurred?"

"No, no!" said the hostess. "Not so bad as that. But I declare now that I will not be drawn into saying another word till you have had your supper. If you ask me fifty questions in the meantime, I won't answer one."

She was so positive, that there was nothing for it but to get the supper over as quickly as possible; and as they had been walking a great many miles, and had fasted since the middle of the day, they did no great violence to their own inclinations in falling on it tooth and nail. It took rather longer to get through than might have been expected; for, half-a-dozen times, when they thought they had finished, Mrs. Lupin exposed the fallacy of that impression triumphantly. But at last, in the course of time and nature, they gave in. Then, sitting with their slippered feet stretched out upon the kitchen hearth (which was wonderfully comforting, for the night had grown by this time raw and chilly), and looking with involuntary admiration at their dimpled, buxom, blooming hostess, as the firelight sparkled in her eyes and glimmered in her raven hair, they composed themselves to listen to her news.

Many were the exclamations of surprise which interrupted her, when she told them of the separation between Mr. Pecksniff and his daughters, and between the same good gentleman and Mr. Pinch. But these were nothing to the indignant demonstrations of Martin, when she related, as the common talk of the neighbourhood, what entire possession he had obtained over the mind and person of old Mr. Chuzzlewit, and what high honour he designed for Mary. On receipt of this intelligence, Martin's slippers flew off in a twinkling, and he began pulling on his wet boots with that indefinite intention of going somewhere instantly, and doing something to somebody, which is the first safety-valve of a hot temper.

"He!" said Martin, "smooth-tongued villain that he is! He! Give me that other boot, Mark!"

"Where was you a thinking of going to, sir?" inquired Mr. Tapley, drying the sole at the fire, and looking coolly at it as he spoke, as if it were a slice of toast.

"Where!" repeated Martin. "You don't suppose I am going to remain here, do you?"

The imperturbable Mark confessed that he did.

"You do!" retorted Martin angrily. "I am much obliged to you. What do you take me for?"

"I take you for what you are, sir," said Mark; "and, consequently, am quite sure that whatever you do, will be right and sensible. The boot, sir."

Martin darted an impatient look at him, without taking it, and walked rapidly up and down the kitchen several times, with one boot and a stocking on. But, mindful of his Eden resolution, he had already gained many victories over himself when Mark was in the case, and he resolved to conquer now. So he came back to the boot-jack, laid his hand on Mark's shoulder to steady himself, pulled the boot off, picked up his slippers, put them on, and sat down again. He could not help thrusting his hands to the very bottom of his pockets, and muttering at intervals, "Pecksniff too! That fellow! Upon my soul! In-deed! What next?" and so forth: nor could he help occasionally shaking his fist at the chimney, with a very threatening countenance: but this did not last long; and he heard Mrs. Lupin out, if not with composure, at all events in silence.

"As to Mr. Pecksniff himself," observed the hostess in conclusion, spreading out the skirts of her gown with both hands, and nodding her head a great many times as she did so, "I don't know what to say. Somebody must have poisoned his mind, or influenced him in some extraordinary way. I cannot believe that such a noble-spoken gentleman would go and do wrong of his own accord!"

A noble-spoken gentleman! How many people are there in the world, who, for no better reason, uphold their Pecksniffs to the last, and abandon virtuous men, when Pecksniffs breathe upon them!

"As to Mr. Pinch," pursued the landlady, "if ever there was a dear, good, pleasant, worthy, soul alive, Pinch, and no other, is his name. But how do we know that old Mr. Chuzzlewit himself was not the cause of difference arising between him and Mr. Pecksniff? No one but themselves can tell: for Mr. Pinch has a proud spirit, though he has such a quiet way; and when he left us, and was so sorry to go, he scorned to make his story good, even to me."

"Poor old Tom!" said Martin, in a tone that sounded like remorse.

"It's a comfort to know," resumed the landlady, "that he has his sister living with him, and is doing well. Only yesterday he sent me back, by post, a little"—here the colour came into her cheeks—"a little trifle I was bold enough to lend him when he went away: saying, with many thanks, that he had good employment, and didn't want it. It was the same note; he hadn't broken it. I never thought I could have been so little pleased to see a bank-note come back to me, as I was to see that."

"Kindly said, and heartily!" said Martin. "Is it not, Mark?"

"She can't say anything as does not possess them qualities," returned Mr. Tapley; "which as much belong to the Dragon as its licence. And now that we have got quite cool and fresh, to the subject again, sir: what will you do? If you're not proud, and can make up your mind to go through with what you spoke of, coming along, that's the course for you to take. If you started wrong with your grandfather (which, you'll excuse my taking the liberty of saying, appears to have been the case), up with you, sir, and tell him so, and make an appeal to his affections. Don't stand out. He's a great deal older than you, and if he was hasty, you was hasty too. Give way, sir, give way."

The eloquence of Mr. Tapley was not without its effect on Martin, but he still hesitated, and expressed his reason thus:

"That's all very true, and perfectly correct, Mark; and if it were a mere question of humbling myself before *him*, I would not consider it twice. But don't you see, that being wholly under this hypocrite's government, and having (if what we hear be true) no mind or will of his own, I throw myself, in fact, not at his feet, but at the feet of Mr. Pecksniff? And when I am rejected and spurned away," said Martin, turning crimson at the thought, "it is not by him: my own blood stirred against me: but by Pecksniff—Pecksniff, Mark!"

"Well, but we know beforehand," returned the politic Mr. Tapley, "that Pecksniff is a wagabond, a scoundrel, and a willain."

"A most pernicious villain!" said Martin.

"A most pernicious willain. We know that beforehand, sir; and, consequently, it's no shame to be defeated by Pecksniff. Blow Pecksniff!" cried Mr. Tapley, in the fervour of his eloquence. "Who's he! It's not in the natur of Pecksniff to shame *us*, unless he agreed with us, or done us a service; and, in case he offered any outdacity of that description, we could express our sentiments in the English language, I hope. Pecksniff!" repeated Mr. Tapley, with ineffable disdain. "What's Pecksniff, who's Pecksniff, where's Pecksniff, that he's to be so much considered? We're not a calculating for ourselves;" he laid uncommon emphasis on the last syllable of that word, and looked full in Martin's face; "we're making a effort for a young lady likewise as has undergone her share; and whatever little hope we have, this here Pecksniff is not to stand in its way, I expect. I never heard of any act of Parliament as was made by Pecksniff. Pecksniff! Why, I wouldn't see the man myself; I wouldn't hear him; I wouldn't choose to know he was in company. I'd scrape my shoes on the scraper of the door, and call that Pecksniff, if you liked; but I wouldn't condescend no further."

The amazement of Mrs. Lupin, and indeed of Mr. Tapley himself for that matter, at this impassioned flow of language, was immense. But Martin, after looking thoughtfully at the fire for a short time, said:

"You are right, Mark. Right or wrong, it shall be done. I'll do it."

"One word more, sir," returned Mark. "Only think of him so far, as not to give him a handle against you. Don't you do anything secret, that he can report before you get there. Don't you even see Miss Mary in the morning, but let this here dear friend of ours;" Mr. Tapley bestowed a smile upon the hostess; "prepare her for what's a going to happen, and carry any little message as may be agreeable. She knows how. Don't you?" Mrs. Lupin laughed and tossed her head. "Then you go in, bold and free as a gentleman should. 'I haven't done nothing under-handed,' says you. 'I haven't been a skulking about the premises, here I am, for-give me, I ask your pardon, God Bless You!'"

Martin smiled, but felt that it was good advice notwithstanding, and resolved to act upon it. When they had

ascertained from Mrs. Lupin that Pecksniff had already returned from the great ceremonial at which they had beheld
him in his glory; and when they had fully arranged the
order of their proceedings; they went to bed, intent upon the
morrow.

In pursuance of their project as agreed upon at this discussion, Mr. Tapley issued forth next morning, after breakfast,
charged with a letter from Martin to his grandfather, requesting
leave to wait upon him for a few minutes. And postponing as
he went along the congratulations of his numerous friends until
a more convenient season, he soon arrived at Mr. Pecksniff's
house. At that gentleman's door; with a face so immovable
that it would have been next to an impossibility for the
most acute physiognomist to determine what he was thinking
about, or whether he was thinking at all : he straightway
knocked.

A person of Mr. Tapley's observation could not long remain
insensible to the fact, that Mr. Pecksniff was making the end
of his nose very blunt against the glass of the parlour window,
in an angular attempt to discover who had knocked at the
door. Nor was Mr. Tapley slow to baffle this movement on
the part of the enemy, by perching himself on the top step,
and presenting the crown of his hat in that direction. But
possibly Mr. Pecksniff had already seen him, for Mark soon
heard his shoes creaking, as he advanced to open the door with
his own hands.

Mr. Pecksniff was as cheerful as ever, and sang a little song
in the passage.

"How d'ye do, sir?" said Mark.

"Oh!" cried Mr. Pecksniff. "Tapley, I believe? The
Prodigal returned! We don't want any beer, my friend."

"Thankee, sir," said Mark. "I couldn't accommodate you,
if you did. A letter, sir. Wait for an answer."

"For me?" cried Mr. Pecksniff. "And an answer, eh?"

"Not for you I think, sir," said Mark, pointing out the
direction. "Chuzzlewit, I believe the name is, sir."

"Oh!" returned Mr. Pecksniff. "Thank you. Yes. Who's it from, my good young man?"

"The gentleman it comes from, wrote his name inside, sir," returned Mr. Tapley with extreme politeness. "I see him a signing of it at the end, while I was a waitin'."

"And he said he wanted an answer, did he?" asked Mr. Pecksniff in his most persuasive manner.

Mark replied in the affirmative.

"He shall have an answer. Certainly," said Mr. Pecksniff, tearing the letter into small pieces, as mildly as if that were the most flattering attention a correspondent could receive. "Have the goodness to give him that, with my compliments, if you please. Good morning!" Whereupon, he handed Mark the scraps; retired; and shut the door.

Mark thought it prudent to subdue his personal emotions, and return to Martin, at the Dragon. They were not unprepared for such a reception, and suffered an hour or so to elapse before making another attempt. When this interval had gone by, they returned to Mr. Pecksniff's house in company. Martin knocked this time, while Mr. Tapley prepared himself to keep the door open with his foot and shoulder, when anybody came, and by that means secure an enforced parley. But this precaution was needless, for the servant-girl appeared almost immediately. Brushing quickly past her as he had resolved in such a case to do, Martin (closely followed by his faithful ally) opened the door of that parlour in which he knew a visitor was most likely to be found; passed at once into the room; and stood, without a word of notice or announcement, in the presence of his grandfather.

Mr. Pecksniff also was in the room; and Mary. In the swift instant of their mutual recognition, Martin saw the old man droop his grey head, and hide his face in his hands.

It smote him to the heart. In his most selfish and most careless day, this lingering remnant of the old man's ancient love, this buttress of a ruined tower he had built up in the

298

time gone by, with so much pride and hope, would have caused a pang in Martin's heart. But now, changed for the better in his worst respect; looking through an altered medium on his former friend, the guardian of his childhood, so broken and bowed down; resentment, sullenness, self-confidence, and pride, were all swept away, before the starting tears upon the withered cheeks. He could not bear to see them. He could not bear to think they fell at sight of him. He could not bear to view reflected in them, the reproachful and irrevocable Past.

He hurriedly advanced, to seize the old man's hand in his, when Mr. Pecksniff interposed himself between them.

"No, young man!" said Mr. Pecksniff, striking himself upon the breast, and stretching out his other arm towards his guest as if it were a wing to shelter him. "No, sir. None of that. Strike here, sir, here! Launch your arrows at me, sir, if you'll have the goodness; not at Him!"

"Grandfather!" cried Martin. "Hear me! I implore you, let me speak!"

"Would you, sir! Would you!" said Mr. Pecksniff, dodging about, so as to keep himself always between them. "Is it not enough, sir, that you come into my house like a thief in the night, or I should rather say, for we can never be too particular on the subject of Truth, like a thief in the day-time: bringing your dissolute companions with you, to plant themselves with their backs against the insides of parlour doors, and prevent the entrance or issuing forth of any of my household;" Mark had taken up this position, and held it quite unmoved; "but would you also strike at venerable Virtue? Would you? Know that it is not defenceless. I will be its shield, young man. Assail me. Come on, sir. Fire away!"

"Pecksniff," said the old man, in a feeble voice. "Calm yourself. Be quiet."

"I can't be calm," cried Mr. Pecksniff, "and I won't be quiet. My benefactor and my friend! Shall even my house be no refuge for your hoary pillow!"

"Stand aside!" said the old man, stretching out his hand; "and let me see what it is I used to love so dearly."

"It is right that you should see it, my friend," said Mr. Pecksniff. "It is well that you should see it, my noble sir. It is desirable that you should contemplate it in its true proportions. Behold it! There it is, sir. There it is!"

Martin could hardly be a mortal man, and not express in his face something of the anger and disdain, with which Mr. Pecksniff inspired him. But beyond this he evinced no knowledge whatever of that gentleman's presence or existence. True, he had once, and that at first, glanced at him involuntarily, and with supreme contempt; but for any other heed he took of him, there might have been nothing in his place save empty air.

As Mr. Pecksniff withdrew from between them, agreeably to the wish just now expressed (which he did during the delivery of the observations last recorded), old Martin, who had taken Mary Graham's hand in his, and whispered kindly to her, as telling her she had no cause to be alarmed, gently pushed her from him, behind his chair; and looked steadily at his grandson.

"And that," he said, "is he. Ah! that is he! Say what you wish to say. But come no nearer."

"His sense of justice is so fine," said Mr. Pecksniff, "that he will hear even him, although he knows beforehand that nothing can come of it. Ingenuous mind!" Mr. Pecksniff did not address himself immediately to any person in saying this, but assuming the position of the Chorus in a Greek Tragedy, delivered his opinion as a commentary on the proceedings.

"Grandfather!" said Martin, with great earnestness. "From a painful journey, from a hard life, from a sick-bed, from privation and distress, from gloom and disappointment, from almost hopelessness and despair, I have come back to you."

"Rovers of this sort," observed Mr. Pecksniff as Chorus, "very commonly come back when they find they don't meet with the success they expected in their marauding ravages."

300

Mr. Pecksniff announces himself as the Shield of Virtue

"But for this faithful man," said Martin, turning towards Mark, "whom I first knew in this place, and who went away with me voluntarily, as a servant, but has been, throughout, my zealous and devoted friend; but for him, I must have died abroad. Far from home, far from any help or consolation: far from the probability even of my wretched fate being ever known to any one who cared to hear it—oh that you would let me say, of being known to you!"

The old man looked at Mr. Pecksniff. Mr. Pecksniff looked at him. "Did you speak, my worthy sir?" said Mr. Pecksniff, with a smile. The old man answered in the negative. "I know what you thought," said Mr. Pecksniff, with another smile. "Let him go on, my friend. The development of self-interest in the human mind is always a curious study. Let him go on, sir."

"Go on!" observed the old man; in a mechanical obedience, it appeared, to Mr. Pecksniff's suggestion.

"I have been so wretched and so poor," said Martin, "that I am indebted to the charitable help of a stranger, in a land of strangers, for the means of returning here. All this tells against me in your mind, I know. I have given you cause to think I have been driven here wholly by want, and have not been led on, in any degree, by affection or regret. When I parted from you, Grandfather, I deserved that suspicion, but I do not now. I do not now."

The Chorus put its hand in its waistcoat, and smiled. "Let him go on, my worthy sir," it said. "I know what you are thinking of, but don't express it prematurely."

Old Martin raised his eyes to Mr. Pecksniff's face, and appearing to derive renewed instruction from his looks and words, said, once again:

"Go on!"

"I have little more to say," returned Martin. "And as I say it now, with little or no hope, Grandfather; whatever dawn of hope I had on entering the room; believe it to be true. At least, believe it to be true."

"Beautiful Truth!" exclaimed the Chorus, looking upward. "How is your name profaned by vicious persons! You don't live in a well, my holy principle, but on the lips of false mankind. It is hard to bear with mankind, dear sir," —addressing the elder Mr. Chuzzlewit; "but let us do so meekly. It is our duty so to do. Let us be among the Few who do their duty. If," pursued the Chorus, soaring up into a lofty flight, "as the poet informs us, England expects Every man to do his duty, England is the most sanguine country on the face of the earth, and will find itself continually disappointed."

"Upon that subject," said Martin, looking calmly at the old man as he spoke, but glancing once at Mary, whose face was now buried in her hands, upon the back of his easy-chair: "upon that subject, which first occasioned a division between us, my mind and heart are incapable of change. Whatever influence they have undergone, since that unhappy time, has not been one to weaken but to strengthen me. I cannot profess sorrow for that, nor irresolution in that, nor shame in that. Nor would you wish me, I know. But that I might have trusted to your love, if I had thrown myself manfully upon it; that I might have won you over, with ease, if I had been more yielding, and more considerate; that I should have best remembered myself in forgetting myself, and re-collecting you; reflection, solitude, and misery, have taught me. I came, resolved to say this, and to ask your forgiveness: not so much in hope for the future, as in regret for the past: for all that I would ask of you, is, that you would aid me to live. Help me to get honest work to do, and I would do it. My condition places me at the disadvantage of seeming to have only my selfish ends to serve, but try if that be so, or not. Try if I be self-willed, obdurate, and haughty, as I was; or have been disciplined in a rough school. Let the voice of nature and association plead between us, Grand-father; and do not, for one fault, however thankless, quite reject me!"

302

As he ceased, the grey head of the old man drooped again ; and he concealed his face behind his outspread fingers.

" My dear sir," cried Mr. Pecksniff, bending over him, " you must not give way to this. It is very natural, and very amiable, but you must not allow the shameless conduct of one whom you long ago cast off, to move you so far. Rouse yourself. Think," said Pecksniff, " think of Me, my friend."

" I will," returned old Martin, looking up into his face. " You recall me to myself. I will."

" Why, what," said Mr. Pecksniff, sitting down beside him in a chair which he drew up for the purpose, and tapping him playfully on the arm, " what is the matter with my strong-minded compatriot, if I may venture to take the liberty of calling him by that endearing expression ? Shall I have to scold my coadjutor, or to reason with an intellect like his ? I think not."

" No, no. There is no occasion," said the old man. " A momentary feeling. Nothing more."

" Indignation," observed Mr. Pecksniff, " *will* bring the scalding tear into the honest eye, I know ; " he wiped his own elaborately. " But we have higher duties to perform than that. Rouse yourself, Mr. Chuzzlewit. Shall I give expression to your thoughts, my friend ? "

" Yes," said old Martin, leaning back in his chair, and looking at him, half in vacancy and half in admiration, as if he were fascinated by the man. " Speak for me, Pecksniff. Thank you. You are true to me. Thank you ! "

" Do not unman me, sir," said Mr. Pecksniff, shaking his hand vigorously, " or I shall be unequal to the task. It is not agreeable to my feelings, my good sir, to address the person who is now before us, for when I ejected him from this house, after hearing of his unnatural conduct from your lips, I re-nounced communication with him for ever. But you desire it ; and that is sufficient. Young man ! The door is imme-diately behind the companion of your infamy. Blush if you can ; begone without a blush, if you can't."

303

Martin looked as steadily at his grandfather as if there had been a dead silence all this time. The old man looked no less steadily at Mr. Pecksniff.

"When I ordered you to leave this house upon the last occasion of your being dismissed from it with disgrace," said Mr. Pecksniff: "when, stung and stimulated beyond endurance by your shameless conduct to this extraordinarily noble-minded individual, I exclaimed 'Go forth!' I told you that I wept for your depravity. Do not suppose that the tear which stands in my eye at this moment, is shed for you. It is shed for him, sir. It is shed for him."

Here Mr. Pecksniff, accidentally dropping the tear in question on a bald part of Mr. Chuzzlewit's head, wiped the place with his pocket-handkerchief, and begged pardon.

"It is shed for him, sir, whom you seek to make the victim of your arts," said Mr. Pecksniff: "whom you seek to plunder, to deceive, and to mislead. It is shed in sympathy with him, and admiration of him; not in pity for him, for happily he knows what you are. You shall not wrong him further, sir, in any way," said Mr. Pecksniff, quite transported with enthusiasm, "while I have life. You may bestride my senseless corse, sir. That is very likely. I can imagine a mind like yours deriving great satisfaction from any measure of that kind. But while I continue to be called upon to exist, sir, you must strike at him through me. Aye!" said Mr. Pecksniff, shaking his head at Martin with indignant jocularity; "and in such a cause you will find me, my young sir, an Ugly Customer!"

Still Martin looked steadily and mildly at his grandfather. "Will you give me no answer," he said, at length, "not a word?"

"You hear what has been said," replied the old man, without averting his eyes from the face of Mr. Pecksniff: who nodded encouragingly.

"I have not heard your voice. I have not heard your spirit," returned Martin.

"Tell him again," said the old man, still gazing up in Mr. Pecksniff's face.

"I only hear," replied Martin, strong in his purpose from the first, and stronger in it as he felt how Pecksniff winced and shrunk beneath his contempt; "I only hear what you say to me, grandfather."

Perhaps it was well for Mr. Pecksniff that his venerable friend found in his (Mr. Pecksniff's) features an exclusive and engrossing object of contemplation, for if his eyes had gone astray, and he had compared young Martin's bearing with that of his zealous defender, the latter disinterested gentleman would scarcely have shown to greater advantage than on the memorable afternoon when he took Tom Pinch's last receipt in full of all demands. One really might have thought there was some quality in Mr. Pecksniff—an emanation from the brightness and purity within him perhaps—which set off and adorned his foes: they looked so gallant and so manly beside him.

"Not a word?" said Martin, for the second time.

"I remember that I have a word to say, Pecksniff," observed the old man. "But a word. You spoke of being indebted to the charitable help of some stranger for the means of returning to England. Who is he? And what help in money did he render you?"

Although he asked this question of Martin, he did not look towards him, but kept his eyes on Mr. Pecksniff as before. It appeared to have become a habit with him, both in a literal and figurative sense, to look to Mr. Pecksniff alone.

Martin took out his pencil, tore a leaf from his pocket-book, and hastily wrote down the particulars of his debt to Mr. Bevan. The old man stretched out his hand for the paper, and took it; but his eyes did not wander from Mr. Pecksniff's face.

"It would be a poor pride and a false humility," said Martin, in a low voice, "to say, I do not wish that to be

305

paid, or that I have any present hope of being able to pay it. But I never felt my poverty so deeply as I feel it now."

"Read it to me, Pecksniff," said the old man.

Mr. Pecksniff, after approaching the perusal of the paper as if it were a manuscript confession of a murder, complied.

"I think, Pecksniff," said old Martin, "I could wish that to be discharged. I should not like the lender, who was abroad; who had no opportunity of making inquiry, and who did (as he thought) a kind action; to suffer."

"An honourable sentiment, my dear sir. Your own entirely. But a dangerous precedent," said Mr. Pecksniff, "permit me to suggest."

"It shall not be a precedent," returned the old man. "It is the only recognition of him. But we will talk of it again. You shall advise me. There is nothing else ? "

"Nothing else," said Mr. Pecksniff buoyantly, "but for you to recover this intrusion—this cowardly and indefensible outrage on your feelings—with all possible dispatch, and smile again."

"You have nothing more to say ? " inquired the old man, laying his hand with unusual earnestness on Mr. Pecksniff's sleeve.

Mr. Pecksniff would not say what rose to his lips. For reproaches, he observed, were useless.

"You have nothing at all to urge ? You are sure of that ? If you have, no matter what it is, speak freely. I will oppose nothing that you ask of me," said the old man.

The tears rose in such abundance to Mr. Pecksniff's eyes at this proof of unlimited confidence on the part of his friend, that he was fain to clasp the bridge of his nose convulsively before he could at all compose himself. When he had the power of utterance again, he said, with great emotion, that he hoped he should live to deserve this; and added, that he had no other observation whatever to make.

For a few moments the old man sat looking at him, with that blank and motionless expression which is not uncommon

in the faces of those whose faculties are on the wane, in age.
But he rose up firmly too, and walked towards the door, from
which Mark withdrew to make way for him.

The obsequious Mr. Pecksniff proffered his arm. The old
man took it. Turning at the door, he said to Martin,
waving him off with his hand,

"You have heard him. Go away. It is all over. Go!"

Mr. Pecksniff murmured certain cheering expressions of
sympathy and encouragement as they retired ; and Martin,
awakening from the stupor into which the closing portion of
this scene had plunged him, to the opportunity afforded by
their departure, caught the innocent cause of all in his embrace,
and pressed her to his heart.

"Dear girl!" said Martin. "He has not changed you.
Why, what an impotent and harmless knave the fellow is!"

"You have restrained yourself so nobly! You have borne
so much!"

"Restrained myself!" cried Martin, cheerfully. "You were
by, and were unchanged, I knew. What more advantage did
I want? The sight of me was such a bitterness to the dog,
that I had my triumph in his being forced to endure it. But
tell me, love—for the few hasty words we can exchange
now are precious—what is this which has been rumoured
to me? Is it true that you are persecuted by this knave's
addresses?"

"I was, dear Martin, and to some extent am now ; but my
chief source of unhappiness has been anxiety for you. Why
did you leave us in such terrible suspense?"

"Sickness, distance ; the dread of hinting at our real condition, the impossibility of concealing it except in perfect
silence ; the knowledge that the truth would have pained you
infinitely more than uncertainty and doubt," said Martin,
hurriedly ; as indeed everything else was done and said, in
those few hurried moments, "were the causes of my writing
only once. But Pecksniff? You needn't fear to tell me the
whole tale : for you saw me with him face to face, hearing

him speak, and not taking him by the throat: what is the history of his pursuit of you? Is it known to my grandfather?"

"Yes."

"And he assists him in it?"

"No," she answered eagerly.

"Thank Heaven!" cried Martin, "that it leaves his mind unclouded in that one respect!"

"I do not think," said Mary, "it was known to him at first. When this man had sufficiently prepared his mind, he revealed it to him by degrees. I think so, but I only know it, from my own impression: not from anything they told me. Then he spoke to me alone."

"My grandfather did?" said Martin.

"Yes—spoke to me alone, and told me—"

"What the hound had said," cried Martin. "Don't repeat it."

"And said I knew well what qualities he possessed; that he was moderately rich; in good repute; and high in his favour and confidence. But seeing me very much distressed, he said that he would not control or force my inclinations, but would content himself with telling me the fact. He would not pain me by dwelling on it, or reverting to it: nor has he ever done so since, but has truly kept his word."

"The man himself?—" asked Martin.

"He has had few opportunities of pursuing his suit. I have never walked out alone, or remained alone an instant in his presence. Dear Martin, I must tell you," she continued, "that the kindness of your grandfather to me remains unchanged. I am his companion still. An indescribable tenderness and compassion seem to have mingled themselves with his old regard; and if I were his only child, I could not have a gentler father. What former fancy or old habit survives in this, when his heart has turned so cold to you, is a mystery I cannot penetrate; but it has been, and it is, a happiness to me, that I remained true to him; that if he should wake

308

from his delusion, even at the point of death, I am here, love, to recall you to his thoughts."

Martin looked with admiration on her glowing face, and pressed his lips to hers.

" I have sometimes heard, and read," she said, " that those whose powers had been enfeebled long ago, and whose lives had faded, as it were, into a dream, have been known to rouse themselves before death, and inquire for familiar faces once very dear to them; but forgotten, unrecognised, hated even, in the meantime. Think, if with his old impressions of this man, he should suddenly resume his former self, and find in him his only friend ! "

" I would not urge you to abandon him, dearest," said Martin, " though I could count the years we are to wear out asunder. But the influence this fellow exercises over him, has steadily increased, I fear."

She could not help admitting that. Steadily, imperceptibly, and surely, until now it was paramount and supreme. She herself had none; and yet he treated her with more affection than at any previous time. Martin thought the inconsistency a part of his weakness and decay.

" Does the influence extend to fear ? " said Martin. " Is he timid of asserting his own opinion in the presence of this infatuation ? I fancied so just now."

" I have thought so, often. Often when we are sitting alone, almost as we used to do, and I have been reading a favourite book to him, or he has been talking quite cheerfully, I have observed that the entrance of Mr. Pecksniff has changed his whole demeanour. He has broken off immediately, and become what you have seen to-day. When we first came here he had his impetuous outbreaks, in which it was not easy for Mr. Pecksniff with his utmost plausibility to appease him. But these have long since dwindled away. He defers to him in everything, and has no opinion upon any question, but that which is forced upon him by this treacherous man."

Such was the account; rapidly furnished in whispers, and

interrupted, brief as it was, by many false alarms of Mr. Pecksniff's return; which Martin received of his grandfather's decline, and of that good gentleman's ascendancy. He heard of Tom Pinch, too, and Jonas too, with not a little about himself into the bargain; for though lovers are remarkable for leaving a great deal unsaid on all occasions, and very properly desiring to come back and say it, they are remarkable also for a wonderful power of condensation; and can, in one way or other, give utterance to more language—eloquent language—in any given short space of time, than all the six hundred and fifty-eight members in the Commons House of Parliament of the United Kingdom of Great Britain and Ireland; who are strong lovers, no doubt, but of their country only, which makes all the difference; for in a passion of that kind (which is not always returned), it is the custom to use as many words as possible, and express nothing whatever.

A caution from Mr. Tapley; a hasty interchange of farewells, and of something else which the proverb says must not be told of afterwards; a white hand held out to Mr. Tapley himself, which he kissed with the devotion of a knight-errant; more farewells, more something else's; a parting word from Martin that he would write from London and would do great things there yet (Heaven knows what, but he quite believed it); and Mark and he stood on the outside of the Pecksniffian halls.

"A short interview after such an absence!" said Martin, sorrowfully. "But we are well out of the house. We might have placed ourselves in a false position by remaining there, even so long, Mark."

"I don't know about ourselves, sir," he returned; "but somebody else would have got into a false position, if he had happened to come back again, while we was there. I had the door all ready, sir. If Pecksniff had showed his head, or had only so much as listened behind it, I would have caught him like a walnut. He's the sort of man," added Mr. Tapley, musing, "as would squeeze soft, I know."

A SALISBURY CARRIAGE

A person who was evidently going to Mr. Pecksniff's house, passed them at this moment. He raised his eyes at the mention of the architect's name; and when he had gone on a few yards, stopped, and gazed at them. Mr. Tapley, also, looked over his shoulder, and so did Martin; for the stranger, as he passed, had looked very sharply at them.

"Who may that be, I wonder!" said Martin. "The face seems familiar to me, but I don't know the man."

"He seems to have a amiable desire that his face should be tolerable familiar to us," said Mr. Tapley, "for he's a staring pretty hard. He'd better not waste his beauty, for he ain't got much to spare."

Coming in sight of the Dragon, they saw a travelling carriage at the door.

"And a Salisbury carriage, eh!" said Mr. Tapley. "That's what he came in, depend upon it. What's in the wind now? A new pupil, I shouldn't wonder. P'raps it's a order for another grammar-school, of the same pattern as the last."

Before they could enter at the door, Mrs. Lupin came running out; and beckoning them to the carriage showed them a portmanteau with the name of CHUZZLEWIT upon it.

"Miss Pecksniff's husband that was," said the good woman to Martin. "I didn't know what terms you might be on, and was quite in a worry till you came back."

"He and I have never interchanged a word yet," observed Martin; "and as I have no wish to be better or worse acquainted with him, I will not put myself in his way. We passed him on the road, I have no doubt. I am glad he timed his coming as he did. Upon my word! Miss Pecksniff's husband travels gaily!"

"A very fine-looking gentleman with him—in the best room now," whispered Mrs. Lupin, glancing up at the window as they went into the house. "He has ordered everything that can be got for dinner; and has the glossiest moustaches and whiskers ever you saw."

"Has he?" cried Martin, "why then we'll endeavour to

311

avoid him too, in the hope that our self-denial may be strong enough for the sacrifice. It is only for a few hours," said Martin, dropping wearily into a chair behind the little screen in the bar. " Our visit has met with no success, my dear Mrs. Lupin, and I must go to London."

" Dear, dear ! " cried the hostess.

" Yes. One foul wind no more makes a winter, than one swallow makes a summer. I'll try it again. Tom Pinch has succeeded. With his advice to guide me, I may do the same. I took Tom under my protection once, God save the mark ! " said Martin, with a melancholy smile; " and promised I would make his fortune. Perhaps Tom will take me under *his* protection now, and teach me how to earn my bread."

CHAPTER XLIV

FURTHER CONTINUATION OF THE ENTERPRISE OF MR. JONAS AND
HIS FRIEND

IT was a special quality, among the many admirable qualities possessed by Mr. Pecksniff, that the more he was found out, the more hypocrisy he practised. Let him be discomforted in one quarter, and he refreshed and recompensed himself by carrying the war into another. If his workings and windings were detected by A, so much the greater reason was there for practising without loss of time on B, if it were only to keep his hand in. He had never been such a saintly and improving spectacle to all about him, as after his detection by Thomas Pinch. He had scarcely ever been at once so tender in his humanity, and so dignified and exalted in his virtue, as when young Martin's scorn was fresh and hot upon him.

Having this large stock of superfluous sentiment and morality on hand which must positively be cleared off at any sacrifice, Mr. Pecksniff no sooner heard his son-in-law announced, than he regarded him as a kind of wholesale or general order, to be immediately executed. Descending, therefore, swiftly to the parlour, and clasping the young man in his arms, he exclaimed, with looks and gestures that denoted the perturbation of his spirit :

"Jonas. My child! She is well! There is nothing the matter?"

"What you're at it again, are you?" replied his son-in-law. "Even with me? Get away with you, will you?"

"Tell me she is well then," said Mr. Pecksniff. "Tell me she is well, my Boy!"

"She's well enough," retorted Jonas, disengaging himself. "There's nothing the matter with *her*."

"There is nothing the matter with her!" cried Mr. Pecksniff, sitting down in the nearest chair, and rubbing up his hair. "Fie upon my weakness! I cannot help it, Jonas. Thank you. I am better now. How is my other child; my eldest; my Cherrywerrychigo?" said Mr. Pecksniff, inventing a playful little name for her, in the restored lightness of his heart.

"She's much about the same as usual," returned Jonas. "She sticks pretty close to the vinegar-bottle. You know she's got a sweetheart, I suppose?"

"I have heard of it," said Mr. Pecksniff, "from head-quarters; from my child herself. I will not deny that it moved me to contemplate the loss of my remaining daughter, Jonas—I am afraid we parents are selfish, I am afraid we are—but it has ever been the study of my life to qualify them for the domestic hearth; and it is a sphere which Cherry will adorn."

"She need adorn some sphere or other," observed his son-in-law, "for she ain't very ornamental in general."

"My girls are now provided for," said Mr. Pecksniff. "They are now happily provided for, and I have not laboured in vain!"

This is exactly what Mr. Pecksniff would have said, if one of his daughters had drawn a prize of thirty thousand pounds in the lottery, or if the other had picked up a valuable purse in the street, which nobody appeared to claim. In either of these cases, he would have invoked a patriarchal blessing on the fortunate head, with great solemnity, and would have taken immense credit to himself, as having meant it from the infant's cradle.

"Suppose we talk about something else, now," observed Jonas, drily; "just for a change. Are you quite agreeable?"

"Quite," said Mr. Pecksniff. "Ah, you wag, you naughty wag! You laugh at poor old fond papa. Well! He deserves it. And he don't mind it either, for his feelings are their own reward. You have come to stay with me, Jonas?"

"No. I've got a friend with me," said Jonas.

"Bring your friend!" cried Mr. Pecksniff, in a gush of hospitality. "Bring any number of your friends!"

"This ain't the sort of man to be brought," said Jonas, contemptuously. "I think I see myself 'bringing' him to your house, for a treat! Thank'ee all the same; but he's a little too near the top of the tree, for that, Pecksniff."

The good man pricked up his ears; his interest was awakened. A position near the top of the tree was greatness, virtue, goodness, sense, genius; or, it should rather be said, a dispensation from all, and in itself something immeasurably better than all; with Mr. Pecksniff. A man who was able to look down upon Mr. Pecksniff could not be looked up at, by that gentleman, with too great an amount of deference, or from a position of too much humility. So it always is with great spirits.

"I'll tell you what you may do, if you like," said Jonas: "you may come and dine with us at the Dragon. We were forced to come down to Salisbury last night, on some business, and I got him to bring me over here this morning, in his carriage; at least, not his own carriage, for we had a breakdown in the night, but one we hired instead; it's all the same. Mind what you're about, you know. He's not used to all sorts; he only mixes with the best!"

"Some young nobleman who has been borrowing money of you at good interest, eh?" said Mr. Pecksniff, shaking his forefinger facetiously. "I shall be delighted to know the gay sprig."

"Borrowing!" echoed Jonas. "Borrowing! When you're a twentieth part as rich as he is, you may shut up shop!

We should be pretty well off, if we could buy his furniture, and plate, and pictures, by clubbing together. A likely man to borrow: Mr. Montague! Why, since I was lucky enough (come! and I'll say, sharp enough, too) to get a share in the Assurance Office that he's President of, I've made—never mind what I've made," said Jonas, seeming to recover all at once his usual caution. "You know me pretty well, and I don't blab about such things. But, Ecod, I've made a trifle."

"Really, my dear Jonas," cried Mr. Pecksniff, with much warmth, "a gentleman like this should receive some attention. Would he like to see the church? Or if he has a taste for the fine arts—which I have no doubt he has, from the description you give of his circumstances—I can send him down a few portfolios. Salisbury Cathedral, my dear Jonas," said Mr. Pecksniff; the mention of the portfolios, and his anxiety to display himself to advantage, suggesting his usual phraseology in that regard; "is an edifice replete with venerable associations, and strikingly suggestive of the loftiest emotions. It is here we contemplate the work of bygone ages. It is here we listen to the swelling organ, as we stroll through the reverberating aisles. We have drawings of this celebrated structure from the North, from the South, from the East, from the West, from the South-East, from the Nor'-West—"

During this digression, and indeed during the whole dialogue, Jonas had been rocking on his chair, with his hands in his pockets, and his head thrown cunningly on one side. He looked at Mr. Pecksniff now with such shrewd meaning twinkling in his eyes, that Mr. Pecksniff stopped, and asked him what he was going to say.

"Ecod!" he answered. "Pecksniff, if I knew how you meant to leave your money, I could put you in the way of doubling it, in no time. It wouldn't be bad to keep a chance like this snug in the family. But you're such a deep one!"

"Jonas!" cried Mr. Pecksniff, much affected, "I am not a diplomatical character: my heart is in my hand. By far the greater part of the inconsiderable savings I have accumulated in the course of—I hope—a not dishonourable or useless career, is already given, devised, and bequeathed (correct me, my dear Jonas, if I am technically wrong), with expressions of confidence, which I will nòt repeat; and in securities which it is unnecessary to mention; to a person whom I cannot, whom I will not, whom I need not, name." Here he gave the hand of his son-in-law a fervent squeeze, as if he would have added, " God bless you; be very careful of it when you get it! "

Mr. Jonas only shook his head and laughed, and, seeming to think better of what he had had in his mind, said, " No. He would keep his own counsel." But as he observed that he would take a walk, Mr. Pecksniff insisted on accompanying him, remarking that he could leave a card for Mr. Montague, as they went along, by way of gentleman-usher to himself at dinner-time. Which he did.

In the course of their walk, Mr. Jonas affected to maintain that close reserve which had operated as a timely check upon him during the foregoing dialogue. And as he made no attempt to conciliate Mr. Pecksniff, but, on the contrary, was more boorish and rude to him than usual, that gentleman, so far from suspecting his real design, laid himself out to be attacked with advantage. For it is in the nature of a knave to think the tools with which he works indispensable to knavery; and knowing what he would do himself in such a case, Mr. Pecksniff argued, " if this young man wanted anything of me for his own ends, he would be polite and deferential."

The more Jonas repelled him in his hints and inquiries, the more solicitous, therefore, Mr. Pecksniff became to be initiated into the golden mysteries at which he had obscurely glanced. Why should there be cold and worldly secrets, he observed, between relations ? What was life without confidence ? If the chosen husband of his daughter, the man to whom he had delivered her with so much pride and hope, such bounding and such beaming joy: if he were not a green spot in the barren waste of life, where was that Oasis to be found ?

Little did Mr. Pecksniff think on what a very green spot he planted one foot at that moment! Little did he foresee when he said, "All is but dust!" how very shortly he would come down with his own!

Inch by inch, in his grudging and ill-conditioned way; sustained to the life, for the hope of making Mr. Pecksniff suffer in that tender place, the pocket, where Jonas smarted so terribly himself, gave him an additional and malicious interest in the wiles he was set on to practise: inch by inch, and bit by bit, Jonas rather allowed the dazzling prospects of the Anglo-Bengalee establishment to escape him, than paraded them before his greedy listener. And in the same niggardly spirit, he left Mr. Pecksniff to infer, if he chose (which he *did* choose, of course), that a consciousness of not having any great natural gifts of speech and manner himself, rendered him desirous to have the credit of introducing to Mr. Montague some one who was well endowed in those respects, and so atone for his own deficiencies. Otherwise he muttered discontentedly, he would have seen his beloved father-in-law "far enough off," before he would have taken him into his confidence.

Primed in this artful manner, Mr. Pecksniff presented himself at dinner-time in such a state of suavity, benevolence, cheerfulness, politeness, and cordiality, as even he had perhaps never attained before. The frankness of the country gentleman, the refinement of the artist, the good-humoured allowance of the man of the world; philanthropy, forbearance, piety, toleration, all blended together in a flexible adaptability to anything and everything; were expressed in Mr. Pecksniff, as he shook hands with the great speculator and capitalist.

"Welcome, respected sir," said Mr. Pecksniff, "to our humble village! We are a simple people; primitive clods, Mr. Montague; but we can appreciate the honour of your visit, as my dear son-in-law can testify. It is very strange," said Mr. Pecksniff, pressing his hand almost reverentially, "but I seem to know you. That towering forehead, my dear Jonas," said Mr. Pecksniff aside, "and those clustering masses of rich hair—I must have seen you, my dear sir, in the sparkling throng."

Nothing was more probable, they all agreed.

"I could have wished," said Mr. Pecksniff, "to have had the honour of introducing you to an elderly inmate of our house : to the uncle of our friend. Mr. Chuzzlewit, sir, would have been proud indeed to have taken you by the hand."

"Is the gentleman here now?" asked Montague, turning deeply red.

"He is," said Mr. Pecksniff.

"You said nothing about that, Chuzzlewit."

"I didn't suppose you'd care to hear of it," returned Jonas. "You wouldn't care to know him, I can promise you."

"Jonas! my dear Jonas!" remonstrated Mr. Pecksniff. "Really!"

"Oh! it's all very well for you to speak up for him," said Jonas. "You have nailed him. You'll get a fortune by him."

"Oho! Is the wind in that quarter?" cried Montague. "Ha, ha, ha!" and here they all laughed—especially Mr. Pecksniff.

"No, no!" said that gentleman, clapping his son-in-law playfully upon the shoulder. "You must not believe all that my young relative says, Mr. Montague. You may believe him in official business, and trust him in official business, but you must not attach importance to his flights of fancy."

"Upon my life, Mr. Pecksniff," cried Montague, "I attach the greatest importance to that last observation of his. I trust and hope it's true. Money cannot be turned and turned again quickly enough in the ordinary course, Mr. Pecksniff. There is nothing like building our fortune on the weaknesses of mankind."

"Oh fie! Oh fie, for shame!" cried Mr. Pecksniff. But they all laughed again—especially Mr. Pecksniff.

"I give you my honour that *we* do it," said Montague.

"Oh fie, fie!" cried Mr. Pecksniff. "You are very pleasant.

That I am sure you don't! That I am sure you don't! How *can* you, you know?"

Again they all laughed in concert; and again Mr. Pecksniff laughed especially.

This was very agreeable indeed. It was confidential, easy, straightforward: and still left Mr. Pecksniff in the position of being in a gentle way the Mentor of the party. The greatest achievements in the article of cookery that the Dragon had ever performed, were set before them; the oldest and best wines in the Dragon's cellar saw the light on that occasion; a thousand bubbles, indicative of the wealth and station of Mr. Montague in the depths of his pursuits, were constantly rising to the surface of the conversation; and they were as frank and merry as three honest men could be. Mr. Pecksniff thought it a pity (he said so) that Mr. Montague should think lightly of mankind and their weaknesses. He was anxious upon this subject; his mind ran upon it; in one way or another he was constantly coming back to it; he must make a convert of him, he said. And as often as Mr. Montague repeated his sentiment about building fortunes on the weaknesses of mankind, and added frankly, " *We* do it!" just as often as Mr. Pecksniff repeated "Oh fie! Oh fie, for shame! I am sure you don't. How *can* you, you know?" laying a greater stress each time on those last words.

The frequent repetition of this playful inquiry on the part of Mr. Pecksniff, led at last to playful answers on the part of Mr. Montague; but after some little sharp-shooting on both sides, Mr. Pecksniff became grave, almost to tears; observing that if Mr. Montague would give him leave, he would drink the health of his young kinsman, Mr. Jonas; congratulating him upon the valuable and distinguished friendship he had formed, but envying him, he would confess, his usefulness to his fellow-creatures. For, if he understood the objects of that Institution with which he was newly and advantageously connected—knowing them but imperfectly—they were calculated to do Good; and for his (Mr. Pecksniff's) part, if he could in any way promote them, he thought he would be able to lay his head upon his pillow every night, with an absolute certainty of going to sleep at once.

The transition from this accidental remark (for it was quite accidental, and had fallen from Mr. Pecksniff in the openness of his soul), to the discussion of the subject as a matter of business, was easy. Books, papers, statements, tables, calculations of various kinds, were soon spread out before them; and as they were all framed with one object, it is not surprising that they should all have tended to one end. But still, whenever Montague enlarged upon the profits of the office, and said that as long as there were gulls upon the wing it must succeed, Mr. Pecksniff mildly said "Oh fie!"—and might indeed have remonstrated with him, but that he knew he was joking. Mr. Pecksniff did know he was joking; because he said so.

There never had been before, and there never would be again, such an opportunity for the investment of a considerable sum (the rate of advantage increased in proportion to the amount invested), as at that moment. The only time that had at all approached it, was the time when Jonas had come into the concern; which made him ill-natured now, and inclined him to pick out a doubt in this place, and a flaw in that, and grumblingly to advise Mr. Pecksniff to think better of it. The sum which would complete the proprietorship in this snug concern, was nearly equal to Mr. Pecksniff's whole hoard: not counting Mr. Chuzzlewit, that is to say, whom he looked upon as money in the Bank, the possession of which inclined him the more to make a dash with his own private sprats for the capture of such a whale as Mr. Montague described. The returns began almost immediately, and were immense. The end of it was, that Mr. Pecksniff agreed to become the last partner and proprietor in the Anglo-Bengalee, and made an appointment to dine with Mr. Montague, at Salisbury, on the next day but one, then and there to complete the negotiation.

It took so long to bring the subject to this head, that it was nearly midnight when they parted. When Mr. Pecksniff walked down stairs to the door, he found Mrs. Lupin standing there, looking out.

"Ah, my good friend!" he said: "not a-bed yet! Contemplating the stars, Mrs. Lupin?"

"It's a beautiful starlight night, sir."

"A beautiful starlight night," said Mr. Pecksniff, looking up. "Behold the planets, how they shine! Behold the—— those two persons who were here this morning, have left your house, I hope, Mrs. Lupin?"

"Yes, sir. They are gone."

"I am glad to hear it," said Mr. Pecksniff. "Behold the wonders of the firmament, Mrs. Lupin! How glorious is the scene! When I look up at those shining orbs, I think that each of them is winking to the other to take notice of the vanity of men's pursuits. My fellow-men!" cried Mr. Pecksniff, shaking his head in pity; "you are much mistaken; my wormy relatives, you are much deceived! The stars are perfectly contented (I suppose so) in their several spheres. Why are not you? Oh! do not strive and struggle to enrich yourselves, or to get the better of each other, my deluded friends, but look up there, with me!"

Mrs. Lupin shook her head, and heaved a sigh. It was very affecting.

"Look up there, with me!" repeated Mr. Pecksniff, stretching out his hand; "with me, an humble individual who is also an Insect like yourselves. Can silver, gold, or precious stones, sparkle like those constellations! I think not. Then do not thirst for silver, gold, or precious stones; but look up there, with me!"

With those words, the good man patted Mrs. Lupin's hand between his own, as if he would have added "think of this, my good woman!" and walked away in a sort of ecstasy or rapture, with his hat under his arm.

Jonas sat in the attitude in which Mr. Pecksniff had left him, gazing moodily at his friend: who, surrounded by a heap of documents, was writing something on an oblong slip of paper.

"You mean to wait at Salisbury over the day after to-morrow, do you, then?" said Jonas.

"You heard our appointment," returned Montague, without raising his eyes. "In any case I should have waited to see after the boy."

They appeared to have changed places again; Montague being in high spirits; Jonas gloomy and lowering.

"You don't want me, I suppose?" said Jonas.

"I want you to put your name here," he returned, glancing at him with a smile, "as soon as I have filled up the stamp. I may as well have your note of hand for that extra capital. That's all I want. If you wish to go home, I can manage Mr. Pecksniff now, alone. There is a perfect understanding between us."

Jonas sat scowling at him as he wrote, in silence. When he had finished his writing, and had dried it on the blotting-paper in his travelling-desk; he looked up, and tossed the pen towards him.

"What, not a day's grace, not a day's trust, eh?" said Jonas, bitterly. "Not after the pains I have taken with to-night's work?"

"To-night's work was a part of our bargain," replied Montague; "and so was this."

"You drive a hard bargain," said Jonas, advancing to the table. "You know best. Give it here!"

Montague gave him the paper. After pausing as if he could not make up his mind to put his name to it, Jonas dipped his pen hastily in the nearest inkstand, and began to write. But he had scarcely marked the paper when he started back, in a panic.

"Why, what the devil's this?" he said. "It's bloody!"

He had dipped the pen, as another moment showed, into red ink. But he attached a strange degree of importance to the mistake. He asked how it had come there, who had brought it, why it had been brought; and looked at Montague, at first, as if he thought he had put a trick upon him. Even when he used a different pen, and the right ink, he made some scratches on another paper first, as half-believing they would turn red also.

"Black enough, this time," he said, handing the note to Montague. "Good-bye."

"Going now! How do you mean to get away from here?"

"I shall cross early in the morning, to the high road, before you are out of bed; and catch the day-coach, going up. "Good-bye!"

"You are in a hurry!"

"I have Something to do," said Jonas. "Good-bye!"

His friend looked after him as he went out, in surprise, which gradually gave place to an air of satisfaction and relief.

"It happens all the better. It brings about what I wanted, without any difficulty. I shall travel home alone."

CHAPTER XLV

Tom Pinch and his sister having to part, for the dispatch
of the morning's business, immediately after the dispersion of
the other actors in the scene upon the Wharf with which the
reader has been already made acquainted, had no opportunity of
discussing the subject at that time. But Tom, in his solitary
office, and Ruth, in the triangular parlour, thought about
nothing else all day ; and, when their hour of meeting in the
afternoon approached, they were very full of it, to be sure.

There was a little plot between them, that Tom should
always come out of the Temple by one way ; and that was
past the fountain. Coming through Fountain Court, he was
just to glance down the steps leading into Garden Court, and
to look once all round him ; and if Ruth had come to meet
him, there he would see her ; not sauntering, you understand
(on account of the clerks), but coming briskly up, with the
best little laugh upon her face that ever played in opposition
to the fountain, and beat it all to nothing. For, fifty to one,
Tom had been looking for her in the wrong direction, and
had quite given her up, while she had been tripping towards
him from the first : jingling that little reticule of hers (with
all the keys in it) to attract his wandering observation.

Whether there was life enough left in the slow vegetation of

325

Fountain Court for the smoky shrubs to have any consciousness of the brightest and purest-hearted little woman in the world, is a question for gardeners, and those who are learned in the loves of plants. But, that it was a good thing for that same paved yard to have such a delicate little figure flitting through it; that it passed like a smile from the grimy old houses, and the worn flagstones, and left them duller, darker, sterner than before; there is no sort of doubt. The Temple fountain might have leaped up twenty feet to greet the spring of hopeful maidenhood, that in her person stole on, sparkling, through the dry and dusty channels of the Law; the chirping sparrows, bred in Temple chinks and crannies, might have held their peace to listen to imaginary skylarks, as so fresh a little creature passed; the dingy boughs, unused to droop, otherwise than in their puny growth, might have bent down in a kindred gracefulness, to shed their benedictions on her graceful head; old love letters, shut up in iron boxes in the neighbouring offices, and made of no account among the heaps of family papers into which they had strayed, and of which, in their degeneracy, they formed a part, might have stirred and fluttered with a moment's recollection of their ancient tenderness, as she went lightly by. Anything might have happened that did not happen, and never will, for the love of Ruth.

Something happened, too, upon the afternoon of which the history treats. Not for her love. Oh no! quite by accident, and without the least reference to her at all.

Either she was a little too soon, or Tom was a little too late—she was so precise in general, that she timed it to half a minute—but no Tom was there. Well! But was anybody else there, that she blushed so deeply, after looking round, and tripped off down the steps with such unusual expedition?

Why, the fact is, that Mr. Westlock was passing at that moment. The Temple is a public thoroughfare; they may write up on the gates that it is not, but so long as the gates are left open it is, and will be; and Mr. Westlock had as good a right to be there as anybody else. But why did she run away, then? Not being ill dressed, for she was much too neat for that, why did she run away? The brown hair that had fallen down beneath her bonnet, and had one impertinent imp of a false flower clinging to it, boastful of its license before all men, *that* could not have been the cause, for it looked charming. Oh! foolish, panting, frightened little heart, why did she run away!

Merrily the tiny fountain played, and merrily the dimples sparkled on its sunny face. John Westlock hurried after her. Softly the whispering water broke and fell; and roguishly the dimples twinkled, as he stole upon her footsteps.

Oh, foolish, panting, timid little heart, why did she feign to be unconscious of his coming! Why wish herself so far away, yet be so flutteringly happy there!

"I felt sure it was you," said John, when he overtook her, in the sanctuary of Garden Court. "I knew I couldn't be mistaken."

She was *so* surprised.

"You are waiting for your brother," said John. "Let me bear you company."

So light was the touch of the coy little hand, that he glanced down to assure himself he had it on his arm. But his glance, stopping for an instant at the bright eyes, forgot its first design, and went no farther.

They walked up and down three or four times, speaking about Tom and his mysterious employment. Now that was a very natural and innocent subject, surely. Then why, whenever Ruth lifted up her eyes, did she let them fall again immediately, and seek the uncongenial pavement of the court? They were not such eyes as shun the light; they were not such eyes as require to be hoarded to enhance their value. They were much too precious and too genuine to stand in need of arts like those. Somebody must have been looking at them!

They found out Tom, though, quickly enough. This pair of eyes descried him in the distance, the moment he appeared. He was staring about him, as usual, in all directions but the right one; and was as obstinate in not looking towards them, as if he had intended it. As it was plain that, being left to himself, he would walk away home, John Westlock darted off to stop him.

This made the approach of poor little Ruth, by herself, one of the most embarrassing of circumstances. There was Tom, manifesting extreme surprise (he had no presence of mind, that Tom, on small occasions); there was John, making as light of it as he could, but explaining at the same time, with most unnecessary elaboration; and here was she, coming towards them, with both of them looking at her, conscious of blushing to a terrible extent, but trying to throw up her eyebrows carelessly, and pout her rosy lips, as if she were the coolest and most unconcerned of little women.

Merrily the fountain plashed and plashed, until the dimples, merging into one another, swelled into a general smile, that covered the whole surface of the basin.

"What an extraordinary meeting!" said Tom. "I should never have dreamed of seeing you two together here."

"Quite accidental," John was heard to murmur.

"Exactly," cried Tom; "that's what I mean, you know. If it wasn't accidental, there would be nothing remarkable in it."

"To be sure," said John.

"Such an out-of-the-way place for you to have met in," pursued Tom, quite delighted. "Such an unlikely spot!"

John rather disputed that. On the contrary, he considered it a very likely spot, indeed. He was constantly passing to and fro there, he said. He shouldn't wonder if it were to happen again. His only wonder was, that it had never happened before.

By this time Ruth had got round on the farther side of her brother, and had taken his arm. She was squeezing it now, as much as to say, "Are you going to stop here all day, you dear, old blundering Tom?"

Tom answered the squeeze as if it had been a speech.

AN INVITATION TO DINNER

"John," he said, "if you'll give my sister your arm, we'll take her between us, and walk on. I have a curious circumstance to relate to you. Our meeting could not have happened better."

Merrily the fountain leaped and danced, and merrily the smiling dimples twinkled and expanded more and more, until they broke into a laugh against the basin's rim, and vanished.

"Tom," said his friend, as they turned into the noisy street, "I have a proposition to make. It is, that you and your sister—if she will so far honour a poor bachelor's dwelling—give me a great pleasure, and come and dine with me."

"What, to-day?" cried Tom.

"Yes, to-day. It's close by, you know. Pray, Miss Pinch, insist upon it. It will be very disinterested, for I have nothing to give you."

"Oh! you must not believe that, Ruth," said Tom. "He is the most tremendous fellow, in his housekeeping, that I ever heard of, for a single man. He ought to be Lord Mayor. Well! what do you say? Shall we go?"

"If you please, Tom," rejoined his dutiful little sister.

"But I mean," said Tom, regarding her with smiling admiration: "is there anything you ought to wear, and haven't got? I am sure I don't know, John: she may not be able to take her bonnet off, for anything I can tell."

There was a great deal of laughing at this, and there were divers compliments from John Westlock—not compliments, *he* said at least (and really he was right), but good, plain, honest truths, which no one could deny. Ruth laughed, and all that, but she made no objection; so it was an engagement.

"If I had known it a little sooner," said John, "I would have tried another pudding. Not in rivalry; but merely to exalt that famous one. I wouldn't on any account have had it made with suet."

"Why not?" asked Tom.

"Because that cookery-book advises suet," said John Westlock; "and ours was made with flour and eggs."

"Oh good gracious!" cried Tom. "Ours was made with flour and eggs, was it? Ha, ha, ha! A beefsteak pudding made with flour and eggs! Why anybody knows better than that. I know better than that! Ha, ha ha!"

It is unnecessary to say that Tom had been present at the making of the pudding, and had been a devoted believer in it all through. But he was so delighted to have this joke against his busy little sister, and was tickled to that degree at having found her out, that he stopped in Temple Bar to laugh; and it was no more to Tom, that he was anathematised and knocked about by the surly passengers, than it would have been to a post; for he continued to exclaim with unabated good humour, "flour and eggs! A beefsteak pudding made with flour and eggs!" until John Westlock and his sister fairly ran away from him, and left him to have his laugh out by himself; which he had; and then came dodging across the crowded street to them, with such sweet temper and tenderness (it was quite a tender joke of Tom's) beaming in his face, God bless it, that it might have purified the air, though Temple Bar had been, as in the golden days gone by, embellished with a row of rotting human heads.

There are snug chambers in those Inns where the bachelors live, and, for the desolate fellows they pretend to be, it is quite surprising how well they get on. John was very pathetic on the subject of his dreary life, and the deplorable makeshifts and apologetic contrivances it involved; but he really seemed to make himself pretty comfortable. His rooms were the perfection of neatness and convenience at any rate; and if he were anything but comfortable, the fault was certainly not theirs.

He had no sooner ushered Tom and his sister into his best room (where there was a beautiful little vase of fresh flowers on the table, all ready for Ruth.—Just as if he had expected her, Tom said), than seizing his hat, he bustled out again, in his most energetically bustling way; and presently came hurrying back, as they saw through the half-opened door, attended by a fiery-faced matron attired in a crunched bonnet, with particularly long strings to it hanging down her back; in conjunction with whom, he instantly began to lay the cloth for dinner, polishing up the wine-glasses with his own hands, brightening the silver top of the pepper-castor on his coat-sleeve, drawing corks and filling decanters, with a skill and expedition that were quite dazzling. And as if, in the course of this rubbing and polishing, he had rubbed an enchanted lamp or a magic ring, obedient to which there were twenty thousand supernatural slaves at least, suddenly there appeared a being in a white waistcoat, carrying under his arm a napkin, and attended by another being with an oblong box upon his head, from which a banquet, piping hot, was taken out and set upon the table.

Salmon, lamb, peas, innocent young potatoes, a cool salad, sliced cucumber, a tender duckling, and a tart—all there. They all came at the right time. Where they came from, didn't appear; but the oblong box was constantly going and coming, and making its arrival known to the man in the white waist-coat by bumping modestly against the outside of the door; for, after its first appearance, it entered the room no more. He was never surprised, this man; he never seemed to wonder at the extraordinary things he found in the box; but took them out with a face expressive of a steady purpose and impenetrable character, and put them on the table. He was a kind man; gentle in his manners, and much interested in what they ate and drank. He was a learned man, and knew the flavour of John Westlock's private sauces, which he softly and feelingly described, as he handed the little bottles round. He was a grave man, and a noiseless; for dinner being done, and wine and fruit arranged upon the board, he vanished, box and all, like something that had never been.

"Didn't I say he was a tremendous fellow in his house-keeping?" cried Tom. "Bless my soul! It's wonderful."

"Ah, Miss Pinch," said John. "This is the bright side of the life we lead in such a place. It would be a dismal life, indeed, if it didn't brighten up to-day."

"Don't believe a word he says," cried Tom. "He lives here like a monarch, and wouldn't change his mode of life for any consideration. He only pretends to grumble."

No, John really did not appear to pretend; for he was uncommonly earnest in his desire to have it understood that he was as dull, solitary, and uncomfortable on ordinary occasions as an unfortunate young man could, in reason, be. It was a wretched life, he said, a miserable life. He thought of getting rid of the chambers as soon as possible; and meant, in fact, to put a bill up very shortly.

"Well!" said Tom Pinch, "I don't know where you can go, John, to be more comfortable. That's all I can say. What do *you* say, Ruth?"

Ruth trifled with the cherries on her plate, and said that she thought Mr. Westlock ought to be quite happy, and that she had no doubt he was.

Ah, foolish, panting, frightened little heart, how timidly she said it!

"But you are forgetting what you had to tell, Tom: what occurred this morning," she added in the same breath.

"So I am," said Tom. "We have been so talkative on other topics, that I declare I have not had time to think of it. I'll tell it you at once, John, in case I should forget it altogether."

On Tom's relating what had passed upon the wharf, his friend was very much surprised, and took such a great interest in the narrative as Tom could not quite understand. He believed he knew the old lady whose acquaintance they had made, he said; and that he might venture to say, from their description of her, that her name was Gamp. But of what nature the communication could have been which Tom had borne so unexpectedly; why its delivery had been entrusted to him; how it happened that the parties were involved together; and what secret lay at the bottom of the whole affair; perplexed him very much. Tom had been sure of his taking some interest in the matter; but was not prepared for the strong interest he showed. It held John Westlock to the subject, even after Ruth had left the room; and evidently made him anxious to pursue it further than as a mere subject of conversation.

"I shall remonstrate with my landlord, of course," said Tom: "though he is a very singular secret sort of man, and not likely to afford me much satisfaction; even if he knew what was in the letter."

"Which you may swear he did," John interposed.

"You think so?"

"I am certain of it."

"Well!" said Tom, "I shall remonstrate with him when I see him (he goes in and out in a strange way, but I will try to catch him to-morrow morning), on his having asked me to execute such an unpleasant commission. And I have been thinking, John, that if I went down to Mrs. What's-her-name's in the City, where I was before, you know—Mrs. Todgers's —to-morrow morning, I might find poor Mercy Pecksniff there, perhaps, and be able to explain to her how I came to have any hand in the business."

"You are perfectly right, Tom," returned his friend, after a short interval of reflection. "You cannot do better. It is quite clear to me that whatever the business is, there is little good in it; and it is so desirable for you to disentangle yourself from any appearance of wilful connection with it, that I would counsel you to see her husband, if you can, and wash your hands of it, by a plain statement of the facts. I have a misgiving that there is something dark at work here, Tom. I will tell you why, at another time: when I have made an inquiry or two myself."

All this sounded very mysterious to Tom Pinch. But as he knew he could rely upon his friend, he resolved to follow this advice.

Ah, but it would have been a good thing to have had a coat of invisibility, wherein to have watched little Ruth, when she was left to herself in John Westlock's chambers, and John and her brother were talking thus, over their wine! The gentle way in which she tried to get up a little conversation with the fiery-faced matron in the crunched bonnet, who was waiting to attend her; after making a desperate rally in regard of her dress, and attiring herself in a washed-out yellow gown with sprigs of the same upon it, so that it looked like a tesselated work of pats of butter. That would have been pleasant. The grim and griffin-like inflexibility with which the fiery-faced matron repelled these engaging advances, as proceeding from a hostile and dangerous power, who could have no business there, unless it were to deprive her of a customer, or suggest what became of the self-consuming tea and sugar, and other general trifles. That would have been agreeable. The bashful, winning, glorious curiosity, with which little Ruth, when fiery-face was gone, peeped into the books and nick-nacks that were lying about, and had a particular interest in some delicate paper-matches on the chimney-piece: wondering who could have made them. That would have been worth seeing. The faltering hand with which she tied those flowers together; with which, almost blushing at her own fair self as imaged in the glass, she arranged them in her breast, and looking at them with her head aside, now half resolved to take them out again, now half resolved to leave them where they were. That would have been delightful!

John seemed to think it all delightful: for coming in with Tom to tea, he took his seat beside her like a man enchanted. And when the tea-service had been removed, and Tom, sitting down at the piano, became absorbed in some of his old organ tunes, he was still beside her at the open window, looking out upon the twilight.

There is little enough to see, in Furnival's Inn. It is a shady, quiet place, echoing to the footsteps of the stragglers who have business there; and rather monotonous and gloomy on summer evenings. What gave it such a charm to them, that they remained at the window as unconscious of the flight of time as Tom himself, the dreamer, while the melodies which had so often soothed his spirit, were hovering again about him!

AN ENCHANTED EVENING

What power infused into the fading light, the gathering darkness; the stars that here and there appeared; the evening air,
the City's hum and stir, the very chiming of the old church
clocks; such exquisite enthralment, that the divinest regions
of the earth spread out before their eyes could not have held
them captive in a stronger chain?

The shadows deepened, deepened, and the room became
quite dark. Still Tom's fingers wandered over the keys of the
piano; and still the window had its pair of tenants.

At length, her hand upon his shoulder, and her breath upon
his forehead, roused Tom from his reverie.

"Dear me!" he cried, desisting with a start. "I am afraid
I have been very inconsiderate and unpolite."

Tom little thought how much consideration and politeness
he had shown!

"Sing something to us, my dear," said Tom. "Let us hear
your voice. Come!"

John Westlock added his entreaties, with such earnestness
that a flinty heart alone could have resisted them. Hers was
not a flinty heart. Oh dear no! Quite another thing.

So down she sat, and in a pleasant voice began to sing the
ballads Tom loved well. Old rhyming stories, with here and
there a pause for a few simple chords, such as a harper might
have sounded in the ancient time while looking upward for the
current of some half-remembered legend; words of old poets,
wedded to such measures that the strain of music might have
been the poet's breath, giving utterance and expression to his
thoughts; and now a melody so joyous and light-hearted,
that the singer seemed incapable of sadness, until in her in-
constancy (oh wicked little singer!) she relapsed, and broke the
listeners' hearts again: these were the simple means she used
to please them. And that these simple means prevailed, and
she *did* please them, let the still darkened chamber, and its
long-deferred illumination witness.

The candles came at last, and it was time for moving home-
ward. Cutting paper carefully, and rolling it about the stalks

of those same flowers, occasioned some delay; but even this was done in time, and Ruth was ready.

"Good night!" said Tom. "A memorable and delightful visit, John! Good night!"

John thought he would walk with them.

"No, no. Don't!" said Tom. "What nonsense! We can get home very well alone. I couldn't think of taking you out."

But John said he would rather.

"Are you sure you would rather?" said Tom. "I am afraid you only say so out of politeness."

John being quite sure, gave his arm to Ruth, and led her out. Fiery-face, who was again in attendance, acknowledged her departure with so cold a curtsey that it was hardly visible; and cut Tom, dead.

Their host was bent on walking the whole distance, and would not listen to Tom's dissuasions. Happy time, happy walk, happy parting, happy dreams! But there are some sweet day-dreams, so there are, that put the visions of the night to shame.

Busily the Temple fountain murmured in the moonlight, while Ruth lay sleeping, with her flowers beside her; and John Westlock sketched a portrait—whose?—from memory.

CHAPTER XLVI

IN WHICH MISS PECKSNIFF MAKES LOVE, MR. JONAS MAKES WRATH,
MRS. GAMP MAKES TEA, AND MR. CHUFFEY MAKES BUSINESS

On the next day's official duties coming to a close, Tom hurried
home without losing any time by the way; and after dinner
and a short rest, sallied out again, accompanied by Ruth, to
pay his projected visit to Todgers's. Tom took Ruth with
him, not only because it was a great pleasure to him to have
her for his companion whenever he could, but because he
wished her to cherish and comfort poor Merry; which she,
for her own part (having heard the wretched history of that
young wife from Tom), was all eagerness to do.

"She was so glad to see me," said Tom, "that I am sure
she will be glad to see you. Your sympathy is certain to be
much more delicate and acceptable than mine."

"I am very far from being certain of that, Tom," she
replied; "and indeed you do yourself an injustice. Indeed
you do. But I hope she may like me, Tom."

"Oh, she is sure to do that!" cried Tom, confidently.

"What a number of friends I should have, if everybody
was of your way of thinking. Shouldn't I, Tom, dear?" said
his little sister, pinching him upon the cheek.

Tom laughed, and said that with reference to this particular
case he had no doubt at all of finding a disciple in Merry.
"For you women," said Tom, "you women, my dear, are so
kind, and in your kindness have such nice perception; you

337

know so well how to be affectionate and full of solicitude without appearing to be; your gentleness of feeling is like your touch: so light and easy, that the one enables you to deal with wounds of the mind as tenderly as the other enables you to deal with wounds of the body. You are such——"

"My goodness, Tom!" his sister interposed. "You ought to fall in love immediately."

Tom put this observation off good humouredly, but somewhat gravely too; and they were soon very chatty again on some other subject.

As they were passing through a street in the City, not very far from Mrs. Todgers's place of residence, Ruth checked Tom before the window of a large Upholstery and Furniture Warehouse, to call his attention to something very magnificent and ingenious, displayed there to the best advantage, for the admiration and temptation of the public. Tom had hazarded some most erroneous and extravagantly wrong guess in relation to the price of this article, and had joined his sister in laughing heartily at his mistake, when he pressed her arm in his, and pointed to two persons at a little distance, who were looking in at the same window with a deep interest in the chests of drawers and tables.

"Hush!" Tom whispered. "Miss Pecksniff, and the young gentleman to whom she is going to be married."

"Why does he look as if he was going to be buried, Tom?" inquired his little sister.

"Why, he is naturally a dismal young gentleman, I believe," said Tom: "but he is very civil and inoffensive."

"I suppose they are furnishing their house," whispered Ruth.

"Yes, I suppose they are," replied Tom. "We had better avoid speaking to them."

They could not very well avoid looking at them, however, especially as some obstruction on the pavement, at a little distance, happened to detain them where they were for a few moments. Miss Pecksniff had quite the air of having taken the unhappy Moddle captive, and brought him up to the contemplation of the furniture like a lamb to the altar. He offered no resistance, but was perfectly resigned and quiet. The melancholy depicted in the turn of his languishing head, and in his dejected attitude, was extreme; and though there was a full-sized four-post bedstead in the window, such a tear stood trembling in his eye, as seemed to blot it out.

"Augustus, my love," said Miss Pecksniff, "ask the price of the eight rosewood chairs, and the loo table."

"Perhaps they are ordered already," said Augustus. "Perhaps they are Another's."

"They can make more like them, if they are," rejoined Miss Pecksniff.

"No, no, they can't," said Moddle. "It's impossible!"

He appeared, for the moment, to be quite overwhelmed and stupefied by the prospect of his approaching happiness; but recovering, entered the shop. He returned immediately: saying in a tone of despair:

"Twenty-four pound ten!"

Miss Pecksniff, turning to receive this announcement, became conscious of the observation of Tom Pinch and his sister.

"Oh, really!" cried Miss Pecksniff, glancing about her, as if for some convenient means of sinking into the earth. "Upon my word, I—there never was such a—to think that one should be so very—Mr. Augustus Moddle, Miss Pinch!"

Miss Pecksniff was quite gracious to Miss Pinch in this triumphant introduction; exceedingly gracious. She was more than gracious; she was kind and cordial. Whether the recollection of the old service Tom had rendered her in knocking Mr. Jonas on the head, had wrought this change in her opinions; or whether her separation from her parent had reconciled her to all human-kind, or to all that increasing portion of human-kind which was not friendly to him; or whether the delight of having some new female acquaintance to whom to communicate her interesting prospects, was paramount to every other consideration; cordial and kind Miss

Pecksniff was. And twice Miss Pecksniff kissed Miss Pinch upon the cheek.

"Augustus—Mr. Pinch, you know. My dear girl!" said Miss Pecksniff, aside. "I never was so ashamed in my life."

Ruth begged her not to think of it.

"I mind your brother less than anybody else," simpered Miss Pecksniff. "But the indelicacy of meeting any gentleman under such circumstances! Augustus, my child, did you—— "

Here Miss Pecksniff whispered in his ear. The suffering Moddle repeated:

"Twenty-four pound ten!"

"Oh, you silly man! I don't mean them," said Miss Pecksniff. "I am speaking of the—— "

Here she whispered him again.

"If it's the same patterned chintz as that in the window; thirty-two, twelve, six," said Moddle, with a sigh. "And very dear."

Miss Pecksniff stopped him from giving any further explanation by laying her hand upon his lips, and betraying a soft embarrassment. She then asked Tom Pinch which way he was going.

"I was going to see if I could find your sister," answered Tom, "to whom I wished to say a few words. We were going to Mrs. Todgers's, where I had the pleasure of seeing her before."

"It's of no use your going on, then," said Cherry, "for we have not long left there; and I know she is not at home. But I'll take you to my sister's house, if you please. Augustus —Mr. Moddle, I mean—and myself, are on our way to tea there, now. You needn't think of *him*," she added, nodding her head, as she observed some hesitation on Tom's part. "He is not at home."

"Are you sure?" asked Tom.

"Oh, I am quite sure of that. I don't want any *more* revenge," said Miss Pecksniff, expressively. "But, really, I must beg you two gentlemen to walk on, and allow me to

Mr. Moddle is led to the Contemplation of his Destiny

follow with Miss Pinch. My dear, I never was so taken by surprise!"

In furtherance of this bashful arrangement, Moddle gave his arm to Tom; and Miss Pecksniff linked her own in Ruth's.

"Of course, my love," said Miss Pecksniff, "it would be useless for me to disguise, after what you have seen, that I am about to be united to the gentleman who is walking with your brother. It would be in vain to conceal it. What do you think of him? Pray, let me have your candid opinion."

Ruth intimated that, as far as she could judge, he was a very eligible swain.

"I am curious to know," said Miss Pecksniff, with loquacious frankness, "whether you have observed, or fancied, in this very short space of time, that he is of a rather melancholy turn?"

"So very short a time," Ruth pleaded.

"No, no; but don't let that interfere with your answer," returned Miss Pecksniff. "I am curious to hear what you say."

Ruth acknowledged that he had impressed her at first sight as looking "rather low."

"No, really?" said Miss Pecksniff. "Well! that is quite remarkable! Everybody says the same. Mrs. Todgers says the same; and Augustus informs me that it is quite a joke among the gentlemen in the house. Indeed, but for the positive commands I have laid upon him, I believe it would have been the occasion of loaded fire-arms being resorted to more than once. What do you think is the cause of his appearance of depression?"

Ruth thought of several things; such as his digestion, his tailor, his mother, and the like. But hesitating to give utterance to any one of them, she refrained from expressing an opinion.

"My dear," said Miss Pecksniff; "I shouldn't wish it to be known, but I don't mind mentioning it to you, having known your brother for so many years—I refused Augustus three times. He is of a most amiable and sensitive nature; always ready to shed tears, if you look at him, which is extremely charming; and he has never recovered the effect of that cruelty. For it *was* cruel," said Miss Pecksniff, with a self-convicting candour that might have adorned the diadem of her own papa. "There is no doubt of it. I look back upon my conduct now with blushes. I always liked him. I felt that he was not to me what the crowd of young men who had made proposals had been, but something very different. Then what right had I to refuse him three times?"

"It was a severe trial of his fidelity, no doubt," said Ruth.

"My dear," returned Miss Pecksniff. "It was wrong. But such is the caprice and thoughtlessness of our sex! Let me be a warning to you. Don't try the feelings of any one who makes you an offer, as I have tried the feelings of Augustus; but if you ever feel towards a person as I really felt towards him, at the very time when I was driving him to distraction, let that feeling find expression, if that person throws himself at your feet, as Augustus Moddle did at mine. Think," said Miss Pecksniff, "what my feelings would have been, if I had goaded him to suicide, and it had got into the papers!"

Ruth observed that she would have been full of remorse, no doubt.

"Remorse!" cried Miss Pecksniff, in a sort of snug and comfortable penitence. "What my remorse is at this moment, even after making reparation by accepting him, it would be impossible to tell you! Looking back upon my giddy self, my dear, now that I am sobered down and made thoughtful, by treading on the very brink of matrimony; and contemplating myself as I was when I was like what you are now; I shudder. I shudder. What is the consequence of my past conduct? Until Augustus leads me to the altar, he is not sure of me. I have blighted and withered the affections of his heart to that extent that he is not sure of me. I see that preying on his mind and feeding on his vitals. What are the reproaches of my conscience, when I see this in the man I love!"

Ruth endeavoured to express some sense of her unbounded and flattering confidence ; and presumed that she was going to be married soon.

"Very soon indeed," returned Miss Pecksniff. "As soon as our house is ready. We are furnishing now as fast as we can."

In the same vein of confidence, Miss Pecksniff ran through a general inventory of the articles that were already bought, with the articles that remained to be purchased; what garments she intended to be married in, and where the ceremony was to be performed; and gave Miss Pinch, in short (as she told her), early and exclusive information on all points of interest connected with the event.

While this was going forward in the rear, Tom and Mr. Moddle walked on, arm in arm, in the front, in a state of profound silence, which Tom at last broke: after thinking for a long time what he could say that should refer to an indifferent topic, in respect of which he might rely, with some degree of certainty, on Mr. Moddle's bosom being unruffled.

"I wonder," said Tom, "that in these crowded streets, the foot-passengers are not oftener run over."

Mr. Moddle, with a dark look, replied :

"The drivers won't do it."

"Do you mean ?" Tom began—

"That there are some men," interrupted Moddle, with a hollow laugh, "who can't get run over. They live a charmed life. Coal waggons recoil from them, and even cabs refuse to run them down. Ah !" said Augustus, marking Tom's astonishment. "There are such men. One of 'em is a friend of mine."

"Upon my word and honour," thought Tom, "this young gentleman is in a state of mind which is very serious indeed !" Abandoning all idea of conversation, he did not venture to say another word; but he was careful to keep a tight hold upon Augustus's arm, lest he should fly into the road, and making another, and a more successful attempt, should get up a private little Juggernaut before the eyes of his betrothed. Tom was so afraid of his committing this rash act, that he had scarcely ever experienced such mental relief as when they arrived in safety at Mrs. Jonas Chuzzlewit's house.

"Walk up, pray, Mr. Pinch," said Miss Pecksniff: for Tom halted, irresolutely, at the door.

"I am doubtful whether I should be welcome," replied Tom, "or, I ought rather to say, I have no doubt about it. I will send up a message, I think."

"But what nonsense that is!" returned Miss Pecksniff, speaking apart to Tom. "He is not at home, I am certain; I know he is not; and Merry hasn't the least idea that you ever——"

"No," interrupted Tom. "Nor would I have her know it, on any account. I am not so proud of that scuffle, I assure you."

"Ah, but then you are so modest, you see," returned Miss Pecksniff, with a smile. "But pray walk up. If you don't wish her to know it, and do wish to speak to her, pray walk up. Pray walk up, Miss Pinch. Don't stand here."

Tom still hesitated; for he felt that he was in an awkward position. But Cherry passing him at this juncture, and leading his sister up stairs, and the house-door being at the same time shut behind them, he followed without quite knowing whether it was well or ill-judged so to do.

"Merry, my darling!" said the fair Miss Pecksniff, opening the door of the usual sitting-room. "Here are Mr. Pinch and his sister come to see you! I thought we should find you here, Mrs. Todgers! How do you do, Mrs. Gamp? And how do you do, Mr. Chuffey, though it's of no use asking you the question, I am well aware."

Honouring each of these parties, as she severally addressed them, with an acid smile, Miss Charity presented Mr. Moddle.

"I believe you have seen *him* before," she pleasantly observed. "Augustus, my sweet child, bring me a chair."

344

The sweet child did as he was told; and was then about to retire into a corner to mourn in secret, when Miss Charity, calling him in an audible whisper "a little pet," gave him leave to come and sit beside her. It is to be hoped, for the general cheerfulness of mankind, that such a doleful little pet was never seen as Mr. Moddle looked when he complied. So despondent was his temper, that he showed no outward thrill of ecstasy, when Miss Pecksniff placed her lily hand in his, and concealed this mark of her favour from the vulgar gaze, by covering it with a corner of her shawl. Indeed, he was infinitely more rueful then than he had been before; and, sitting uncomfortably upright in his chair, surveyed the company with watery eyes, which seemed to say, without the aid of language, "Oh, good gracious! look here! Won't some kind Christian help me!"

But the ecstasies of Mrs. Gamp were sufficient to have furnished forth a score of young lovers: and they were chiefly awakened by the sight of Tom Pinch and his sister. Mrs. Gamp was a lady of that happy temperament which can be ecstatic without any other stimulating cause than a general desire to establish a large and profitable connection. She added daily so many strings to her bow, that she made a perfect harp of it; and upon that instrument she now began to perform an extemporaneous concerto.

"Why, goodness me!" she said, "Mrs. Chuzzlewit! To think as I should see beneath this blessed ouse, which well I know it, Miss Pecksniff, my sweet young lady, to be a ouse as there is not a many like, worse luck, and wishin' it ware not so, which then this tearful walley would be changed into a flowerin' guardian, Mr. Chuffey; to think as I should see beneath this indiwidge roof, identically comin', Mr. Pinch (I take the liberty, though almost unbeknown), and do assure you of it, sir, the smilinest and sweetest face as ever, Mrs. Chuzzlewit, I see, exceptin' yourn, my dear good lady, and *your* good lady's too, sir, Mr. Moddle, if I may make so bold as speak so plain of what is plain enough to them as needn't look through millstones, Mrs. Todgers, to find out wot is wrote upon the wall behind. Which no offence is meant, ladies and gentlemen; none bein' took, I hope. To think as I should see that smilinest and sweetest face which me and another friend of mine, took notige of among the packages down London Bridge, in this promiscous place, is a surprige in-deed!"

Having contrived, in this happy manner, to invest every member of her audience with an individual share and immediate personal interest in her address, Mrs. Gamp dropped several curtseys to Ruth, and smilingly shaking her head a great many times, pursued the thread of her discourse:

"Now, ain't we rich in beauty this here joyful arternoon, I'm sure. I knows a lady, which her name, I'll not deceive you, Mrs. Chuzzlewit, is Harris, her husband's brother bein' six foot three, and marked with a mad bull in Wellington boots upon his left arm, on account of his precious mother havin' been worrited by one into a shoemaker's shop, when in a sitiwation which blessed is the man as has his quiver full of sech, as many times I've said to Gamp when words has roge betwixt us on account of the expense—and often have I said to Mrs. Harris, 'Oh, Mrs. Harris, ma'am! your countenance is quite a angel's!' Which, but for Pimples, it would be. 'No, Sairey Gamp,' says she, 'you best of hard-working and industrious creeturs as ever was underpaid at any price, which underpaid you are, quite diff'rent. Harris had it done afore marriage at ten and six,' she says, 'and wore it faithful next his heart 'till the colour run, when the money was declined to be give back, and no arrangement could be come to. But he never said it was a angel's, Sairey, wotever he might have thought.' If Mrs. Harris's husband was here now," said Mrs. Gamp, looking round, and chuckling as she dropped a general curtsey, "he'd speak out plain, he would, and his dear wife would be the last to blame him! For if ever a woman lived as know'd not wot it was to form a wish to pizon them as had good looks, and had no reagion give her by the best of husbands, Mrs. Harris is that ev'nly dispogician!"

MRS. GAMP AND MR. CHUFFEY

With these words the worthy woman, who appeared to have dropped in to take tea as a delicate little attention, rather than to have any engagement on the premises in an official capacity, crossed to Mr. Chuffey, who was seated in the same corner as of old, and shook him by the shoulder.

"Rouge yourself, and look up! Come!" said Mrs. Gamp. "Here's company, Mr. Chuffey."

"I am sorry for it," cried the old man, looking humbly round the room. "I know I'm in the way. I ask pardon, but I've nowhere else to go to. Where is she?"

Merry went to him.

"Ah!" said the old man, patting her on the cheek. "Here she is. Here she is! She's never hard on poor old Chuffey. Poor old Chuff!"

As she took her seat upon a low chair by the old man's side, and put herself within the reach of his hand, she looked up once at Tom. It was a sad look that she cast upon him, though there was a faint smile trembling on her face. It was a speaking look, and Tom knew what it said. "You see how misery has changed me. I can feel for a dependant *now*, and set some value on his attachment."

"Ay, ay!" cried Chuffey in a soothing tone. "Ay, ay, ay! Never mind him. It's hard to bear, but never mind him. He'll die one day. There are three hundred and sixty-five days in the year—three hundred and sixty-six in leap year— and he may die on any one of 'em."

"You're a wearing old soul. and that's the sacred truth," said Mrs. Gamp, contemplating him from a little distance with anything but favour, as he continued to mutter to himself. "It's a pity that you don't know wot you say, for you'd tire your own patience out if you did, and fret yourself into a happy releage for all as knows you."

"His son," murmured the old man lifting up his hand. "His son!"

"Well I'm sure!" said Mrs. Gamp, "you're a settlin' of it, Mr. Chuffey. To your satigefaction, sir, I hope. But I wouldn't lay a new pin-cushion on it myself, sir, though you *are* so well informed. Drat the old creetur, he's a layin' down the law tolerable confident, too! A deal he knows of sons! Or darters either! Suppose you was to favour us with some remarks on twins, sir, *would* you be so good!"

The bitter and indignant sarcasm which Mrs. Gamp conveyed into these taunts was altogether lost on the unconscious Chuffey, who appeared to be as little cognizant of their delivery as of his having given Mrs. Gamp offence. But that high-minded woman being sensitively alive to any invasion of her professional province, and imagining that Mr. Chuffey had given utterance to some prediction on the subject of sons, which ought to have emanated in the first instance from herself as the only lawful authority, or which should at least have been on no account proclaimed without her sanction and concurrence, was not so easily appeased. She continued to sidle at Mr. Chuffey with looks of sharp hostility, and to defy him with many other ironical remarks, uttered in that low key which commonly denotes suppressed indignation; until the entrance of the tea-board, and a request from Mrs. Jonas that she would make tea at a side-table for the party that had unexpectedly assembled, restored her to herself. She smiled again, and entered on her ministration with her own particular urbanity.

"And quite a family it is to make tea for," said Mrs. Gamp; "and wot a happiness to do it! My good young 'ooman"—to the servant-girl—"p'raps somebody would like to try a new-laid egg or two, not biled too hard. Likeways, a few rounds o' buttered toast, first cuttin' off the crust, in consequence of tender teeth, and not too many of 'em; which Gamp himself, Mrs. Chuzzlewit, at one blow, being in liquor, struck out four, two single, and two double, as was took by Mrs. Harris for a keepsake, and is carried in her pocket at this present hour, along with two cramp-bones, a bit o' ginger, and a grater like a blessed infant's shoe, in tin, with a little heel to put the nutmeg in: as many times

Mrs. Gamp makes Tea

I've seen and said, and used for caudle when required, within the month."

As the privileges of the side-table—besides including the small prerogatives of sitting next the toast, and taking two cups of tea to other people's one, and always taking them at a crisis, that is to say, before putting fresh water into the tea-pot, and after it had been standing for some time—also comprehended a full view of the company, and an opportunity of addressing them as from a rostrum, Mrs. Gamp discharged the functions entrusted to her with extreme good-humour and affability. Sometimes, resting her saucer on the palm of her outspread hand, and supporting her elbow on the table, she stopped between her sips of tea to favour the circle with a smile, a wink, a roll of the head, or some other mark of notice ; and at those periods, her countenance was lighted up with a degree of intelligence and vivacity, which it was almost impossible to separate from the benignant influence of distilled waters.

But for Mrs. Gamp, it would have been a curiously silent party. Miss Pecksniff only spoke to her Augustus, and to him in whispers. Augustus spoke to nobody, but sighed for every one, and occasionally gave himself such a sounding slap upon the forehead as would make Mrs. Todgers, who was rather nervous, start in her chair with an involuntary exclamation. Mrs. Todgers was occupied in knitting, and seldom spoke. Poor Merry held the hand of cheerful little Ruth between her own, and listening with evident pleasure to all she said, but rarely speaking herself, sometimes smiled, and sometimes kissed her on the cheek, and sometimes turned aside to hide the tears that trembled in her eyes. Tom felt this change in her so much, and was so glad to see how tenderly Ruth dealt with her, and how she knew and answered to it, that he had not the heart to make any movement towards their departure, although he had long since given utterance to all he came to say.

The old clerk, subsiding into his usual state, remained

profoundly silent, while the rest of the little assembly were thus occupied, intent upon the dreams, whatever they might be, which hardly seemed to stir the surface of his sluggish thoughts. The bent of these dull fancies combining probably with the silent feasting that was going on about him, and some struggling recollection of the last approach to revelry he had witnessed, suggested a strange question to his mind. He looked round upon a sudden, and said,

"Who's lying dead up stairs?"

"No one," said Merry, turning to him. "What is the matter? We are all here."

"All here!" cried the old man. "All here! Where is he then—my old master, Mr. Chuzzlewit, who had the only son? Where is he?"

"Hush! Hush!" said Merry, speaking kindly to him. "That happened long ago. Don't you recollect?"

"Recollect!" rejoined the old man, with a cry of grief. "As if I could forget! As if I ever could forget!"

He put his hand up to his face for a moment; and then repeated turning round exactly as before,

"Who's lying dead up stairs?"

"No one!" said Merry.

At first he gazed angrily upon her, as upon a stranger who endeavoured to deceive him; but, peering into her face, and seeing that it was indeed she, he shook his head in sorrowful compassion.

"You think not. But they don't tell you. No, no, poor thing! They don't tell you. Who are these, and why are they merry-making here, if there is no one dead? Foul play! Go see who it is!"

She made a sign to them not to speak to him, which indeed they had little inclination to do; and remained silent herself. So did he for a short time; but then he repeated the same question with an eagerness that had a peculiar terror in it.

"There's some one dead," he said, "or dying; and I want to know who it is. Go see, go see! Where's Jonas?"

" In the country," she replied.

The old man gazed at her as if he doubted what she said, or had not heard her; and, rising from his chair, walked across the room and up stairs, whispering as he went, " Foul play ! " They heard his footsteps overhead, going up into that corner of the room in which the bed stood (it was there old Anthony had died); and then they heard him coming down again immediately. His fancy was not so strong or wild that it pictured to him anything in the deserted bed-chamber which was not there; for he returned much calmer, and appeared to have satisfied himself.

" They don't tell you," he said to Merry in his quavering voice, as he sat down again, and patted her upon the head. " They don't tell me either; but I'll watch, I'll watch. They shall not hurt you; don't be frightened. When you have sat up watching, I have sat up watching too. Ay, ay, I have ! " he piped out, clenching his weak, shrivelled hand. " Many a night I have been ready ! "

He said this with such trembling gaps and pauses in his want of breath, and said it in his jealous secrecy so closely in her ear, that little or nothing of it was understood by the visitors. But they had heard and seen enough of the old man to be disquieted, and to have left their seats and gathered about him; thereby affording Mrs. Gamp, whose professional coolness was not so easily disturbed, an eligible opportunity for concentrating the whole resources of her powerful mind and appetite upon the toast and butter, tea and eggs. She had brought them to bear upon those viands with such vigour that her face was in the highest state of inflammation, when she now (there being nothing left to eat or drink) saw fit to interpose.

" Why, highty tighty, sir ! " cried Mrs. Gamp, " is these your manners ? You want a pitcher of cold water throw'd over you to bring you round; that's my belief; and if you was under Betsey Prig you'd have it, too, I do assure you, Mr. Chuffey. Spanish Flies is the only thing to draw this nonsense out of you; and if anybody wanted to do you a kindness, they'd clap a blister of 'em on your head, and put a mustard poultige on your back. Who's dead, indeed! It wouldn't be no grievous loss if some one was, I think!"

"He's quiet now, Mrs. Gamp," said Merry. "Don't disturb him."

"Oh, bother the old wictim, Mrs. Chuzzlewit," replied that zealous lady, "I ain't no patience with him. You give him his own way too much by half. A worritin' wexagious creetur!"

No doubt with the view of carrying out the precepts she enforced, and "bothering the old wictim" in practice as well as in theory, Mrs. Gamp took him by the collar of his coat, and gave him some dozen or two of hearty shakes backward and forward in his chair; that exercise being considered by the disciples of the Prig school of nursing (who are very numerous among professional ladies) as exceedingly conducive to repose, and highly beneficial to the performance of the nervous functions. Its effect in this instance was to render the patient so giddy and addle-headed, that he could say nothing more; which Mrs. Gamp regarded as the triumph of her art.

"There!" she said, loosening the old man's cravat, in consequence of his being rather black in the face, after this scientific treatment. "Now, I hope, you're easy in your mind. If you should turn at all faint, we can soon revive you, sir, I promige you. Bite a person's thumbs, or turn their fingers the wrong way," said Mrs. Gamp, smiling with the consciousness of at once imparting pleasure and instruction to her auditors, "and they comes to, wonderful, Lord bless you!"

As this excellent woman had been formally entrusted with the care of Mr. Chuffey on a previous occasion, neither Mrs. Jonas nor anybody else had the resolution to interfere directly with her mode of treatment: though all present (Tom Pinch and his sister especially) appeared to be disposed to differ from her views. For such is the rash boldness of the uninitiated, that they will frequently set up some monstrous abstract principle, such as humanity, or tenderness, or the like idle folly, in obstinate defiance of all precedent and usage; and will even venture to maintain the same against the persons who have made the precedents and established the usage, and who must therefore be the best and most impartial judges of the subject.

"Ah, Mr. Pinch!" said Miss Pecksniff. "It all comes of this unfortunate marriage. If my sister had not been so precipitate, and had not united herself to a Wretch, there would have been no Mr. Chuffey in the house."

'Hush!" cried Tom. "She'll hear you."

"I should be very sorry if she did hear me, Mr. Pinch," said Cherry, raising her voice a little: "for it is not in my nature to add to the uneasiness of any person : far less of my own sister. *I* know what a sister's duties are, Mr. Pinch, and I hope I always showed it in my practice. Augustus, my dear child, find my pocket-handkerchief, and give it to me."

Augustus obeyed, and took Mrs. Todgers aside to pour his griefs into her friendly bosom.

"I am sure, Mr. Pinch," said Charity, looking after her betrothed and glancing at her sister, "that I ought to be very grateful for the blessings I enjoy, and those which are yet in store for me. When I contrast Augustus "—here she was modest and embarrassed—" who, I don't mind saying to you, is all softness, mildness, and devotion, with the detestable man who is my sister's husband ; and when I think, Mr. Pinch, that in the dispensations of this world, our cases might have been reversed ; I have much to be thankful for, indeed, and much to make me humble and contented."

Contented she might have been, but humble she assuredly was not. Her face and manner experienced something so widely different from humility, that Tom could not help understanding and despising the base motives that were working in her breast. He turned away, and said to Ruth, that it was time for them to go.

353

"I will write to your husband," said Tom to Merry, "and explain to him, as I would have done if I had met him here, that if he has sustained any inconvenience through my means, it is not my fault: a postman not being more innocent of the news he brings, than I was when I handed him that letter."

"I thank you!" said Merry. "It may do some good."

She parted tenderly from Ruth, who with her brother was in the act of leaving the room, when a key was heard in the lock of the door below, and immediately afterwards a quick footstep in the passage. Tom stopped, and looked at Merry.

It was Jonas, she said timidly.

"I had better not meet him on the stairs, perhaps," said Tom, drawing his sister's arm through his, and coming back a step or two. "I'll wait for him here, a moment."

He had scarcely said it when the door opened, and Jonas entered. His wife came forward to receive him; but he put her aside with his hand, and said in a surly tone:

"I didn't know you'd got a party."

As he looked, at the same time, either by accident or design, towards Miss Pecksniff; and as Miss Pecksniff was only too delighted to quarrel with him, she instantly resented it.

"Oh dear!" she said, rising. "Pray don't let us intrude upon your domestic happiness! That would be a pity. We have taken tea here, sir, in your absence; but if you will have the goodness to send us a note of the expense, receipted, we shall be happy to pay it. Augustus, my love, we will go, if you please. Mrs. Todgers, unless you wish to remain here, we shall be happy to take you with us. It would be a pity, indeed, to spoil the bliss which this gentleman always brings with him: especially into his own home."

"Charity! Charity!" remonstrated her sister, in such a heartfelt tone that she might have been imploring her to show the cardinal virtue whose name she bore.

"Merry, my dear, I am much obliged to you for your advice," returned Miss Pecksniff, with a stately scorn: by the way, she had not been offered any: "but I am not his slave——"

354

"No, nor wouldn't have been if you could," interrupted Jonas. "We know all about it."

"What did you say, sir?" cried Miss Pecksniff, sharply.

"Didn't you hear?" retorted Jonas, lounging down upon a chair. "I am not a-going to say it again. If you like to stay, you may stay. If you like to go, you may go. But if you stay, please to be civil."

"Beast!" cried Miss Pecksniff, sweeping past him. "Augustus! He is beneath your notice!" Augustus had been making some faint and sickly demonstration of shaking his fist. "Come away, child," screamed Miss Pecksniff, "I command you!"

The scream was elicited from her by Augustus manifesting an intention to return and grapple with him. But Miss Pecksniff giving the fiery youth a pull, and Mrs. Todgers giving him a push, they all three tumbled out of the room together, to the music of Miss Pecksniff's shrill remonstrances.

All this time, Jonas had seen nothing of Tom and his sister; for they were almost behind the door when he opened it, and he had sat down with his back towards them, and had purposely kept his eyes upon the opposite side of the street during his altercation with Miss Pecksniff, in order that his seeming carelessness might increase the exasperation of that wronged young damsel. His wife now faltered out that Tom had been waiting to see him; and Tom advanced.

The instant he presented himself, Jonas got up from his chair, and swearing a great oath, caught it in his grasp, as if he would have felled Tom to the ground with it. As he most unquestionably would have done, but that his very passion and surprise made him irresolute, and gave Tom, in his calmness, an opportunity of being heard.

"You have no cause to be violent, sir," said Tom. "Though what I wish to say relates to your own affairs, I know nothing of them, and desire to know nothing of them."

Jonas was too enraged to speak. He held the door open; and stamping his foot upon the ground, motioned Tom away.

"As you cannot suppose," said Tom, "that I am here, with any view of conciliating you or pleasing myself, I am quite indifferent to your reception of me, or your dismissal of me. Hear what I have to say, if you are not a madman! I gave you a letter the other day, when you were about to go abroad."

"You Thief, you did!" retorted Jonas. "I'll pay you for the carriage of it one day, and settle an old score besides. I will!"

"Tut, tut," said Tom, "you needn't waste words or threats. I wish you to understand—plainly because I would rather keep clear of you and everything that concerns you: not because I have the least apprehension of your doing me any injury: which would be weak indeed—that I am no party to the contents of that letter. That I know nothing of it. That I was not even aware that it was to be delivered to you; and that I had it from—— "

"By the Lord!" cried Jonas, fiercely catching up the chair, "I'll knock your brains out, if you speak another word."

Tom, nevertheless, persisting in his intention, and opening his lips to speak again, Jonas set upon him like a savage; and in the quickness and ferocity of his attack would have surely done him some grievous injury, defenceless as he was, and embarrassed by having his frightened sister clinging to his arm, if Merry had not run between them, crying to Tom for the love of Heaven to leave the house. The agony of this poor creature, the terror of his sister, the impossibility of making himself audible, and the equal impossibility of bearing up against Mrs. Gamp, who threw herself upon him like a feather-bed, and forced him backwards down the stairs by the mere oppression of her dead-weight, prevailed. Tom shook the dust of that house off his feet, without having mentioned Nadgett's name.

If the name could have passed his lips; if Jonas, in the insolence of his vile nature, had never roused him to do that old act of manliness, for which (and not for his last offence) he hated him with such malignity; if Jonas could have learned, as then he could and would have learned, through Tom's means, what unsuspected spy there was upon him; he would have been saved from the commission of a Guilty Deed, then drawing on towards its black accomplishment. But the fatality was of his own working; the pit was of his own digging; the gloom that gathered round him, was the shadow of his own life.

His wife had closed the door, and thrown herself before it, on the ground, upon her knees. She held up her hands to him now, and besought him not to be harsh with her, for she had interposed in fear of bloodshed.

"So, so!" said Jonas, looking down upon her, as he fetched his breath. "These are your friends, are they, when I am away? You plot and tamper with this sort of people, do you?"

"No, indeed! I have no knowledge of these secrets, and no clue to their meaning. I have never seen him since I left home but once—but twice—before to-day."

"Oh!" sneered Jonas, catching at this correction. "But once, but twice, eh? Which do you mean? Twice and once perhaps. Three times! How many more, you lying jade?"

As he made an angry motion with his hand, she shrunk down hastily. A suggestive action! Full of a cruel truth!

"How many more times?" he repeated.

"No more. The other morning, and to-day, and once besides."

He was about to retort upon her, when the clock struck. He started, stopped, and listened: appearing to revert to some engagement, or to some other subject, a secret within his own breast, recalled to him by this record of the progress of the hours.

"Don't lie there! Get up!"

Having helped her to rise, or rather hauled her up by the arm, he went on to say:

"Listen to me, young lady; and don't whine when you have no occasion, or I may make some for you. If I find him in my house again, or find that you have seen him in anybody else's house, you'll repent it. If you are not deaf and dumb to everything that concerns me, unless you have my leave to hear and speak, you'll repent it. If you don't obey exactly what I order, you'll repent it. Now, attend. What's the time?"

"It struck Eight a minute ago."

He looked towards her intently; and said, with a laboured distinctness, as if he had got the words off by heart:

"I have been travelling day and night, and am tired. I have lost some money, and that don't improve me. Put my supper in the little off-room below, and have the truckle-bed made. I shall sleep there to-night, and maybe to-morrow night; and if I can sleep all day to-morrow, so much the better, for I've got trouble to sleep off, if I can. Keep the house quiet, and don't call me. Mind! Don't call me. Don't let anybody call me. Let me lie there."

She said it should be done. Was that all?

"All what! You must be prying and questioning?" he angrily retorted. "What more do you want to know?"

"I want to know nothing, Jonas, but what you tell me. All hope of confidence between us has long deserted me!"

"Ecod, I should hope so!" he muttered.

"But if you will tell me what you wish, I will be obedient and will try to please you. I make no merit of that, for I have no friend in my father or my sister, but am quite alone. I am very humble and submissive. You told me you would break my spirit, and you have done so. Do not break my heart too!"

She ventured, as she said these words, to lay her hand upon his shoulder. He suffered it to rest there, in his exultation; and the whole mean, abject, sordid, pitiful soul of the man, looked at her, for the moment, through his wicked eyes.

For the moment only: for, with the same hurried return to something within himself, he bade her, in a surly tone, show her obedience by executing his commands without delay.

When she had withdrawn, he paced up and down the room several times; but always with his right hand clenched, as if it held something; which it did not, being empty. When he was tired of this, he threw himself into a chair, and thoughtfully turned up the sleeve of his right arm, as if he were rather musing about its strength than examining it; but, even then, he kept the hand clenched.

He was brooding in this chair, with his eyes cast down upon the ground, when Mrs. Gamp came in to tell him that the little room was ready. Not being quite sure of her reception after interfering in the quarrel, Mrs. Gamp, as a means of interesting and propitiating her patron, affected a deep solicitude in Mr. Chuffey.

"How is he now, sir?" she said.

"Who?" cried Jonas, raising his head, and staring at her.

"To be sure?" returned the matron with a smile and a curtsey. "What am I thinking of! You wasn't here, sir, when he was took so strange. I never see a poor dear creetur took so strange in all my life, except a patient much about the same age, as I once nussed, which his calling was the custom-'us, and his name was Mrs. Harris's own father, as pleasant a singer, Mr. Chuzzlewit, as ever you heerd, with a voice like a Jew's-harp in the bass notes, that it took six men to hold at sech times, foaming frightful."

"Chuffey, eh?" said Jonas carelessly, seeing that she went up to the old clerk, and looked at him. "Ha!"

"The creetur's head's so hot," said Mrs. Gamp, "that you might eat a flat-iron at it. And no wonder I am sure, considerin' the things he said!"

"Said!" cried Jonas. "What did he say?"

Mrs. Gamp laid her hand upon her heart, to put some check upon its palpitations, and turning up her eyes replied in a faint voice:

"The awfullest things, Mr. Chuzzlewit, as ever I heerd! Which Mrs. Harris's father never spoke a word when took so, some does and some don't, except sayin' when he come round, 'Where is Sairey Gamp?' But raly, sir, when Mr. Chuffey comes to ask who's lyin' dead up stairs, and——"

"Who's lying dead up stairs!" repeated Jonas, standing aghast.

Mrs. Gamp nodded, made as if she were swallowing, and went on.

"Who's lying dead up stairs; such was his Bible language; and where was Mr. Chuzzlewit as had the only son; and when he goes up stairs a looking in the beds and wandering about the rooms, and comes down again a whisperin' softly to his-self about foul play and that; it give me sich a turn, I don't deny it, Mr. Chuzzlewit, that I never could have kep myself up but for a little drain of spirits, which I seldom touches, but could always wish to know where to find, if so dispoged, never knowin' wot may happen next, the world bein' so uncertain."

"Why, the old fool's mad!" cried Jonas, much disturbed.

"That's my opinion, sir," said Mrs. Gamp, "and I will not deceive you. I believe as Mr. Chuffey, sir, rekwires attention (if I may make so bold), and should not have his liberty to wex and worrit your sweet lady as he doos."

"Why, who minds what he says?" retorted Jonas.

"Still he is worritin', sir," said Mrs. Gamp. "No one don't mind him, but he *is* a ill conwenience."

"Ecod you're right," said Jonas, looking doubtfully at the subject of this conversation. "I have half a mind to shut him up."

Mrs. Gamp rubbed her hands, and smiled, and shook her head, and sniffed expressively, as scenting a job.

"Could you—could you take care of such an idiot, now, in some spare room up stairs?" asked Jonas.

"Me and a friend of mine, one off, one on, could do it, Mr. Chuzzlewit," replied the nurse; "our charges not bein' high, but wishin' they was lower, and allowance made considerin' not strangers. Me and Betsey Prig, sir, would undertake Mr. Chuffey, reasonable," said Mrs. Gamp, looking at him with her head on one side, as if he had been a piece of goods, for which she was driving a bargain; "and give every satigefaction. Betsey Prig has nussed a many lunacies, and well she knows their ways, which puttin' 'em right close afore the fire, when fractious, is the certainest and most compoging."

While Mrs. Gamp discoursed to this effect, Jonas was walking up and down the room again: glancing covertly at the old clerk, as he did so. He now made a stop, and said:

"I must look after him, I suppose, or I may have him doing some mischief. What say you?"

"Nothin' more likely!" Mrs. Gamp replied. "As well I have experienged, I do assure you, sir."

"Well! Look after him for the present, and—let me see— three days from this time let the other woman come here, and we'll see if we can make a bargain of it. About nine or ten o'clock at night, say. Keep your eye upon him in the meanwhile, and don't talk about it. He's as mad as a March hare!"

"Madder!" cried Mrs. Gamp. "A deal madder!"

"See to him, then; take care that he does no harm; and recollect what I have told you."

Leaving Mrs. Gamp in the act of repeating all she had been told, and of producing in support of her memory and trustworthiness, many commendations selected from among the most remarkable opinions of the celebrated Mrs. Harris, he descended to the little room prepared for him, and pulling off his coat and his boots, put them outside the door before he locked it. In locking it, he was careful so to adjust the key, as to baffle any curious person who might try to peep in through the key-hole; and when he had taken these precautions, he sat down to his supper.

"Mr. Chuff," he muttered, "it'll be pretty easy to be even with *you*. It's of no use doing things by halves, and as long as I stop here, I'll take good care of you. When I'm off you may say what you please. But it's a d—d strange thing," he added, pushing away his untouched plate, and striding moodily

361

to and fro, " that his drivellings should have taken this turn just now."

After pacing the little room from end to end several times, he sat down in another chair.

" I say just now, but for anything I know, he may have been carrying on the same game all along. Old dog! He shall be gagged ! "

He paced the room again in the same restless and unsteady way; and then sat down upon the bedstead, leaning his chin upon his hand, and looking at the table. When he had looked at it for a long time, he remembered his supper; and resuming the chair he had first occupied, began to eat with great rapacity: not like a hungry man, but as if he were determined to do it. He drank too, roundly; sometimes stopping in the middle of a draught to walk, and change his seat and walk again, and dart back to the table and fall to, in a ravenous hurry, as before.

It was now growing dark. As the gloom of evening, deepening into night, came on, another dark shade emerging from within him seemed to overspread his face, and slowly change it. Slowly, slowly; darker and darker; more and more haggard; creeping over him by little and little; until it was black night within him and without.

The room in which he had shut himself up, was on the ground floor, at the back of the house. It was lighted by a dirty skylight, and had a door in the wall, opening into a narrow covered passage or blind-alley, very little frequented after five or six o'clock in the evening, and not in much use as a thoroughfare at any hour. But it had an outlet in a neighbouring street.

The ground on which this chamber stood, had, at one time, not within his recollection, been a yard; and had been converted to its present purpose, for use as an office. But the occasion for it, died with the man who built it; and saving that it had sometimes served as an apology for a spare bedroom, and that the old clerk had once held it (but that was years ago) as his recognised apartment, it had been little troubled by Anthony Chuzzlewit and Son. It was a blotched, stained, mouldering room, like a vault; and there were water-pipes running through it, which at unexpected times in the night, when other things were quiet, clicked and gurgled suddenly, as if they were choking.

The door into the court had not been open for a long, long time; but the key had always hung in one place, and there it hung now. He was prepared for its being rusty; for he had a little bottle of oil in his pocket and the feather of a pen, with which he lubricated the key, and the lock too, carefully. All this while he had been without his coat, and had nothing on his feet but his stockings. He now got softly into bed, in the same state, and tossed from side to side to tumble it. In his restless condition, that was easily done.

When he arose, he took from his portmanteau, which he had caused to be carried into that place when he came home, a pair of clumsy shoes, and put them on his feet; also a pair of leather leggings, such as countrymen are used to wear, with straps to fasten them to the waistband. In these he dressed himself at leisure. Lastly, he took out a common frock of coarse dark jean, which he drew over his own underclothing; and a felt hat—he had purposely left his own up stairs. He then sat himself down by the door, with the key in his hand, waiting.

He had no light; the time was dreary, long, and awful. The ringers were practising in a neighbouring church, and the clashing of the bells was almost maddening. Curse the clamouring bells, they seemed to know that he was listening at the door, and to proclaim it in a crowd of voices to all the town! Would they never be still?

They ceased at last, and then the silence was so new and terrible that it seemed the prelude to some dreadful noise. Footsteps in the court! Two men. He fell back from the door on tiptoe, as if they could have seen him through its wooden panels.

They passed on, talking (he could make out) about a skeleton which had been dug up yesterday, in some work of excavation near at hand, and was supposed to be that of a murdered man. "So murder is not always found out, you see," they said to one another as they turned the corner.

Hush!

He put the key into the lock, and turned it. The door resisted for a while, but soon came stiffly open; mingling with the sense of fever in his mouth, a taste of rust, and dust, and earth, and rotting wood. He looked out; passed out; locked it after him.

All was clear and quiet, as he fled away.

CHAPTER XLVII

DID no men passing through the dim streets shrink without knowing why, when he came stealing up behind them? As he glided on, had no child in its sleep an indistinct perception of a guilty shadow falling on its bed, that troubled its innocent rest? Did no dog howl, and strive to break its rattling chain, that it might tear him; no burrowing rat, scenting the work he had in hand, essay to gnaw a passage after him, that it might hold a greedy revel at the feast of his providing? When he looked back, across his shoulder, was it to see if his quick footsteps still fell dry upon the dusty pavement, or were already moist and clogged with the red mire that stained the naked feet of Cain!

He shaped his course for the main western road, and soon reached it: riding a part of the way, then alighting and walking on again. He travelled for a considerable distance upon the roof of a stage-coach, which came up while he was afoot; and when it turned out of his road, bribed the driver of a return post-chaise to take him on with him; and then made across the country at a run, and saved a mile or two before he struck again into the road. At last, as his plan was, he came up with a certain lumbering, slow, night-coach, which stopped wherever it could, and was stopping then at a public-house, while the guard and coachman ate and drank within.

He bargained for a seat outside this coach, and took it. And he quitted it no more until it was within a few miles of its destination, but occupied the same place all night.

All night! It is a common fancy that nature seems to sleep by night. It is a false fancy, as who should know better than he?

The fishes slumbered in the cold, bright, glistening streams and rivers, perhaps; and the birds roosted on the branches of the trees; and in their stalls and pastures beasts were quiet; and human creatures slept. But what of that, when the solemn night was watching, when it never winked, when its darkness watched no less than its light! The stately trees, the moon and shining stars, the softly-stirring wind, the over-shadowed lane, the broad, bright country-side, they all kept watch. There was not a blade of growing grass or corn, but watched; and the quieter it was, the more intent and fixed its watch upon him seemed to be.

And yet he slept. Riding on among those sentinels of God, he slept, and did not change the purpose of his journey. If he forgot it in his troubled dreams, it came up steadily, and woke him. But it never woke him to remorse, or to abandonment of his design.

He dreamed at one time that he was lying calmly in his bed, thinking of a moonlight night and the noise of wheels, when the old clerk put his head in at the door, and beckoned him. At this signal he arose immediately: being already dressed, in the clothes he actually wore at that time: and accompanied him into a strange city, where the names of the streets were written on the walls in characters quite new to him; which gave him no surprise or uneasiness, for he remembered in his dream to have been there before. Although these streets were very precipitous, insomuch that to get from one to another, it was necessary to descend great heights by ladders that were too short, and ropes that moved deep bells, and swung and swayed as they were clung to, the danger gave him little emotion beyond the first thrill of terror: his anxieties being concentrated on his dress, which was quite unfitted for some festival that was about to be holden there, and in which he had come to take a part. Already, great crowds began to fill the streets, and in one direction myriads of people came rushing down an interminable perspective, strewing flowers and making way for others on white horses, when a terrible figure started from the throng, and cried out that it was the Last Day for all the world. The cry being spread, there was a wild hurrying on to Judgment; and the press became so great that he and his companion (who was constantly changing, and was never the same man two minutes together, though he never saw one man come or another go), stood aside in a porch, fearfully surveying the multitude; in which there were many faces that he knew, and many that he did not know, but dreamed he did; when all at once a struggling head rose up among the rest—livid and deadly, but the same as he had known it— and denounced him as having appointed that direful day to happen. They closed together. As he strove to free the hand in which he held a club, and strike the blow he had so often thought of, he started to the knowledge of his waking purpose and the rising of the sun.

The sun was welcome to him. There were life and motion, and a world astir, to divide the attention of Day. It was the eye of Night: of wakeful, watchful, silent, and attentive Night, with so much leisure for the observation of his wicked thoughts: that he dreaded most. There is no glare in the night. Even Glory shows to small advantage in the night, upon a crowded battle-field. How then shows Glory's blood-relation, bastard Murder!

Ay! He made no compromise, and held no secret with himself now. Murder. He had come to do it.

"Let me get down here," he said.

"Short of the town, eh!" observed the coachman.

"I may get down where I please, I suppose?"

"You got up to please yourself, and may get down to

please yourself. It won't break our hearts to lose you, and it wouldn't have broken 'em if we'd never found you. Be a little quicker. That's all."

The guard had alighted, and was waiting in the road to take his money. In the jealousy and distrust of what he contemplated, he thought this man looked at him with more than common curiosity.

"What are you staring at?" said Jonas.

"Not at a handsome man," returned the guard. "If you want your fortune told, I'll tell you a bit of it. You won't be drowned. That's a consolation for you."

Before he could retort or turn away, the coachman put an end to the dialogue by giving him a cut with his whip, and bid him get out for a surly dog. The guard jumped up to his seat at the same moment, and they drove off, laughing; leaving him to stand in the road, and shake his fist at them. He was not displeased though, on second thoughts, to have been taken for an ill-conditioned common country fellow; but rather congratulated himself upon it as a proof that he was well disguised.

Wandering into a copse by the road-side—but not in that place: two or three miles off—he tore out from a fence a thick, hard, knotted stake; and, sitting down beneath a hay-rick, spent some time in shaping it, in peeling off the bark, and fashioning its jagged head, with his knife.

The day passed on. Noon, afternoon, evening. Sunset.

At that serene and peaceful time two men, riding in a gig, came out of the city by a road not much frequented. It was the day on which Mr. Pecksniff had agreed to dine with Montague. He had kept his appointment, and was now going home. His host was riding with him for a short distance; meaning to return by a pleasant track, which Mr. Pecksniff had engaged to show him, through some fields. Jonas knew their plans. He had hung about the inn-yard while they were at dinner and had heard their orders given.

They were loud and merry in their conversation, and might

have been heard at some distance : far above the sound of their carriage wheels or horses' hoofs. They came on noisily, to where a stile and footpath indicated their point of separation. Here they stopped.

"It's too soon. Much too soon," said Mr. Pecksniff. "But this is the place, my dear sir. Keep the path, and go straight through the little wood you'll come to. The path is narrower there, but you can't miss it. When shall I see you again? Soon I hope?"

"I hope so," replied Montague.

"Good-night!"

"Good-night. And a pleasant ride!"

So long as Mr. Pecksniff was in sight, and turned his head, at intervals, to salute him, Montague stood in the road smiling, and waving his hand. But when his new partner had disappeared, and this show was no longer necessary, he sat down on the stile with looks so altered, that he might have grown ten years older in the meantime.

He was flushed with wine, but not gay. His scheme had succeeded, but he showed no triumph. The effort of sustaining his difficult part before his late companion had fatigued him, perhaps, or it may be, that the evening whispered to his conscience, or it may be (as it *has* been) that a shadowy veil was dropping round him, closing out all thoughts but the presentiment and vague foreknowledge of impending doom.

If there be fluids, as we know there are, which, conscious of a coming wind, or rain, or frost, will shrink and strive to hide themselves in their glass arteries; may not that subtle liquor of the blood perceive by properties within itself, that hands are raised to waste and spill it; and in the veins of men run cold and dull as his did, in that hour!

So cold, although the air was warm: so dull, although the sky was bright: that he rose up shivering, from his seat, and hastily resumed his walk. He checked himself as hastily: undecided whether to pursue the footpath which was lonely and retired, or to go back by the road.

He took the footpath.

The glory of the departing sun was on his face. The music of the birds was in his ears. Sweet wild flowers bloomed about him. Thatched roofs of poor men's homes were in the distance; and an old grey spire, surmounted by a Cross, rose up between him and the coming night.

He had never read the lesson which these things conveyed; he had ever mocked and turned away from it; but, before going down into a hollow place, he looked round, once, upon the evening prospect, sorrowfully. Then he went down, down, down, into the dell.

It brought him to the wood; a close, thick, shadowy wood, through which the path went winding on, dwindling away into a slender sheep-track. He paused before entering; for the stillness of this spot almost daunted him.

The last rays of the sun were shining in, aslant, making a path of golden light along the stems and branches in its range, which, even as he looked, began to die away, yielding gently to the twilight that came creeping on. It was so very quiet that the soft and stealthy moss about the trunks of some old trees, seemed to have grown out of the silence, and to be its proper offspring. Those other trees which were subdued by blasts of wind in winter time, had not quite tumbled down, but being caught by others, lay all bare and scathed across their leafy arms, as if unwilling to disturb the general repose by the crash of their fall. Vistas of silence opened everywhere, into the heart and innermost recesses of the wood; beginning with the likeness of an aisle, a cloister, or a ruin open to the sky; then tangling off into a deep green rustling mystery, through which gnarled trunks, and twisted boughs, and ivy-covered stems, and trembling leaves, and bark-stripped bodies of old trees stretched out at length, were faintly seen in beautiful confusion.

As the sunlight died away, and evening fell upon the wood, he entered it. Moving, here and there, a bramble or a drooping bough which stretched across his path, he slowly disappeared. At intervals a narrow opening showed him passing on, or the sharp cracking of some tender branch denoted where he went: then, he was seen or heard no more.

Never more beheld by mortal eye or heard by mortal ear: one man excepted. That man, parting the leaves and branches on the other side, near where the path emerged again, came leaping out soon afterwards.

What had he left within the wood, that he sprang out of it, as if it were a hell!

The body of a murdered man. In one thick solitary spot, it lay among the last year's leaves of oak and beech, just as it had fallen headlong down. Sopping and soaking in among the leaves that formed its pillow; oozing down into the boggy ground, as if to cover itself from human sight; forcing its way between and through the curling leaves, as if those sense-less things rejected and forswore it, and were coiled up in abhorrence; went a dark, dark stain that dyed the whole summer night from earth to heaven.

The doer of this deed came leaping from the wood so fiercely, that he cast into the air a shower of fragments of young boughs, torn away in his passage, and fell with violence upon the grass. But he quickly gained his feet again, and keeping underneath a hedge with his body bent, went running on towards the road. The road once reached, he fell into a rapid walk, and set on towards London.

And he was not sorry for what he had done. He was frightened when he thought of it—when did he not think of it!—but he was not sorry. He had had a terror and dread of the wood when he was in it; but being out of it, and having committed the crime, his fears were now diverted, strangely, to the dark room he had left shut up at home. He had a greater horror, infinitely greater, of that room than of the wood. Now that he was on his return to it, it seemed beyond com-parison more dismal and more dreadful than the wood. His hideous secret was shut up in the room, and all its terrors were there; to his thinking it was not in the wood at all.

He walked on for ten miles; and then stopped at an ale-house for a coach, which he knew would pass through, on its way to London, before long; and which he also knew was not the coach he had travelled down by, for it came from another place. He sat down outside the door here, on a bench, beside a man who was smoking his pipe. Having called for some beer, and drunk, he offered it to this companion, who thanked him, and took a draught. He could not help thinking that, if the man had known all, he might scarcely have relished drinking out of the same cup with him.

"A fine night, master!" said this person. "And a rare sunset."

"I didn't see it," was his hasty answer.

"Didn't see it?" returned the man.

"How the devil could I see it, if I was asleep?"

"Asleep! Ay, ay." The man appeared surprised by his unexpected irritability, and saying no more, smoked his pipe in silence. They had not sat very long, when there was a knocking within.

"What's that?" cried Jonas.

"Can't say, I'm sure," replied the man.

He made no further inquiry, for the last question had escaped him, in spite of himself. But he was thinking, at the moment, of the closed-up room; of the possibility of their knocking at the door on some special occasion; of their being alarmed at receiving no answer; of their bursting it open; of their finding the room empty; of their fastening the door into the court, and rendering it impossible for him to get into the house, without showing himself in the garb he wore; which would lead to rumour, rumour to detection, detection to death. At that instant, as if by some design and order of circumstances, the knocking had come.

It still continued; like a warning echo of the dread reality he had conjured up. As he could not sit and hear it, he paid for his beer and walked on again. And having slunk about, in places unknown to him, all day; and being out at night,

in a lonely road, in an unusual dress, and in that wandering
and unsettled frame of mind; he stopped more than once to
look about him, hoping he might be in a dream.

Still he was not sorry. No. He had hated the man too
much, and had been bent, too desperately and too long, on
setting himself free. If the thing could have come over again,
he would have done it again. His malignant and revengeful
passions were not so easily laid. There was no more penitence
or remorse within him now, than there had been while the
deed was brewing.

Dread and fear were upon him. To an extent he had never
counted on, and could not manage in the least degree. He
was so horribly afraid of that infernal room at home. This
made him, in a gloomy, murderous, mad way, not only fearful
for himself but *of* himself; for being, as it were, a part of
the room : a something supposed to be there, yet missing from
it : he invested himself with its mysterious terrors; and when
he pictured in his mind the ugly chamber, false and quiet,
false and quiet, through the dark hours of two nights; and
the tumbled bed, and he not in it, though believed to be; he
became in a manner his own ghost and phantom, and was at
once the haunting spirit and the haunted man.

When the coach came up, which it soon did, he got a place
outside, and was carried briskly onward towards home. Now,
in taking his seat among the people behind, who were chiefly
country people, he conceived a fear that they knew of the
murder, and would tell him that the body had been found;
which, considering the time and place of the commission of
the crime, were events almost impossible to have happened
yet, as he very well knew. But, although he did know it,
and had therefore no reason to regard their ignorance as
anything but the natural sequence to the facts, still this very
ignorance of theirs encouraged him. So far encouraged him,
that he began to believe the body never would be found, and
began to speculate on that probability. Setting off from this
point, and measuring time by the rapid hurry of his guilty

thoughts, and what had gone before the bloodshed, and the troops of incoherent and disordered images, of which he was the constant prey; he came by daylight to regard the murder as an old murder, and to think himself comparatively safe, because it had not been discovered yet. Yet! When the sun which looked into the wood, and gilded with its rising light a dead man's face, had seen that man alive, and sought to win him to a thought of Heaven, on its going down last night!

But here were London streets again. Hush!

It was but five o'clock. He had time enough to reach his own house unobserved, and before there were many people in the streets, if nothing had happened so far, tending to his discovery. He slipped down from the coach without troubling the driver to stop his horses: and hurrying across the road, and in and out of every by-way that lay near his course, at length approached his own dwelling. He used additional caution in his immediate neighbourhood; halting first to look all down the street before him; then gliding swiftly through that one, and stopping to survey the next; and so on.

The passage-way was empty when his murderer's face looked into it. He stole on, to the door, on tiptoe, as if he dreaded to disturb his own imaginary rest.

He listened. Not a sound. As he turned the key with a trembling hand, and pushed the door softly open with his knee, a monstrous fear beset his mind.

What if the murdered man were there before him!

He cast a fearful glance all round. But there was nothing there.

He went in, locked the door, drew the key through and through the dust and damp in the fire-place to sully it again, and hung it up as of old. He took off his disguise, tied it up in a bundle ready for carrying away and sinking in the river before night, and locked it up in a cupboard. These precautions taken, he undressed, and went to bed.

The raging thirst, the fire that burnt within him as he lay

beneath the clothes, the augmented horror of the room, when they shut it out from his view; the agony of listening, in which he paid enforced regard to every sound, and thought the most unlikely one the prelude to that knocking which should bring the news; the starts with which he left his couch, and looking in the glass, imagined that his deed was broadly written in his face, and lying down and burying himself once more beneath the blankets, heard his own heart beating Murder, Murder, Murder, in the bed; what words can paint tremendous truths like these!

The morning advanced. There were footsteps in the house. He heard the blinds drawn up, and shutters opened; and now and then a stealthy tread outside his own door. He tried to call out, more than once, but his mouth was dry as if it had been filled with sand. At last he sat up in his bed, and cried:

" Who's there ! "

It was his wife.

He asked her what it was o'clock? Nine.

" Did—did no one knock at my door yesterday ? " he faltered. "Something disturbed me; but unless you had knocked the door down, you would have got no notice from me."

"No one," she replied. That was well. He had waited, almost breathless, for her answer. It was a relief to him, if anything could be.

" Mr. Nadgett wanted to see you," she said, "but I told him you were tired, and had requested not to be disturbed. He said it was of little consequence, and went away. As I was opening my window to let in the cool air, I saw him passing through the street this morning, very early; but he hasn't been again."

Passing through the street that morning? Very early! Jonas trembled at the thought of having had a narrow chance of seeing him himself: even him, who had no object but to avoid people, and sneak on unobserved, and keep his own secrets: and who saw nothing.

He called to her to get his breakfast ready, and prepared

to go up stairs: attiring himself in the clothes he had taken off when he came into that room, which had been, ever since, outside the door. In his secret dread of meeting the household for the first time, after what he had done, he lingered at the door on slight pretexts that they might see him without looking in his face; and left it ajar while he dressed; and called out, to have the windows opened, and the pavement watered, that they might become accustomed to his voice. Even when he had put off the time, by one means or other, so that he had seen or spoken to them all, he could not muster courage for a long while to go in among them, but stood at his own door listening to the murmur of their distant conversation.

He could not stop there for ever, and so joined them. His last glance at the glass had seen a tell-tale face, but that might have been because of his anxious looking in it. He dared not look at them to see if they observed him, but he thought them very silent.

And whatsoever guard he kept upon himself, he could not help listening, and showing that he listened. Whether he attended to their talk, or tried to think of other things, or talked himself, or held his peace, or resolutely counted the dull tickings of a hoarse clock at his back, he always lapsed, as if a spell were on him, into eager listening. For he knew it must come; and his present punishment, and torture, and distraction, were, to listen for its coming.

Hush!

CHAPTER XLVIII

BEARS TIDINGS OF MARTIN, AND OF MARK, AS WELL AS OF A
THIRD PERSON NOT QUITE UNKNOWN TO THE READER.
EXHIBITS FILIAL PIETY IN AN UGLY ASPECT; AND CASTS
A DOUBTFUL RAY OF LIGHT UPON A VERY DARK PLACE

Tom Pinch and Ruth were sitting at their early breakfast,
with the window open, and a row of the freshest little plants
ranged before it on the inside by Ruth's own hands; and
Ruth had fastened a sprig of geranium in Tom's button-hole,
to make him very smart and summer-like for the day (it was
obliged to be fastened in, or that dear old Tom was certain
to lose it); and people were crying flowers up and down the
street; and a blundering bee, who had got himself in between
the two sashes of the window, was bruising his head against
the glass, endeavouring to force himself out into the fine morning, and considering himself enchanted because he couldn't
do it; and the morning was as fine a morning as ever was
seen; and the fragrant air was kissing Ruth and rustling
about Tom, as if it said, " How are you, my dears : I came
all this way on purpose to salute you;" and it was one of
those glad times when we form, or ought to form, the wish
that every one on earth were able to be happy, and catching
glimpses of the summer of the heart, to feel the beauty of
the summer of the year.

It was even a pleasanter breakfast than usual; and it was
always a pleasant one. For little Ruth had now two pupils

to attend, each three times a week, and each two hours at a time; and besides this, she had painted some screens and card-racks, and, unknown to Tom (was there ever anything so delightful!) had walked into a certain shop which dealt in such articles, after often peeping through the window; and had taken courage to ask the mistress of that shop whether she would buy them. And the mistress had not only bought them, but had ordered more; and that very morning Ruth had made confession of these facts to Tom, and had handed him the money in a little purse she had worked expressly for the purpose. They had been in a flutter about this, and per-haps had shed a happy tear or two for anything the history knows to the contrary; but it was all over now; and a brighter face than Tom's, or a brighter face than Ruth's, the bright sun had not looked on, since he went to bed last night.

"My dear girl," said Tom, coming so abruptly on the subject, that he interrupted himself in the act of cutting a slice of bread, and left the knife sticking in the loaf, "what a queer fellow our landlord is! I don't believe he has been home once, since he got me into that unsatisfactory scrape. I begin to think he will never come home again. What a mysterious life that man does lead, to be sure!"

"Very strange. Is it not, Tom!"

"Really," said Tom, "I hope it is only strange. I hope there may be nothing wrong in it. Sometimes I begin to be doubtful of that. I must have an explanation with him," said Tom, shaking his head as if this were a most tremendous threat, "when I can catch him!"

A short double knock at the door put Tom's menacing looks to flight, and awakened an expression of surprise instead.

"Heyday!" said Tom. "An early hour for visitors! It must be John, I suppose."

"I—I—don't think it was his knock, Tom," observed his little sister.

"No?" said Tom. "It surely can't be my employer suddenly arrived in town; directed here by Mr. Fips; and come for the key of the office. It's somebody inquiring for me, I declare! Come in, if you please!"

But when the person came in, Tom Pinch, instead of saying, "Did you wish to speak with me, sir?" or, "My name is Pinch, sir; what is your business, may I ask?" or addressing him in any such distant terms; cried out, "Good gracious Heaven!" and seized him by both hands, with the liveliest manifestations of astonishment and pleasure.

The visitor was not less moved than Tom himself, and they shook hands a great many times, without another word being spoken on either side. Tom was the first to find his voice.

"Mark Tapley, too!" said Tom, running towards the door, and shaking hands with somebody else. "My dear Mark, come in. How are you, Mark? He don't look a day older than he used to do, at the Dragon. How *are* you, Mark!"

"Uncommonly jolly, sir, thank'ee," returned Mr. Tapley, all smiles and bows. "I hope I see you well, sir."

"Good gracious me!" cried Tom, patting him tenderly on the back. "How delightful it is to hear his old voice again! My dear Martin, sit down. My sister, Martin. Mr. Chuzzlewit, my love. Mark Tapley from the Dragon, my dear. Good gracious me, what a surprise this is! Sit down. Lord bless me!"

Tom was in such a state of excitement that he couldn't keep himself still for a moment, but was constantly running between Mark and Martin, shaking hands with them alternately, and presenting them over and over again to his sister.

"I remember the day we parted, Martin, as well as if it were yesterday," said Tom. "What a day it was! and what a passion you were in! And don't you remember my overtaking you in the road that morning, Mark, when I was going to Salisbury in the gig to fetch him, and you were looking out for a situation? And don't you recollect the dinner we had at Salisbury, Martin, with John Westlock, eh? Good gracious me! Ruth, my dear, Mr. Chuzzlewit. Mark Tapley, my love, from the Dragon. More cups and saucers, if you please. Bless my soul, how glad I am to see you both!"

And then Tom (as John Westlock had done on his arrival) ran off to the loaf to cut some bread and butter for them; and before he had spread a single slice, remembered something else, and came running back again to tell it; and then he shook hands with them again; and then he introduced his sister again; and then he did everything he had done already all over again; and nothing Tom could do, and nothing Tom could say, was half sufficient to express his joy at their safe return.

Mr. Tapley was the first to resume his composure. In a very short space of time, he was discovered to have somehow installed himself in office as waiter, or attendant upon the party; a fact which was first suggested to them by his temporary absence in the kitchen, and speedy return with a kettle of boiling water, from which he replenished the tea-pot with a self-possession that was quite his own.

"Sit down, and take your breakfast, Mark," said Tom. "Make him sit down and take his breakfast, Martin."

"Oh! I gave him up, long ago, as incorrigible," Martin replied. "He takes his own way, Tom. You would excuse him, Miss Pinch, if you knew his value."

"She knows it, bless you!" said Tom. "I have told her all about Mark Tapley. Have I not, Ruth?"

"Yes, Tom."

"Not all," returned Martin, in a low voice. "The best of Mark Tapley is only known to one man, Tom; and but for Mark he would hardly be alive to tell it."

"Mark!" said Tom Pinch, energetically: "if you don't sit down this minute, I'll swear at you!"

"Well, sir," returned Mr. Tapley, "sooner than you should do that, I'll com-ply. It's a considerable invasion of a man's jollity to be made so partickler welcome, but a Werb is a word as signifies to be, to do, or to suffer (which is all the grammar, and enough too, as ever I wos taught); and if there's a Werb alive, I'm it. For I'm always a bein', some-times a doin', and continually a sufferin'."

"Not jolly yet?" asked Tom, with a smile.

"Why, I was rather so, over the water, sir," returned Mr. Tapley; "and not entirely without credit. But Human Natur' is in a conspiracy again' me; I can't get on. I shall have to leave it in my will, sir, to be wrote upon my tomb: 'He was a man as might have come out strong if he could have got a chance. But it was denied him.'"

Mr. Tapley took this occasion of looking about him with a grin, and subsequently attacking the breakfast, with an appetite not at all expressive of blighted hopes, or insurmount-able despondency.

In the meanwhile, Martin drew his chair a little nearer to Tom and his sister, and related to them what had passed at Mr. Pecksniff's house; adding in few words a general sum-mary of the distresses and disappointments he had undergone since he left England.

"For your faithful stewardship in the trust I left with you, Tom," he said, "and for all your goodness and disinterested-ness, I can never thank you enough. When I add Mary's thanks to mine——"

Ah, Tom! The blood retreated from his cheeks, and came rushing back, so violently, that it was pain to feel it; ease though, ease, compared with the aching of his wounded heart.

"When I add Mary's thanks to mine," said Martin, "I have made the only poor acknowledgment it is in our power to offer; but if you knew how much we feel, Tom, you would set some store by it, I am sure."

And if they had known how much Tom felt—but that no human creature ever knew—they would have set some store by him. Indeed they would.

Tom changed the topic of discourse. He was sorry he could not pursue it, as it gave Martin pleasure; but he was unable, at that moment. No drop of envy or bitterness was in his soul; but he could not master the firm utterance of her name.

He inquired what Martin's projects were.

" No longer to make your fortune, Tom," said Martin, " but to try to live. I tried that once in London, Tom; and failed. If you will give me the benefit of your advice and friendly counsel, I may succeed better under your guidance. I will do anything, Tom, anything, to gain a livelihood by my own exertions. My hopes do not soar above that, now."

High-hearted, noble Tom! Sorry to find the pride of his old companion humbled, and to hear him speaking in this altered strain, at once, at once, he drove from his breast the inability to contend with its deep emotions, and spoke out bravely.

" Your hopes do not soar above that!" cried Tom. " Yes they do. How can you talk so! They soar up to the time when you will be happy with her, Martin. They soar up to the time when you will be able to claim her, Martin. They soar up to the time when you will not be able to believe that you were ever cast down in spirit, or poor in pocket, Martin. Advice, and friendly counsel! Why, of course. But you shall have better advice and counsel (though you cannot have more friendly) than mine. You shall consult John Westlock. We'll go there immediately. It is yet so early that I shall have time to take you to his chambers before I go to business; they are in my way; and I can leave you there, to talk over your affairs with him. So come along. Come along. I am a man of occupation now, you know," said Tom, with his pleasantest smile; "and have no time to lose. Your hopes don't soar higher than that? I dare say they don't. *I* know you, pretty well. They'll be soaring out of sight soon, Martin, and leaving all the rest of us leagues behind."

" Ay! But I may be a little changed," said Martin, " since you knew me pretty well, Tom."

" What nonsense!" exclaimed Tom. " Why should you be changed? You talk as if you were an old man. I never heard such a fellow! Come to John Westlock's, come. Come along, Mark Tapley. It's Mark's doing, I have no doubt;

and it serves you right for having such a grumbler for your companion."   •

"There's no credit to be got through being jolly with *you*, Mr. Pinch, anyways," said Mark, with his face all wrinkled up with grins. "A parish doctor might be jolly with you. There's nothing short of goin' to the U-nited States for a second trip, as would make it at all creditable to be jolly, arter seein' you again!"

Tom laughed, and taking leave of his sister, hurried Mark and Martin out into the street, and away to John Westlock's by the nearest road; for his hour of business was very near at hand, and he prided himself on always being exact to his time.

John Westlock was at home, but, strange to say, was rather embarrassed to see them; and when Tom was about to go into the room where he was breakfasting, said he had a stranger there. It appeared to be a mysterious stranger, for John shut that door as he said it, and led them into the next room.

He was very much delighted, though, to see Mark Tapley; and received Martin with his own frank courtesy. But Martin felt that he did not inspire John Westlock with any unusual interest; and twice or thrice observed that he looked at Tom Pinch doubtfully; not to say compassionately. He thought, and blushed to think, that he knew the cause of this.

"I apprehend you are engaged," said Martin, when Tom had announced the purport of their visit. "If you will allow me to come again at your own time, I shall be glad to do so."

"I *am* engaged," replied John, with some reluctance; "but the matter on which I am engaged is one, to say the truth, more immediately demanding your knowledge than mine."

"Indeed!" cried Martin.

"It relates to a member of your family, and is of a serious nature. If you will have the kindness to remain here, it will be a satisfaction to me to have it privately communicated to you, in order that you may judge of its importance for yourself."

"And in the meantime," said Tom, "I must really take myself off, without any further ceremony."

"Is your business so very particular," asked Martin, "that you cannot remain with us for half an hour? I wish you could. What *is* your business, Tom?"

It was Tom's turn to be embarrassed now : but he plainly said, after a little hesitation :

"Why, I am not at liberty to say what it is, Martin : though I hope soon to be in a condition to do so, and am aware of no other reason to prevent my doing so now, than the request of my employer. It's an awkward position to be placed in," said Tom, with an uneasy sense of seeming to doubt his friend, "as I feel every day ; but I really cannot help it, can I, John?"

John Westlock replied in the negative ; and Martin, expressing himself perfectly satisfied, begged them not to say another word : though he could not help wondering very much, what curious office Tom held, and why he was so secret, and embarrassed, and unlike himself, in reference to it. Nor could he help reverting to it, in his own mind, several times after Tom went away, which he did as soon as this conversation was ended, taking Mr. Tapley with him, who, as he laughingly said, might accompany him as far as Fleet Street, without injury.

"And what do *you* mean to do, Mark?" asked Tom, as they walked on together.

"Mean to do, sir?" returned Mr. Tapley.

"Ay. What course of life do you mean to pursue?"

"Well, sir," said Mr. Tapley. "The fact is, that I have been a-thinking rather of the matrimonial line, sir."

"You don't say so, Mark!" cried Tom.

"Yes, sir. I've been a-turnin' of it over."

"And who is the lady, Mark?"

"The which, sir?" said Mr. Tapley.

"The lady. Come! You know what I said," replied Tom, laughing, "as well as I do!"

384

Mr. Tapley suppressed his own inclination to laugh ; and with one of his most whimsically-twisted looks, replied,

"You couldn't guess, I suppose, Mr. Pinch ? "

"How is it possible?" said Tom. "I don't know any of your flames, Mark. Except Mrs. Lupin, indeed."

"Well, sir!" retorted Mr. Tapley. "And supposing it was her ! "

Tom stopping in the street to look at him, Mr. Tapley for a moment presented to his view, an utterly stolid and expressionless face : a perfect dead wall of countenance. But opening window after window in it, with astonishing rapidity, and lighting them all up as for a general illumination, he repeated :

"Supposin', for the sake of argument, as it was her, sir ! "

"Why, I thought such a connexion wouldn't suit you, Mark, on any terms ! " cried Tom.

"Well, sir, I used to think so myself, once," said Mark. "But I ain't so clear about it now. A dear, sweet creetur, sir ! "

"A dear, sweet creature ? To be sure she is," cried Tom. "But she always was a dear sweet creature, was she not ? "

" *Was* she not ! " assented Mr. Tapley.

"Then why on earth didn't you marry her at first, Mark, instead of wandering abroad, and losing all this time, and leaving her alone by herself, liable to be courted by other people ? "

"Why, sir," retorted Mr. Tapley, in a spirit of unbounded confidence, " I'll tell you how it come about. You know me, Mr. Pinch, sir; there ain't a gentleman alive as knows me better. You're acquainted with my constitution, and you're acquainted with my weakness. My constitution is, to be jolly ; and my weakness is, to wish to find a credit in it. Wery good, sir. In this state of mind, I gets a notion in my head that she looks on me with a eye of—with what you may call a favourable sort of a eye in fact," said Mr. Tapley, with modest hesitation.

"No doubt," replied Tom. " We knew that perfectly well

when we spoke on this subject long ago; before you left the Dragon."

Mr. Tapley nodded assent. "Well, sir! But bein' at that time full of hopeful wisions, I arrives at the conclusion that no credit is to be got out of such a way of life as that, where everything agreeable would be ready to one's hand. Lookin' on the bright side of human life in short, one of my hopeful wisions is, that there's a deal of misery a-waitin' for me; in the midst of which I may come out tolerable strong, and be jolly under circumstances as reflects some credit. I goes into the world, sir, wery boyant, and I tries this. I goes aboard ship first, and wery soon discovers (by the ease with which I'm jolly, mind you) as there's no credit to be got *there*. I might have took warning by this, and gave it up; but I didn't. I gets to the U-nited States; and then I *do* begin, I won't deny it, to feel some little credit in sustaining my spirits. What follows? Jest as I'm a beginning to come out, and am a treadin' on the werge, my master deceives me."

"Deceives you!" cried Tom.

"Swindles me," retorted Mr. Tapley with a beaming face. "Turns his back on ev'ry thing as made his service a creditable one, and leaves me, high and dry, without a leg to stand upon. In which state, I returns home. Wery good. Then all my hopeful wisions bein' crushed; and findin' that there ain't no credit for me nowhere; I abandons myself to despair, and says, 'Let me do that as has the least credit in it, of all; marry a dear, sweet creetur, as is wery fond of me: me being, at the same time, wery fond of her: lead a happy life, and struggle no more again' the blight which settles on my prospects.'"

"If your philosophy, Mark," said Tom, who laughed heartily at this speech, "be the oddest I ever heard of, it is not the least wise. Mrs. Lupin has said 'yes,' of course?"

"Why, no, sir," replied Mr. Tapley; "she hasn't gone so far as that yet. Which I attribute principally to my not havin' asked her. But we was wery agreeable together—

comfortable, I may say—the night I come home. It's all right, sir."

"Well!" said Tom, stopping at the Temple Gate. "I wish you joy, Mark, with all my heart. I shall see you again to-day, I dare say. Good-bye for the present."

"Good-bye, sir! Good-bye, Mr. Pinch!" he added, by way of soliloquy, as he stood looking after him: "Although you *are* a damper to a honourable ambition. You little think it, but you was the first to dash my hopes. Pecksniff would have built me up for life, but your sweet temper pulled me down. Good-bye, Mr. Pinch!"

While these confidences were interchanged between Tom Pinch and Mark, Martin and John Westlock were very differently engaged. They were no sooner left alone together than Martin said, with an effort he could not disguise:

"Mr. Westlock, we have met only once before, but you have known Tom a long while, and that seems to render you familiar to me. I cannot talk freely with you on any subject unless I relieve my mind of what oppresses it just now. I see with pain that you so far mistrust me that you think me likely to impose on Tom's regardlessness of himself, or on his kind nature, or some of his good qualities."

"I had no intention," replied John, "of conveying any such impression to you, and am exceedingly sorry to have done so."

"But you entertain it?" said Martin.

"You ask me so pointedly and directly," returned the other, "that I cannot deny the having accustomed myself to regard you as one who, not in wantonness but in mere thoughtlessness of character, did not sufficiently consider his nature and did not quite treat it as it deserves to be treated. It is much easier to slight than to appreciate Tom Pinch."

This was not said warmly, but was energetically spoken too; for there was no subject in the world (but one) on which the speaker felt so strongly

"I grew into the knowledge of Tom," he pursued, "as I grew

387

towards manhood; and I have learned to love him as something infinitely better than myself. I did not think that you understood him when we met before. I did not think that you greatly cared to understand him. The instances of this which I observed in you, were, like my opportunities for observation, very trivial—and were very harmless I dare say. But they were not agreeable to me, and they forced themselves upon me; for I was not upon the watch for them, believe me. You will say," added John, with a smile, as he subsided into more of his accustomed manner, "that I am not by any means agreeable to you. I can only assure you, in reply, that I would not have originated this topic on any account"

"I originated it," said Martin; "and so far from having any complaint to make against you, highly esteem the friendship you entertain for Tom, and the very many proofs you have given him of it. Why should I endeavour to conceal from you:" he coloured deeply though: "that I neither understood him nor cared to understand him when I was his companion; and that I am very truly sorry for it now!"

It was so sincerely said, at once so modestly and manfully, that John offered him his hand as if he had not done so before; and Martin giving his in the same open spirit, all constraint between the young men vanished.

"Now pray," said John, "when I tire your patience very much in what I am going to say, recollect that it has an end to it, and that the end is the point of the story."

With this preface, he related all the circumstances connected with his having presided over the illness and slow recovery of the patient at the Bull; and tacked on to the skirts of that narrative Tom's own account of the business on the wharf. Martin was not a little puzzled when he came to an end, for the two stories seemed to have no connexion with each other, and to leave him, as the phrase is, all abroad.

"If you will excuse me for one moment," said John, rising, "I will beg you almost immediately to come into the next room."

Upon that, he left Martin to himself, in a state of considerable astonishment; and soon came back again to fulfil his
promise. Accompanying him into the next room, Martin
found there a third person; no doubt the stranger of whom
his host had spoken when Tom Pinch introduced him.

He was a young man; with deep black hair and eyes. He
was gaunt and pale; and evidently had not long recovered
from a severe illness. He stood as Martin entered, but sat
again at John's desire. His eyes were cast downward; and
but for one glance at them both, half in humiliation and half
in entreaty, he kept them so, and sat quite still and silent.

"This person's name is Lewsome," said John Westlock,
"whom I have mentioned to you as having been seized with
an illness at the Inn near here, and undergone so much. He
has had a very hard time of it, ever since he began to recover;
but, as you see, he is now doing well."

As he did not move or speak, and John Westlock made a
pause, Martin, not knowing what to say, said that he was
glad to hear it.

"The short statement that I wish you to hear from his own
lips, Mr. Chuzzlewit," John pursued: looking attentively at
him, and not at Martin: "he made to me for the first time
yesterday, and repeated to me this morning, without the least
variation of any essential particular. I have already told
you that he informed me before he was removed from the
Inn, that he had a secret to disclose to me which lay heavy
on his mind. But, fluctuating between sickness and health,
and between his desire to relieve himself of it, and his dread
of involving himself by revealing it, he has, until yesterday,
avoided the disclosure. I never pressed him for it (having
no idea of its weight or import, or of my right to so), until
within a few days past; when, understanding from him, on
his own voluntary avowal, in a letter from the country, that
it related to a person whose name was Jonas Chuzzlewit;
and thinking that it might throw some light on that little
mystery which made Tom anxious now and then; I urged the

point upon him, and heard his statement, as you will now, from his own lips. It is due to him to say, that in the apprehension of death, he committed it to writing sometime since, and folded it in a sealed paper, addressed to me: which he could not resolve, however, to place of his own act in my hands. He has the paper in his breast, I believe, at this moment."

The young man touched it hastily; in corroboration of the fact.

"It will be well to leave that in our charge, perhaps," said John. "But do not mind it now."

As he said this, he held up his hand to bespeak Martin's attention. It was already fixed upon the man before him, who, after a short silence said, in a low, weak, hollow voice:

"What relation was Mr. Anthony Chuzzlewit, who—"

"—Who died—to me?" said Martin. "He was my grandfather's brother."

"I fear he was made away with. Murdered!"

"My God!" said Martin. "By whom?"

The young man, Lewsome, looked up in his face, and casting down his eyes again, replied:

"I fear, by me."

"By you?" cried Martin.

"Not by my act, but I fear by my means."

"Speak out!" said Martin, "and speak the truth."

"I fear this *is* the truth."

Martin was about to interrupt him again, but John Westlock saying softly, "Let him tell his story in his own way," Lewsome went on thus:

"I have been bred a surgeon, and for the last few years have served a general practitioner in the City, as his assistant. While I was in his employment I became acquainted with Jonas Chuzzlewit. He is the principal in this deed."

"What do you mean?" demanded Martin, sternly. "Do you know he is the son of the old man of whom you have spoken?"

"I do," he answered.

390

He remained silent for some moments, when he resumed at the point where he had left off.

"I have reason to know it; for I have often heard him wish his old father dead, and complain of his being wearisome to him, and a drag upon him. He was in the habit of doing so, at a place of meeting we had—three or four of us— at night. There was no good in the place, you may suppose, when you hear that he was the chief of the party. I wish I had died myself, and never seen it!"

He stopped again; and again resumed as before.

"We met to drink and game; not for large sums, but for sums that were large to us. He generally won. Whether or no, he lent money at interest to those who lost; and in this way, though I think we all secretly hated him, he came to be the master of us. To propitiate him, we made a jest of his father: it began with his debtors; I was one: and we used to toast a quicker journey to the old man, and a swift inheritance to the young one."

He paused again.

"One night he came there in a very bad humour. He had been greatly tried, he said, by the old man that day. He and I were alone together: and he angrily told me, that the old man was in his second childhood; that he was weak, imbecile, and drivelling; as unbearable to himself as he was to other people; and that it would be a charity to put him out of the way. He swore that he had often thought of mixing something with the stuff he took for his cough, which should help him to die easily. People were sometimes smothered who were bitten by mad dogs, he said; and why not help these lingering old men out of their troubles too? He looked full at me as he said so, and I looked full at him; but it went no farther that night."

He stopped once more, and was silent for so long an interval that John Westlock said "Go on." Martin had never removed his eyes from his face, but was so absorbed in horror and astonishment, that he could not speak.

"It may have been a week after that, or it may have been less, or more—the matter was in my mind all the time, but I cannot recollect the time, as I should any other period— when he spoke to me again. We were alone then, too; being there before the usual hour of assembling. There was no appointment between us; but I think I went there to meet him, and I know he came there to meet me. He was there first. He was reading a newspaper when I went in, and nodded to me without looking up, or leaving off reading. I sat down opposite and close to him. He said, immediately, that he wanted me to get him some of two sorts of drugs. One that was instantaneous in its effect; of which he wanted very little. One that was slow, and not suspicious in appearance; of which he wanted more. While he was speaking to me he still read the newspaper. He said 'Drugs,' and never used any other word. Neither did I."

"This all agrees with what I have heard before," observed John Westlock.

"I asked him what he wanted the drugs for? He said for no harm; to physic cats; what did it matter to me? I was going out to a distant colony (I had recently got the appointment, which, as Mr. Westlock knows, I have since lost by my sickness, and which was my only hope of salvation from ruin), and what did it matter to me? He could get them without my aid at half a hundred places, but not so easily as he could get them of me. This was true. He might not want them at all, he said, and he had no present idea of using them; but he wished to have them by him. All this time he still read the newspaper. We talked about the price. He was to forgive me a small debt—I was quite in his power—and to pay me five pounds; and there the matter dropped, through others coming in. But, next night, under exactly similar circumstances, I gave him the drugs, on his saying I was a fool to think that he should ever use them for any harm; and he gave me the money. We have never met since. I only know that the poor old father died soon afterwards, just as he would have died from this cause : and that I have undergone, and suffer now, intolerable misery. Nothing," he added, stretching out his hands, "can paint my misery! It is well deserved, but nothing can paint it."

With that he hung his head, and said no more. Wasted and wretched, he was not a creature upon whom to heap reproaches that were unavailing.

"Let him remain at hand," said Martin, turning from him ; "but out of sight, in Heaven's name !"

"He will remain here," John whispered. "Come with me !" Softly turning the key upon him as they went out, he conducted Martin into the adjoining room, in which they had been before.

Martin was so amazed, so shocked, and confounded by what he had heard, that it was some time before he could reduce it to any order in his mind, or could sufficiently comprehend the bearing of one part upon another, to take in all the details at one view. When he, at length, had the whole narrative clearly before him, John Westlock went on to point out the great probability of the guilt of Jonas being known to other people, who traded in it for their own benefit, and who were, by such means, able to exert that control over him which Tom Pinch had accidentally witnessed, and unconsciously assisted. This appeared so plain, that they agreed upon it without difficulty ; but instead of deriving the least assistance from this source, they found that it embarrassed them the more.

They knew nothing of the real parties, who possessed this power. The only person before them was Tom's landlord. They had no right to question Tom's landlord, even if they could find him, which, according to Tom's account, it would not be easy to do. And granting that they did question him, and he answered (which was taking a good deal for granted), he had only to say, with reference to the adventure on the wharf, that he had been sent from such and such a place to summon Jonas back on urgent business, and there was an end of it.

Besides, there was the great difficulty and responsibility of moving at all in the matter. Lewsome's story might be false; in his wretched state it might be greatly heightened by a diseased brain; or admitting it to be entirely true, the old man might have died a natural death. Mr. Pecksniff had been there at the time; as Tom immediately remembered, when he came back in the afternoon, and shared their counsels; and there had been no secrecy about it. Martin's grandfather was of right the person to decide upon the course that should be taken; but to get at his views would be impossible, for Mr. Pecksniff's views were certain to be his. And the nature of Mr. Pecksniff's views in reference to his own son-in-law, might be easily reckoned upon.

Apart from these considerations, Martin could not endure the thought of seeming to grasp at this unnatural charge against his relative, and using it as a stepping-stone to his grandfather's favour. But, that he would seem to do so, if he presented himself before his grandfather in Mr. Pecksniff's house again, for the purpose of declaring it; and that Mr. Pecksniff, of all men, would represent his conduct in that despicable light, he perfectly well knew. On the other hand, to be in possession of such a statement, and take no measures of further inquiry in reference to it, was tantamount to being a partner in the guilt it professed to disclose.

In a word, they were wholly unable to discover any outlet from this maze of difficulty, which did not lie through some perplexed and entangled thicket. And although Mr. Tapley was promptly taken into their confidence; and the fertile imagination of that gentleman suggested many bold expedients, which, to do him justice, he was quite ready to carry into instant operation on his own personal responsibility; still 'bating the general zeal of Mr. Tapley's nature, nothing was made particularly clearer by these offers of service.

It was in this position of affairs that Tom's account of the strange behaviour of the decayed clerk, on the night of the tea-party, became of great moment, and finally convinced them that to arrive at a more accurate knowledge of the workings of that old man's mind and memory, would be to take a most important stride in their pursuit of the truth. So, having first satisfied themselves that no communication had ever taken place between Lewsome and Mr. Chuffey (which would have accounted at once for any suspicions the latter might entertain), they unanimously resolved that the old clerk was the man they wanted.

But, like the unanimous resolution of a public meeting, which will oftentimes declare that this or that grievance is not to be borne a moment longer, which is nevertheless borne for a century or two afterwards, without any modification, they only reached in this the conclusion that they were all of one mind. For, it was one thing to want Mr. Chuffey, and another thing to get at him; and to do that without alarming him, or without alarming Jonas, or without being discomfited by the difficulty of striking, in an instrument so out of tune and so unused, the note they sought, was an end as far from their reach as ever.

The question then became, who of those about the old clerk had had most influence with him that night? Tom said his young mistress clearly. But Tom and all of them shrunk from the thought of entrapping her, and making her the innocent means of bringing retribution on her cruel husband. Was there nobody else? Why yes. In a very different way, Tom said, he was influenced by Mrs. Gamp, the nurse: who had once had the control of him, as he understood, for some time.

They caught at this immediately. Here was a new way out, developed in a quarter until then overlooked. John Westlock knew Mrs. Gamp; he had given her employment; he was acquainted with her place of residence: for that good lady had obligingly furnished him, at parting, with a pack of her professional cards for general distribution. It was decided that Mrs. Gamp should be approached with caution, but approached without delay; and that the depths of that discreet matron's knowledge of Mr. Chuffey, and means of bringing them, or one of them, into communication with him, should be carefully sounded.

On this service, Martin and John Westlock determined to proceed that night; waiting on Mrs. Gamp first, at her lodgings; and taking their chance of finding her in the repose of private life, or of having to seek her out, elsewhere, in the exercise of her professional duties. Tom returned home, that he might lose no opportunity of having an interview with Nadgett, by being absent in the event of his reappearance. And Mr. Tapley remained (by his own particular desire) for the time being in Furnival's Inn, to look after Lewsome; who might safely have been left to himself, however, for any thought he seemed to entertain of giving them the slip.

Before they parted on their several errands, they caused him to read aloud, in the presence of them all, the paper which he had about him, and the declaration he had attached to it, which was to the effect, that he had written it voluntarily, in the fear of death and in the torture of his mind. And when he had done so, they all signed it, and taking it from him, of his free will, locked it in a place of safety.

Martin also wrote, by John's advice, a letter to the trustees of the famous Grammar School, boldly claiming the successful design as his, and charging Mr. Pecksniff with the fraud he had committed. In this proceeding also, John was hotly interested: observing with his usual irreverence, that Mr. Pecksniff had been a successful rascal all his life through, and that it would be a lasting source of happiness to him (John) if he could help to do him justice in the smallest particular.

A busy day! But Martin had no lodgings yet; so when these matters were disposed of, he excused himself from dining with John Westlock and was fain to wander out alone, and look for some. He succeeded, after great trouble, in engaging two garrets for himself and Mark, situated in a court in the Strand, not far from Temple Bar. Their luggage, which was waiting for them at a coach-office, he conveyed to this new place of refuge; and it was with a glow of satisfaction, which as a selfish man he never could have known and never had, that, thinking how much pains and trouble he had saved Mark, and how pleased and astonished Mark would be, he afterwards walked up and down, in the Temple, eating a meat-pie for his dinner.

CHAPTER XLIX

Mrs. Gamp's apartment in Kingsgate Street, High Holborn, wore, metaphorically speaking, a robe of state. It was swept and garnished for the reception of a visitor. That visitor was Betsey Prig : Mrs. Prig, of Bartlemy's ; or as some said Barklemy's, or as some said Bardlemy's : for by all these endearing and familiar appellations, had the hospital of Saint Bartholomew become a household word among the sisterhood which Betsey Prig adorned.

Mrs. Gamp's apartment was not a spacious one, but, to a contented mind, a closet is a palace ; and the first-floor front at Mr. Sweedlepipe's may have been, in the imagination of Mrs. Gamp, a stately pile. If it were not exactly that, to restless intellects, it at least comprised as much accommodation as any person, not sanguine to insanity, could have looked for in a room of its dimensions. For only keep the bedstead always in your mind ; and you were safe. That was the grand secret. Remembering the bedstead, you might even stoop to look under the little round table for anything you had dropped, without hurting yourself much against the chest of drawers, or qualifying as a patient of Saint Bartholomew, by falling into the fire.

Visitors were much assisted in their cautious efforts to preserve an unflagging recollection of this piece of furniture, by its size: which was great. It was not a turn-up bedstead, nor yet a French bedstead, nor yet a four-post bedstead, but what is poetically called a tent: the sacking whereof, was low and bulgy, insomuch that Mrs. Gamp's box would not go under it, but stopped half-way, in a manner which while it did violence to the reason, likewise endangered the legs, of a stranger. The frame too, which would have supported the canopy and hangings if there had been any, was ornamented with divers pippins carved in timber, which on the slightest provocation, and frequently on none at all, came tumbling down; harassing the peaceful guest with inexplicable terrors.

The bed itself was decorated with a patchwork quilt of great antiquity; and at the upper end, upon the side nearest to the door, hung a scanty curtain of blue check, which prevented the Zephyrs that were abroad in Kingsgate Street, from visiting Mrs. Gamp's head too roughly. Some rusty gowns and other articles of that lady's wardrobe depended from the posts; and these had so adapted themselves by long usage to her figure, that more than one impatient husband coming in precipitately, at about the time of twilight, had been for an instant stricken dumb by the supposed discovery that Mrs. Gamp had hanged herself. One gentleman, coming on the usual hasty errand, had said indeed, that they looked like guardian angels "watching of her in her sleep." But that, as Mrs. Gamp said, "was his first;" and he never repeated the sentiment, though he often repeated his visit.

The chairs in Mrs. Gamp's apartment were extremely large and broad-backed, which was more than a sufficient reason for there being but two in number. They were both elbow-chairs, of ancient mahogany; and were chiefly valuable for the slippery nature of their seats, which had been originally horsehair, but were now covered with a shiny substance of a bluish tint, from which the visitor began to slide away with a dismayed countenance, immediately after sitting down. What Mrs. Gamp wanted in chairs she made up in bandboxes; of which she had a great collection, devoted to the reception of various miscellaneous valuables, which were not, however, as well protected as the good woman, by a pleasant fiction, seemed to think: for, though every bandbox had a carefully closed lid, not one among them had a bottom: owing to which cause, the property within was merely, as it were, extinguished. The chest of drawers having been originally made to stand upon the top of another chest, had a dwarfish, elfin look, alone; but, in regard of its security it had a great advantage over the bandboxes, for as all the handles had been long ago pulled off, it was very difficult to get at its contents. This indeed was only to be done by one of two devices; either by tilting the whole structure forward until all the drawers fell out together, or by opening them singly with knives, like oysters.

Mrs. Gamp stored all her household matters in a little cupboard by the fire-place; beginning below the surface (as in nature) with the coals, and mounting gradually upwards to the spirits, which, from motives of delicacy, she kept in a tea-pot. The chimney-piece was ornamented with a small almanack, marked here and there in Mrs. Gamp's own hand, with a memorandum of the date at which some lady was expected to fall due. It was also embellished with three profiles: one, in colours, of Mrs. Gamp herself in early life; one, in bronze, of a lady in feathers, supposed to be Mrs. Harris, as she appeared when dressed for a ball; and one, in black, of Mr. Gamp, deceased. The last was a full length, in order that the likeness might be rendered more obvious and forcible, by the introduction of the wooden leg.

A pair of bellows, a pair of pattens, a toasting-fork, a kettle, a pap-boat, a spoon for the administration of medicine to the refractory, and lastly, Mrs. Gamp's umbrella, which as something of great price and rarity was displayed with particular ostentation, completed the decorations of the chimney-piece and adjacent wall. Towards these objects, Mrs. Gamp raised her eyes in satisfaction when she had arranged the tea-board, and had concluded her arrangements for the reception of

PREPARATIONS FOR A VISITOR

Betsey Prig, even unto the setting forth of two pounds of Newcastle salmon, intensely pickled.

"There! Now drat you, Betsey, don't be long!" said Mrs. Gamp, apostrophising her absent friend. "For I can't abear to wait, I do assure you. To wotever place I goes, I sticks to this one mortar, 'I'm easy pleased; it is but little as I wants; but I must have that little of the best, and to the minute when the clock strikes, else we do not part as I could wish, but bearin' malice in our arts.'"

Her own preparations were of the best, for they comprehended a delicate new loaf, a plate of fresh butter, a basin of fine white sugar, and other arrangements on the same scale. Even the snuff with which she now refreshed herself, was so choice in quality, that she took a second pinch.

"There's the little bell a ringing now," said Mrs. Gamp, hurrying to the stair-head and looking over. "Betsey Prig, my—why it's that there disapintin' Sweedlepipes, I do believe."

"Yes, it's me," said the barber in a faint voice; "I've just come in."

"You're always a comin' in, I think," muttered Mrs. Gamp to herself, "except wen you're a going out. I ha'n't no patience with that man!"

"Mrs. Gamp," said the barber. "I say! Mrs. Gamp!"

"Well," cried Mrs. Gamp, impatiently, as she descended the stairs. "What is it? Is the Thames a-fire, and cooking its own fish, Mr. Sweedlepipes? Why wot's the man gone and been a-doin' of to himself? He's as white as chalk!"

She added the latter clause of inquiry, when she got down stairs, and found him seated in the shaving-chair, pale and disconsolate.

"You recollect," said Poll. "You recollect young—"

"Not young Wilkins!" cried Mrs. Gamp. "Don't say young Wilkins, wotever you do. If young Wilkins's wife is took—"

"It isn't anybody's wife," exclaimed the little barber. "Bailey, young Bailey!"

"Why, wot do you mean to say that chit's been a-doin' of?" retorted Mrs. Gamp, sharply. "Stuff and nonsense, Mr. Sweedlepipes!"

"He hasn't been a-doing anything!" exclaimed poor Poll, quite desperate. "What do you catch me up so short for, when you see me put out, to that extent, that I can hardly speak? He'll never do anything again. He's done for. He's killed. The first time I ever see that boy," said Poll, "I charged him too much for a red-poll. I asked him three-halfpence for a penny one, because I was afraid he'd beat me down. But he didn't. And now he's dead; and if you was to crowd all the steam-engines and electric fluids that ever was, into this shop, and set 'em every one to work their hardest, they couldn't square the account, though it's only a ha'penny!"

Mr. Sweedlepipe turned aside to the towel, and wiped his eyes with it.

"And what a clever boy he was!" he said. "What a surprising young chap he was! How he talked! and what a deal he know'd! Shaved in this very chair he was; only for fun; it was all his fun; he was full of it. Ah! to think that he'll never be shaved in earnest! The birds might every one have died, and welcome," cried the little barber, looking round him at the cages, and again applying to the towel, "sooner than I'd have heard this news!"

"How did you ever come to hear it?" said Mrs. Gamp. "Who told you?"

"I went out," returned the little barber, "into the City, to meet a sporting Gent, upon the Stock Exchange, that wanted a few slow pigeons to practise at; and when I'd done with him, I went to get a little drop of beer, and there I heard everybody a-talking about it. It's in the papers."

"You are in a nice state of confugion, Mr. Sweedlepipes, you are!" said Mrs. Gamp, shaking her head; "and my opinion is, as half-a-dudgeon fresh young lively leeches on your temples, wouldn't be too much to clear your mind, which so I tell you. Wot were they a-talkin' on, and wot was in the papers?"

"All about it!" cried the barber. "What else do you suppose? Him and his master were upset on a journey, and he was carried to Salisbury, and was breathing his last when the account came away. He never spoke afterwards. Not a single word. That's the worst of it to me; but that ain't all. His master can't be found. The other manager of their office in the city: Crimple, David Crimple: has gone off with the money, and is advertised for, with a reward, upon the walls. Mr. Montague, poor young Bailey's master (what a boy he was!) is advertised for, too. Some say he's slipped off, to join his friend abroad; some say he mayn't have got away yet; and they're looking for him high and low. Their office is a smash; a swindle altogether. But what's a Life Assurance Office to a Life! And what a Life Young Bailey's was!"

"He was born into a wale," said Mrs. Gamp, with philosophical coolness; "and he lived in a wale; and he must take the consequences of sech a sitiwation. But don't you hear nothink of Mr. Chuzzlewit in all this?"

"No," said Poll, "nothing to speak of. His name wasn't printed as one of the board, though some people say it was just going to be. Some believe he was took in, and some believe he was one of the takers-in; but however that may be, they can't prove nothing against him. This morning he went up of his own accord afore the Lord Mayor or some of them City big-wigs, and complained that he'd been swindled, and that these two persons had gone off and cheated him, and that he had just found out that Montague's name wasn't even Montague, but something else. And they do say that he looked like Death, owing to his losses. But, Lord forgive me," cried the barber, coming back again to the subject of his individual grief, "what's his looks to me! He might have died and welcome, fifty times, and not been such a loss as Bailey!"

At this juncture the little bell rang, and the deep voice of Mrs. Prig struck into the conversation.

" Oh! You're a-talkin' about it, are you!" observed that lady. " Well, I hope you've got it over, for I ain't interested in it myself."

" My precious Betsey," said Mrs. Gamp, " how late you are!"

The worthy Mrs. Prig replied, with some asperity, " that if perwerse people went off dead, when they was least expected, it warn't no fault of her'n." And further, " that it was quite aggrawation enough to be made late when one was dropping for one's tea, without hearing on it again."

Mrs. Gamp, deriving from this exhibition of repartee some clue to the state of Mrs. Prig's feelings, instantly conducted her up stairs : deeming that the sight of pickled salmon might work a softening change.

But Betsey Prig expected pickled salmon. It was obvious that she did ; for her first words, after glancing at the table, were :

" I know'd she wouldn't have a coucumber!"

Mrs. Gamp changed colour, and sat down upon the bedstead.

" Lord bless you, Betsey Prig, your words is true. I quite forgot it!"

Mrs. Prig, looking steadfastly at her friend, put her hand in her pocket, and, with an air of surly triumph drew forth either the oldest of lettuces or youngest of cabbages, but at any rate, a green vegetable of an expansive nature, and of such magnificent proportions that she was obliged to shut it up like an umbrella before she could pull it out. She also produced a handful of mustard and cress, a trifle of the herb called dandelion, three bunches of radishes, an onion rather larger than an average turnip, three substantial slices of beet-root, and a short prong or antler of celery ; the whole of this garden-stuff having been publicly exhibited, but a short time before, as a twopenny salad, and purchased by Mrs. Prig, on condition that the vendor could get it all into her pocket. Which had been happily accomplished, in High Holborn, to the breathless interest of a hackney-coach stand. And she laid so little stress on this surprising forethought, that she did not even smile, but returning her pocket into its accustomed sphere, merely recommended that these productions of nature should be sliced up, for immediate consumption, in plenty of vinegar.

"And don't go a dropping none of your snuff in it," said Mrs. Prig. "In gruel, barley-water, apple-tea, mutton-broth, and that, it don't signify. It stimilates a patient. But I don't relish it myself."

"Why, Betsey Prig!" cried Mrs. Gamp, "how *can* you talk so!"

"Why, ain't your patients, wotever their diseases is, always a sneezin' their wery heads off, along of your snuff?" said Mrs. Prig.

"And wot if they are!" said Mrs. Gamp.

"Nothing if they are," said Mrs. Prig. "But don't deny it, Sairah."

"Who deniges of it?" Mrs. Gamp inquired.

Mrs. Prig returned no answer.

"Who deniges of it, Betsey?" Mrs. Gamp inquired again. Then Mrs. Gamp, by reversing the question, imparted a deeper and more awful character of solemnity to the same. "Betsey, who deniges of it?"

It was the nearest possible approach to a very decided difference of opinion between these ladies; but Mrs. Prig's impatience for the meal being greater at the moment than her impatience of contradiction, she replied, for the present, "Nobody, if you don't, Sairah," and prepared herself for tea. For a quarrel can be taken up at any time, but a limited quantity of salmon cannot.

Her toilet was simple. She had merely to "chuck" her bonnet and shawl upon the bed; give her hair two pulls, one upon the right side and one upon the left, as if she were ringing a couple of bells; and all was done. The tea was already made, Mrs. Gamp was not long over the salad, and they were soon at the height of their repast.

The temper of both parties was improved, for the time being, by the enjoyments of the table. When the meal came to a termination (which it was pretty long in doing), and Mrs. Gamp having cleared away, produced the tea-pot from the top-shelf, simultaneously with a couple of wine-glasses, they were quite amiable.

"Betsey," said Mrs. Gamp, filling her own glass, and passing the tea-pot, "I will now propoge a toast. My frequent pardner, Betsey Prig!"

"Which, altering the name to Sairah Gamp; I drink," said Mrs. Prig, "with love and tenderness."

From this moment symptoms of inflammation began to lurk in the nose of each lady; and perhaps, notwithstanding all appearances to the contrary, in the temper also.

"Now, Sairah," said Mrs. Prig, "joining business with pleasure, wot is this case in which you wants me?"

Mrs. Gamp betraying in her face some intention of returning an evasive answer, Betsey added:

"*Is* it Mrs. Harris!"

"No, Betsey Prig, it ain't," was Mrs. Gamp's reply.

"Well!" said Mrs. Prig, with a short laugh. "I'm glad of that, at any rate."

"Why should you be glad of that, Betsey?" Mrs. Gamp retorted, warmly. "She is unbeknown to you except by hearsay, why should you be glad? If you have anythink to say contrairy to the character of Mrs. Harris, which well I knows behind her back, afore her face, or anywheres, is not to be impeaged, out with it, Betsey. I have know'd that sweetest and best of women," said Mrs. Gamp, shaking her head, and shedding tears, "ever since afore her First, which Mr. Harris who was dreadful timid went and stopped his ears in a empty dog-kennel, and never took his hands away or come out once till he was showed the baby, wen bein' took with fits, the doctor collared him and laid him on his back upon the airy stones, and she was told to ease her mind, his owls was organs. And I have know'd her, Betsey Prig, when he has hurt her feelin' art by sayin' of his Ninth that it was one too many, if not two, while that dear innocent was cooin' in his face, which thrive it did though bandy, but I have never know'd as you had occagion to be glad, Betsey, on accounts of Mrs. Harris not requiring you. Require she never will, depend upon it, for her constant words in sickness is, and will be, 'Send for Sairey!'"

During this touching address, Mrs. Prig adroitly feigning to be the victim of that absence of mind which has its origin in excessive attention to one topic, helped herself from the tea-pot without appearing to observe it. Mrs. Gamp observed it, however, and came to a premature close in consequence.

"Well it ain't her, it seems," said Mrs. Prig, coldly: "who is it then?"

"You have heerd me mention, Betsey," Mrs. Gamp replied, after glancing in an expressive and marked manner at the tea-pot, "a person as I took care on at the time as you and me was pardners off and on, in that there fever at the Bull?"

"Old Snuffey," Mrs. Prig observed.

Sarah Gamp looked at her with an eye of fire, for she saw in this mistake of Mrs. Prig, another wilful and malignant stab at that same weakness or custom of hers, an ungenerous allusion to which, on the part of Betsey, had first disturbed their harmony that evening. And she saw it still more clearly, when, politely but firmly correcting that lady by the distinct enunciation of the word "Chuffey," Mrs. Prig received the correction with a diabolical laugh.

The best among us have their failings, and it must be conceded of Mrs. Prig, that if there were a blemish in the goodness of her disposition, it was a habit she had of not bestowing all its sharp and acid properties upon her patients (as a thoroughly amiable woman would have done), but of keeping a considerable remainder for the service of her friends. Highly pickled salmon, and lettuces chopped up in vinegar, may, as viands possessing some acidity of their own, have encouraged and increased this failing in Mrs. Prig; and every application to the tea-pot, certainly did; for it was often remarked of her by her friends, that she was most contradictory when most elevated. It is certain that her countenance became about this time derisive and defiant, and that she sat with her arms folded, and one eye shut up, in a somewhat offensive, because obtrusively intelligent, manner.

Mrs. Gamp observing this, felt it the more necessary that Mrs. Prig should know her place, and be made sensible of her exact station in society, as well as of her obligations to herself. She therefore assumed an air of greater patronage and importance, as she went on to answer Mrs. Prig a little more in detail.

"Mr. Chuffey, Betsey," said Mrs. Gamp, "is weak in his mind. Excuge me if I makes remark, that he may neither be so weak as people thinks, nor people may not think he is so weak as they pretends, and what I knows, I knows; and what you don't, you don't; so do not ask me, Betsey. But Mr. Chuffey's friends has made propojals for his bein' took care on, and has said to me, 'Mrs. Gamp, *will* you undertake it? We couldn't think,' they says, 'of trusting him to nobody but you, for, Sairey, you are gold as has passed the furnage. Will you undertake it, at your own price, day and night, and by your own self?' 'No,' I says, 'I will not. Do not reckon on it. There is,' I says, 'but one creetur in the world as I would undertake on sech terms, and her name is Harris. But,' I says, 'I am acquainted with a friend, whose name is Betsey Prig, that I can recommend, and will assist me. Betsey,' I says, 'is always to be trusted, under me, and will be guided as I could desire.'"

Here Mrs. Prig, without any abatement of her offensive manner, again counterfeited abstraction of mind, and stretched out her hand to the tea-pot. It was more than Mrs. Gamp could bear. She stopped the hand of Mrs. Prig with her own, and said, with great feeling:

"No, Betsey! Drink fair, wotever you do!"

Mrs. Prig, thus baffled, threw herself back in her chair,

408

and closing the same eye more emphatically, and folding her arms tighter, suffered her head to roll slowly from side to side, while she surveyed her friend with a contemptuous smile.

Mrs. Gamp resumed:

"Mrs. Harris, Betsey—"

"Bother Mrs. Harris!" said Betsey Prig.

Mrs. Gamp looked at her with amazement, incredulity, and indignation; when Mrs. Prig, shutting her eye still closer, and folding her arms still tighter, uttered these memorable and tremendous words:

"I don't believe there's no sich a person!"

After the utterance of which expressions, she leaned forward, and snapped her fingers once, twice, thrice; each time nearer to the face of Mrs. Gamp, and then rose to put on her bonnet, as one who felt that there was now a gulf between them, which nothing could ever bridge across.

The shock of this blow was so violent and sudden, that Mrs. Gamp sat staring at nothing with uplifted eyes, and her mouth open as if she were gasping for breath, until Betsey Prig had put on her bonnet and her shawl, and was gathering the latter about her throat. Then Mrs. Gamp rose—morally and physically rose—and denounced her.

"What!" said Mrs. Gamp, "you bage creetur, have I know'd Mrs. Harris five and thirty year, to be told at last that there ain't no sech a person livin'! Have I stood her friend in all her troubles, great and small, for it to come at last to sech a end as this, which her own sweet picter hanging up afore you all the time, to shame your Bragian words! But well you mayn't believe there's no sech a creetur, for she wouldn't demean herself to look at you, and often has she said, when I have made mention of your name, which, to my sinful sorrow, I have done, 'What, Sairey Gamp! debage yourself to her!' Go along with you!"

"I'm a goin', ma'am, ain't I?" said Mrs. Prig, stopping as she said it.

"You had better, ma'am," said Mrs. Gamp.

"Do you know who you're talking to, ma'am?" inquired her visitor.

"Aperiently," said Mrs. Gamp, surveying her with scorn from head to foot, "to Betsey Prig. Aperiently so. *I* know her. No one better. Go along with you!"

"And *you* was a going to take me under you!" cried Mrs. Prig, surveying Mrs. Gamp from head to foot in her turn. "*You* was, was you? Oh, how kind! Why, deuce take your imperence," said Mrs. Prig, with a rapid change from banter to ferocity, "what do you mean?"

"Go along with you!" said Mrs. Gamp. "I blush for you."

"You had better blush a little for yourself, while you *are* about it!" said Mrs. Prig. "You and your Chuffeys! What, the poor old creetur isn't mad enough, isn't he? Aha!"

"He'd very soon be mad enough, if you had anything to do with him," said Mrs. Gamp.

"And that's what I was wanted for, is it?" cried Mrs. Prig, triumphantly. "Yes. But you'll find yourself deceived. I won't go near him. We shall see how you get on without me. I won't have nothink to do with him."

"You never spoke a truer word than that!" said Mrs. Gamp. "Go along with you!"

She was prevented from witnessing the actual retirement of Mrs. Prig from the room, notwithstanding the great desire she had expressed to behold it, by that lady, in her angry withdrawal, coming into contact with the bedstead, and bringing down the previously mentioned pippins; three or four of which came rattling on the head of Mrs. Gamp so smartly, that when she recovered from this wooden shower-bath, Mrs. Prig was gone.

She had the satisfaction, however, of hearing the deep voice of Betsey, proclaiming her injuries and her determination to have nothing to do with Mr. Chuffey, down the stairs, and along the passage, and even out in Kingsgate Street. Likewise of seeing in her own apartment, in the place of Mrs. Prig, Mr. Sweedlepipe and two gentlemen.

TWO VISITORS CONSOLE MRS. GAMP

"Why, bless my life!" exclaimed the little barber, "what's amiss? The noise you ladies have been making, Mrs. Gamp! Why, these two gentlemen have been standing on the stairs, outside the door, nearly all the time, trying to make you hear, while you were pelting away, hammer and tongs! It'll be the death of the little bullfinch in the shop, that draws his own water. In his fright, he's been a straining himself all to bits, drawing more water than he could drink in a twelve-month. He must have thought it was Fire!"

Mrs. Gamp had in the meanwhile sunk into her chair, from whence, turning up her overflowing eyes, and clasping her hands, she delivered the following lamentation:

"Oh, Mr. Sweedlepipes, which Mr. Westlock also, if my eyes do not deceive, and a friend not havin' the pleasure of bein' beknown, wot I have took from Betsey Prig this blessed night, no mortial creetur knows! If she had abuged me, bein' in liquor, which I thought I smelt her wen she come, but could not so believe, not bein' used myself"—Mrs. Gamp, by the way, was pretty far gone, and the fragrance of the tea-pot was strong in the room—"I could have bore it with a thankful art. But the words she spoke of Mrs. Harris, lambs could not forgive. No, Betsey!" said Mrs. Gamp, in a violent burst of feeling, "nor worms forget!"

The little barber scratched his head, and shook it, and looked at the tea-pot, and gradually got out of the room. John Westlock, taking a chair, sat down on one side of Mrs. Gamp. Martin, taking the foot of the bed, supported her on the other.

"You wonder what we want, I dare say," observed John. "I'll tell you presently, when you have recovered. It's not pressing, for a few minutes or so. How do you find yourself? Better?"

Mrs. Gamp shed more tears, shook her head and feebly pronounced Mrs. Harris's name.

"Have a little—" John was at a loss what to call it.

"Tea," suggested Martin.

"It ain't tea," said Mrs. Gamp.

"Physic of some sort, I suppose," cried John. "Have a little."

Mrs. Gamp was prevailed upon to take a glassful. "On condition," she passionately observed, "as Betsey never has another stroke of work from me."

"Certainly not," said John. "She shall never help to nurse *me.*"

"To think," said Mrs. Gamp, "as she should ever have helped to nuss that friend of yourn, and been so near of hearing things that—Ah!"

John looked at Martin.

"Yes," he said. "That was a narrow escape, Mrs. Gamp."

"Narrer, in-deed!" she returned. "It was only my having the night, and hearin' of him in his wanderins; and her the day, that saved it. Wot would she have said and done, if she had know'd what *I* know; that perfeejus wretch! Yet, oh good gracious me!" cried Mrs. Gamp, trampling on the floor, in the absence of Mrs. Prig, "that I should hear from that same woman's lips what I have heerd her speak of Mrs. Harris!"

"Never mind," said John. "You know it is not true."

"Isn't true!" cried Mrs. Gamp. "True! Don't I know as that dear woman is expecting of me at this minnit, Mr. Westlock, and is a lookin' out of window down the street, with little Tommy Harris in her arms, as calls me his own Gammy, and truly calls, for bless the mottled little legs of that there precious child (like Canterbury Brawn his own dear father says, which so they are) his own I have been, ever since I found him, Mr. Westlock, with his small red worsted shoe a gurglin' in his throat, where he had put it in his play, a chick, wile they was leavin' of him on the floor a looking for it through the ouse and him a choakin' sweetly in the parlour! Oh, Betsey Prig, what wickedness you've showed this night, but never shall you darken Sairey's doors agen, you twining serpiant!"

412

"You were always so kind to her, too!" said John, consolingly.

"That's the cutting part. That's where it hurts me, Mr. Westlock," Mrs. Gamp replied; holding out her glass unconsciously, while Martin filled it.

"Chosen to help you with Mr. Lewsome!" said John. "Chosen to help you with Mr. Chuffey!"

"Chose once, but chose no more," cried Mrs. Gamp. "No pardnership with Betsey Prig agen, sir!"

"No, no," said John. "That would never do."

"I don't know as it ever would have done, sir," Mrs. Gamp replied, with the solemnity peculiar to a certain stage of intoxication. "Now that the marks," by which Mrs. Gamp is supposed to have meant mask, "is off that creetur's face, I do not think it ever would have done. There are reagions in families for keeping things a secret, Mr. Westlock, and havin' only them about you as you knows you can repoge in. Who could repoge in Betsey Prig, arter her words of Mrs. Harris, setting in that chair afore my eyes!"

"Quite true," said John; "quite. I hope you have time to find another assistant, Mrs. Gamp?"

Between her indignation and the tea-pot, her powers of comprehending what was said to her began to fail. She looked at John with tearful eyes, and murmuring the well-remembered name which Mrs. Prig had challenged—as if it were a talisman against all earthly sorrows—seemed to wander in her mind.

"I hope," repeated John, "that you have time to find another assistant?"

"Which short it is, indeed," cried Mrs. Gamp, turning up her languid eyes, and clasping Mr. Westlock's wrist with matronly affection. "To-morrow evenin', sir, I waits upon his friends. Mr. Chuzzlewit apinted it from nine to ten."

"From nine to ten," said John, with a significant glance at Martin; "and then Mr. Chuffey retires into safe keeping, does he?"

"He needs to be kep safe, I do assure you," Mrs. Gamp

replied, with a mysterious air. "Other people besides me has had a happy deliverance from Betsey Prig. I little know'd that woman. She'd have let it out!"

"Let *him* out, you mean," said John.

"Do I !" retorted Mrs. Gamp. "Oh !"

The severely ironical character of this reply was strengthened by a very slow nod, and a still slower drawing down of the corners of Mrs. Gamp's mouth. She added with extreme stateliness of manner, after indulging in a short doze :

"But I am a keepin' of you gentlemen, and time is precious."

Mingling with that delusion of the tea-pot which inspired her with the belief that they wanted her to go somewhere immediately, a shrewd avoidance of any further reference to the topics into which she had lately strayed, Mrs. Gamp rose ; and putting away the tea-pot in its accustomed place, and locking the cupboard with much gravity, proceeded to attire herself for a professional visit.

This preparation was easily made, as it required nothing more than the snuffy black bonnet, the snuffy black shawl, the pattens, and the indispensable umbrella, without which neither a lying-in nor a laying-out could by any possibility be attempted. When Mrs. Gamp had invested herself with these appendages she returned to her chair, and sitting down again, declared herself quite ready.

"It's a appiness to know as one can benefit the poor sweet creetur," she observed, "I'm sure. It isn't all as can. The torters Betsey Prig inflicts is frightful !"

Closing her eyes as she made this remark, in the acuteness of her commiseration for Betsey's patients, she forgot to open them again until she dropped a patten. Her nap was also broken at intervals, like the fabled slumbers of Friar Bacon, by the dropping of the other patten, and of the umbrella. But when she had got rid of those incumbrances, her sleep was peaceful.

The two young men looked at each other, ludicrously

enough; and Martin, stifling his disposition to laugh, whispered in John Westlock's ear,

"What shall we do now?"

"Stay here," he replied.

Mrs. Gamp was heard to murmur "Mrs. Harris" in her sleep.

"Rely upon it," whispered John, looking cautiously towards her, "that you shall question this old clerk, though you go as Mrs. Harris herself. We know quite enough to carry her our own way now, at all events; thanks to this quarrel, which confirms the old saying that when rogues fall out, honest people get what they want. Let Jonas Chuzzlewit look to himself; and let her sleep as long as she likes. We shall gain our end in good time."

CHAPTER L

It was the next evening; and Tom and his sister were sitting together before tea, talking, in their usual quiet way, about a great many things, but not at all about Lewsome's story or anything connected with it; for John Westlock—really John, for so young a man, was one of the most considerate fellows in the world—had particularly advised Tom not to mention it to his sister just yet, in case it should disquiet her. "And I wouldn't, Tom," he said, with a little hesitation, "I wouldn't have a shadow on her happy face, or an uneasy thought in her gentle heart, for all the wealth and honours of the universe!" Really John was uncommonly kind; extraordinarily kind. If he had been her father, Tom said, he could not have taken a greater interest in her.

But although Tom and his sister were extremely conversational, they were less lively, and less cheerful, than usual. Tom had no idea that this originated with Ruth, but took it for granted that he was rather dull himself. In truth he was; for the lightest cloud upon the Heaven of her quiet mind, cast its shadow upon Tom.

And there was a cloud on little Ruth that evening. Yes, indeed. When Tom was looking in another direction, her bright eyes, stealing on towards his face, would sparkle still more brightly than their custom was, and then grow dim. When Tom was silent, looking out upon the summer weather

416

she would sometimes make a hasty movement, as if she were about to throw herself upon his neck; then check the impulse, and when he looked round, show a laughing face, and speak to him very merrily; when she had anything to give Tom, or had any excuse for coming near him, she would flutter about him, and lay her bashful hand upon his shoulder, and not be willing to withdraw it; and would show by all such means that there was something on her heart which in her great love she longed to say to him, but had not the courage to utter.

So they were sitting, she with her work before her, but not working, and Tom with his book beside him, but not reading, when Martin knocked at the door. Anticipating who it was, Tom went to open it: and he and Martin came back into the room together. Tom looked surprised, for in answer to his cordial greeting Martin had hardly spoken a word.

Ruth also saw that there was something strange in the manner of their visitor, and raised her eyes inquiringly to Tom's face, as if she were seeking an explanation there. Tom shook his head, and made the same mute appeal to Martin.

Martin did not sit down, but walked up to the window, and stood there, looking out. He turned round after a few moments to speak, but hastily averted his head again, without doing so.

"What has happened, Martin?" Tom anxiously inquired. "My dear fellow, what bad news do you bring?"

"Oh, Tom!" replied Martin, in a tone of deep reproach. "To hear you feign that interest in anything that happens to me, hurts me even more than your ungenerous dealing."

"My ungenerous dealing! Martin! My—" Tom could say no more.

"How could you, Tom, how could you suffer me to thank you so fervently and sincerely for your friendship; and not tell me, like a man, that you had deserted me! Was it true, Tom! Was it honest! Was it worthy of what you used to be: of what I am sure you used to be: to tempt me, when

417

you had turned against me, into pouring out my heart! Oh, Tom!"

His tone was one of such strong injury and yet of so much grief for the loss of a friend he had trusted in; it expressed such high past love for Tom, and so much sorrow and compassion for his supposed unworthiness; that Tom, for a moment, put his hand before his face, and had no more power of justifying himself, than if he had been a monster of deceit and falsehood.

"I protest, as I must die," said Martin, "that I grieve over the loss of what I thought you; and have no anger in the recollection of my own injuries. It is only at such a time, and after such a discovery, that we know the full measure of our old regard for the subject of it. I swear, little as I showed it; little as I know I showed it; that when I had the least consideration for you, Tom, I loved you like a brother."

Tom was composed by this time, and might have been the Spirit of Truth, in a homely dress—it very often wears a homely dress, thank God!—when he replied to him.

"Martin," he said, "I don't know what is in your mind, or who has abused it, or by what extraordinary means. But the means are false. There is no truth whatever in the impression under which you labour. It is a delusion from first to last; and I warn you that you will deeply regret the wrong you do me. I can honestly say that I have been true to you, and to myself. You will be very sorry for this. Indeed, you will be very sorry for it, Martin."

"I *am* sorry," returned Martin, shaking his head. "I think I never knew what it was to be sorry in my heart, until now."

"At least," said Tom, "if I had always been what you charge me with being now, and had never had a place in your regard, but had always been despised by you, and had always deserved it, you should tell me in what you have found me to be treacherous; and on what grounds you proceed. I do not intreat you, therefore, to give me that satisfaction as a favour, Martin, but I ask it of you as a right."

"My own eyes are my witnesses," returned Martin. "Am I to believe them?"

"No," said Tom, calmly. "Not if they accuse me."

"Your own words. Your own manner," pursued Martin. "Am I to believe *them*?"

"No," replied Tom, calmly. "Not if they accuse me. But they never have accused me. Whoever has perverted them to such a purpose, has wronged me, almost as cruelly;" his calmness rather failed him here; "as you have done."

"I came here," said Martin; "and I appeal to your good sister to hear me—"

"Not to her," interrupted Tom. "Pray, do not appeal to her. She will never believe you."

He drew her arm through his own, as he said it.

"*I* believe it, Tom!"

"No, no," cried Tom, "of course not. I said so. Why, tut, tut, tut. What a silly little thing you are!"

"I never meant," said Martin, hastily, "to appeal to you against your brother. Do not think me so unmanly and unkind. I merely appealed to you to hear my declaration, that I came here for no purpose of reproach—I have not one reproach to vent—but in deep regret. You could not know in what bitterness of regret, unless you knew how often I have thought of Tom; how long in almost hopeless circumstances, I have looked forward to the better estimation of his friendship; and how steadfastly I have believed and trusted in him."

"Tut, tut," said Tom, stopping her as she was about to speak. "He is mistaken. He is deceived. Why should you mind? He is sure to be set right at last."

"Heaven bless the day that sets me right!" cried Martin, "if it could ever come!"

"Amen!" said Tom. "And it will!"

Martin paused, and then said in a still milder voice:

"You have chosen for yourself, Tom, and will be relieved by our parting. It is not an angry one. There is no anger on my side—"

419

" There is none on mine," said Tom.

" —It is merely what you have brought about, and worked to bring about. I say again, you have chosen for yourself. You have made the choice that might have been expected in most people situated as you are, but which I did not expect in you. For that, perhaps, I should blame my own judgment more than you. There is wealth and favour worth having, on one side ; and there is the worthless friendship of an abandoned, struggling fellow, on the other. You were free to make your election, and you made it; and the choice was not difficult. But those who have not the courage to resist such temptations, should have the courage to avow what they have yielded to them ; and I *do* blame you for this, Tom : that you received me with a show of warmth, encouraged me to be frank and plain-spoken, tempted me to confide in you, and professed that you were able to be mine ; when you had sold yourself to others. I do not believe," said Martin, with emotion : " hear me say it from my heart ; I *cannot* believe, Tom, now that I am standing face to face with you, that it would have been in your nature to do me any serious harm, even though I had not discovered, by chance, in whose employment you were. But I should have encumbered you ; I should have led you into more double-dealing ; I should have hazarded your retaining the favour for which you have paid so high a price, bartering away your former self; and it is best for both of us that I have found out what you so much desired to keep secret."

"Be just," said Tom ; who had not removed his mild gaze from Martin's face since the commencement of this last address ; "be just even in your injustice, Martin. You forget. You have not yet told me what your accusation is !"

"Why should I ?" returned Martin, waving his hand, and moving towards the door. "You could not know it the better for my dwelling on it, and though it would be really none the worse, it might seem to me to be. No, Tom. Bygones shall be bygones between us. I can take leave of you at this moment, and in this place : in which you are so amiable and so good: as heartily, if not as cheerfully, as ever I have done since we first met. All good go with you, Tom!—I—"

"You leave me so? You can leave me so, can you?" said Tom.

"I—you—you have chosen for yourself, Tom! I—I hope it was a rash choice," Martin faltered. "I think it was. I am sure it was! Good-bye!"

And he was gone.

Tom led his little sister to her chair, and sat down in his own. He took his book, and read, or seemed to read. Presently he said aloud: turning a leaf as he spoke: "He will be very sorry for this." And a tear stole down his face, and dropped upon the page.

Ruth nestled down beside him on her knees, and clasped her arms about his neck.

"No, Tom! No no! Be comforted! Dear Tom!"

"I am quite—comforted," said Tom. "It will be set right."

"Such a cruel, bad return!" cried Ruth.

"No, no," said Tom. "He believes it. I cannot imagine why. But it will be set right."

More closely yet, she nestled down about him; and wept as if her heart would break.

"Don't. Don't," said Tom. "Why do you hide your face, my dear!"

Then in a burst of tears, it all broke out at last.

"Oh Tom, dear Tom, I know your secret heart. I have found it out; you couldn't hide the truth from me. Why didn't you tell me? I am sure I could have made you happier, if you had! You love her, Tom, so dearly!"

Tom made a motion with his hand as if he would have put his sister hurriedly away; but it clasped upon hers, and all his little history was written in the action. All its pathetic eloquence was in the silent touch.

"In spite of that," said Ruth, "you have been so faithful and so good, dear; in spite of that, you have been so true and self-denying, and have struggled with yourself; in spite of that, you have been so gentle, and so kind, and even-tempered, that I have never seen you give a hasty look, or heard you say one irritable word. In spite of all, you have been so cruelly mistaken. Oh Tom, dear Tom, will *this* be set right too! Will it, Tom? Will you always have this sorrow in your breast; you who deserve to be so happy: or is there any hope!"

And still she hid her face from Tom, and clasped him round the neck, and wept for him, and poured out all her woman's heart and soul in the relief and pain of this disclosure.

It was not very long before she and Tom were sitting side by side, and she was looking with an earnest quietness in Tom's face. Then Tom spoke to her thus: cheerily, though gravely.

"I am very glad, my dear, that this has passed between us. Not because it assures me of your tender affection (for I was well assured of that before), but because it relieves my mind of a great weight."

Tom's eyes glistened when he spoke of her affection; and he kissed her on the cheek.

" My dear girl," said Tom: "with whatever feeling I regard her;" they seemed to avoid the name by mutual consent; "I have long ago—I am sure I may say from the very first—looked upon it as a dream. As something that might possibly have happened under very different circumstances, but which can never be. Now, tell me. What would you have set right?"

She gave Tom such a significant little look, that he was obliged to take it for an answer whether he would or no; and to go on.

" By her own choice and free consent, my love, she is betrothed to Martin; and was, long before either of them knew of my existence. You would have her betrothed to me?"

" Yes," she said directly.

" Yes," rejoined Tom, "but that might be setting it wrong, instead of right. Do you think," said Tom, with a grave smile, "that even if she had never seen him, it is very likely she would have fallen in love with Me?"

SUBDUED SORROW

"Why not, dear Tom?"

Tom shook his head, and smiled again.

"You think of me, Ruth," said Tom, "and it is very natural that you should, as if I were a character in a book; and you make it a sort of poetical justice that I should, by some impossible means or other, come, at last, to marry the person I love. But there is a much higher justice than poetical justice, my dear, and it does not order events upon the same principle. Accordingly, people who read about heroes in books, and choose to make heroes of themselves out of books, consider it a very fine thing to be discontented and gloomy, and misanthropical, and perhaps a little blasphemous, because they cannot have everything ordered for their individual accommodation. Would you like me to become one of that sort of people?"

"No, Tom. But still I know," she added timidly, "that this is a sorrow to you in your own better way."

Tom thought of disputing the position. But it would have been mere folly, and he gave it up.

"My dear," said Tom, "I will repay your affection with the Truth, and all the Truth. It is a sorrow to me. I have proved it to be so sometimes, though I have always striven against it. But somebody who is precious to you may die, and you may dream that you are in heaven with the departed spirit, and you may find it a sorrow to wake to the life on earth, which is no harder to be borne than when you fell asleep. It is sorrowful to me to contemplate my dream, which I always knew was a dream, even when it first presented itself; but the realities about me are not to blame. They are the same as they were. My sister, my sweet companion, who makes this place so dear, is she less devoted to me, Ruth, than she would have been, if this vision had never troubled me? My old friend John, who might so easily have treated me with coldness and neglect, is he less cordial to me? The world about me, is there less good in that? Are my words to be harsh and my looks to be sour, and is my heart to grow cold, because there has fallen in my way a good and beautiful creature, who but for the selfish regret that I cannot call her my own, would, like all other good and beautiful creatures, make me happier and better! No, my dear sister. No," said Tom stoutly. "Remembering all my means of happiness, I hardly dare to call this lurking something, a sorrow; but whatever name it may justly bear, I thank Heaven that it renders me more sensible of affection and attachment, and softens me in fifty ways. Not less happy. Not less happy, Ruth!"

She could not speak to him, but she loved him, as he well deserved. Even as he deserved, she loved him.

"She will open Martin's eyes," said Tom, with a glow of pride, " and that (which is indeed wrong) will be set right. Nothing will persuade her, I know, that I have betrayed him. It will be set right through her, and he will be very sorry for it. Our secret, Ruth, is our own, and lives and dies with us. I don't believe I ever could have told it you," said Tom, with a smile, " but how glad I am to think you have found it out!"

They had never taken such a pleasant walk as they took that night. Tom told her all so freely, and so simply, and was so desirous to return her tenderness with his fullest confidence, that they prolonged it far beyond their usual hour, and sat up late when they came home. And when they parted for the night there was such a tranquil, beautiful expression in Tom's face, that she could not bear to shut it out, but going back on tip-toe to his chamber-door, looked in and stood there till he saw her, and then embracing him again, withdrew. And in her prayers, and in her sleep—good times to be remembered with such fervour, Tom!—his name was uppermost.

When he was left alone, Tom pondered very much on this discovery of hers, and greatly wondered what had led her to it. "Because," thought Tom, "I have been so very careful. It was foolish and unnecessary in me, as I clearly see now, when I am so relieved by her knowing it; but I have been so very careful to conceal it from her. Of course I knew that she was intelligent and quick, and for that reason was more upon my guard; but I was not in the least prepared for this. I am sure her discovery has been sudden too. Dear me!" said Tom. "It's a most singular instance of penetration!"

Tom could not get it out of his head. There it was, when his head was on his pillow.

"How she trembled when she began to tell me she knew it!" thought Tom, recalling all the little incidents and circumstances; "and how her face flushed! But that was natural! Oh, quite natural! That needs no accounting for."

Tom little thought how natural it was. Tom little knew that there was that in Ruth's own heart, but newly set there, which had helped her to the reading of his mystery. Ah, Tom! He didn't understand the whispers of the Temple Fountain, though he passed it every day.

Who so lively and cheerful as busy Ruth next morning! Her early tap at Tom's door, and her light foot outside, would have been music to him though she had not spoken. But she said it was the brightest morning ever seen; and so it was; and if it had been otherwise, she would have made it so to Tom.

She was ready with his neat breakfast when he went down stairs, and had her bonnet ready for the early walk, and was so full of news, that Tom was lost in wonder. She might have been up all night, collecting it for his entertainment. There was Mr. Nadgett not come home yet, and there was bread down a penny a loaf, and there was twice as much strength in this tea as in the last, and the milkwoman's husband had come out of the hospital cured, and the curly-headed child over the way had been lost all yesterday, and she was going to make all sorts of preserves in a desperate hurry, and there happened to be a saucepan in the house which was the very saucepan for the purpose; and she knew all about the last book Tom had brought home, all through, though it was a teazer to read; and she had so much to tell him that she had finished breakfast first. Then she had her

425

little bonnet on, and the tea and sugar locked up, and the keys in her reticule, and the flower, as usual, in Tom's coat, and was in all respects quite ready to accompany him, before Tom knew she had begun to prepare. And in short, as Tom said, with a confidence in his own assertion which amounted to a defiance of the public in general, there never was such a little woman.

She made Tom talkative. It was impossible to resist her. She put such enticing questions to him; about books, and about dates of churches, and about organs, and about the Temple, and about all kinds of things. Indeed, she lightened the way (and Tom's heart with it) to that degree, that the Temple looked quite blank and solitary when he parted from her at the gate.

"No Mr. Fips's friend to-day, I suppose," thought Tom, as he ascended the stairs.

Not yet, at any rate, for the door was closed as usual, and Tom opened it with his key. He had got the books into perfect order now, and had mended the torn leaves, and had pasted up the broken backs, and substituted neat labels for the worn-out letterings. It looked a different place, it was so orderly and neat. Tom felt some pride in contemplating the change he had wrought, though there was no one to approve or disapprove of it.

He was at present occupied in making a fair copy of his draught of the catalogue; on which, as there was no hurry, he was painfully concentrating all the ingenious and laborious neatness he had ever expended on map or plan in Mr. Pecksniff's workroom. It was a very marvel of a catalogue; for Tom sometimes thought he was really getting his money too easily, and he had determined within himself that this document should take a little of his superfluous leisure out of him.

So, with pens and ruler, and compasses and india-rubber, and pencil and black ink, and red ink, Tom worked away all the morning. He thought a good deal about Martin, and their interview of yesterday, and would have been far easier in his mind if he could have resolved to confide it to his friend John, and to have taken his opinion on the subject. But besides that he knew what John's boiling indignation would be, he bethought himself that he was helping Martin now in a matter of great moment, and that to deprive the latter of his assistance at such a crisis of affairs, would be to inflict a serious injury upon him.

"So I'll keep it to myself," said Tom, with a sigh. "I'll keep it to myself."

And to work he went again, more assiduously than ever, with the pens, and the ruler, and the india-rubber, and the pencil, and the black ink, and the red ink, that he might forget it.

He had laboured away for another hour or more, when he heard a footstep in the entry, down below.

"Ah!" said Tom, looking towards the door; "time was, not long ago either, when that would have set me wondering and expecting. But I have left off now."

The footstep came on, up the stairs.

"Thirty-six, thirty-seven, thirty-eight," said Tom, counting. "Now you'll stop. Nobody ever comes past the thirty-eighth stair."

The person did stop, certainly, but only to take breath; for up the footstep came again. Forty, forty-one, forty-two, and so on.

The door stood open. As the tread advanced, Tom looked impatiently and eagerly towards it. When a figure came upon the landing, and arriving in the doorway, stopped and gazed at him, he rose up from his chair, and half believed he saw a spirit.

Old Martin Chuzzlewit! The same whom he had left at Mr. Pecksniff's, weak and sinking!

The same? No, not the same, for this old man, though old, was strong, and leaned upon his stick with a vigorous hand, while with the other he signed to Tom to make no noise. One glance at the resolute face, the watchful eye, the vigorous hand upon the staff, the triumphant purpose in the figure, and such a light broke in on Tom as blinded him.

"You have expected me," said Martin, "a long time."

"I was told that my employer would arrive soon," said Tom; "but—"

"I know. You were ignorant who he was. It was my desire. I am glad it has been so well observed. I intended to have been with you much sooner. I thought the time had come. I thought I could know no more, and no worse, of him, than I did on that day when I saw you last. But I was wrong."

He had by this time come up to Tom, and now he grasped his hand.

"I have lived in his house, Pinch, and had him fawning on me days and weeks, and months. You know it. I have suffered him to treat me like his tool and instrument. You know it; you have seen me there. I have undergone ten thousand times as much as I could have endured if I had been the miserable weak old man he took me for. You know it. I have seen him offer love to Mary. You know it; who better—who better, my true heart! I have had his base soul bare before me, day by day, and have not betrayed myself once. I never could have undergone such torture but for looking forward to this time."

He stopped, even in the passion of his speech; if that can be called passion which was so resolute and steady; to press Tom's hand again. Then he said, in great excitement:

"Close the door, close the door. He will not be long after me, but may come too soon. The time now drawing on," said the old man, hurriedly: his eyes and whole face brightening as he spoke: "will make amends for all. I wouldn't have him die or hang himself, for millions of golden pieces! Close the door!"

Tom did so, hardly knowing yet whether he was awake, or in a dream.

Mr. Pinch is amazed by an Unexpected Apparition

CHAPTER LI

THE night had now come, when the old clerk was to be delivered over to his keepers. In the midst of his guilty distractions, Jonas had not forgotten it.

It was a part of his guilty state of mind to remember it; for on his persistence in the scheme depended one of his precautions for his own safety. A hint, a word, from the old man, uttered at such a moment in attentive ears, might fire the train of suspicion, and destroy him. His watchfulness of every avenue by which the discovery of his guilt might be approached, sharpened with his sense of the danger by which he was encompassed. With murder on his soul, and its innumerable alarms and terrors dragging at him night and day, he would have repeated the crime, if he had seen a path of safety stretching out beyond. It was in his punishment; it was in his guilty condition. The very deed which his fears rendered insupportable, his fears would have impelled him to commit again.

But keeping the old man close, according to his design, would serve his turn. His purpose was, to escape, when the first alarm and wonder had subsided : and when he could make the attempt without awakening instant suspicion. In the meanwhile these women would keep him quiet; and if the talking humour came upon him, would not be easily startled. He knew their trade.

Nor had he spoken idly when he said the old man should be gagged. He had resolved to ensure his silence; and he looked to the end, not the means. He had been rough and rude and cruel to the old man all his life; and violence was natural to his mind in connection with him. "He shall be gagged if he speaks, and pinioned if he writes," said Jonas, looking at him; for they sat alone together. "He is mad enough for that; I'll go through with it!"

Hush!

Still listening! To every sound. He had listened ever since, and it had not come yet. The exposure of the Assurance office; the flight of Crimple and Bullamy with the plunder, and among the rest, as he feared, with his own bill, which he had not found in the pocket-book of the murdered man, and which with Mr. Pecksniff's money had probably been remitted to one or other of those trusty friends for safe deposit at the banker's; his immense losses, and peril of being still called to account as a partner in the broken firm; all these things rose in his mind at one time and always, but he could not contemplate them. He was aware of their presence, and of the rage, discomfiture, and despair, they brought along with them; but he thought—of his own controlling power and direction he thought—of the one dread question only. When they would find the body in the wood.

He tried—he had never left off trying—not to forget it was there, for that was impossible, but to forget to weary himself by drawing vivid pictures of it in his fancy: by going softly about it and about it among the leaves, approaching it nearer and nearer through a gap in the boughs, and startling the very flies that were thickly sprinkled all over it, like heaps of dried currants. His mind was fixed and fastened on the discovery, for intelligence of which he listened intently to every cry and shout; listened when any one came in, or went out; watched from the window the people who passed up and down the street; mistrusted his own looks and words. And the more his thoughts were set upon the discovery, the stronger was the fascination which attracted them to the thing itself: lying alone in the wood. He was for ever showing and presenting it, as it were, to every creature whom he saw. "Look here! Do you know of this? Is it found? Do you suspect *me*?" If he had been condemned to bear the body in his arms, and lay it down for recognition at the feet of every one he met, it could not have been more constantly with him, or a cause of more monotonous and dismal occupation than it was in this state of his mind.

Still he was not sorry. It was no contrition or remorse for what he had done that moved him; it was nothing but alarm for his own security. The vague consciousness he possessed of having wrecked his fortune in the murderous venture, intensified his hatred and revenge, and made him set the greater store by what he had gained. The man was dead; nothing could undo that. He felt a triumph yet, in the reflection.

He had kept a jealous watch on Chuffey, ever since the deed; seldom leaving him but on compulsion, and then for as short intervals as possible. They were alone together now. It was twilight, and the appointed time drew near at hand. Jonas walked up and down the room. The old man sat in his accustomed corner.

The slightest circumstance was matter of disquiet to the murderer, and he was made uneasy at this time by the absence of his wife, who had left home early in the afternoon, and had not returned yet. No tenderness for her was at the bottom of this; but he had a misgiving that she might have been waylaid, and tempted into saying something that would criminate him when the news came. For anything he knew, she might have knocked at the door of his room, while he was away, and discovered his plot. Confound her, it was like her pale face, to be wandering up and down the house! Where was she now?

"She went to her good friend, Mrs. Todgers," said the old man, when he asked the question with an angry oath.

Aye! To be sure! Always stealing away into the company of that woman. She was no friend of his. Who could tell what devil's mischief they might hatch together! Let her be fetched home directly.

The old man, muttering some words softly, rose as if he would have gone himself, but Jonas thrust him back into his chair with an impatient imprecation, and sent a servant-girl to fetch her. When he had charged her with her errand he walked to and fro again, and never stopped till she came back, which she did pretty soon: the way being short, and the woman having made good haste.

Well! Where was she? Had she come?

No. She had left there, full three hours.

"Left there! Alone?"

The messenger had not asked; taking that for granted.

"Curse you for a fool. Bring candles!"

She had scarcely left the room, when the old clerk, who had been unusually observant of him ever since he had asked about his wife, came suddenly upon him.

"Give her up!" cried the old man. "Come! Give her up to me! Tell me what you have done with her. Quick! I have made no promises on that score. Tell me what you have done with her."

He laid his hands upon his collar as he spoke, and grasped it: tightly too.

"You shall not leave me!" cried the old man. "I am strong enough to cry out to the neighbours, and I will, unless you give her up. Give her up to me!"

Jonas was so dismayed and conscience-stricken, that he had not even hardihood enough to unclench the old man's hands with his own; but stood looking at him as well as he could in the darkness, without moving a finger. It was as much as he could do to ask him what he meant.

"I will know what you have done with her!' retorted

Chuffey. "If you hurt a hair of her head, you shall answer it. Poor thing! Poor thing! Where is she?"

"Why, you old madman!" said Jonas, in a low voice, and with trembling lips. "What Bedlam fit has come upon you now?"

"It is enough to make me mad, seeing what I have seen in this house!" cried Chuffey. "Where is my dear old master! Where is his only son that I have nursed upon my knee, a child! Where is she, she who was the last; she that I've seen pining day by day, and heard weeping in the dead of night! She was the last, the last of all my friends! Heaven help me, she was the very last!"

Seeing that the tears were stealing down his face, Jonas mustered courage to unclench his hands, and push him off before he answered:

"Did you hear me ask for her? Did you hear me send for her? How can I give you up what I haven't got, idiot! Ecod, I'd give her up to you and welcome, if I could; and a precious pair you'd be!"

"If she has come to any harm," cried Chuffey, "mind! I'm old and silly; but I have my memory sometimes; and if she has come to any harm—"

"Devil take you," interrupted Jonas, but in a suppressed voice still; "what harm do you suppose she has come to? I know no more where she is than you do; I wish I did. Wait till she comes home, and see; she can't be long. Will that content you?"

"Mind!" exclaimed the old man. "Not a hair of her head! not a hair of her head ill-used! I won't bear it. I—I —have borne it too long, Jonas. I am silent, but I—I—I can speak. I—I—I can speak—" he stammered, as he crept back to his chair, and turned a threatening, though a feeble, look upon him.

"You can speak, can you!" thought Jonas. "So, so, we'll stop your speaking. It's well I knew of this in good time. Prevention is better than cure."

He had made a poor show of playing the Bully and evincing a desire to conciliate at the same time, but was so afraid of the old man that great drops had started out upon his brow; and they stood there yet. His unusual tone of voice and agitated manner had sufficiently expressed his fear; but his face would have done so now, without that aid, as he again walked to and fro, glancing at him by the candle-light.

He stopped at the window to think. An opposite shop was lighted up; and the tradesman and a customer were reading some printed bill together across the counter. The sight brought him back, instantly, to the occupation he had forgotten. "Look here! Do you know of this? Is it found? Do you suspect *me?*"

A hand upon the door. "What's that!"

"A pleasant evenin'," said the voice of Mrs. Gamp, "though warm, which, bless you, Mr. Chuzzlewit, we must expect when cowcumbers is three for twopence. How does Mr. Chuffey find his self to-night, sir?"

Mrs. Gamp kept particularly close to the door in saying this, and curtseyed more than usual. She did not appear to be quite so much at her ease as she generally was.

"Get him to his room," said Jonas, walking up to her, and speaking in her ear. "He has been raving to-night—stark mad. Don't talk while he's here, but come down again."

"Poor sweet dear!' cried Mrs. Gamp, with uncommon tenderness. "He's all of a tremble."

"Well he may be," said Jonas, "after the mad fit he has had. Get him up stairs."

She was by this time assisting him to rise.

"There's my blessed old chick!" cried Mrs. Gamp, in a tone that was at once soothing and encouraging. "There's my darlin' Mr. Chuffey! Now come up to your own room, sir, and lay down on your bed a bit; for you're a shakin' all over, as if your precious jints was hung upon wires. That's a good creetur! Come with Sairey!"

"Is she come home?" inquired the old man.

"She'll be here directly minnit," returned Mrs. Gamp. "Come with Sairey, Mr. Chuffey. Come with your own Sairey!"

The good woman had no reference to any female in the world in promising this speedy advent of the person for whom Mr. Chuffey inquired, but merely threw it out as a means of pacifying the old man. It had its effect, for he permitted her to lead him away: and they quitted the room together.

Jonas looked out of the window again. They were still reading the printed paper in the shop opposite, and a third man had joined in the perusal. What could it be, to interest them so?

A dispute or discussion seemed to arise among them, for they all looked up from their reading together, and one of the three, who had been glancing over the shoulder of another, stepped back to explain or illustrate some action by his gestures.

Horror! How like the blow he had struck in the wood!

It beat him from the window as if it had lighted on himself. As he staggered into a chair he thought of the change in Mrs. Gamp, exhibited in her new-born tenderness to her charge. Was that because it was found?—because she knew of it?—because she suspected him?

"Mr. Chuffey is a lyin' down," said Mrs. Gamp, returning, "and much good may it do him, Mr. Chuzzlewit, which harm it can't and good it may, be joyful!"

"Sit down," said Jonas, hoarsely, "and let us get this business done. Where is the other woman?"

"The other person's with him now," she answered.

"That's right," said Jonas. "He is not fit to be left to himself. Why, he fastened on me to-night; here, upon my coat; like a savage dog. Old as he is, and feeble as he is usually, I had some trouble to shake him off. You—Hush!— It's nothing. You told me the other woman's name. I forget it."

"I mentioned Betsey Prig," said Mrs. Gamp.

"She is to be trusted, is she?"

"That she ain't!" said Mrs. Gamp; "nor have I brought her, Mr. Chuzzlewit. I've brought another, which engages to give every satigefaction."

"What is her name?" asked Jonas.

Mrs. Gamp looked at him in an odd way without returning any answer, but appeared to understand the question too.

"What is her name?" repeated Jonas.

"Her name," said Mrs. Gamp, "is Harris."

It was extraordinary how much effort it cost Mrs. Gamp to pronounce the name she was commonly so ready with. She made some three or four gasps before she could get it out; and, when she had uttered it, pressed her hand upon her side, and turned up her eyes, as if she were going to faint away. But, knowing her to labour under a complication of internal disorders, which rendered a few drops of spirits indispensable at certain times to her existence, and which came on very strong when that remedy was not at hand, Jonas merely supposed her to be the victim of one of these attacks.

"Well!" he said, hastily, for he felt how incapable he was of confining his wandering attention to the subject. "You and she have arranged to take care of him, have you?"

Mrs. Gamp replied in the affirmative, and softly discharged herself of her familiar phrase, "Turn and turn about; one off, one on." But she spoke so tremulously that she felt called upon to add, "which fiddle-strings is weakness to expredge my nerves this night!"

Jonas stopped to listen. Then said, hurriedly:

"We shall not quarrel about terms. Let them be the same as they were before. Keep him close, and keep him quiet. He must be restrained. He has got it in his head to-night that my wife's dead, and has been attacking me as if I had killed her. It's—it's common with mad people to take the worst fancies of those they like best. Isn't it?"

Mrs. Gamp assented with a short groan.

"Keep him close, then, or in one of his fits he'll be doing me a mischief. And don't trust him at any time; for when he seems most rational, he's wildest in his talk. But that you know already. Let me see the other."

"The t'other person, sir?" said Mrs. Gamp.

"Ay! Go you to him and send the other. Quick! I'm busy."

Mrs. Gamp took two or three backward steps towards the door, and stopped there.

"It is your wishes, Mr. Chuzzlewit," she said, in a sort of quavering croak, "to see the t'other person. Is it?"

But the ghastly change in Jonas told her that the other person was already seen. Before she could look round towards the door, she was put aside by old Martin's hand; and Chuffey and John Westlock entered with him.

"Let no one leave the house," said Martin. "This man is my brother's son. Ill-met, ill-trained, ill-begotten. If he moves from the spot on which he stands, or speaks a word above his breath to any person here, open the window, and call for help!"

"What right have you to give such directions in this house?" asked Jonas faintly.

"The right of your wrong-doing. Come in there!"

An irrepressible exclamation burst from the lips of Jonas, as Lewsome entered at the door. It was not a groan, or a shriek, or a word, but was wholly unlike any sound that had ever fallen on the ears of those who heard it, while at the same time it was the most sharp and terrible expression of what was working in his guilty breast, that nature could have invented.

He had done murder for this! He had girdled himself about with perils, agonies of mind, innumerable fears, for this! He had hidden his secret in the wood; pressed and stamped it down into the bloody ground; and here it started up when least expected, miles upon miles away; known to many; proclaiming itself from the lips of an old man who had renewed

his strength and vigour as by a miracle, to give it voice
against him!

He leaned his hand on the back of a chair, and looked at
them. It was in vain to try to do so, scornfully; or with
his usual insolence. He required the chair for his support.
But he made a struggle for it.

"I know that fellow," he said, fetching his breath at every
word, and pointing his trembling finger towards Lewsome.
"He's the greatest liar alive. What's his last tale? Ha, ha!
You're rare fellows, too! Why, that uncle of mine is childish;
he's even a greater child than his brother, my father, was, in
his old age; or than Chuffey is. What the devil do you
mean," he added, looking fiercely at John Westlock and Mark
Tapley (the latter had entered with Lewsome), "by coming
here, and bringing two idiots and a knave with you to take
my house by storm? Hallo, there! Open the door! Turn
these strangers out!

"I tell you what," cried Mr. Tapley, coming forward, "if
it wasn't for your name, I'd drag you through the streets of
my own accord, and single-handed, I would! Ah, I would!
Don't try and look bold at me. You can't do it! Now go
on, sir," this was to old Martin. "Bring the murderin'
wagabond upon his knees! If he wants noise, he shall have
enough of it; for as sure as he's a shiverin' from head to foot,
I'll raise a uproar at this winder that shall bring half London
in. Go on, sir! Let him try me once, and see whether I'm
a man of my word or not."

With that, Mark folded his arms, and took his seat upon
the window-ledge, with an air of general preparation for anything, which seemed to imply that he was equally ready to
jump out himself, or to throw Jonas out, upon receiving the
slightest hint that it would be agreeable to the company.

Old Martin turned to Lewsome:

"This is the man," he said, extending his hand towards
Jonas. "Is it?"

"You need do no more than look at him to be sure

438

of that, or of the truth of what I have said," was the reply. "He is my witness."

"Oh, brother!" cried old Martin, clasping his hands and lifting up his eyes. "Oh, brother, brother! Were we strangers half our lives that you might breed a wretch like this, and I make life a desert by withering every flower that grew about me! Is it the natural end of your precepts and mine, that this should be the creature of your rearing, training, teaching, hoarding, striving for: and I the means of bringing him to punishment, when nothing can repair the wasted past!"

He sat down upon a chair as he spoke, and turning away his face, was silent for a few moments. Then with recovered energy he proceeded:

"But the accursed harvest of our mistaken lives shall be trodden down. It is not too late for that. You are confronted with this man, yon monster there; not to be spared, but to be dealt with justly. Hear what he says! Reply, be silent, contradict, repeat, defy, do what you please. My course will be the same. Go on! And you," he said to Chuffey, "for the love of your old friend, speak out, good fellow!"

"I have been silent for his love!" cried the old man. "He urged me to it. He made me promise it, upon his dying bed. I never would have spoken, but for your finding out so much. I have thought about it ever since: I couldn't help that: and sometimes I have had it all before me in a dream: but in the day-time, not in sleep. Is there such a kind of dream?" said Chuffey, looking anxiously in old Martin's face.

As Martin made him an encouraging reply, he listened attentively to his voice; and smiled.

"Ah, ay!" he cried. "He often spoke to me like that. We were at school together, he and I. I couldn't turn against his son, you know—his only son, Mr. Chuzzlewit!"

"I would to heaven you had been his son!" said Martin.

"You speak so like my dear old master," cried the old man with a childish delight, "that I almost think I hear him. I can hear you quite as well as I used to hear him. It makes me young again. He never spoke unkindly to me, and I always understood him. I could always see him too, though my sight was dim. Well, well! He's dead, he's dead. He was very good to me, my dear old master!"

He shook his head mournfully over the brother's hand. At this moment Mark, who had been glancing out of the window, left the room.

"I couldn't turn against his only son, you know," said Chuffey. "He has nearly driven me to do it sometimes; he very nearly did to-night. Ah!" cried the old man, with a sudden recollection of the cause. "Where is she! She's not come home!"

"Do you mean his wife?" said Mr. Chuzzlewit.

"Yes."

"I have removed her. She is in my care, and will be spared the present knowledge of what is passing here. She has known misery enough, without that addition."

Jonas heard this with a sinking heart. He knew that they were on his heels, and felt that they were resolute to run him to destruction. Inch by inch the ground beneath him was sliding from his feet; faster and faster the encircling ruin contracted and contracted towards himself, its wicked centre, until it should close in and crush him.

And now he heard the voice of his accomplice stating to his face, with every circumstance of time and place and incident; and openly proclaiming, with no reserve, suppression, passion, or concealment; all the truth. The truth, which nothing would keep down; which blood would not smother, and earth would not hide; the truth, whose terrible inspiration seemed to change dotards into strong men; and on whose avenging wings, one whom he had supposed to be at the extremest corner of the earth came swooping down upon him.

He tried to deny it, but his tongue would not move. He conceived some desperate thought of rushing away, and tearing through the streets; but his limbs would as little answer to his will as his stark, stiff, staring face. All this time the voice went slowly on, denouncing him. It was as if every drop of blood in the wood had found a voice to jeer him with.

When it ceased, another voice took up the tale, but strangely: for the old clerk, who had watched, and listened to the whole, and had wrung his hands from time to time, as if he knew its truth and could confirm it, broke in with these words:

"No, no, no! you're wrong; you're wrong—all wrong together! Have patience, for the truth is only known to me!"

"How can that be," said his old master's brother, "after what you have heard? Besides, you said just now, above stairs, when I told you of the accusation against him, that you knew he was his father's murderer."

"Ay, yes! and so he was!" cried Chuffey, wildly. "But not as you suppose—not as you suppose. Stay! Give me a moment's time. I have it all here—all here! It was foul, foul, cruel, bad; but not as you suppose. Stay, stay!"

He put his hands up to his head, as if it throbbed or pained him. After looking about him in a wandering and vacant manner for some moments, his eyes rested upon Jonas, when they kindled up with sudden recollection and intelligence.

"Yes!" cried old Chuffey, "yes! That's how it was. It's all upon me now. He—he got up from his bed before he died, to be sure, to say that he forgave him; and he came down with me into this room; and when he saw him—his only son, the son he loved—his speech forsook him: he had no speech for what he knew—and no one understood him except me. But I did—I did!"

Old Martin regarded him in amazement; so did his companions. Mrs. Gamp, who had said nothing yet; but had kept two-thirds of herself behind the door, ready for escape, and one-third in the room, ready for siding with the strongest party; came a little further in and remarked, with a sob, that Mr. Chuffey was "the sweetest old creetur goin'."

"He bought the stuff," said Chuffey, stretching out his arm towards Jonas, while an unwonted fire shone in his eye, and lightened up his face; "he bought the stuff, no doubt, as you have heard, and brought it home. He mixed the stuff—look at him!—with some sweetmeat in a jar, exactly as the medicine for his father's cough was mixed, and put it in a drawer; in that drawer yonder in the desk; he knows which drawer I mean! He kept it there locked up. But his courage failed him, or his heart was touched—my God! I hope it was his heart! He was his only son!—and he did not put it in the usual place, where my old master would have taken it twenty times a-day."

The trembling figure of the old man shook with the strong emotions that possessed him. But, with the same light in his eye, and with his arm outstretched, and with his grey hair stirring on his head, he seemed to grow in size, and was like a man inspired. Jonas shrunk from looking at him, and cowered down into the chair by which he had held. It seemed as if this tremendous Truth could make the dumb speak.

"I know it every word now!" cried Chuffey. "Every word! He put it in that drawer, as I have said. He went so often there, and was so secret, that his father took notice of it; and when he was out, had it opened. We were there together, and we found the mixture—Mr. Chuzzlewit and I. He took it into his possession, and made light of it at the time; but in the night he came to my bedside, weeping, and told me that his own son had it in his mind to poison him. 'Oh, Chuff,' he said, 'oh, dear old Chuff! a voice came into my room to-night, and told me that this crime began with me. It began when I taught him to be too covetous of what I have to leave, and made the expectation of it his great business!' Those were his words; ay, they are his very words! If he was a hard man now and then, it was for his only son. He loved his only son, and he was always good to me!"

Jonas listened with increased attention. Hope was breaking in upon him.

"'He shall not weary for my death, Chuff:' that was what he said next," pursued the old clerk, as he wiped his eyes; "that was what he said next, crying like a little child: 'He shall not weary for my death, Chuff. He shall have it now; he shall marry where he has a fancy, Chuff, although it don't please me; and you and I will go away and live upon a little. I always loved him; perhaps he'll love *me* then. It's a dreadful thing to have my own child thirsting for my death. But I might have known it. I have sown, and I must reap. He shall believe that I am taking this; and when I see that he is sorry, and has all he wants, I'll tell him that I found it out, and I'll forgive him. He'll make a better man of his own son, and be a better man himself, perhaps, Chuff!'"

Poor Chuffey paused to dry his eyes again. Old Martin's face was hidden in his hands. Jonas listened still more keenly, and his breast heaved like a swollen water, but with hope. With growing hope.

"My dear old master made believe next day," said Chuffey, "that he had opened the drawer by mistake with a key from the bunch, which happened to fit it (we had one made and hung upon it); and that he had been surprised to find his fresh supply of cough medicine in such a place, but supposed it had been put there in a hurry when the drawer stood open. We burnt it; but his son believed that he was taking it—he knows he did. Once Mr. Chuzzlewit to try him took heart to say it had a strange taste; and he got up directly, and went out."

Jonas gave a short, dry cough; and, changing his position for an easier one, folded his arms without looking at them, though they could now see his face.

"Mr. Chuzzlewit wrote to her father; I mean the father of the poor thing who's his wife;" said Chuffey; "and got him to come up: intending to hasten on the marriage. But his mind, like mine, went a little wrong through grief, and then his heart broke. He sank and altered from the time when he came to me in the night; and never held up his head again. It was only a few days, but he had never changed so much in twice the years. 'Spare him, Chuff!' he said, before he died. They were the only words he could speak. 'Spare him, Chuff!' I promised him I would. I've tried to do it. He's his only son."

In his recollection of the last scene in his old friend's life, poor Chuffey's voice, which had grown weaker and weaker, quite deserted him. Making a motion with his hand, as if he would have said that Anthony had taken it, and had died with it in his, he retreated to the corner where he usually concealed his sorrows; and was silent.

Jonas could look at his company now, and vauntingly too. " Well!" he said, after a pause. " Are you satisfied? Or have you any more of your plots to broach? Why that fellow, Lewsome, can invent 'em for you by the score. Is this all? Have you nothing else?"

Old Martin looked at him steadily.

" Whether you are what you seemed to be at Pecksniff's, or are something else and a mountebank, I don't know and I don't care," said Jonas, looking downward with a smile, " but I don't want you here. You were here so often when your brother was alive, and were always so fond of him (your dear, dear brother, and you would have been cuffing one another before this, ecod!), that I am not surprised at your being attached to the place; but the place is not attached to you, and you can't leave it too soon, though you may leave it too late. And for my wife, old man, send her home straight, or it will be the worse for her. Ha ha! You carry it with a high hand too! But it isn't hanging yet for a man to keep a penn'orth of poison for his own purposes, and have it taken from him by two old crazy jolter-heads who go and act a play about it. Ha, ha! Do you see the door?"

His base triumph, struggling with his cowardice, and shame, and guilt, was so detestable, that they turned away from him, as if he were some obscene and filthy animal, repugnant to the sight. And here that last black crime was busy with

444

him too; working within him to his perdition. But for that, the old clerk's story might have touched him, though never so lightly; but for that, the sudden removal of so great a load might have brought about some wholesome change even in him. With that deed done, however; with that unnecessary wasteful danger haunting him; despair was in his very triumph and relief; wild, ungovernable, raging despair, for the uselessness of the peril into which he had plunged; despair that hardened him and maddened him, and set his teeth a grinding in a moment of his exultation.

"My good friend!" said old Martin, laying his hand on Chuffey's sleeve. "This is no place for you to remain in. Come with me."

"Just his old way!" cried Chuffey, looking up into his face. "I almost believe it's Mr. Chuzzlewit alive again. Yes! Take me with you! Stay, though, stay."

"For what?" asked old Martin.

"I can't leave her, poor thing!" said Chuffey. "She has been very good to me. I can't leave her, Mr. Chuzzlewit. Thank you kindly. I'll remain here. I hav'n't long to remain; it's no great matter."

As he meekly shook his poor, grey head, and thanked old Martin in these words, Mrs. Gamp, now entirely in the room, was affected to tears.

"The mercy as it is!" she said, "as sech a dear, good, reverend creetur, never got into the clutches of Betsey Prig, which but for me he would have done, undoubted, facts bein' stubborn and not easy drove!"

"You heard me speak to you just now, old man," said Jonas to his uncle. "I'll have no more tampering with my people, man or woman. Do you see the door?"

"Do *you* see the door?" returned the voice of Mark, coming from that direction. "Look at it!"

He looked, and his gaze was nailed there. Fatal, ill-omened, blighted threshold, cursed by his father's footsteps in his dying hour, cursed by his young wife's sorrowing tread, cursed by the daily shadow of the old clerk's figure, cursed by the crossing of his murderer's feet—what men were standing in the doorway!

Nadgett foremost.

Hark! It came on, roaring like a sea! Hawkers burst into the street, crying it up and down; windows were thrown open that the inhabitants might hear it; people stopped to listen in the road and on the pavement; the bells, the same bells, began to ring: tumbling over one another in a dance of boisterous joy at the discovery (that was the sound they had in his distempered thoughts), and making their airy playground rock.

"That is the man," said Nadgett. "By the window!"

Three others came in, laid hands upon him, and secured him. It was so quickly done, that he had not lost sight of the informer's face for an instant when his wrists were manacled together.

"Murder," said Nadgett, looking round on the astonished group. "Let no one interfere."

The sounding street repeated Murder; barbarous and dreadful Murder; Murder, Murder, Murder. Rolling on from house to house, and echoing from stone to stone, until the voices died away into the distant hum, which seemed to mutter the same word!

They all stood silent: listening, and gazing in each other's faces, as the noise passed on.

Old Martin was the first to speak. "What terrible history is this?" he demanded.

"Ask *him*," said Nadgett. "You're his friend, sir. He can tell you, if he will. He knows more of it than I do, though I know much."

"How do you know much?"

"I have not been watching him so long for nothing," returned Nadgett. "I never watched a man so close as I have watched him."

Another of the phantom forms of this terrific Truth!

Another of the many shapes in which it started up about him, out of vacancy. This man, of all men in the world, a spy upon him; this man, changing his identity: casting off his shrinking, purblind, unobservant character, and springing up into a watchful enemy! The dead man might have come out of his grave, and not confounded and appalled him more.

The game was up. The race was at an end; the rope was woven for his neck. If, by a miracle, he could escape from this strait, he had but to turn his face another way, no matter where, and there would rise some new avenger front to front with him; some infant in an hour grown old, or old man in an hour grown young, or blind man with his sight restored, or deaf man with his hearing given him. There was no chance. He sank down in a heap against the wall, and never hoped again from that moment.

"I am not his friend, although I have the dishonour to be his relative," said Mr. Chuzzlewit. "You may speak to me. Where have you watched, and what have you seen?"

"I have watched in many places," returned Nadgett, "night and day. I have watched him lately, almost without rest or relief;" his anxious face and bloodshot eyes confirmed it. "I little thought to what my watching was to lead. As little as he did when he slipped out in the night, dressed in those clothes which he afterwards sunk in a bundle at London Bridge!"

Jonas moved upon the ground like a man in bodily torture. He uttered a suppressed groan, as if he had been wounded by some cruel weapon; and plucked at the iron band upon his wrists, as though (his hands being free) he would have torn himself.

"Steady, kinsman?" said the chief officer of the party. "Don't be violent."

"Whom do you call kinsman?" asked old Martin sternly.

"You," said the man, "among others."

Martin turned his scrutinising gaze upon him. He was sitting lazily across a chair with his arms resting on the

447

back; eating nuts, and throwing the shells out of window as he cracked them; which he still continued to do while speaking.

"Ay," he said, with a sulky nod. "You may deny your nephews till you die, but Chevy Slyme is Chevy Slyme still, all the world over. Perhaps even you may feel it some disgrace to your own blood to be employed in this way. I'm to be bought off.".

"At every turn!" cried Martin. "Self, self, self. Every one among them for himself!"

"You had better save one or two among them the trouble then, and be for them as well as *your*self," replied his nephew. "Look here at me! Can you see the man of your family who has more talent in his little finger than all the rest in their united brains, dressed as a police officer without being ashamed? I took up with this trade on purpose to shame you. I didn't think I should have to make a capture in the family, though."

"If your debauchery, and that of your chosen friends, has really brought you to this level," returned the old man, "keep it. You are living honestly, I hope, and that's something."

"Don't be hard upon my chosen friends," returned Slyme, "for they were sometimes your chosen friends too. Don't say you never employed my friend Tigg, for I know better. We quarrelled upon it."

"I hired the fellow," retorted Mr. Chuzzlewit, "and I paid him."

"It's well you paid him," said his nephew, "for it would be too late to do so now. He has given his receipt in full— or had it forced from him rather."

The old man looked at him as if he were curious to know what he meant, but scorned to prolong the conversation.

"I have always expected that he and I would be brought together again in the course of business," said Slyme, taking a fresh handful of nuts from his pocket; "but I thought he would be wanted for some swindling job; it never entered my head that I should hold a warrant for the apprehension of his murderer."

"*His* murderer!" cried Mr. Chuzzlewit, looking from one to another.

"His or Mr. Montague's," said Nadgett. "They are the same, I am told. I accuse him yonder of the murder of Mr. Montague, who was found last night, killed, in a wood. You will ask me why I accuse him, as you have already asked me how I know so much. I'll tell you. It can't remain a secret long."

The ruling passion of the man expressed itself even then, in the tone of regret in which he deplored the approaching publicity of what he knew.

"I told you I had watched him," he proceeded. "I was instructed to do so by Mr. Montague, in whose employment I have been for some time. We had our suspicions of him; and you know what they pointed at, for you have been discussing it since we have been waiting here, outside the room. If you care to hear now it's all over, in what our suspicions began, I'll tell you plainly: in a quarrel (it first came to our ears through a hint of his own) between him and another office in which his father's life was insured, and which had so much doubt and distrust upon the subject, that he compounded with them, and took half the money; and was glad to do it. Bit by bit, I ferreted out more circumstances against him, and not a few. It required a little patience, but it's my calling. I found the nurse—here she is to confirm me; I found the doctor, I found the undertaker, I found the undertaker's man. I found out how the old gentleman there, Mr. Chuffey, had behaved at the funeral; and I found out what this man," touching Lewsome on the arm, "had talked about in his fever. I found out how he conducted himself before his father's death, and how since, and how at the time; and writing it all down, and putting it carefully together, made case enough for Mr. Montague to tax him with the crime, which (as he himself believed until to-night) he had committed.

449

I was by when this was done. You see him now. He is only worse than he was then."

Oh, miserable, miserable fool! oh, insupportable, excruciating torture! To find alive and active—a party to it all —the brain and right-hand of the secret he had thought to crush! In whom, though he had walled the murdered man up, by enchantment in a rock, the story would have lived and walked abroad! He tried to stop his ears with his fettered arms, that he might shut out the rest.

As he crouched upon the floor, they drew away from him as if a pestilence were in his breath. They fell off, one by one, from that part of the room, leaving him alone upon the ground. Even those who had him in their keeping shunned him, and (with the exception of Slyme, who was still occupied with his nuts) kept apart.

"From that garret-window opposite," said Nadgett, pointing across the narrow street, "I have watched this house and him for days and nights. From that garret-window opposite I saw him return home, alone, from a journey on which he had set out with Mr. Montague. That was my token that Mr. Montague's end was gained; and I might rest easy on my watch, though I was not to leave it until he dismissed me. But, standing at the door opposite, after dark that same night, I saw a countryman steal out of this house, by a side-door in the court, who had never entered it. I knew his walk, and that it was himself, disguised. I followed him immediately. I lost him on the western road, still travelling westward."

Jonas looked up at him for an instant, and muttered an oath.

"I could not comprehend what this meant," said Nadgett; "but, having seen so much, I resolved to see it out, and through. And I did. Learning, on inquiry at his house from his wife, that he was supposed to be sleeping in the room from which I had seen him go out, and that he had given strict orders not to be disturbed, I knew that he was

coming back; and for his coming back I watched. I kept
my watch in the street—in doorways, and such places—all
that night; at the same window, all next day; and when
night came on again, in the street once more. For I knew
he would come back, as he had gone out, when this part of
the town was empty. He did. Early in the morning, the
same countryman came creeping, creeping, creeping home."

"Look sharp!" interposed Slyme, who had now finished
his nuts. "This is quite irregular, Mr. Nadgett."

"I kept at the window all day," said Nadgett, without
heeding him. "I think I never closed my eyes. At night,
I saw him come out with a bundle. I followed him again.
He went down the steps at London Bridge, and sunk it in
the river. I now began to entertain some serious fears, and
made a communication to the Police, which caused that
bundle to be—"

"To be fished up," interrupted Slyme. "Be alive, Mr.
Nadgett."

"It contained the dress I had seen him wear," said Nadgett;
"stained with clay, and spotted with blood. Information of
the murder was received in town last night. The wearer of
that dress is already known to have been seen near the place;
to have been lurking in that neighbourhood; and to have
alighted from a coach coming from that part of the country,
at a time exactly tallying with the very minute when I
saw him returning home. The warrant has been out, and
these officers have been with me, some hours. We chose our
time; and seeing you come in, and seeing this person at the
window—"

"Beckoned to him," said Mark, taking up the thread of
the narrative, on hearing this allusion to himself, "to open
the door; which he did with a deal of pleasure."

"That's all at present," said Nadgett, putting up his great
pocket-book, which from mere habit he had produced when
he began his revelation, and had kept in his hand all the
time; "but there is plenty more to come. You asked me

451

for the facts, so far I have related them, and need not detain these gentlemen any longer. Are you ready, Mr. Slyme?"

"And something more," replied that worthy, rising. "If you walk round to the office, we shall be there as soon as you. Tom! Get a coach!"

The officer to whom he spoke departed for that purpose. Old Martin lingered for a few moments, as if he would have addressed some words to Jonas; but looking round, and seeing him still seated on the floor, rocking himself in a savage manner to and fro, took Chuffey's arm, and slowly followed Nadgett out. John Westlock and Mark Tapley accompanied them. Mrs. Gamp had tottered out first, for the better display of her feelings, in a kind of walking swoon; for Mrs. Gamp performed swoons of different sorts, upon a moderate notice, as Mr. Mould did Funerals.

"Ha!" muttered Slyme, looking after them. "Upon my soul! As insensible of being disgraced by having such a nephew as myself, in such a situation, as he was of my being an honour and a credit to the family! That's the return I get for having humbled my spirit—such a spirit as mine—to earn a livelihood, is it?"

He got up from his chair, and kicked it away indignantly.

"And such a livelihood too! When there are hundreds of men, not fit to hold a candle to me, rolling in carriages and living on their fortunes. Upon my soul it's a nice world!"

His eyes encountered Jonas, who looked earnestly towards him, and moved his lips as if he were whispering.

"Eh?" said Slyme.

Jonas glanced at the attendant whose back was towards him, and made a clumsy motion with his bound hands towards the door.

"Humph!" said Slyme, thoughtfully. "I couldn't hope to disgrace him into anything when you have shot so far ahead of me though. I forgot that."

Jonas repeated the same look and gesture.

"Jack!" said Slyme.

452

"Hallo!" returned his man.

"Go down to the door, ready for the coach. Call out when it comes. I'd rather have you there. Now then," he added, turning hastily to Jonas, when the man was gone. "What's the matter?"

Jonas essayed to rise.

"Stop a bit," said Slyme. "It's not so easy when your wrists are tight together. Now then! Up! What is it?"

"Put your hand in my pocket. Here! The breast pocket, on the left!" said Jonas.

He did so; and drew out a purse.

"There's a hundred pound in it," said Jonas, whose words were almost unintelligible; as his face, in its pallor and agony, was scarcely human.

Slyme looked at him; gave it into his hands; and shook his head.

"I can't. I daren't. I couldn't if I dared. Those fellows below—"

"Escape's impossible," said Jonas. "I know it. One hundred pound for only five minutes in the next room!"

"What to do?" he asked.

The face of his prisoner as he advanced to whisper in his ear, made him recoil involuntarily. But he stopped and listened to him. The words were few, but his own face changed as he heard them.

"I have it about me," said Jonas, putting his hands to his throat, as though whatever he referred to, were hidden in his neck-kerchief. "How should you know of it? How could you know? A hundred pound for only five minutes in the next room! The time's passing. Speak!"

"It would be more—more creditable to the family," observed Slyme, with trembling lips. "I wish you hadn't told me half so much. Less would have served your purpose. You might have kept it to yourself."

"A hundred pound for only five minutes in the next room! Speak!" cried Jonas, desperately.

He took the purse. Jonas, with a wild unsteady step, retreated to the door in the glass partition.

"Stop!" cried Slyme, catching at his skirts. "I don't know about this. Yet it must end so at last. Are you guilty?"

"Yes!" said Jonas.

"Are the proofs as they were told just now?"

"Yes!" said Jonas.

"Will you—will you engage to say a—a Prayer, now, or something of that sort?" faltered Slyme.

Jonas broke from him without replying, and closed the door between them.

Slyme listened at the keyhole. After that, he crept away on tiptoe, as far off as he could; and looked awfully towards the place. He was roused by the arrival of the coach, and their letting down the steps.

"He's getting a few things together," he said, leaning out of window, and speaking to the two men below, who stood in the full light of a street-lamp. "Keep your eye upon the back, one of you, for form's sake."

One of the men withdrew into the court. The other, seating himself on the steps of the coach, remained in conversation with Slyme at the window : who perhaps had risen to be his superior, in virtue of his old propensity (one so much lauded by the murdered man) of being always round the corner. A useful habit in his present calling.

"Where is he?" asked the man.

Slyme looked into the room for an instant and gave his head a jerk, as much as to say, "Close at hand. I see him."

"He's booked," observed the man.

"Through," said Slyme.

They looked at each other, and up and down the street. The man on the coach-steps took his hat off, and put it on again, and whistled a little.

"I say! He's taking his time!" he remonstrated.

"I allowed him five minutes," said Slyme. "Time's more than up, though. I'll bring him down."

454

He withdrew from the window accordingly, and walked on tiptoe to the door in the partition. He listened. There was not a sound within. He set the candles near it, that they might shine through the glass.

It was not easy, he found, to make up his mind to the opening of the door. But he flung it wide open suddenly, and with a noise; then retreated. After peeping in and listening again, he entered.

He started back as his eyes met those of Jonas, standing in an angle of the wall, and staring at him. His neck-kerchief was off; his face was ashy pale.

"You're too soon," said Jonas, with an abject whimper. "I've not had time. I have not been able to do it. I—five minutes more—two minutes more!—Only one!"

Slyme gave him no reply, but thrusting the purse upon him and forcing it back into his pocket, called up his men.

He whined, and cried, and cursed, and entreated them, and struggled, and submitted, in the same breath, and had no power to stand. They got him away and into the coach, where they put him on a seat; but he soon fell moaning down among the straw at the bottom, and lay there.

The two men were with him; Slyme being on the box with the driver; and they let him lie. Happening to pass a fruiterer's on their way; the door of which was open, though the shop was by this time shut; one of them remarked how faint the peaches smelt.

The other assented at the moment, but presently stooped down in quick alarm, and looked at the prisoner.

"Stop the coach! He has poisoned himself! The smell comes from this bottle in his hand!"

The hand had shut upon it tight. With that rigidity of grasp with which no living man, in the full strength and energy of life, can clutch a prize he has won.

They dragged him out, into the dark street; but jury, judge, and hangman, could have done no more, and could do nothing now. Dead, dead, dead.

455

CHAPTER LII

IN WHICH THE TABLES ARE TURNED, COMPLETELY UPSIDE DOWN.

OLD MARTIN's cherished projects, so long hidden in his own breast, so frequently in danger of abrupt disclosure through the bursting forth of the indignation he had hoarded up, during his residence with Mr. Pecksniff, were retarded, but not beyond a few hours, by the occurrences just now related. Stunned, as he had been at first by the intelligence conveyed to him through Tom Pinch and John Westlock, of the supposed manner of his brother's death; overwhelmed as he was by the subsequent narratives of Chuffey and Nadgett, and the forging of that chain of circumstances ending in the death of Jonas, of which catastrophe he was immediately informed; scattered as his purposes and hopes were for the moment, by the crowding in of all these incidents between him and his end; still their very intensity and the tumult of their assemblage nerved him to the rapid and unyielding execution of his scheme. In every single circumstance, whether it were cruel, cowardly, or false, he saw the flowering of the same pregnant seed. Self; grasping, eager, narrow-ranging, over-reaching self; with its long train of suspicions, lusts, deceits, and all their growing consequences; was the root of the vile tree. Mr. Pecksniff had so presented his character before the old man's eyes, that he—the good, the tolerant, enduring Pecksniff—had become the incarnation of all selfishness and treachery; and the more odious the shapes in which those vices ranged themselves

456

before him now, the sterner consolation he had in his design of setting Mr. Pecksniff right, and Mr. Pecksniff's victims too.

To this work he brought, not only the energy and determination natural to his character (which, as the reader may have observed in the beginning of his or her acquaintance with this gentleman, was remarkable for the strong development of those qualities), but all the forced and unnaturally nurtured energy consequent upon their long suppression. And these two tides of resolution setting into one and sweeping on, became so strong and vigorous, that, to prevent themselves from being carried away before it, Heaven knows where, was as much as John Westlock and Mark Tapley together (though they were tolerably energetic too) could manage to effect.

He had sent for John Westlock immediately on his arrival; and John, under the conduct of Tom Pinch, had waited on him. Having a lively recollection of Mr. Tapley, he had caused that gentleman's attendance to be secured, through John's means, without delay; and thus, as we have seen, they had all repaired, together, to the City. But his grandson he had refused to see until to-morrow, when Mr. Tapley was instructed to summon him to the Temple at ten o'clock in the forenoon. Tom he would not allow to be employed in anything, lest he should be wrongfully suspected; but he was a party to all their proceedings, and was with them until late at night—until after they knew of the death of Jonas; when he went home to tell all these wonders to little Ruth, and to prepare her for accompanying him to the Temple in the morning, agreeably to Mr. Chuzzlewit's particular injunction.

It was characteristic of old Martin, and his looking on to something which he had distinctly before him, that he communicated to them nothing of his intentions, beyond such hints of reprisal on Mr. Pecksniff as they gathered from the game he had played in that gentleman's house, and the brightening of his eyes whenever his name was mentioned. Even to John Westlock, in whom he was evidently disposed to place great confidence (which may indeed be said of every one of them), he gave no explanation whatever. He merely requested him to return in the morning; and with this for their utmost satisfaction, they left him, when the night was far advanced, alone.

The events of such a day might have worn out the body and spirit of a much younger man than he, but he sat in deep and painful meditation until the morning was bright. Nor did he even then seek any prolonged repose, but merely slumbered in his chair, until seven o'clock, when Mr. Tapley had appointed to come to him by his desire: and came—as fresh and clean and cheerful as the morning itself.

"You are punctual," said Mr. Chuzzlewit, opening the door to him in reply to his light knock, which had roused him instantly.

"My wishes, sir," replied Mr. Tapley, whose mind would appear from the context to have been running on the matrimonial service, "is to love, honour, and obey. The clock's a-striking now, sir."

"Come in!"

"Thank'ee, sir," rejoined Mr. Tapley, "what could I do for you first, sir?"

"You gave my message to Martin?" said the old man, bending his eyes upon him.

"I did, sir," returned Mark; "and you never see a gentleman more surprised in all your born days than he was."

"What more did you tell him?" Mr. Chuzzlewit inquired.

"Why, sir," said Mr. Tapley, smiling, "I should have liked to tell him a deal more, but not being able, sir, I didn't tell it him."

"You told him all you knew?"

"But it was precious little, sir," retorted Mr. Tapley. "There was very little respectin' you that I was able to tell him, sir. I only mentioned my opinion that Mr. Pecksniff would find himself deceived, sir, and that you would find yourself deceived, and that he would find himself deceived, sir."

"In what?" asked Mr. Chuzzlewit.

"Meaning him, sir?"

"Meaning both him and me."

"Well, sir," said Mr. Tapley. "In your old opinions of each other. As to him, sir, and his opinions, I know he's a altered man. I know it. I know'd it long afore he spoke to you t'other day, and I must say it. Nobody don't know half as much of him as I do. Nobody can't. There was always a deal of good in him, but a little of it got crusted over, somehow. I can't say who rolled the paste of that 'ere crust myself, but—— "

"Go on," said Martin. "Why do you stop?"

"But it—well! I beg your pardon, but I think it may have been you, sir. Unintentional I think it may have been you. I don't believe that neither of you gave the other quite a fair chance. There! Now I've got rid on it," said Mr. Tapley in a fit of desperation: "I can't go a carryin' it about in my own mind, bustin' myself with it; yesterday was quite long enough. It's out now. I can't help it. I'm sorry for it. Don't wisit it on him, sir, that's all."

It was clear that Mark expected to be ordered out immediately, and was quite prepared to go.

"So you think," said Martin, "that his old faults are, in some degree, of my creation, do you?"

"Well, sir," retorted Mr. Tapley, "I'm wery sorry, but I can't unsay it. It's hardly fair of you, sir, to make a ignorant man conwict himself in this way, but I do think so. I am as respectful disposed to you, sir, as a man can be; but I *do* think so."

The light of a faint smile seemed to break through the dull steadiness of Martin's face, as he looked attentively at him, without replying.

"Yet you are an ignorant man, you say," he observed after a long pause.

"Wery much so," Mr. Tapley replied.

"And I a learned, well-instructed man, you think?"

"Likewise wery much so," Mr. Tapley answered.

The old man, with his chin resting on his hand, paced the room twice or thrice before he added:

"You have left him this morning?"

"Come straight from him now, sir."

"For what: does he suppose?"

"He don't know what to suppose, sir, no more than myself. I told him jest wot passed yesterday, sir, and that you had said to me, 'Can you be here by seven in the morning?' and that you had said to him, through me, 'Can you be here by ten in the morning?' and that I had said 'Yes' to both. That's all, sir."

His frankness was so genuine that it plainly *was* all.

"Perhaps," said Martin, "he may think you are going to desert him, and to serve me?"

"I have served him in that sort of way, sir," replied Mark, without the loss of any atom of his self-possession; "and we have been that sort of companions in misfortune, that my opinion is, he don't believe a word on it. No more than you do, sir."

"Will you help me to dress? and get me some breakfast from the hotel?" asked Martin.

"With pleasure, sir," said Mark.

"And by-and-by," pursued Martin, "remaining in the room, as I wish you to do, will you attend to the door yonder— give admission to visitors, I mean, when they knock?"

"Certainly, sir," said Mr. Tapley.

"You will not find it necessary to express surprise at their appearance," Martin suggested.

"Oh dear no, sir!" said Mr. Tapley, "not at all."

Although he pledged himself to this with perfect confidence, he was in a state of unbounded astonishment even now. Martin appeared to observe it, and to have some sense of the ludicrous bearing of Mr. Tapley under these perplexing circumstances; for in spite of the composure of his voice and the gravity of his face, the same indistinct light flickered on the latter several times. Mark bestirred himself, however, to execute the offices with which he was entrusted; and soon lost all tendency to any outward expression of his surprise, in the occupation of being brisk and busy.

But when he had put Mr. Chuzzlewit's clothes in good order for dressing, and when that gentleman was dressed and sitting at his breakfast, Mr. Tapley's feelings of wonder began to return upon him with great violence; and, standing beside the old man with a napkin under his arm (it was as natural and easy a joke to Mark to be a butler in the Temple, as it had been to volunteer as cook on board the Screw), he found it difficult to resist the temptation of casting sidelong glances at him very often. Nay, he found it impossible; and accordingly yielded to this impulse so often, that Martin caught him in the fact some fifty times. The extraordinary things Mr. Tapley did with his own face when any of these detections occurred; the sudden occasions he had to rub his eyes or his nose or his chin; the look of wisdom with which he immediately plunged into the deepest thought, or became intensely interested in the habits and customs of the flies upon the ceiling, or the sparrows out of doors; or the overwhelming politeness with which he endeavoured to hide his confusion by handing the muffin; may not unreasonably be assumed to have exercised the utmost power of feature that even Martin Chuzzlewit the elder possessed.

But he sat perfectly quiet and took his breakfast at his leisure, or made a show of doing so, for he scarcely ate or drank, and frequently lapsed into long intervals of musing. When he had finished, Mark sat down to his breakfast at the same table; and Mr. Chuzzlewit, quite silent still, walked up and down the room.

Mark cleared away in due course, and set a chair out for him, in which, as the time drew on towards ten o'clock, he took his seat, leaning his hands upon his stick, and clenching them upon the handle, and resting his chin on them again. All his impatience and abstraction of manner had vanished now; and as he sat there, looking, with his keen eyes, steadily towards the door, Mark could not help thinking what a firm, square, powerful face it was; or exulting in the thought that Mr. Pecksniff, after playing a pretty long game of bowls with its owner, seemed to be at last in a very fair way of coming in for a rubber or two.

Mark's uncertainty in respect of what was going to be done or said, and by whom to whom, would have excited him in itself. But knowing for a certainty besides, that young Martin was coming, and in a very few minutes must arrive, he found it by no means easy to remain quiet and silent. But, excepting that he occasionally coughed in a hollow and unnatural manner to relieve himself, he behaved with great decorum through the longest ten minutes he had ever known.

A knock at the door. Mr. Westlock. Mr. Tapley, in admitting him, raised his eyebrows to the highest possible pitch, implying thereby that he considered himself in an unsatisfactory position. Mr. Chuzzlewit received him very courteously.

Mark waited at the door for Tom Pinch and his sister, who were coming up the stairs. The old man went to meet them; took their hands in his; and kissed her on the cheek. As this looked promising, Mr. Tapley smiled benignantly.

Mr. Chuzzlewit had resumed his chair, before young Martin, who was close behind them, entered. The old man, scarcely looking at him, pointed to a distant seat. This was less encouraging; and Mr. Tapley's spirits fell again.

He was quickly summoned to the door by another knock. He did not start, or cry, or tumble down, at sight of Miss Graham and Mrs. Lupin, but he drew a very long breath, and came back perfectly resigned, looking on them and on the rest with an expression which seemed to say, that nothing could surprise him any more; and that he was rather glad to have done with that sensation for ever.

The old man received Mary no less tenderly than he had received Tom Pinch's sister. A look of friendly recognition passed between himself and Mrs. Lupin, which implied the existence of a perfect understanding between them. It engendered no astonishment in Mr. Tapley; for, as he afterwards observed, he had retired from the business, and sold off the stock.

Not the least curious feature in this assemblage was, that everybody present was so much surprised and embarrassed by the sight of everybody else, that nobody ventured to speak. Mr. Chuzzlewit alone broke silence.

"Set the door open, Mark!" he said; "and come here." Mark obeyed.

The last appointed footstep sounded now upon the stairs. They all knew it. It was Mr. Pecksniff's; and Mr. Pecksniff was in a hurry too, for he came bounding up with such uncommon expedition that he stumbled twice or thrice.

"Where is my venerable friend?" he cried upon the upper landing; and then with open arms came darting in.

Old Martin merely looked at him; but Mr. Pecksniff started back as if he had received the charge of an electric battery.

"My venerable friend is well?" cried Mr. Pecksniff.

"Quite well."

It seemed to reassure the anxious inquirer. He clasped his hands, and, looking upwards with a pious joy, silently expressed his gratitude. He then looked round on the assembled group, and shook his head reproachfully. For such a man severely, quite severely.

"Oh, vermin!" said Mr. Pecksniff. "Oh, bloodsuckers! Is it not enough that you have embittered the existence of an individual, wholly unparalleled in the biographical records of amiable persons; but must you now, even now, when he has made his election, and reposed his trust in a Numble, but at least sincere and disinterested relative; must you now, vermin and swarmers (I regret to make use of these strong expressions, my dear sir, but there are times when honest indignation will not be controlled), must you now, vermin and swarmers (for I WILL repeat it), taking advantage of his unprotected state, assemble round him from all quarters, as wolves and vultures, and other animals of the feathered tribe assemble round—I will not say round carrion or a carcass, for Mr. Chuzzlewit is quite the contrary—but round their prey—their prey—to rifle and despoil; gorging their voracious maws, and staining their offensive beaks, with every description of carnivorous enjoyment!"

As he stopped to fetch his breath, he waved them off, in a solemn manner, with his hand.

"Horde of unnatural plunderers and robbers!" he continued; "leave him! leave him, I say! Begone! Abscond! You had better be off! Wander over the face of the earth, young sirs, like vagabonds as you are, and do not presume to remain in a spot which is hallowed by the grey hairs of the patriarchal gentleman to whose tottering limbs I have the honour to act as an unworthy, but I hope an unassuming, prop and staff. And you, my tender sir," said Mr. Pecksniff, addressing himself in a tone of gentle remonstrance to the old man, "how could you ever leave me, though even for this short period! You have absented yourself, I do not doubt, upon some act of kindness to me; bless you for it: but you must not do it; you must not be so venturesome. I should really be angry with you if I could, my friend!"

He advanced with outstretched arms to take the old man's hand. But he had not seen how the hand clasped and clutched the stick within its grasp. As he came smiling on, and got within his reach, old Martin, with his burning indignation crowded into one vehement burst, and flashing out of every line and wrinkle in his face, rose up, and struck him down upon the ground.

With such a well-directed nervous blow, that down he went, as heavily and true as if the charge of a Life-Guardsman had tumbled him out of a saddle. And whether he was stunned by the shock, or only confused by the wonder and novelty of this warm reception, he did not offer to get up again; but lay there, looking about him, with a disconcerted meekness in his face so enormously ridiculous, that neither Mark Tapley nor John Westlock could repress a smile, though both were actively interposing to prevent a repetition of the blow; which the old man's gleaming eyes and vigorous attitude seemed to render one of the most probable events in the world.

"Drag him away! Take him out of my reach!" said Martin; "or I can't help it. The strong restraint I have put upon my hands has been enough to palsy them. I am not master of myself, while he is within their range. Drag him away!"

Seeing that he still did not rise, Mr. Tapley, without any compromise about it, actually did drag him away, and stick him up on the floor, with his back against the opposite wall.

"Hear me, rascal!" said Mr. Chuzzlewit. "I have summoned you here to witness your own work. I have summoned you here to witness it, because I know it will be gall and wormwood to you! I have summoned you here to witness it, because I know the sight of everybody here must be a dagger in your mean false heart! What! do you know me as I am, at last!"

Mr. Pecksniff had cause to stare at him, for the triumph in his face and speech and figure was a sight to stare at.

"Look there!" said the old man, pointing at him, and appealing to the rest. "Look there! And then—come hither, my dear Martin—look here! here! here!" At every repetition of the word he pressed his grandson closer to his breast.

"The passion I felt, Martin, when I dared not do this," he said, "was in the blow I struck just now. Why did we ever part! How could we ever part! How could you ever fly from me to him!"

Martin was about to answer, but he stopped him, and went on.

"The fault was mine no less than yours. Mark has told me so to-day, and I have known it long; though not so long as I might have done. Mary, my love, come here."

As she trembled and was very pale, he sat her in his own

chair, and stood beside it with her hand in his; and Martin standing by him.

"The curse of our house," said the old man, looking kindly down upon her, "has been the love of self; has ever been the love of self. How often have I said so, when I never knew that I had wrought it upon others!"

He drew one hand through Martin's arm, and standing so, between them, proceeded thus:

"You all know how I bred this orphan up, to tend me. None of you can know by what degrees I have come to regard her as a daughter; for she has won upon me, by her self-forgetfulness, her tenderness, her patience, all the goodness of her nature, when Heaven is her witness that I took but little pains to draw it forth. It blossomed without cultivation, and it ripened without heat. I cannot find it in my heart to say that I am sorry for it now, or yonder fellow might be holding up his head."

Mr. Pecksniff put his hand into his waistcoat, and slightly shook that part of him to which allusion had been made: as if to signify that it was still uppermost.

"There is a kind of selfishness," said Martin: "I have learned it in my own experience of my own breast; which is constantly upon the watch for selfishness in others; and holding others at a distance by suspicions and distrusts, wonders why they don't approach, and don't confide, and calls that selfishness in them. Thus I once doubted those about me—not without reason in the beginning—and thus I once doubted you, Martin."

"Not without reason," Martin answered; "either."

"Listen, hypocrite! Listen, smooth-tongued, servile, crawling knave!" said Martin. "Listen, you shallow dog. What! When I was seeking him, you had already spread your nets; you were already fishing for him, were ye? When I lay ill in this good woman's house, and your meek spirit pleaded for my grandson, you had already caught him, had ye? Counting on the restoration of the love you knew I bore him, you

466

Warm Reception of Mr. Pecksniff by his Venerable Friend

designed him for one of your two daughters, did ye? Or failing that, you traded in him as a speculation which at any rate should blind me with the lustre of your charity, and found a claim upon me! Why, even then I knew you, and I told you so. Did I tell you that I knew you, even then?

"I am not angry, sir," said Mr. Pecksniff, softly. "I can bear a great deal from you. I will never contradict you, Mr. Chuzzlewit."

"Observe!" said Martin, looking round. "I put myself in that man's hands on terms as mean and base, and as degrading to himself as I could render them in words. I stated them at length to him, before his own children, syllable by syllable, as coarsely as I could, and with as much offence, and with as plain an exposition of my contempt, as words—not looks and manner merely—could convey. If I had only called the angry blood into his face, I would have wavered in my purpose. If I had only stung him into being a man for a minute I would have abandoned it. If he had offered me one word of remonstrance, in favour of the grandson whom he supposed I had disinherited; if he had pleaded with me, though never so faintly, against my appeal to him to abandon him to misery and cast him from his house; I think I could have borne with him for ever afterwards. But not a word, not a word. Pandering to the worst of human passions was the office of his nature; and faithfully he did his work!"

"I am not angry," observed Mr. Pecksniff. "I am hurt, Mr. Chuzzlewit: wounded in my feelings: but I am not angry, my good sir."

Mr. Chuzzlewit resumed.

"Once resolved to try him, I was resolute to pursue the trial to the end; but while I was bent on fathoming the depth of his duplicity, I made a sacred compact with myself that I would give him credit on the other side for any latent spark of goodness, honour, forbearance—any virtue—that might glimmer in him. From first to last, there has been no such thing. Not once. He cannot say I have not given him opportunity. He cannot say I have ever led him on. He cannot say I have not left him freely to himself in all things; or that I have not been a passive instrument in his hands, which he might have used for good as easily as evil. Or if he can, he Lies! And that's his nature too."

"Mr. Chuzzlewit," interrupted Pecksniff, shedding tears. "I am not angry, sir. I cannot be angry with you. But did you never, my dear sir, express a desire that the unnatural young man who by his wicked arts has estranged your good opinion from me, for the time being: only for the time being: that your grandson, Mr. Chuzzlewit, should be dismissed my house? Recollect yourself, my Christian friend."

"I have said so, have I not?" retorted the old man, sternly. "I could not tell how far your specious hypocrisy had deceived him, knave; and knew no better way of opening his eyes than by presenting you before him in your own servile character. Yes. I did express that desire. And you leaped to meet it; and you met it; and turning in an instant on the hand you had licked and beslavered, as only such hounds can, you strengthened, and confirmed, and justified me in my scheme."

Mr. Pecksniff made a bow; a submissive, not to say, a grovelling and an abject bow. If he had been complimented on his practice of the loftiest virtues, he never could have bowed as he bowed then.

"The wretched man who has been murdered," Mr. Chuzzlewit went on to say; "then passing by the name of——"

"Tigg," suggested Mark.

"Of Tigg—brought begging messages to me, on behalf of a friend of his, and an unworthy relative of mine; and finding him a man well enough suited to my purpose, I employed him to glean some news of you, Martin, for me. It was from him I learned that you had taken up your abode with yonder fellow. It was he, who meeting you here, in town, one evening —you remember where?"

"At the pawnbroker's shop," said Martin.

"Yes; watched you to your lodging, and enabled me to send you a Bank note."

"I little thought," said Martin, greatly moved, "that it had come from you. I little thought that you were interested in my fate. If I had——"

"If you had," returned the old man, sorrowfully, "you would have shown less knowledge of me as I seemed to be, and as I really was. I hoped to bring you back, Martin, penitent and humbled. I hoped to distress you into coming back to me. Much as I loved you, I had that to acknowledge which I could not reconcile it to myself to avow, then, unless you made submission to me, first. Thus it was I lost you. If I have had, indirectly, any act or part in the fate of that unhappy man, by putting means, however small, within his reach; Heaven forgive me! I might have known, perhaps, that he would misuse money; that it was ill-bestowed upon him; and that sown by his hands, it could engender mischief only. But I never thought of him at that time, as having the disposition or ability to be a serious impostor, or otherwise than as a thoughtless, idle-humoured, dissipated spendthrift, sinning more against himself than others, and frequenting low haunts and indulging vicious tastes, to his own ruin only."

"Beggin' your pardon, sir," said Mr. Tapley, who had Mrs. Lupin on his arm by this time, quite agreeably: "if I may make so bold as say so, my opinion is, as you was quite correct, and that he turned out perfectly nat'ral for all that. There's a surprisin' number of men, sir, who as long as they've only got their own shoes and stockings to depend upon, will walk down-hill, along the gutters quiet enough, and by themselves, and not do much harm. But set any on 'em up with a coach and horses, sir; and it's wonderful what a knowledge of drivin' he'll show, and how he'll fill his wehicle with passengers, and start off in the middle of the road, neck or nothing, to the Devil! Bless your heart, sir, there's ever so many Tiggs a passing this here Temple-gate any hour in the day, that only want a chance, to turn out full-blown Montagues every one!"

" Your ignorance, as you call it, Mark," said Mr. Chuzzlewit, "is wiser than some men's enlightenment, and mine among them. You are right; not for the first time to-day. Now hear me out, my dears. And hear me, you, who, if what I have been told be accurately stated, are Bankrupt in pocket no less than in good name! And when you have heard me, leave this place, and poison my sight no more!"

Mr. Pecksniff laid his hand upon his breast, and bowed again.

"The penance I have done in his house," said Mr. Chuzzlewit, "has carried this reflection with it constantly, above all others. That if it had pleased Heaven to visit such infirmity on my old age as really had reduced me to the state in which I feigned to be, I should have brought its misery upon myself. Oh you whose wealth, like mine, has been a source of continual unhappiness, leading you to distrust the nearest and dearest, and to dig yourself a living grave of suspicion and reserve; take heed that, having cast off all whom you might have bound to you, and tenderly, you do not become in your decay the instrument of such a man as this, and waken in another world to the knowledge of such wrong, as would embitter Heaven itself, if wrong or you could ever reach it!"

And then he told them, how he had sometimes thought, in the beginning, that love might grow up between Mary and Martin; and how he had pleased his fancy with the picture of observing it when it was new, and taking them to task, apart, in counterfeited doubt, and then confessing to them that it had been an object dear to his heart; and by his sympathy with them, and generous provision for their young fortunes, establishing a claim on their affection and regard which nothing should wither, and which should surround his old age with means of happiness. How in the first dawn of this design, and when the pleasure of such a scheme for the happiness of others was new and indistinct within him, Martin had come to tell him that he had already chosen for himself; knowing that he, the old man, had some faint project on that head, but ignorant whom it concerned. How it was little comfort to him to know that Martin had chosen Her, because the grace of his design was lost, and because finding that she had returned his love, he tortured himself with the reflection that they, so young, to whom he had been so kind a benefactor, were already like the world, and bent on their own selfish, stealthy ends. How in the bitterness of this impression, and of his past experience, he had reproached Martin so harshly (forgetting that he had never invited his confidence on such a point, and confounding what he had meant to do with what he had done), that high words sprung up between them, and they separated in wrath. How he loved him still, and hoped he would return. How on the night of his illness at the Dragon, he had secretly written tenderly of him, and made him his heir, and sanctioned his marriage with Mary; and how, after his interview with Mr. Pecksniff, he had distrusted him again, and burnt the paper to ashes, and had lain down in his bed distracted by suspicions, doubts, and regrets.

And then he told them how, resolved to probe this Pecksniff, and to prove the constancy and truth of Mary (to himself no less than Martin), he had conceived and entered on his plan; and how, beneath her gentleness and patience, he had softened more and more; still more and more beneath the goodness and simplicity, the honour and the manly faith of Tom. And when he spoke of Tom, he said God bless him; and the tears were in his eyes; for he said that Tom, mistrusted and disliked by him at first, had come like summer rain upon his heart; and had disposed it to believe in better things. And Martin took him by the hand, and Mary too, and John, his old friend, stoutly too: and Mark, and Mrs. Lupin, and his sister, little Ruth. And peace of mind, deep, tranquil peace of mind was on Tom Pinch.

The old man then related how nobly Mr. Pecksniff had performed the duty in which he stood indebted to society, in the matter of Tom's dismissal; and how, having often heard disparagement of Mr. Westlock from Pecksniffian lips, and knowing him to be a friend to Tom, he had used, through his confidential agent and solicitor, that little artifice which had kept him in readiness to receive his unknown friend in London. And he called on Mr. Pecksniff (by the name of Scoundrel) to remember that there again he had not trapped him to do evil, but that he had done it of his own free will and agency; nay, that he had cautioned him against it. And once again he called on Mr. Pecksniff (by the name of Hangdog) to remember that when Martin coming home at last, an altered man, had sued for the forgiveness which awaited him, he, Pecksniff, had rejected him in language of his own, and had remorselessly stepped in between him and the least touch of natural tenderness. "For which," said the old man, "if the bending of my finger would remove a halter from your neck, I wouldn't bend it!"

"Martin," he added, "your rival has not been a dangerous one, but Mrs. Lupin here, has played duenna for some weeks; not so much to watch your love as to watch her lover. For that Ghoul" —his fertility in finding names for Mr. Pecksniff was astonishing—"would have crawled into her daily walks otherwise, and polluted the fresh air. What's this? Her hand is trembling strangely. See if you can hold it."

Hold it! If he clasped it half as tightly as he did her waist.——Well, well!

But it was good in him that even then, in his high fortune and happiness, with her lips nearly printed on his own, and her proud young beauty in his close embrace, he had a hand still left to stretch out to Tom Pinch.

"Oh, Tom! Dear Tom! I saw you, accidentally, coming here. Forgive me!"

"Forgive!" cried Tom. "I'll never forgive you as long as I live, Martin, if you say another syllable about it. Joy to you both! Joy, my dear fellow, fifty thousand times."

Joy! There is not a blessing on earth that Tom did not wish them. There is not a blessing on earth that Tom would not have bestowed upon them, if he could.

"I beg your pardon, sir," said Mr. Tapley, stepping forward, "but you was mentionin', just now, a lady of the name of Lupin, sir."

"I was," returned old Martin.

"Yes, sir. It's a pretty name, sir?"

"A very good name," said Martin.

"It seems a'most a pity to change such a name into Tapley. Don't it, sir?" said Mark.

"That depends upon the lady. What is *her* opinion?"

"Why, sir," said Mr. Tapley, retiring, with a bow, towards the buxom hostess, "her opinion is as the name ain't a change for the better, but the indiwidual may be, and therefore, if nobody ain't acquainted with no jest cause or impediment, et cetrer, the Blue Dragon will be con-werted into the Jolly Tapley. A sign of my own inwention, sir. Wery new, conwivial, and expressive!"

The whole of these proceedings were so agreeable to Mr. Pecksniff, that he stood with his eyes fixed upon the floor and his hands clasping one another alternately, as if a host of penal sentences were being passed upon him. Not only did his figure appear to have shrunk, but his discomfiture seemed to have extended itself, even to his dress. His clothes seemed to have grown shabbier, his linen to have turned yellow, his hair to have become lank and frowsy; his very boots looked villanous and dim, as if their gloss had departed with his own.

Feeling, rather than seeing, that the old man now pointed to the door, he raised his eyes, picked up his hat, and thus addressed him:

"Mr. Chuzzlewit, sir! you have partaken of my hospitality."

"And paid for it," he observed.

"Thank you. That savours," said Mr. Pecksniff, taking out his pocket-handkerchief, "of your old familiar frankness. You have paid for it. I was about to make the remark. You have deceived me, sir. Thank you again. I am glad of it. To see you in the possession of your health and faculties on any terms, is, in itself, a sufficient recompense. To have been deceived, implies a trusting nature. Mine is a trusting nature. I am thankful for it. I would rather have a trusting nature, do you know, sir, than a doubting one!"

Here Mr. Pecksniff, with a sad smile, bowed, and wiped his eyes.

" There is hardly any person present, Mr. Chuzzlewit," said Pecksniff, " by whom I have *not* been deceived. I have forgiven those persons on the spot. That was my duty; and, of course, I have done it. Whether it was worthy of you to partake of my hospitality, and to act the part you did act in my house, that, sir, is a question which I leave to your own conscience. And your conscience does not acquit you. No, sir, no!"

Pronouncing these last words in a loud and solemn voice, Mr. Pecksniff was not so absolutely lost in his own fervour as to be unmindful of the expediency of getting a little nearer to the door.

"I have been struck this day," said Mr. Pecksniff, " with a walking-stick (which I have every reason to believe has knobs upon it), on that delicate and exquisite portion of the human anatomy, the brain. Several blows have been inflicted, sir, without a walking-stick, upon that tenderer portion of my frame: my heart. You have mentioned, sir, my being bankrupt in my purse. Yes, sir, I am. By an unfortunate speculation, combined with treachery, I find myself reduced to poverty; at a time, sir, when the child of my bosom is widowed, and affliction and disgrace are in my family."

Here Mr. Pecksniff wiped his eyes again, and gave himself two or three little knocks upon the breast, as if he were answering two or three other little knocks from within, given by the tinkling hammer of his conscience, to express " Cheer up, my boy!"

"I know the human mind, although I trust it. That is my weakness. Do I not know, sir;" here he became exceedingly plaintive, and was observed to glance towards Tom Pinch;

" that my misfortunes bring this treatment on me? Do I not know, sir, that but for them I never should have heard what I have heard to-day? Do I not know, that in the silence and the solitude of night, a little voice will whisper in your ear, Mr. Chuzzlewit, 'This was not well. This was not well, sir!' Think of this, sir (if you will have the goodness), remote from the impulses of passion, and apart from the specialities, if I may use that strong remark, of prejudice. And if you ever contemplate the silent tomb, sir, which you will excuse me for entertaining some doubt of your doing, after the conduct into which you have allowed yourself to be betrayed this day; if you ever contemplate the silent tomb, sir, think of me. If you find yourself approaching to the silent tomb, sir, think of me. If you should wish to have anything inscribed upon your silent tomb, sir, let it be, that I—ah, my remorseful sir! that I—the humble individual who has now the honour of reproaching you, forgave you. That I forgave you when my injuries were fresh, and when my bosom was newly wrung. It may be bitterness to you to hear it now, sir, but you will live to seek a consolation in it. May you find a consolation in it when you want it, sir! Good morning!"

With this sublime address, Mr. Pecksniff departed. But the effect of his departure was much impaired by his being immediately afterwards run against, and nearly knocked down by, a monstrously-excited little man in velveteen shorts and a very tall hat; who came bursting up the stairs, and straight into the chambers of Mr. Chuzzlewit, as if he were deranged.

"Is there anybody here that knows him?" cried the little man. "Is there anybody here that knows him? Oh, my stars, is there anybody here that knows him!"

They looked at each other for an explanation, but nobody knew anything more than that here was an excited little man with a very tall hat on, running in and out of the room as hard as he could go; making his single pair of bright blue stockings appear at least a dozen; and constantly repeating in a shrill voice, "*Is* there anybody here that knows him?"

"If your brains is not turned topjy turjey, Mr. Sweedle-pipes!" exclaimed another voice, "hold that there nige of yourn, I beg you, sir."

At the same time Mrs. Gamp was seen in the doorway; out of breath from coming up so many stairs, and panting fearfully; but dropping curtseys to the last.

"Excuge the weakness of the man," said Mrs. Gamp, eyeing Mr. Sweedlepipe with great indignation; "and well I might expect it, as I should have know'd, and wishin' he was drownded in the Thames afore I had brought him here, which not a blessed hour ago he nearly shaved the noge off from the father of as lovely a family as ever, Mr. Chuzzlewit, was born three sets of twins, and would have done it, only he see it a goin' in the glass, and dodged the rager. And never, Mr. Sweedlepipes, I do assure you, sir, did I so well know what a misfortun it was to be acquainted with you, as now I do, which so I say, sir, and I don't deceive you!"

"I ask your pardon, ladies and gentlemen all," cried the little barber, taking off his hat, "and yours too, Mrs. Gamp. But—but," he added this, half-laughing and half-crying, "*Is* there anybody here that knows him!"

As the barber said these words, a something in top-boots, with its head bandaged up, staggered into the room, and began going round and round and round, apparently under the impression that it was walking straight forward.

"Look at him!" cried the excited little barber. "Here he is! That'll soon wear off, and then he'll be all right again. He's no more dead than I am. He's all alive and hearty. Ain't you, Bailey?"

"R—r—reether so, Poll!" replied that gentleman.

"Look here!" cried the little barber, laughing and crying in the same breath. "When I steady him he comes all right. There! He's all right now. Nothing's the matter with him now, except that he's a little shook and rather giddy; is there, Bailey?"

"R—r—reether shook, Poll—reether so!" said Mr. Bailey. "What, my lovely Sairey! There you air!"

"What a boy he is!" cried the tender-hearted Poll, actually sobbing over him. "I never see sech a boy! It's all his fun. He's full of it. He shall go into the business along with me. I am determined he shall. We'll make it Sweedlepipe and Bailey. He shall have the sporting branch (what a one he'll be for the matches!) and me the shavin'. I'll make over the birds to him as soon as ever he's well enough. He shall have the little bullfinch in the shop, and all. He's sech a boy! I ask your pardon, ladies and gentlemen, but I thought there might be some one here that know'd him!"

Mrs. Gamp had observed, not without jealousy and scorn, that a favourable impression appeared to exist in behalf of Mr. Sweedlepipe and his young friend; and that she had fallen rather into the background in consequence. She now struggled to the front, therefore, and stated her business.

"Which, Mr. Chuzzlewit," she said, "is well beknown to Mrs. Harris as has one sweet infant (though she *do* not wish it known) in her own family by the mother's side, kep in spirits in a bottle; and that sweet babe she see at Greenwich Fair, a travelling in company with the pink-eyed lady, Prooshan dwarf, and livin' skelinton, which judge her feelins when the barrel organ played, and she was showed her own dear sister's child, the same not bein' expected from the outside picter, where it was painted quite contrairy in a livin' state, a many sizes larger, and performing beautiful upon the Arp, which never did that dear child know or do: since breathe it never did, to speak on, in this wale! And Mrs. Harris, Mr. Chuzzlewit, has knowed me many year, and can give you information that the lady which is widdered can't do better and may do worse, than let me wait upon her, which I hope to do. Permittin' the sweet faces as I see afore me."

"Oh!" said Mr. Chuzzlewit. "Is that your business? Was this good person paid for the trouble we gave her?"

"I paid her, sir," returned Mark Tapley; "liberal."

477

"The young man's words is true," said Mrs. Gamp, "and thank you kindly."

"Then here we will close our acquaintance, Mrs. Gamp," retorted Mr. Chuzzlewit. "And Mr. Sweedlepipe—is that your name?"

"That is my name, sir," replied Poll, accepting with a profusion of gratitude, some chinking pieces which the old man slipped into his hand.

"Mr. Sweedlepipe, take as much care of your lady-lodger as you can, and give her a word or two of good advice now and then. Such," said old Martin, looking gravely at the astonished Mrs. Gamp, "as hinting at the expediency of a little less liquor, and a little more humanity, and a little less regard for herself, and a little more regard for her patients, and perhaps a trifle of additional honesty. Or when Mrs. Gamp gets into trouble, Mr. Sweedlepipe, it had better not be at a time when I am near enough to the Old Bailey, to volunteer myself as a witness to her character. Endeavour to impress that upon her at your leisure, if you please."

Mrs. Gamp clasped her hands, turned up her eyes until they were quite invisible, threw back her bonnet for the admission of fresh air to her heated brow; and in the act of saying faintly—"Less liquor!—Sairey Gamp—Bottle on the chimney-piece, and let me put my lips to it, when I am so dispoged!"—fell into one of the walking swoons; in which pitiable state she was conducted forth by Mr. Sweedlepipe, who, between his two patients, the swooning Mrs. Gamp and the revolving Bailey, had enough to do, poor fellow.

The old man looked about him, with a smile, until his eyes rested on Tom Pinch's sister; when he smiled the more.

"We will all dine here together," he said; "and as you and Mary have enough to talk of, Martin, you shall keep house for us until the afternoon, with Mr. and Mrs. Tapley. I must see your lodgings in the meanwhile, Tom."

Tom was quite delighted. So was Ruth. She would go with them.

"Thank you, my love," said Mr. Chuzzlewit. "But I am afraid I must take Tom a little out of the way, on business. Suppose you go on first, my dear?"

Pretty little Ruth was equally delighted to do that.

"But not alone," said Martin, "not alone. Mr. Westlock, I dare say, will escort you."

Why, of course he would: what else had Mr. Westlock in his mind? How dull these old men are!

"You are sure you have no engagement?" he persisted.

Engagement! As if he could have any engagement!

So they went off arm in arm. When Tom and Mr. Chuzzlewit went off arm in arm a few minutes after them, the latter was still smiling: and really, for a gentleman of his habits, in rather a knowing manner.

CHAPTER LIII

BRILLIANTLY the Temple Fountain sparkled in the sun, and
laughingly its liquid music played, and merrily the idle drops
of water danced and danced, and peeping out in sport among
the trees, plunged lightly down to hide themselves, as little
Ruth and her companion came towards it.

And why they came towards the Fountain at all is a mystery;
for they had no business there. It was not in their way. It
was quite out of their way. They had no more to do with
the Fountain, bless you, than they had with—with Love, or
any out-of-the-way thing of that sort.

It was all very well for Tom and his sister to make appointments by the Fountain, but that was quite another affair.
Because, of course, when she had to wait a minute or two,
it would have been very awkward for her to have had to wait
in any but a tolerably quiet spot; and that was as quiet a
spot, everything considered, as they could choose. But when
she had John Westlock to take care of her, and was going
home with her arm in his (home being in a different direction
altogether), their coming anywhere near that Fountain, was
quite extraordinary.

However, there they found themselves. And another extraordinary part of the matter was, that they seemed to have

480

come there, by a silent understanding. Yet when they got there, they were a little confused by being there, which was the strangest part of all; because there is nothing naturally confusing in a Fountain. We all know that.

What a good old place it was! John said. With quite an earnest affection for it.

"A pleasant place indeed," said little Ruth. "So shady!" Oh wicked little Ruth!

They came to a stop when John began to praise it. The day was exquisite; and stopping at all, it was quite natural —nothing could be more so—that they should glance down Garden Court; because Garden Court ends in the Garden, and the Garden ends in the River, and that glimpse is very bright and fresh and shining on a summer's day. Then, oh little Ruth, why not look boldly at it! Why fit that tiny precious, blessed little foot into the cracked corner of an insensible old flagstone in the pavement; and be so very anxious to adjust it to a nicety!

If the Fiery-faced matron in the crunched bonnet could have seen them as they walked away, how many years' purchase might Fiery Face have been disposed to take for her situation in Furnival's Inn as laundress to Mr. Westlock!

They went away, but not through London's streets! Through some enchanted city, where the pavements were of air; where all the rough sounds of a stirring town were softened into gentle music; where every thing was happy; where there was no distance, and no time. There were two good-tempered burly draymen letting down big butts of beer into a cellar, somewhere; and when John helped her—almost lifted her—the lightest, easiest, neatest thing you ever saw—across the rope, they said he owed them a good turn for giving him the chance. Celestial draymen!

Green pastures in the summer tide, deep-littered straw-yards in the winter, no stint of corn and clover, ever, to that noble horse who *would* dance on the pavement with a gig behind him, and who frightened her, and made her clasp his arm with both hands (both hands: meeting one upon the other, so endearingly!), and caused her to implore him to take refuge in the pastry-cook's; and afterwards to peep out at the door so shrinkingly; and then: looking at him with those eyes: to ask him was he sure—now was he sure—they might go safely on! Oh for a string of rampant horses! For a lion, for a bear, for a mad bull, for anything to bring the little hands together on his arm, again!

They talked, of course. They talked of Tom, and all these changes, and the attachment Mr. Chuzzlewit had conceived for him, and the bright prospects he had in such a friend, and a great deal more to the same purpose. The more they talked, the more afraid this fluttering little Ruth became of any pause; and sooner than have a pause she would say the same things over again; and if she hadn't courage or presence of mind enough for that (to say the truth she very seldom had), she was ten thousand times more charming and irresistible than she had been before.

"Martin will be married very soon now, I suppose?" said John.

She supposed he would. Never did a bewitching little woman suppose anything in such a faint voice as Ruth supposed that.

But seeing that another of those alarming pauses was approaching, she remarked that he would have a beautiful wife. Didn't Mr. Westlock think so?

"Ye—yes," said John; "oh, yes."

She feared he was rather hard to please—he spoke so coldly.

"Rather say already pleased," said John. "I have scarcely seen her. I had no care to see her. I had no eyes for *her*, this morning."

Oh, good gracious!

It was well they had reached their destination. She never could have gone any further. It would have been impossible to walk in such a tremble.

482

Tom had not come in. They entered the triangular parlour together, and alone. Fiery Face, Fiery Face, how many years' purchase *now*!

She sat down on the little sofa, and untied her bonnet-strings. He sat down by her side, and very near her : very, very near her. Oh, rapid, swelling, bursting little heart, you knew that it would come to this, and hoped it would. Why beat so wildly, heart!

"Dear Ruth! Sweet Ruth! If I had loved you less, I could have told you that I loved you, long ago. I have loved you from the first. There never was a creature in the world more truly loved than you, dear Ruth, by me!"

She clasped her little hands before her face. The gushing tears of joy, and pride, and hope, and innocent affection, would not be restrained. Fresh from her full young heart they came to answer him.

"My dear love! If this is—I almost dare to hope it is, now—not painful or distressing to you, you make me happier than I can tell, or you imagine. Darling Ruth! My own good, gentle, winning Ruth! I hope I know the value of your heart, I hope I know the worth of your angel nature. Let me try and show you that I do ; and you will make me happier, Ruth—— "

"Not happier," she sobbed, "than you make me. No one can be happier, John, than you make me!"

Fiery Face, provide yourself! The usual wages or the usual warning. It's all over, Fiery Face. We needn't trouble you any further.

The little hands could meet each other now, without a rampant horse to urge them. There was no occasion for lions, bears, or mad bulls. It could all be done, and infinitely better, without their assistance. No burly drayman or big butts of beer, were wanted for apologies. No apology at all was wanted. The soft light touch fell coyly, but quite naturally, upon the lover's shoulder ; the delicate waist, the drooping head, the blushing cheek, the beautiful eyes, the exquisite mouth itself, were all as natural as possible. If all the horses in Araby had run away at once, they couldn't have improved upon it.

They soon began to talk of Tom again.

"I hope he will be glad to hear of it!" said John, with sparkling eyes.

Ruth drew the little hands a little tighter when he said it, and looked up seriously into his face.

"I am never to leave him, *am* I, dear? I could never leave Tom. I am sure you know that."

"Do you think I would ask you?" he returned, with a—well! Never mind with what.

"I am sure you never would," she answered, the bright tears standing in her eyes.

"And I will swear it, Ruth, my darling, if you please. Leave Tom! That would be a strange beginning. Leave Tom, dear! If Tom and we be not inseparable, and Tom (God bless him) have not all honour and all love in our home, my little wife, may that home never be! And that's a strong oath, Ruth."

Shall it be recorded how she thanked him? Yes, it shall. In all simplicity and innocence and purity of heart, yet with a timid, graceful, half-determined hesitation, she set a little rosy seal upon the vow, whose colour was reflected in her face, and flashed up to the braiding of her dark brown hair.

"Tom will be so happy, and so proud, and glad," she said, clasping her little hands. "But so surprised! I am sure he had never thought of such a thing."

Of course John asked her immediately—because you know they were in that foolish state when great allowances must be made—when *she* had begun to think of such a thing, and this made a little diversion in their talk; a charming diversion to them, but not so interesting to us; at the end of which, they came back to Tom again.

"Ah! dear Tom!" said Ruth. "I suppose I ought to tell you everything now. I should have no secrets from you. Should I, John, love?"

484

ABOUT TELLING TOM

It is of no use saying how that preposterous John answered her, because he answered in a manner which is untranslatable on paper, though highly satisfactory in itself. But what he conveyed was, No no no, sweet Ruth; or something to that effect.

Then she told him Tom's great secret; not exactly saying how she had found it out, but leaving him to understand it if he liked; and John was sadly grieved to hear it, and was full of sympathy and sorrow. But they would try, he said, only the more, on this account, to make him happy, and to beguile him with his favourite pursuits. And then, in all the confidence of such a time, he told her how he had a capital opportunity of establishing himself in his old profession in the country; and how he had been thinking, in the event of that happiness coming upon him which had actually come— there was another slight diversion here—how he had been thinking that it would afford occupation to Tom, and enable them to live together in the easiest manner, without any sense of dependence on Tom's part; and to be as happy as the day was long. And Ruth receiving this with joy, they went on catering for Tom to that extent that they had already purchased him a select library and built him an organ, on which he was performing with the greatest satisfaction : when they heard him knocking at the door.

Though she longed to tell him what had happened, poor little Ruth was greatly agitated by his arrival ; the more so because she knew that Mr. Chuzzlewit was with him. So she said, all in a tremble :

" What shall I do, dear John ! I can't bear that he should hear it from any one but me, and I could not tell him, unless we were alone."

" Do, my love," said John, " whatever is natural to you on the impulse of the moment, and I am sure it will be right."

He had hardly time to say thus much, and Ruth had hardly time to—just to get a little farther off—upon the sofa, when

Tom and Mr. Chuzzlewit came in. Mr. Chuzzlewit came first, and Tom was a few seconds behind him.

Now Ruth had hastily resolved that she would beckon Tom up stairs after a short time, and would tell him in his little bed-room. But when she saw his dear old face come in, her heart was so touched that she ran into his arms, and laid her head down on his breast, and sobbed out, "Bless me, Tom! My dearest brother!"

Tom looked up, in surprise, and saw John Westlock close beside him, holding out his hand.

"John!" cried Tom. "John!"

"Dear Tom," said his friend, "give me your hand. We are brothers, Tom."

Tom wrung it with all his force, embraced his sister fervently, and put her in John Westlock's arms.

"Don't speak to me, John. Heaven is very good to us. I——" Tom could find no further utterance, but left the room; and Ruth went after him.

And when they came back, which they did by-and-by, she looked more beautiful, and Tom more good and true (if that were possible) than ever. And though Tom could not speak upon the subject even now; being yet too newly glad: he put both his hands in both of John's with emphasis sufficient for the best speech ever spoken.

"I am glad you chose to-day," said Mr. Chuzzlewit to John; with the same knowing smile as when they had left him. "I thought you would. I hoped Tom and I lingered behind a discreet time. It's so long since I had any practical knowledge of these subjects, that I have been anxious, I assure you."

"Your knowledge is still pretty accurate, sir," returned John, laughing, "if it led you to foresee what would happen to-day."

"Why, I am not sure, Mr. Westlock," said the old man, "that any great spirit of prophecy was needed, after seeing you and Ruth together. Come hither, pretty one. See what Tom and I purchased this morning, while you were dealing in exchange with that young merchant there."

A BEAUTIFUL PRESENT

The old man's way of seating her beside him, and humouring his voice as if she were a child, was whimsical enough, but full of tenderness, and not ill adapted, somehow, to little Ruth.

"See here!" he said, taking a case from his pocket, "what a beautiful necklace. Ah! How it glitters! Earrings, too, and bracelets, and a zone for your waist. This set is yours, and Mary has another like it. Tom couldn't understand why I wanted two. What a short-sighted Tom! Earrings and bracelets, and a zone for your waist! Ah! beautiful! Let us see how brave they look. Ask Mr. Westlock to clasp them on."

It was the prettiest thing to see her holding out her round, white arm; and John (oh deep, deep John!) pretending that the bracelet was very hard to fasten; it was the prettiest thing to see her girding on the precious little zone, and yet obliged to have assistance because her fingers were in such terrible perplexity; it was the prettiest thing to see her so confused and bashful, with the smiles and blushes playing brightly on her face, like the sparkling light upon the jewels; it was the prettiest thing that you would see, in the common experiences of a twelvemonth, rely upon it.

"The set of jewels and the wearer are so well matched," said the old man, "that I don't know which becomes the other most. Mr. Westlock could tell me, I have no doubt, but I'll not ask him, for he is bribed. Health to wear them, my dear, and happiness to make you forgetful of them, except as a remembrance from a loving friend!"

He patted her upon the cheek, and said to Tom:

"I must play the part of a father here, Tom, also. There are not many fathers who marry two such daughters on the same day: but we will overlook the improbability for the gratification of an old man's fancy. I may claim that much indulgence," he added, "for I have gratified few fancies enough in my life tending to the happiness of others, Heaven knows!"

These various proceedings had occupied so much time, and they fell into such a pleasant conversation now, that it was within a quarter of an hour of the time appointed for dinner before any of them thought about it. A hackney-coach soon carried them to the Temple, however; and there they found everything prepared for their reception.

Mr. Tapley having been furnished with unlimited credentials relative to the ordering of dinner, had so exerted himself for the honour of the party, that a prodigious banquet was served, under the joint direction of himself and his Intended. Mr. Chuzzlewit would have had them of the party, and Martin urgently seconded his wish, but Mark could by no means be persuaded to sit down at table; observing, that in having the honour of attending to their comforts, he felt himself, indeed, the landlord of the Jolly Tapley, and could almost delude himself into the belief that the entertainment was actually being held under the Jolly Tapley's roof.

For the better encouragement of himself in this fable, Mr. Tapley took it upon him to issue divers general directions to the waiters from the hotel, relative to the disposal of the dishes and so forth; and as they were usually in direct opposition to all precedent, and were always issued in his most facetious form of thought and speech, they occasioned great merriment among those attendants; in which Mr. Tapley participated, with an infinite enjoyment of his own humour. He likewise entertained them with short anecdotes of his travels, appropriate to the occasion; and now and then with some comic passage or other between himself and Mrs. Lupin; so that explosive laughs were constantly issuing from the sideboard, and from the backs of chairs; and the head-waiter (who wore powder, and knee-smalls, and was usually a grave man) got to be a bright scarlet in the face, and broke his waistcoat-strings, audibly.

Young Martin sat at the head of the table, and Tom Pinch at the foot; and if there were a genial face at that board, it was Tom's. They all took their tone from Tom. Everybody drank to him, everybody looked to him, everybody thought of him, everybody loved him. If he so much as laid down his knife and fork, somebody put out a hand to shake with him. Martin and Mary had taken him aside before dinner, and spoken to him so heartily of the time to come : laying such fervent stress upon the trust they had in his completion of their felicity, by his society and closest friendship : that Tom was positively moved to tears. He couldn't bear it. His heart was full, he said, of happiness. And so it was. Tom spoke the honest truth. It was. Large as thy heart was, dear Tom Pinch, it had no room that day, for anything but happiness and sympathy !

And there was Fips, old Fips of Austin Friars, present at the dinner, and turning out to be the jolliest old dog that ever did violence to his convivial sentiments by shutting himself up in a dark office. " Where is he ! " said Fips, when he came in. And then he pounced on Tom, and told him that he wanted to relieve himself of all his old constraint : and in the first place shook him by one hand, and in the second place shook him by the other, and in the third place nudged him in the waistcoat, and in the fourth place, said, " How *are* you ! " and in a great many other places did a great many other things to show his friendliness and joy. And he sang songs, did Fips ; and made speeches, did Fips ; and knocked off his wine pretty handsomely, did Fips ; and in short, he showed himself a perfect Trump, did Fips, in all respects.

But ah ! the happiness of strolling home at night—obstinate little Ruth, she wouldn't hear of riding !—as they had done on that dear night, from Furnival's Inn ! The happiness of being able to talk about it, and to confide their happiness to each other ! The happiness of stating all their little plans to Tom, and seeing his bright face grow brighter as they spoke !

When they reached home, Tom left John and his sister in the parlour, and went up stairs into his own room, under pretence of seeking a book. And Tom actually winked to himself, when he got up stairs : he thought it such a deep thing to have done.

" They like to be by themselves, of course," said Tom ; " and

I came away so naturally, that I have no doubt they are expecting me, every moment, to return. That's capital!"

But he had not sat reading very long, when he heard a tap at his door.

"May I come in?" said John.

"Oh, surely!" Tom replied.

"Don't leave us, Tom. Don't sit by yourself. We want to make you merry; not melancholy."

"My dear friend," said Tom, with a cheerful smile.

"Brother, Tom. Brother."

"My dear brother," said Tom; "there is no danger of my being melancholy, how can I be melancholy, when I know that you and Ruth are so blest in each other! I think I can find my tongue to-night, John," he added, after a moment's pause. "But I never can tell you what unutterable joy this day has given me. It would be unjust to you to speak of your having chosen a portionless girl, for I feel that you know her worth; I am sure you know her worth. Nor will it diminish in your estimation, John, which money might."

"Which money would, Tom," he returned. "Her worth! Oh, who could see her here, and not love her! Who could know her, Tom, and not honour her! Who could ever stand possessed of such a heart as hers, and grow indifferent to the treasure! Who could feel the rapture that I feel to-day, and love as I love her, Tom, without knowing something of her worth! Your joy unutterable! No, no, Tom. It's mine, it's mine."

"No, no, John," said Tom. "It's mine, it's mine."

Their friendly contention was brought to a close by little Ruth herself, who came peeping in at the door. And oh, the look, the glorious, half-proud, half-timid look she gave Tom, when her lover drew her to his side! As much as to say, "Yes indeed, Tom, he will do it. But then he has a right, you know. Because I *am* fond of him, Tom."

As to Tom, he was perfectly delighted. He could have sat and looked at them, just as they were, for hours.

"I have told Tom, love, as we agreed, that we are not going to permit him to run away, and that we cannot possibly allow it. The loss of one person, and such a person as Tom, too, out of our small household of three, is not to be endured; and so I have told him. Whether he is considerate, or whether he is only selfish, I don't know. But he needn't be considerate, for he is not the least restraint upon us. Is he, dearest Ruth?"

Well! He really did not seem to be any particular restraint upon them. Judging from what ensued.

Was it folly in Tom to be so pleased by their remembrance of him, at such a time? Was their graceful love a folly, were their dear caresses follies, was their lengthened parting folly? Was it folly in him to watch her window from the street, and rate its scantiest gleam of light above all diamonds; folly in her to breathe his name upon her knees, and pour out her pure heart before that Being, from whom such hearts and such affections come?

If these be follies, then Fiery Face go on and prosper! If they be not, then Fiery Face avaunt! But set the crunched bonnet at some other single gentleman, in any case, for one is lost to thee for ever!

CHAPTER LIV

Todgers's was in high feather, and mighty preparations for
a late breakfast were astir in its commercial bowers. The
blissful morning had arrived when Miss Pecksniff was to be
united in holy matrimony, to Augustus.

Miss Pecksniff was in a frame of mind, equally becoming
to herself and the occasion. She was full of clemency and
conciliation. She had laid in several chaldrons of live coals,
and was prepared to heap them on the heads of her enemies.
She bore no spite nor malice in her heart. Not the least.

Quarrels, Miss Pecksniff said, were dreadful things in families;
and though she never could forgive her dear papa, she was
willing to receive her other relations. They had been separated,
she observed, too long. It was enough to call down a judgment upon the family. She believed the death of Jonas *was* a
judgment on them for their internal dissensions. And Miss
Pecksniff was confirmed in this belief, by the lightness with
which the visitation had fallen on herself.

By way of doing sacrifice—not in triumph; not, of course,
in triumph, but in humiliation of spirit—this amiable young
person wrote, therefore, to her kinswoman of the strong mind,
and informed her, that her nuptials would take place on such
a day. That she had been much hurt by the unnatural
conduct of herself and daughters, and hoped they might not

492

have suffered in their consciences. That being desirous to forgive her enemies, and make her peace with the world before entering into the most solemn of covenants with the most devoted of men, she now held out the hand of friendship. That if the strong-minded woman took that hand, in the temper in which it was extended to her, she, Miss Pecksniff, did invite her to be present at the ceremony of her marriage, and did furthermore invite the three red-nosed spinsters, her daughters (but Miss Pecksniff did not particularise their noses), to attend as bridesmaids.

The strong-minded woman returned for answer, that herself and daughters were, as regarded their consciences, in the enjoyment of robust health, which she knew Miss Pecksniff would be glad to hear. That she had received Miss Pecksniff's note with unalloyed delight, because she never had attached the least importance to the paltry and insignificant jealousies with which herself and circle had been assailed ; otherwise than as she found them, in the contemplation, a harmless source of innocent mirth. That she would joyfully attend Miss Pecksniff's bridal ; and that her three dear daughters would be happy to assist, on so interesting, and *so very unexpected*— which the strong-minded woman underlined—*so very unexpected* an occasion.

On the receipt of this gracious reply, Miss Pecksniff extended her forgiveness and her invitations to Mr. and Mrs. Spottletoe ; to Mr. George Chuzzlewit the bachelor cousin ; to the solitary female who usually had the tooth-ache ; and to the hairy young gentleman with the outline of a face ; surviving remnants of the party that had once assembled in Mr. Pecksniff's parlour. After which Miss Pecksniff remarked, that there was a sweetness in doing our duty, which neutralised the bitter in our cups.

The wedding guests had not yet assembled, and indeed it was so early that Miss Pecksniff herself was in the act of dressing at her leisure, when a carriage stopped near the Monument ; and Mark, dismounting from the rumble, assisted Mr. Chuzzlewit to alight. The carriage remained in waiting ;

so did Mr. Tapley. Mr. Chuzzlewit betook himself to Todgers's.

He was shown, by the degenerate successor of Mr. Bailey, into the dining-parlour; where—for his visit was expected—Mrs. Todgers immediately appeared.

"You are dressed, I see, for the wedding," he said.

Mrs. Todgers, who was greatly flurried by the preparations, replied in the affirmative.

"It goes against my wishes to have it in progress just now, I assure you, sir," said Mrs. Todgers; "but Miss Pecksniff's mind was set upon it, and it really is time that Miss Pecksniff was married. That cannot be denied, sir."

"No," said Mr. Chuzzlewit, "assuredly not. Her sister takes no part in the proceedings?"

"Oh dear, no, sir. Poor thing!" said Mrs. Todgers, shaking her head, and dropping her voice. "Since she has known the worst, she has never left my room; the next room."

"Is she prepared to see me?" he inquired.

"Quite prepared, sir."

"Then let us lose no time."

Mrs. Todgers conducted him into the little back chamber commanding the prospect of the cistern; and there, sadly different from when it had first been her lodging, sat poor Merry, in mourning weeds. The room looked very dark and sorrowful; and so did she; but she had one friend beside her, faithful to the last. Old Chuffey.

When Mr. Chuzzlewit sat down at her side, she took his hand and put it to her lips. She was in great grief. He too was agitated; for he had not seen her since their parting in the churchyard.

"I judged you hastily," he said, in a low voice. "I fear I judged you cruelly. Let me know that I have your forgiveness."

She kissed his hand again; and retaining it in hers, thanked him, in a broken voice, for all his kindness to her, since.

"Tom Pinch," said Martin, "has faithfully related to me

494

all that you desired him to convey; at a time when he deemed it very improbable that he would ever have an opportunity of delivering your message. Believe me, that if I ever deal again with an ill-advised and unawakened nature, hiding the strength it thinks its weakness, I will have long and merciful consideration for it."

"You had for me; even for me," she answered. "I quite believe it. I said the words you have repeated, when my distress was very sharp and hard to bear; I say them now for others; but I cannot urge them for myself. You spoke to me after you had seen and watched me day by day. There was great consideration in that. You might have spoken, perhaps, more kindly; you might have tried to invite my confidence by greater gentleness; but the end would have been the same."

He shook his head in doubt, and not without some inward self-reproach.

"How can I hope," she said, "that your interposition would have prevailed with me, when I know how obdurate I was! I never thought at all; dear Mr. Chuzzlewit, I never thought at all; I had no thought, no heart, no care to find one; at that time. It has grown out of my trouble. I have felt it in my trouble. I wouldn't recall my trouble, such as it is, and has been—and it is light in comparison with trials which hundreds of good people suffer every day, I know—I wouldn't recall it to-morrow, if I could. It has been my friend, for without it, no one could have changed me; nothing could have changed me. Do not mistrust me because of these tears; I cannot help them. I am grateful for it, in my soul. Indeed I am!"

"Indeed she is!" said Mrs. Todgers. "I believe it, sir."

"And so do I!" said Mr. Chuzzlewit. "Now, attend to me, my dear. Your late husband's estate, if not wasted by the confession of a large debt to the broken office (which document, being useless to the runaways, has been sent over to England by them: not so much for the sake of the creditors as for the gratification of their dislike to him, whom they suppose to be still living), will be seized upon by law; for it is not exempt, as I learn, from the claims of those who have suffered by the fraud in which he was engaged. Your father's property was all, or nearly all, embarked in the same transaction. If there be any left, it will be seized on, in like manner. There is no home *there*."

"I couldn't return to him," she said, with an instinctive reference to his having forced her marriage on. "I could not return to him!"

"I know it," Mr. Chuzzlewit resumed; "and I am here, because I know it. Come with me! From all who are about me, you are certain (I have ascertained it) of a generous welcome. But until your health is re-established, and you are sufficiently composed to bear that welcome, you shall have your abode in any quiet retreat of your own choosing, near London; not so far removed but that this kind-hearted lady may still visit you as often as she pleases. You have suffered much; but you are young, and have a brighter and a better future stretching out before you. Come with me. Your sister is careless of you, I know. She hurries on and publishes her marriage, in a spirit which (to say no more of it) is barely decent, is unsisterly, and bad. Leave the house before her guests arrive. She means to give you pain. Spare her the offence, and come with me!"

Mrs. Todgers, though most unwilling to part with her, added her persuasions. Even poor old Chuffey (of course included in the project) added his. She hurriedly attired herself, and was ready to depart, when Miss Pecksniff dashed into the room.

Miss Pecksniff dashed in so suddenly, that she was placed in an embarrassing position. For, though she had completed her bridal toilette as to her head, on which she wore a bridal bonnet with orange flowers, she had not completed it as to her skirts, which displayed no choicer decoration than a dimity bedgown. She had dashed in, in fact, about half-way through, to console her sister in her affliction with a sight of the aforesaid bonnet; and being quite unconscious of the presence of a visitor, until she found Mr. Chuzzlewit standing face to face with her, her surprise was an uncomfortable one.

"So, young lady!" said the old man, eyeing her with strong disfavour. "You are to be married to-day!"

"Yes, sir," returned Miss Pecksniff, modestly. "I am. I—my dress is rather—really, Mrs. Todgers!"

"Your delicacy," said old Martin, "is troubled, I perceive. I am not surprised to find it so. You have chosen the period of your marriage, unfortunately."

"I beg your pardon, Mr. Chuzzlewit," retorted Cherry; very red and angry in a moment: "but if you have anything to say on that subject, I must beg to refer you to Augustus. You will scarcely think it manly, I hope, to force an argument on me, when Augustus is at all times ready to discuss it with you. I have nothing to do with any deceptions that may have been practised on my parent," said Miss Pecksniff, pointedly; "and as I wish to be on good terms with everybody at such a time, I should have been glad if you would have favoured us with your company at breakfast. But I will not ask you as it is: seeing that you have been prepossessed and set against me in another quarter. I hope I have my natural affections for another quarter, and my natural pity for another quarter; but I cannot always submit to be subservient to it, Mr. Chuzzlewit. That would be a little too much. I trust I have more respect for myself, as well as for the man who claims me as his Bride."

"Your sister, meeting—as I think: not as she says, for she has said nothing about it—with little consideration from you, is going away with me," said Mr. Chuzzlewit.

"I am very happy to find that she has some good fortune at last," returned Miss Pecksniff, tossing her head. "I congratulate her, I am sure. I am not surprised that this event should be painful to her—painful to her—but I can't help that, Mr. Chuzzlewit. It's not my fault."

"Come, Miss Pecksniff!" said the old man, quietly. "I should like to see a better parting between you. I should like to see a better parting on your side, in such circumstances. It would make me your friend. You may want a friend one day or other."

"Every relation of life, Mr. Chuzzlewit, begging your pardon: and every friend in life:" returned Miss Pecksniff, with dignity, "is now bound up and cemented in Augustus. So long as Augustus is my own, I cannot want a friend. When you speak of friends, sir, I must beg, once for all, to refer you to Augustus. That is my impression of the religious ceremony in which I am so soon to take a part at that altar to which Augustus will conduct me. I bear no malice at any time, much less in a moment of triumph, towards any one ; much less towards my sister. On the contrary, I congratulate her. If you didn't hear me say so, I am not to blame. And as I owe it to Augustus, to be punctual on an occasion when he may naturally be supposed to be—to be impatient—really, Mrs. Todgers!—I must beg your leave, sir, to retire."

After these words the bridal bonnet disappeared; with as much state, as the dimity bedgown left in it.

Old Martin gave his arm to the younger sister without speaking; and led her out. Mrs. Todgers, with her holiday garments fluttering in the wind, accompanied them to the carriage, clung round Merry's neck at parting, and ran back to her own dingy house, crying the whole way. She had a lean lank body, Mrs. Todgers, but a well-conditioned soul within. Perhaps the Good Samaritan was lean and lank, and found it hard to live. Who knows !

Mr. Chuzzlewit followed her so closely with his eyes, that, until she had shut her own door, they did not encounter Mr. Tapley's face.

"Why, Mark !" he said, as soon as he observed it, "what's the matter !"

"The wonderfullest ewent, sir!" returned Mark, pumping at his voice in a most laborious manner, and hardly able to articulate with all his efforts. "A coincidence as never was equalled! I'm blessed if here ain't two old neighbours of ourn, sir!"

"What neighbours!" cried old Martin, looking out of window. "Where?"

"*I* was a walkin' up and down not five yards from this spot," said Mr. Tapley, breathless, "and they come upon me like their own ghosts, as I thought they was! It's the wonderfullest ewent that ever happened. Bring a feather, somebody, and knock me down with it!"

"What do you mean!" exclaimed old Martin, quite as much excited by the spectacle of Mark's excitement, as that strange person was himself. "Neighbours, where!"

"Here, sir!" replied Mr. Tapley. "Here in the city of London! Here upon these very stones! Here they are, sir! Don't I know 'em? Lord love their welcome faces, don't I know 'em!"

With which ejaculations Mr. Tapley not only pointed to a decent-looking man and woman standing by, but commenced embracing them alternately, over and over again, in Monument Yard.

"Neighbours, WHERE!" old Martin shouted: almost maddened by his ineffectual efforts to get out at the coach-door.

"Neighbours in America! Neighbours in Eden!" cried Mark. "Neighbours in the swamp, neighbours in the bush, neighbours in the fever. Didn't she nurse us! Didn't he help us! Shouldn't we both have died without 'em! Hav'n't they come a strugglin' back, without a single child for their consolation! And talk to me of neighbours!"

Away he went again, in a perfectly wild state, hugging them, and skipping round them, and cutting in between them, as if he were performing some frantic and outlandish dance.

Mr. Chuzzlewit no sooner gathered who these people were, than he burst open the coach-door somehow or other, and came tumbling out among them; and as if the lunacy of Mr.

Tapley were contagious, he immediately began to shake hands too, and exhibit every demonstration of the liveliest joy.

"Get up behind!" he said. "Get up in the rumble. Come along with me! Go you on the box, Mark. Home! Home!"

"Home!" cried Mr. Tapley, seizing the old man's hand in a burst of enthusiasm. "Exactly my opinion, sir. Home, for ever! Excuse the liberty, sir, I can't help it. Success to the Jolly Tapley! There's nothin' in the house they shan't have for the askin' for, except a bill. Home to be sure! Hurrah!"

Home they rolled accordingly, when he had got the old man in again, as fast as they could go; Mark abating nothing of his fervour by the way, but allowing it to vent itself as unrestrainedly as if he had been on Salisbury Plain.

And now the wedding party began to assemble at Todgers's. Mr. Jinkins, the only boarder invited, was on the ground first. He wore a white favour in his button-hole, and a brand new extra super double-milled blue saxony dress coat (that was its description in the bill), with a variety of tortuous embellishments about the pockets, invented by the artist to do honour to the day. The miserable Augustus no longer felt strongly even on the subject of Jinkins. He hadn't strength of mind enough to do it. "Let him come!" he had said, in answer to Miss Pecksniff, when she urged the point. "Let him come! He has ever been my rock ahead through life. 'Tis meet he should be there. Ha, ha! Oh, yes! let Jinkins come!"

Jinkins had come, with all the pleasure in life; and there he was. For some few minutes he had no companion but the breakfast, which was set forth in the drawing-room, with unusual taste and ceremony. But Mrs. Todgers soon joined him; and the bachelor cousin, the hairy young gentleman, and Mr. and Mrs. Spottletoe, arrived in quick succession.

Mr. Spottletoe honoured Jinkins with an encouraging bow. "Glad to know you, sir," he said. "Give you joy!" Under the impression that Jinkins was the happy man.

Mr. Jinkins explained. He was merely doing the honours for his friend Moddle, who had ceased to reside in the house, and had not yet arrived.

"Not arrived, sir!" exclaimed Spottletoe, in a great heat.

"Not yet," said Mr. Jinkins.

"Upon my soul!" cried Spottletoe. "He begins well! Upon my life and honour this young man begins well! But I should very much like to know how it is that every one who comes into contact with this family is guilty of some gross insult to it. Death! Not arrived yet. Not here to receive us!"

The nephew with the outline of a countenance, suggested that perhaps he had ordered a new pair of boots, and they hadn't come home.

"Don't talk to me of Boots, sir!" retorted Spottletoe, with immense indignation. "He is bound to come here in his slippers then; he is bound to come here barefoot. Don't offer such a wretched and evasive plea to me on behalf of your friend, as Boots, sir."

"He is not *my* friend," said the nephew. "I never saw him."

"Very well, sir," returned the fiery Spottletoe. "Then don't talk to me!"

The door was thrown open at this juncture, and Miss Pecksniff entered, tottering, and supported by her three bridesmaids. The strong-minded woman brought up the rear; having waited outside until now, for the purpose of spoiling the effect.

"How do you do, ma'am!" said Spottletoe to the strong-minded woman in a tone of defiance. "I believe you see Mrs. Spottletoe, ma'am?"

The strong-minded woman with an air of great interest in Mrs. Spottletoe's health, regretted that she was not more easily seen. Nature erring, in that lady's case, upon the slim side.

"Mrs. Spottletoe is at least more easily seen than the bridegroom, ma'am," returned that lady's husband. "That is, unless he has confined his attentions to any particular part or branch of this family, which would be quite in keeping with its usual proceedings."

" If you allude to me, sir——" the strong-minded woman began.

" Pray," interposed Miss Pecksniff, " do not allow Augustus, at this awful moment of his life and mine, to be the means of disturbing that harmony which it is ever Augustus's and my wish to maintain. Augustus has not been introduced to any of my relations now present. He preferred not."

" Why, then, I venture to assert," cried Mr. Spottletoe, " that the man who aspires to join this family, and ' prefers not ' to be introduced to its members, is an impertinent Puppy. That is my opinion of *him !* "

The strong-minded woman remarked with great suavity, that she was afraid he must be. Her three daughters observed aloud that it was " shameful ! "

" You do not know Augustus," said Miss Pecksniff, tearfully, " indeed you do not know him. Augustus is all mildness and humility. Wait till you see Augustus, and I am sure he will conciliate your affections."

" The question arises," said Spottletoe, folding his arms : " How long we are to wait. I am not accustomed to wait ; that's the fact. And I want to know how long we are expected to wait."

" Mrs. Todgers ! " said Charity, " Mr. Jinkins ! I am afraid there must be some mistake. I think Augustus must have gone straight to the Altar ! "

As such a thing was possible, and the church was close at hand, Mr. Jinkins ran off to see : accompanied by Mr. George Chuzzlewit the bachelor cousin, who preferred anything to the aggravation of sitting near the breakfast, without being able to eat it. But they came back with no other tidings than a familiar message from the clerk, importing that if they wanted to be married that morning they had better look sharp, as the curate wasn't going to wait there all day.

502

THE BRIDEGROOM FORBIDS THE BANNS

The bride was now alarmed; seriously alarmed. Good Heavens, what could have happened! Augustus! Dear Augustus!

Mr. Jinkins volunteered to take a cab, and seek him at the newly-furnished house. The strong-minded woman administered comfort to Miss Pecksniff. "It was a specimen of what she had to expect. It would do her good. It would dispel the romance of the affair." The red-nosed daughters also administered the kindest comfort. "Perhaps he'd come," they said. The sketchy nephew hinted that he might have fallen off a bridge. The wrath of Mr. Spottletoe resisted all the entreaties of his wife. Everybody spoke at once, and Miss Pecksniff, with clasped hands, sought consolation everywhere and found it nowhere, when Jinkins, having met the postman at the door, came back with a letter: which he put into her hand.

Miss Pecksniff opened it; glanced at it; uttered a piercing shriek; threw it down upon the ground; and fainted away.

They picked it up; and crowding round, and looking over one another's shoulders, read, in the words and dashes following, this communication:

> "OFF GRAVESEND.
> "CLIPPER SCHOONER, CUPID.
> "*Wednesday night.*

"EVER-INJURED MISS PECKSNIFF,

"Ere this reaches you, the undersigned will be—if not a corpse—on the way to Van Dieman's Land. Send not in pursuit. I never will be taken alive!

"The burden—300 tons per register—forgive, if in my distraction, I allude to the ship—on my mind—has been truly dreadful. Frequently—when you have sought to soothe my brow with kisses—has self-destruction flashed across me. Frequently—incredible as it may seem—have I abandoned the idea.

"I love another. She is Another's. Everything appears

503

to be somebody else's. Nothing in the world is mine—not even my Situation—which I have forfeited—by my rash conduct—in running away.

"If you ever loved me, hear my last appeal! The last appeal of a miserable and blighted exile. Forward the inclosed—it is the key of my desk—to the office—by hand. Please address to Bobbs and Cholberry—I mean to Chobbs and Bolberry—but my mind is totally unhinged. I left a penknife—with a buckhorn handle—in your work-box. It will repay the messenger. May it make him happier than ever it did me!

"Oh, Miss Pecksniff, why didn't you leave me alone! Was it not cruel, *cruel!* Oh, my goodness, have you not been a witness of my feelings—have you not seen them flowing from my eyes—did you not, yourself, reproach me with weeping more than usual on that dreadful night when last we met—in that house—where I once was peaceful—though blighted—in the society of Mrs. Todgers!

"But it was written—in the Talmud—that you should involve yourself in the inscrutable and gloomy Fate which it is my mission to accomplish, and which wreathes itself —e'en now—about my—temples. I will not reproach, for I have wronged you. May the Furniture make some amends!

"Farewell! Be the proud bride of a ducal coronet, and forget me! Long may it be before you know the anguish with which I now subscribe myself—amid the tempestuous howlings of the—sailors,

"Unalterably, never yours,
"AUGUSTUS."

They thought as little of Miss Pecksniff, while they greedily perused this letter, as if she were the very last person on earth whom it concerned. But Miss Pecksniff really had fainted away. The bitterness of her mortification; the bitterness of having summoned witnesses, and such witnesses, to behold it; the bitterness of knowing that the strong-minded

504

The Nuptials of Miss Pecksniff receive a Temporary Check

woman and the red-nosed daughters towered triumphant in this hour of their anticipated overthrow; was too much to be borne. Miss Pecksniff had fainted away in earnest.

What sounds are these that fall so grandly on the ear! What darkening room is this!

And that mild figure seated at an organ, who is he! Ah Tom, dear Tom, old friend!

Thy head is prematurely grey, though Time has passed between thee and our old association, Tom. But, in those sounds with which it is thy wont to bear the twilight company, the music of thy heart speaks out: the story of thy life relates itself.

Thy life is tranquil, calm, and happy, Tom. In the soft strain which ever and again comes stealing back upon the ear, the memory of thine old love may find a voice perhaps; but it is a pleasant, softened, whispering memory, like that in which we sometimes hold the dead, and does not pain or grieve thee, God be thanked!

Touch the notes lightly, Tom, as lightly as thou wilt, but never will thine hand fall half so lightly on that Instrument as on the head of thine old tyrant brought down very, very low; and never will it make as hollow a response to any touch of thine, as he does always.

For a drunken, squalid, begging-letter-writing man, called Pecksniff (with a shrewish daughter), haunts thee, Tom; and when he makes appeals to thee for cash, reminds thee that he built thy fortunes better than his own; and when he spends it, entertains the alehouse company, with tales of thine ingratitude and his munificence towards thee once upon a time; and then he shows his elbows worn in holes, and puts his soleless shoes up on a bench, and begs his auditors look there, while thou art comfortably housed and clothed. All known to thee, and yet all borne with, Tom!

So, with a smile upon thy face, thou passest gently to

another measure—to a quicker and more joyful one—and little feet are used to dance about thee at the sound, and bright young eyes to glance up into thine. And there is one slight creature, Tom—her child; not Ruth's—whom thine eyes follow in the romp and dance: who, wondering sometimes to see thee look so thoughtful, runs to climb up on thy knee, and put her cheek to thine: who loves thee, Tom, above the rest, if that can be: and falling sick once, chose thee for her nurse, and never knew impatience, Tom, when Thou wert by her side.

Thou glidest now, into a graver air; an air devoted to old friends and bygone times; and in thy lingering touch upon the keys, and the rich swelling of the mellow harmony, they rise before thee. The spirit of that old man dead, who delighted to anticipate thy wants, and never ceased to honour thee, is there, among the rest: repeating, with a face composed and calm, the words he said to thee upon his bed, and blessing thee!

And coming from a garden, Tom, bestrewn with flowers by children's hands, thy sister, little Ruth, as light of foot and heart as in old days, sits down beside thee. From the Present, and the Past, with which she is so tenderly entwined in all thy thoughts, thy strain soars onward to the Future. As it resounds within thee and without, the noble music, rolling round ye both, shuts out the grosser prospect of an earthly parting, and uplifts ye both to Heaven!

POSTSCRIPT

At a Public Dinner given to me on Saturday the 18th of April, 1868, in the City of New York, by two hundred representatives of the Press of the United States of America, I made the following observations among others:

"So much of my voice has lately been heard in the land, that I might have been contented with troubling you no further from my present standing-point, were it not a duty with which I henceforth charge myself, not only here but on every suitable occasion, whatsoever and wheresoever, to express my high and grateful sense of my second reception in America, and to bear my honest testimony to the national generosity and magnanimity. Also, to declare how astounded I have been by the amazing changes I have seen around me on every side,—changes moral, changes physical, changes in the amount of land subdued and peopled, changes in the rise of vast new cities, changes in the growth of older cities almost out of recognition, changes in the graces and amenities of life, changes in the Press, without whose advancement no advancement can take place anywhere. Nor am I, believe me, so arrogant as to suppose that in five and twenty years there have been no changes in me, and that I had nothing to learn and no extreme impressions to correct when I was here first. And this brings me to a point on which I have, ever since I landed in the United States last November, observed a strict silence, though sometimes tempted to break it, but in reference to which I will, with your good leave, take you into my confidence now. Even the Press, being human, may be sometimes mistaken or misinformed, and I rather think that I have in one or two rare instances observed its information to be not strictly accurate with reference to myself. Indeed, I have, now and again, been more surprised by printed news that I have read of myself, than by any printed news that I have ever read in my present state of existence. Thus, the vigour and perseverance with which I have for some months past been collecting materials for, and hammering away at, a new book on America has much astonished me ; seeing that all that time my declaration has been perfectly well known to my publishers on both sides of the Atlantic, that no consideration on earth would induce me to write one. But what I have intended, what I have resolved upon (and this is the confidence I seek to place in you) is, on my return to England, in my own person, in my own Journal, to bear, for the behoof of my countrymen, such testimony to the gigantic changes in this country as I have hinted at to-night. Also, to record that wherever I have been, in the smallest places equally with the largest, I have been received with unsurpassable politeness, delicacy, sweet temper, hospitality, consideration, and with unsurpassable respect for the privacy daily enforced upon me by the nature of my avocation here and the state of my health. This testimony, so long as I live, and so long as my descendants have any legal right in my books, I shall cause to be republished, as an appendix to every copy of those two books of mine in which I have referred to

POSTSCRIPT

America. And this I will do and cause to be done, not in mere love and thankfulness, but because I regard it as an act of plain justice and honour."

I said these words with the greatest earnestness that I could lay upon them, and I repeat them in print here with equal earnestness. So long as this book shall last, I hope that they will form a part of it, and will be fairly read as inseparable from my experiences and impressions of America.

CHARLES DICKENS.

May, 1868.

This book, designed by
William B. Taylor
is a production of
Edito-Service S.A., Geneva

Printed in Switzerland